THE DEPTH OF
YOU

Written by
Corrie MacKay

Content Warning: This novel explores aspects of psychology and mental health and contains occasionally descriptive references to past traumas, including child abuse, stalking, physical and mental abuse, cult/religious abuse, sexual abuse, domestic violence, and murder. Please read with care.

The Depth of You is a work of fiction. Names, characters, places, and incidents either are the product of the author's imagination or are used fictitiously. Any resemblance to actual persons, living or dead, events, or locales is entirely coincidental.

ISBN 979-8-9887445-3-5
Digital ISBN 979-8-9887445-2-8

Cover Design by Katarina, @nskvsky
Book Editing by Corrie MacKay
Book Design by Deborah June, @deborah_june

Author Instagram: @writefreemackay
Author Email: writefreemackay@gmail.com

This book is dedicated to women, all women everywhere who are surviving, struggling, and thriving in a world that says we cannot and should not. Hold your heads high, darlings, even if they feel heavy, and never, ever, apologize for wanting, seeking, and striving. Your power is right at the depth of you, in the very essence of who you are. Womanhood is magic. You are magic, and you can, and you should keep going. Keep going.

"There is no timestamp on trauma. There isn't a formula that you can insert yourself into to get from horror to healed. Be patient. Take up space. Let your journey be the balm."

– Dawn Serra

1

Sweat hewed to her skin like a thickly applied lotion. She wiped the excess from her brow and upper lip, then lifted her copper hair to let the air cool the back of her neck as she strode down the creaky stairs, through the foyer, and into her large kitchen. At the sink, she filled a glass with cold water and aimed to sip it but chugged instead. The muscles in her legs and arms twitched. Even her abdomen ached from sustained tension.

As she filled her glass a second time, she stretched her neck from side to side, then yawned her mouth open to give her jaw the same relief. She enjoyed it, that absolute need to twist and stretch and hydrate. She experienced it not as discomfort but as relief and perhaps a bit of pride, like the immense exhaustion and sense of accomplishment that married in the body and buzzed about the brain after a great workout.

A cool hand settled on her naked hip, and she hummed, pleased. Long, deliberate fingers walked atop the arch of her hipbone and down. They scratched through the dewy, dark red curls at the junc-ture of her thighs, and settled there. Dosie smiled into her next sip of water and eased herself back to rest against the bare body framing her from behind.

"I hope you didn't think we were finished," said the voice at her ear.

Dosie freed an airy laugh. "You can't be serious."

Her lover nosed through her hair and kissed her nape. "I'm not known for my humor."

"No, just your endurance," Dosie teased as she set her glass aside and turned.

"*Just* my endurance?" Jennifer's sex-mussed, panther-black hair was longer than ever, draping down her back and bushing behind her ears where Dosie's hands had earlier been buried. Her bright blue eyes were blackberry-rich in the shadowy kitchen as she explored the expanse of flesh at her fingertips uninhibited, mapping Dosie's torso with a maddening back-and-forth of deep, massaging pulls and featherlight teases. She flashed a devilish grin as she leaned in to kiss the corner of Dosie's mouth. "Surely, there are other things."

A warm, dizzying flutter erupted in Dosie's belly. She tilted her head to allow better access for the promising kisses traveling her jawline to the lobe of her ear, then just below, over the steady rhythm of her pulse. She loved the way Jennifer touched her now. There had always been heat between them, care and desire in their connections even when they were strangers to one another, but there had also been timidity and uncertainty. A subtle underlying trepidation once colored every interaction, whether of words or flesh or both, but nearly six months into their established relationship, that apprehension had whittled away and left the richest, most addictive knowing in its place. They communicated without words as often as with and read each other's bodies like well-loved, spine-cracked paperbacks. They touched each other with affection and familiarity, a near innate awareness of the other's preferences and needs and shifting moods.

They were in each other now, deeply, and Dosie had never experienced anything like it. She couldn't explain how such familiarity still afforded them excitement and discovery, but it did. Dosie felt she discovered something new about herself or Jennifer or their dynamic every day, every week. She shocked herself every time she woke up next to Jennifer and somehow found her more beautiful than the day before, found herself more in love. Surely, there was a limit. Surely, they could grow no more, could go no deeper. But then they always did.

"Dosie." Her name, messily wrapped in Jennifer's thirst-dried voice, crackled through her thoughts like delicious static, pulling her out of her head. "Where did you go?"

Dosie smiled. "Just my thoughts," she said. "Good ones."

"Thoughts of...? Wait, I know: the many things I'm known for beyond my endurance," Jennifer said. "No wonder you glitched like a broken robot. Your poor, horny brain got overheated."

Dosie laughed, loud and uninhibited, and drew Jennifer in by the back of her neck to kiss her. Pleasure zapped along her skin like an electrical current when Jennifer's hands coiled in her hair and scratched behind her ears, then back down her neck, over the arches of her shoulders. It was a lazy kiss that Dosie still felt down to her toes.

"Do you want to know what I was really thinking?" Dosie said as she rung her arms around Jennifer's shoulders and pressed their foreheads together. Their naked bodies slowly swayed in the dark kitchen, a rhythm just shy of a dance. Jennifer rubbed her fingers over the downy-soft hairs in the triangle dip of her lower back, and Dosie took it as the confirmation she knew it was. "I was thinking about how much I feel for you. I keep thinking there's got to be a limit, because we're so used to each other now, but instead, it's like that just makes it even better. Everything I learn about you makes me want to know you more. I know it sounds ridiculous, but I swear, I fall in love with you a little bit more every day. Sometimes a lot more."

Jennifer's hands tightened around Dosie's back and waist, pulled her closer, held her harder. She wasn't one to talk openly about her feelings often, and when she did, she needed a good amount of build-up to get her there. But that didn't mean she wasn't affected. It didn't mean she didn't feel the same. It didn't mean she wasn't right there with Dosie every step of the way, feeling and wanting just as much.

Dosie had learned all Jennifer's languages, and many of them were written in her skin. Despite her general distaste for physical affection with anyone who wasn't Dosie, she possessed a deep understanding of the body and of physicality in general, and so it was only natural that she communicated with hers. She cared with her body when she couldn't find her words or her voice. She kissed in place of Dosie's long-winded love confessions. She touched and, better, she allowed touch. Avidly. Often. She listened and accommodated, adjusted as needed, and she never judged. She gave Dosie everything she had, and she often managed to do so entirely in silence, something Dosie found so incredibly beautiful and intense that she struggled, at times, to accept it. She struggled not to interrupt her girlfriend's precious, quiet devotion to ask for verbal reassurance, yet somehow, Jennifer always recognized that struggle, and just as she'd done since the beginning, set aside her own hang-ups and gave it without request.

"You say the worst, best things," she murmured into a chaste kiss, and a laugh bloomed in Dosie's throat.

"I *know*," she groaned and shifted them into a proper embrace, her chin tucked over Jennifer's shoulder, arms tightly looped. "I'm so sappy."

"You're maple syrup. It's why you're always in the kitchen."

Dosie's next laugh jumped free in a bright burst of sound, and she pulled back to poke at Jennifer's armpits where she knew she was most ticklish. She laughed even harder when Jennifer squawked like a shocked hen and swatted her hands away. Her breath caught in her throat when one swat snatched her wrist like practiced choreography and yanked, reeling Dosie sharply in again.

Their chests collided. Their gazes locked in place, and suddenly Jennifer was serious. The air thickened as Dosie's laugh croaked to silence, and Jennifer's next words sent three hot, little puffs of air over her lips. "Kiss me again."

Dosie's pulse jumped under Jennifer's fingers, still curled around her wrist. It raced up her arm and into her neck as she watched Jennifer's gaze drop to her mouth. When Dosie leaned in only to have Jennifer's free hand catch her chin and stop her, it appeared like magic between her thighs. *Whump-whump. Whump-whump. Whump-whump.*

"Not there," Jennifer said, and a shiver coursed Dosie's spine. That voice. It wasn't just Jennifer. It was Jennifer at her career best, her most delicious and dangerous. It was the voice of her work persona, the one that had once wound through Dosie's body like a siren song and taught her desire, changed her life. The voice of the Director.

"*Oh,*" Dosie said, a pathetic whimper of sudden awareness as their eyes met again.

The hand at her chin shifted, slid up Dosie's cheek to her mussed hair. Jennifer's short fingernails scraped along her scalp, sending bursts of pleasure rippling down her neck and back. When she palmed the top of her head with one insistent, downward push, the throb between Dosie's legs turned violent.

Without further prompting, Dosie dropped to her bony knees on the kitchen floor and sank her face right into the manicured thicket above Jennifer's sex. She inhaled deeply through her nose, and the heady scent of Jennifer's arousal, both lingering and new, made her mouth water. Her abdomen clenched as she shuffled closer and breathed her in again, let her hands wander up Jennifer's thighs and over the slopes of her ass. Desire lanced through her body, white-hot and invasive, until she was breathless with it as she dug her fingers into Jennifer's hips and slid her tongue between her swollen labia.

A moan curled up from the butterfly pit of Dosie's gut as Jennifer's perfect, familiar tang smeared her lips and coated her mouth. The sound crested into a whine when Jennifer hiked her leg without warning. She braced her foot against the opposite counter-top, and her pink velvet vulva opened in front of Dosie like a sun-drenched summer rose.

"Suck me." Jennifer's sharp order struck Dosie's libido like a battering ram.

"God, *yes.*" She dove back in, her lover's urging hand at her nape, and drew Jennifer's straining clitoris into her mouth. Just as she hollowed her cheeks to suck at her, an ear-splitting melody rent the air. Shock jerked them apart, and Jennifer's leg dropped from the counter only to bonk into Dosie's head like a cushioned hammer, and any semblance of balance they had fled the room. Down they went, toppling between the kitchen counter and island with their hands flailing for something other than each other to anchor them. Jennifer caught herself on the floor a microsecond before Dosie's back hit the tile and the rest of Jennifer hit *her.* Dosie grunted on impact, heard Jennifer's knee strike the floor beside her head and slide, and as if fate was insisting Dosie finish her sacred work, Jennifer's cunt smash-landed on her face.

"Motherfucker," Jennifer groaned from somewhere above her.

Dosie couldn't help herself. She could hardly breathe, but she let the last of her precious air go in a loud, unrelenting laugh that vibrated into the wet flesh smushed against her. Then she hooked her arms around Jennifer's thighs and licked a broad stripe up the core of her.

Jennifer gasped at the sudden burst of pleasure then dissolved into laughter herself. Grabbing the counter edge above her, she shifted herself up and back onto her knees, positioned herself perfectly over Dosie's mouth. "Do it again," she said and rutted once against Dosie's mouth.

The shrill melody echoed through the kitchen again, and Jennifer growled her frustration. "Is that your fucking phone?" she asked as she shifted off of Dosie and hauled herself back up onto her feet. "Why is it so loud?"

Dosie wiped her mouth and chin with the back of her wrist and said, "It's still in the bowl from earlier."

It was a trick Natalie had shown her some years prior. Placing her phone at the bottom of a deep bowl while playing music would amplify the sound without the use of an external speaker. It especially worked with bowls made of metal or glass. Dosie had used the trick ever since.

"Kaylia," Jennifer said as she reached for Dosie's arm to help her up, then handed her the still-ringing phone. "Tell her a text would suffice. We're in the middle of dinner here."

Dosie giggled into the phone as she answered. "Hi! Did you just land? Are you in Spain?!"

"Yes, and it's hellishly early." Kaylia's voice was scratchy as if she had woken only a moment before. "The entire country is still asleep. Hey, is Jennifer there?"

"Yeah." Dosie flashed a suspicious glance toward the woman in question. "Why?"

"Good," Kaylia said, "because I'm actually calling for her."

Dosie's mouth went dry, not because of the words but because of Jennifer. Because Jennifer's hands were on her again, cupping her breasts, thumbing her nipples. Jennifer's mouth was on her neck, sucking the soft skin over her pulse, and Dosie, easily and properly flustered, briefly lost track of reality.

"Wait, what?" Dosie asked, and Kaylia huffed as if Dosie was accusing her of something rather than simply asking her to repeat herself.

"Just give her the phone," Kaylia said. "I'll tell you later."

Confused, Dosie handed the phone to Jennifer and said, "Um, she wants to talk to you."

Jennifer's eyebrow jumped, her expression equally bewildered as she put the phone to her ear. Stark naked, she crossed her legs at the ankles and leaned against the counter. A stone-carved goddess made flesh, just casually taking a call in Dosie's kitchen. "Jennifer speaking." A second later, her face went slack, and her voice droned. "Really, Kaylia? For this, you interrupt my orgasm?"

Dosie choked on her sip of water and let it dribble down her chin into the sink. "Jen!"

"You are a lawyer," Jennifer said into the phone. "I assume you know how to do a basic internet search."

"Stop teasing her," Dosie said, wishing she was privy to more than one side of the exchange.

"Fine," Jennifer sighed. "I'm just winding you up. How much time do you have? Oh, he's meeting you at the airport."

"She's meeting a guy?! I thought she was going to stay at the vineyard with her parents!" Dosie felt like she was reading a book with half its pages ripped out. The longer it went on, the more maddening it became. She whined. "Why is she telling you and not me? I want to know too!" Then it dawned on her. "Wait, is this about sex?"

Jennifer nodded, though Dosie wasn't sure if it was in answer to her question or something Kaylia had said that she was simply considering and reacting to. "Well, my personal opinion is to not wait until the last second to seek answers," Jennifer said, "and my professional opinion, on such short notice, is to buy the thickest condoms you can find."

Dosie's eyebrows had never experienced such hyperactivity. Up then down then up then down again. *What is happening?*

"Mhm, good luck." Jennifer ended the call and set Dosie's phone back on the table, then she caught Dosie's gaze and slowly drew one leg up to bridge the gap between the countertop and island again. "Now..." Tingles pinpricked Dosie's lower back as she watched Jennifer's hand waterfall down her torso and slide between her legs, watched her fingers spread herself wide and button her clitoris. "... back on your knees, please."

Arousal twitched Dosie's nerves. She could smell Jennifer, the scent still heavy in her nose and on her breath, and now imagined it wafting up like steam off of freshly baked bread. She went to her knees again, eager, and shuffled forward. She looked up at Jennifer before diving in. "Are you really not going to tell me what that was about?"

Jennifer's stony, challenging gaze communicated she wouldn't be speaking further until she got what she wanted, and what she wanted was Dosie's mouth.

"Fine," Dosie laughed and licked her relentlessly, reveling in the hard press of Jennifer's hand at the back of her head, holding her in place. "You taste so good."

Jennifer shuddered. "I fucking love when you talk to me," she said and rutted harder against Dosie's tongue. "Don't stop."

Dosie stopped and looked up at her, feeling a bit of Jennifer's own mischief hopping about her soul. "Wait," she said, feigning confusion as Jennifer growled her annoyance. "Don't stop talking to you? Or don't stop *fucking* you?"

She couldn't help her satisfied giggle when Jennifer moaned and yanked her back in by the hair. It always had an effect when she spoke during sex, but when she cussed, something she did sparingly, it really riled Jennifer up. "Finish me, or so help me, I will—"

Dosie drew Jennifer's clit into her mouth and sucked it like a siphon, and Jennifer's idle threat cracked around a shout that turned her voice raw. Holding her breath, Dosie let herself be smashed into place as Jennifer rode out her orgasm in fleeting hurricane waves. When the tension released, Jennifer eased her leg down, and Dosie kissed up her sweat-slicked skin, over her perked nipples, and along one collarbone. She kissed the edge of Jennifer's jaw then the corner of her mouth. Then right on her still-huffing lips.

"Is it just me or am I getting really good at that?" she asked with a grin. She could feel it growing wider until she no doubt looked ridiculous but couldn't bring herself to care. Even with all the sex they'd had over the course of their relationship and before, every time she gave Jennifer pleasure, made her moan, made her come, Dosie felt like she could burst with pride.

Jennifer laughed, breathy and sweet. "I think my ego is starting to rub off on you," she said and poked the tip of her finger into Dosie's one dimpled cheek. "But yes, my love, you have gotten very, *very* good at that."

"Good." Dosie wrapped her arms around Jennifer's waist and

painted their bodies together, touching at every point possible. "And just for the record, I like it when your parts rub off on me."

"Damn right you do," Jennifer said as she started to wobble-walk them backward through the kitchen to the foyer.

Dosie laughed and held on, did her best to aid the shuffle without tripping them. "Where are we going?"

"Bed."

"So you can rub your parts on me some more?"

"So I can kiss you goodnight before I have to go."

Dosie's heart plummeted. "Ugh, no," she whined as they stopped at the bottom of the stairs. "Don't speak of the cursed goodbye."

"I know." Jennifer's voice gentled as she tucked Dosie's messy hair back. "I'm sorry." And it sounded so sincere, so full of yearning, that it made Dosie ache.

"Don't be. Come here." She drew her in by the neck and kissed her. "I just hate missing you."

"Mm, me too." Her sexy, little smile as she leaned in for another kiss turned Dosie's aches to air. Once again, she was floating on the high of attraction and tenderness, on the whirlwind of being in love. "It has led to some truly spectacular reunions, though."

Warmth invaded, rushing up from Dosie's chest to her cheeks. "That's true," she whispered as Jennifer swept her up, feet fully off the ground, and slowly carouseled her around as they kissed. She sighed as her toes met the cold floor again, and Jennifer turned to lead her up the stairs. "Babe?"

"Hm?"

"Can you go ahead, and I'll catch up?" She tried to stop it from happening, but as usual, Dosie couldn't help herself. She was too wide awake, too alive, too full of joy and desire and ridiculous hot air. Her laugh burst out of her before Jennifer could even ask her why, and the answer shook itself free in the process. "I just want to look at your butt while you go up the stairs."

Jennifer's brief confusion morphed into amusement. Her shoulders bounced with it. Her smile spread until her eyes crinkled at the edges, and Dosie had to kiss her again. "Happy to oblige, lover," Jennifer said as she headed up the stairs, her tall, gorgeous figure on shady, moonlit display.

Dosie trailed behind her. "Ooh, *lover*. I like it when you call me that." When Jennifer responded by reaching back to slap one gorgeous glute for her, Dosie's goofy grin stretched until it hurt.

The night neared its peak when Jennifer finally managed to talk herself into leaving the warmth of Dosie's bed. She peeled her tacky skin off Dosie's sweat-sheened back and braced herself for the cool air outside their cocoon of blankets and body heat. It pricked at her, ready or not, as she tiptoed to the bathroom with her teeth gritted and her nipples turning to stone.

She eased the door shut behind her, and the automatic light Dosie had installed the week before spilled through the dark in an instant. Jennifer squinted and shielded her eyes until they adjusted then switched on the sink to splash some warm water over her face. She took a moment to relieve herself then washed up and donned the clothes she'd set out ahead of time. A simple sweater and joggers. Her toothbrush clinked against Dosie's as she freed it from the ceramic cup on the sink, then she coated it with minty paste and stuck it in her mouth, trying and failing not to grin like a fool as she did. She had a toothbrush at Dosie's house, not one she traveled with but one that remained.

A toothbrush had been there for her since the first one magically appeared beside Dosie's six weeks into their relationship. *"You got me a toothbrush?"* Jennifer asked her that very day, to which Dosie, in a cute but hopeless effort to appear casual, shrugged her shoulders and said, "One less thing to have to pack, right?" And somehow, Jennifer managed not to wander off into the air like an overinflated balloon. Her heart had sat in her throat for nearly a minute before she kissed Dosie as if she intended to send her soaring, too.

Two days later, Jennifer found a spare case for her contacts on Dosie's bedside table and stared at it as if she'd discovered a small creature sitting there instead. She had rarely worn her contacts before, as she only needed her prescription for reading and night driving, but since her driving had increased, her use of them had as well. So, she often had them with her when staying at her girlfriend's.

Three weeks after that, Dosie showed Jennifer the two drawers she'd emptied for her in her dresser and the space in her closet that was meant to house whatever clothes Jennifer might want to hang while visiting or keep there while gone. Dosie said nothing about the significance of any of it, the combining of their possessions, the weaving of their two individual lives. And somewhere in the center of the tangle: a new life, not solely Jennifer's and not solely Dosie's, but both of theirs. Instead, Dosie had kissed her tenderly and said, *"I just like the idea of your things and my things in the same place."*

Jennifer liked it too, more than she would have ever imagined herself capable. The idea of having deliberate, dedicated space not only in a woman's heart but in her home, in her bedroom, in all her most private, sacred places, elated her. She'd spent all her adult life feeling the immensity of others' desire for her, thriving on it, but this kind of desire, this kind of care and need and respect, was something altogether new. It shook her, leveled her some days. Lifted her higher than any drug or orgasm ever had or could. That very night, she had returned home and redesigned her own spaces, and when Dosie next visited her, Jennifer said nothing about any of it. She let Dosie discover it all herself—bathroom essentials and empty drawers and the air freshener scents that Dosie preferred—and when Dosie returned to the living room with tears in her eyes and a smile on her face, she knew she'd done well. Her girlfriend leapt on her back like a monkey and peppered Jennifer's cheek with loud, happy kisses as she shouted, *"You're in love with me,"* as if Jennifer didn't already know that right down to her bones. A good day.

But then, all her days with Dosie felt good. Even when they talked little or barely got through the door before going to sleep, it felt

Corrie MacKay

good. It felt right, so right that their time apart had begun to feel wrong. At first, Jennifer needed the space. She needed the time to adjust to sharing so much of herself and her life and her privacy with another person after two decades of being on her own. But then her needs shifted. She still wanted her time alone, but she wanted it with Dosie nearby. It felt odd to be without her, like she had briefly misplaced some part of herself and wouldn't feel properly at ease again until she had it back. It was the strangest, simplest, most frustrating and thrilling experience of Jennifer's life. *Well, maybe not the strangest.*

With one last slap of water to her cheeks to ensure she was awake, Jennifer finished in the bathroom and returned to Dosie's bed. She crawled up, careful not to stir her girl, and nosed along the naked slope of her shoulder. Dosie's messy hair embraced her as she buried her face and breathed her in a final time, wanting her lazy-day scent to invade and linger. She hated leaving like this, with Dosie asleep, but she had long since learned that leaving a wide-awake Dosie was much harder. This was better and made more sense for Jennifer anyway. She was a night owl by nature, and while she had never loved driving, she preferred to do it at night. The less traffic she had to endure on the freeway, the more peaceful her mind and the more regulated her blood pressure.

"I'll see you soon," she whispered despite Dosie's small snores indicating she wouldn't hear. It didn't matter. Jennifer always said it and always meant it. She *would* see Dosie soon, as soon as she was able. She never let any other thought enter her mind, the idea that Dosie might not be there someday, that they might be separated somehow; that losing her was possible. When those thoughts started to creep in, she—*No.* She took a breath, another whiff of her love, and banished those fears from her mind. Here Dosie was. Safe. Warm. Perfect. "I love you."

She didn't say it often, not when they were awake, at least. It still sometimes felt like pulling teeth, and it wasn't because she didn't feel it. She did. Constantly. So much sometimes that she feared it might explode out of her like water from a burst ballon. But people who were in love didn't say it as often as they felt it, right? Otherwise, how would anyone ever stop? The sheer number of times Jennifer felt drenched in the sensation and found herself stricken with the impulse to shout the words at the woman responsible surely exceeded an acceptable amount. How the hell would they ever have any other conversation?

Ugh. Being in love was disgusting. She was disgusted with herself. And delighted. *For fuck's sake.*

"Okay, I'm going," she grumbled to no one but herself and backed off the bed for the hall.

It was close to three in the morning when she keyed into her building, weary from the long drive; rather, from the many, *many* long drives. Every week, she or Dosie made the trip from one place to the other. They kept it fair, trading off often to prevent privileging one location over the other, but on occasion, Dosie took the brunt of the travel. Sometimes, she did so because Jennifer lived closer to her two best friends than she did, and it gave her better access. Other times, she simply needed a break.

Dosie's childhood home was full of ghosts, and most days, they lived there with her in peace. Other days, they traded that peace for violence, latching onto all her most vulnerable spots like starving leeches seeking a final burst of life at their host's expense. Those days, Dosie couldn't be there, so she would make the drive to Jennifer's instead. Those nights, she slept in Jennifer's bed, some part of her always touching. Her hand on Jennifer's back or belly. Her thigh tossed over Jennifer's hip. Her icy feet jammed between Jennifer's warmer ones. Her breath would puff at the back of Jennifer's neck, nose squashed into the fine, silky hairs there, and she would stay right there until Jennifer's was the only presence she could feel anymore. The only touch left, the only real one. The one that mattered.

In the building's skinny foyer, Jennifer unlocked her mailbox to grab the latest stash of envelopes smushed inside, then she headed up the old staircase to her condo. Once inside, she toed off her sneakers and made a beeline for the bathroom. Her bladder was screaming after a few hours of slurping down an oversized, shockingly not terrible, gas-station coffee with one too many creamers. Road trip snacks had become the bane of her existence; well, road trip snacks *and* asshole drivers who didn't signal to change lanes. She was so fucking tired of driving, and of long rides and longer separations. It was starting to itch at her, like a scab still too fresh to fall. She wanted to pick at it until it bled.

Bill. Ad. Ad. Junk. Bill. Bank. Political. Junk. Jennifer only glanced at each piece of mail before tossing it onto the bathroom countertop and, for the moment, out of her mind. The final envelope was larger and folded over, its manila exterior rumpled around the corners. Jennifer shifted the fold to see the writing on the envelope's face and froze right where she sat. She knew the name, recognized the handwriting. Couldn't stop staring.

She hadn't heard from her aunt in nearly two years, not that that was uncommon for them. They had never been very close. Much like herself, her aunt was, for all but business intents and purposes, allergic to other people. Jennifer had only ever experienced two exceptions for herself: her sister, Lauren, and many, *many* years later, Theodosia Grace Fisher, who'd swept into her life like the most timid, beautiful storm and washed all her natural resistance away.

Her father, she knew, had been her aunt's one special exception, the big brother she had loved and leaned on all her young life. Jennifer had wondered many times over the years if her aunt ever found another person to let in. It had never been and never would be Jennifer. As much as they loved one another, and as similar as they were, so too was their grief. So much so that it often sat in the room with them like a long-lost friend that they both desperately wished would've remained gone.

Jennifer carried her aunt's mail to her bed, clicked on the bedside lamp, and sat. She tore a strip off the top of the envelope to open it and frowned when she found another envelope inside. It was older, postmarked nearly three months before, and also addressed to Jennifer but at her aunt's residence. Then she noticed it: a formal seal stamped in the corner. Her blood chilled. Her eyes slid over the sender's details. She was holding an official notice from the *Massachusetts Parole Board*.

Jennifer's late-night coffee resurfaced in an instant, scorching up her throat from her gut like magma from the mantle. Where it failed to give her much energy before, it now electrified. Adrenaline sparked as the bitter mix of a dark Colombian roast and bile lapped at the back of her tongue like a sour tide, and Jennifer had to suck in several fast, cold breaths through her nose just to keep it down. She swallowed, breathed again. Swallowed. Another breath. Then she ripped open the second envelope.

Dosie woke to an empty bed and banana-pie sunshine speckling her sheets. It stretched across the cool pillow beside her, so that her hand cast a shadow as it slid over the soft lump. She yanked the pillow over and wrapped her arms around it, buried her face in the lingering scent of her girlfriend's hair.

Was it too soon to miss her? *Ugh.*

She breathed her fill of Jennifer's shampoo until the pillow smelled like her own breath more than anything and shoved it away with a huff. Her phone lay where she left it, end still attached to the charger, and Dosie was surprised to see she had no new messages. Her brow wrinkled. That wasn't right. Jennifer always messaged her when she got home, so that Dosie would know she made the trip safely. Her stomach lurched. *Relax.* There was no need to panic yet.

Corrie MacKay

Maybe she had woken at some point in the night and sleepily checked her phone, dismissed her notifications in the haze, and had no memory of it. Because she'd been asleep. *Right?*

Relax, she told herself again, though it felt more like a reprimand as it sank through her body to her noncompliant heart. Her pulse fluttered as she opened her messages, telling herself she would find what she sought, what she expected: a message she had likely already read without remembering, in which Jennifer, as Jennifer always did, let Dosie know she was home in one piece.

Nothing.

Nothing?!

The last message sitting in their text exchange was from five days before when Jennifer had been on the way *to* Dosie, not home. *Stopping for gas*, she'd written. *Thirty minutes out.* Dosie's own reply now glared up at her from her bright screen. *Honey mustard pretzels! I'll kiss you BEFORE I eat them this time. I promise.*

And that was it.

Dread sank through Dosie's body like an anchor to the ocean floor. Where was the message? Why wasn't it there? Where was Jennifer? Did she even make it home? Was she lying on the side of the freeway unable to move, hurt and helpless and—"Stop!"

Dosie clutched her phone to her chest and closed her eyes, breathed in through her nose and out through her mouth. "Stop," she said again, softer but still firm. "These aren't facts. This is my anxiety making assumptions." Another breath eased in and out as she covered her eyes with her hand and leaned into the cup of her palm. "There's no need to panic about what I don't know." *I need to know.* Fear bubbled at the back of her mouth. *I need to know.* "Don't panic. Just act."

She looked at her phone again, at the haunting lack of message, but didn't let herself linger. With two taps, she switched from text to call and raised the phone to her ear, waited as it began to ring. *Please answer. Please be okay. Please answer. Please be okay.* On the third unanswered ring, Dosie's fearful pleas became shameful scolds. *She's probably fine. Asleep. She's not on the side of the road somewhere. She's in bed! Exhausted! You're being stupid and dramatic, and now you're going to wake her up at the crack of dawn.* Tears burned along her eyelids. *She just forgot to text. It's fine. It happens. You're being ridiculous. You're being stupid.*

The fifth ring cracked at its midpoint, and silence came through where Dosie expected Jennifer's voicemail. It stretched for nearly a minute, then she heard it. Jennifer's quiet breath, a tired sigh, slithered through the speaker. Her voice rattled through a beat later, a whisper of Dosie's name, and Dosie's doubt turned certain. *Something's wrong.* She could hear it in Jennifer's voice. It wasn't anything she could explain or put a name to. She doubted she could even describe what it was that set the hairs at the back of her neck on end, but at the core of her, she knew. *Something's wrong.* "I forgot to text. I'm sorry."

"It's okay," Dosie said and heard the tightness in her own voice. Her throat felt as if it had been coated in sand. She didn't know if she should ask. Jennifer hadn't volunteered any information. Technically, Dosie had no reason to think there was an issue, except that feeling. It wouldn't go away. In fact, it was growing, ballooning outward like a smoke plume the longer the silence stretched between them. *Something's wrong.* "I was worried about you."

"I'm home. I'm okay." *Are you? Really? No. She's not. Something's wrong.*

She couldn't take it anymore. "You're not, though."

Silence.

"I'm sorry," Dosie said, hating herself for prying. Jennifer had worked so hard on being more open about her feelings and anxieties, and Dosie always did her best to give her the space to do it voluntarily and in her own time. She had learned to trust that, for the most part, if Jennifer needed to talk with her about something, she would. Except... "I have a terrible feeling that something's wrong."

Again, Jennifer said nothing. Dosie heard her breathe, heard her swallow. She listened to her silence for so long that she began to hear

Corrie MacKay

everything in the background too. Jennifer's bedside fan buzzing. The morning birds calling outside her own bedroom window. A tinkling sound, like a spoon stirring inside a cup.

"I can't talk." It came after what felt like hours, coated in a voice so strained that Dosie was on her feet before she'd even processed what Jennifer said.

"I'm coming." She tucked her phone between her ear and shoulder and jerked open her dresser drawer. Started grabbing what she could get her hands on. T-shirt. Sweats. Socks.

"No, Dosie. Don't." She barely got the words out, and it terrified Dosie. *Something's seriously wrong.* "You don't need—"

"Stop, Jen. I'm already out the door." *She wasn't.* It didn't matter. She would be. In seconds. She raced down the stairs half-dressed. "Whatever it is, it'll be okay. Okay? I love you. Okay?" Jennifer's only answer was a tight squeak of a breath that caused Dosie's heart to plummet into her gut. She spilled into the sunlit morning chill, one shoe on and the other dangling as she hopped her way to the car. "Just a few hours, and I'll be there. I'm on my way."

2

A text notification chimed from the passenger seat as Dosie passed the exit for Cordelia, CA. She wasn't far now. With a glance, she saw the text was from Jennifer, and her anxiety kicked up like a bad case of indigestion. Her chest hurt. Her throat did, too. The backs of her ears were hot. It was as if all her nerves were pinched, all her muscles rigid. She couldn't relax, yet she resisted the urge to check the message. As badly as she wanted to know what it said, she believed it was more urgent that she *get there*. Then Jennifer could say whatever it was to Dosie's face, and Dosie could be there, tangible and in real time, to soothe her. To help. To figure out a solution, if whatever it was even required a solution. She huffed at her lack of information and took one hand from the wheel to fan her eyes dry. *It's okay*, she told herself. *Everything will be okay. I'll be there soon. I'll be there soon.*

Positive thinking only helped for so long, though, and by the time she reached Jennifer's place, the words had faded to an ambient buzz in her head while the rest of her dissolved into a puddle of panic. There was no way of knowing how much of that was because she hadn't eaten yet and her blood sugar was low, and how much of it was because she had, against all sense, managed to half-convince herself in the last thirty minutes of her drive that Jennifer was dying of some terrible disease, and she only had two weeks to live, and she didn't know how to tell Dosie or even process it herself. Because who the hell *did* know how to process something like that?

At the curb, she threw her car in park and pulled the emergency brake. San Francisco's hills were not a joke. Then she grabbed her phone. She needed to know what Jennifer's message said in case it was vital to whatever mood she was about to be confronted with, so she swiped to see. To her surprise, it said nothing. It wasn't words at all but a picture, a picture of a piece of paper with Jennifer's fingers pinched at one edge to hold it in front of the camera. It was formatted like a letter or notice, but Dosie couldn't tell the significance. The words were too small. She used her fingers to enlarge the image and began to read.

Her breath stalled. "Oh God," she whispered to no one but her empty vehicle. An ache pinged through her. "Oh Jen."

All Dosie's earlier worries, all the random, wretched fears and anxieties that had crept through her head like spreading sickness dissipated, and she was left with something perhaps worse. As much as she hated not knowing, she had learned over and over that having the knowledge could sometimes be just as terrible. Because once you knew something, once you had answers, the world would unfreeze. The stagnant stasis of not knowing would pass, and the wheel would begin to turn again. Which meant action. Decision. Consequence. As awesome as those steps could sometimes be, they could also be some of the worst experiences of a person's life.

Dosie left her car and walked up the skinny concrete path to the building. *Calm. Steady. Strong. Calm. Steady. Strong.* She didn't know exactly how she was going to approach the situation, but she knew she needed to be in control of herself and her emotions. Jennifer's anxiety only showed itself on rare occasions, and when it did, it was unpredictable. Impulsive. Moody. Biting, at times. Matching that kind of untamed energy would do neither of them any good. Besides, Jennifer wasn't one to seek commiseration when suffering. She wouldn't wallow. Despite how she typically loved to be looked at, when she was emotional, she could hardly stand to have eyes on her. So, she would fake it. She would pretend she was fine, be strong, be the Director, or if she couldn't do that, she would run. She would seek a life raft, a haven. Somewhere to hide. Somewhere safe. Dosie *needed* to be that safe place. She wanted to be that safe place, any time, in any way, for however long Jennifer agreed to let her. She was determined.

When she reached the condo door, she hesitated. *Should I knock?* She knocked. Nothing. She knocked again, a little louder, and waited. One moment passed, then another. No answer came. Dosie got out the key that Jennifer had made for her two months into their relationship after she accidentally slept through Dosie's arrival and left her sitting in her car outside, calling and calling before the ringing phone finally woke her. Jennifer had apologized profusely with both words and *deeds* despite Dosie's repeated assurances that it was fine, and by the end of the day, the freshly cut key was in Dosie's pocket.

Dosie let herself in just as an angry cry thundered through the room. The wall next to Jennifer's large bay window cracked, puckering where the heavy lamp's base made contact. A millisecond, a ripple of energy that lasted only as long as it took Dosie to wince, and then the porcelain shattered. Thick shards shot from the point of impact before clattering to the floor and skidding out of sight.

"Dosie."

A wisp of a word, a crackle of breath and hurt. When Dosie looked up, the shock of what she'd walked into sapped away. Pain took its place, the kind of heartache she'd not felt in ages. The familiarity of it stole her breath.

Jennifer stood across the room in a pair of running shorts and a sports bra, her long hair pulled back in a frizzy ponytail and earbuds stuck in her ears. The music pumping through them was so loud that Dosie could hear it from where she stood. Jennifer's skin was sheened with sweat and every muscle was taut. Her chest heaved, breaths shallow and wet, and fresh tears puddled around her red-rimmed eyes. One of her hands still jutted slightly forward from throwing the lamp. It fell to her side as their eyes met. "You shouldn't have come."

Dosie's eyes stung. Her throat constricted. She had never seen Jennifer like this, this emotional, this out of control, this devastated and *angry*. "I was worried about you. You didn't sound like yourself on the phone."

"That's because I'm not," Jennifer snapped, a sudden burst of irritation splintering the brief surprise of Dosie's arrival. She yanked out her earbuds and tossed them on the couch. "I'm not myself. That's why you shouldn't be here."

"Or maybe it's why I should be," Dosie argued and chanced a step toward her. She willed her voice steady despite how badly she wanted to cry. Jennifer looked like a lost animal, like a puppy left on the side of the road—bereft and broken, hurt and scared and mad enough to bite. "You don't have to be alone with this. No one should be alone with something like this."

The tension in Jennifer's body wobbled then gave. Tremors rolled through her as her rigid jaw unset around a breath. Her voice turned to rubble. "I don't want you to see me like this."

Dosie shook her head. "You're beautiful." She moved closer, and when Jennifer didn't tense or warn her off, she closed the gap between them and reached for her. First her hands, a tight grip, a grounding one. She massaged Jennifer fingers and palms, her wrists and forearms and elbows. Then her shoulders. Her neck. She rubbed away the tension at the base of Jennifer's head then shifted to her cheeks to wipe through her tears. "I don't ever want you to be afraid to show me every part of you, even this part. Especially this part."

Jennifer collapsed into Dosie like she was a warm bed to fall into after a long day. She ringed her arms around Dosie's waist and hid her face in her neck and hair. The broken sound of her next words zinged through Dosie's soul. "It doesn't scare you?"

"Yes," she admitted as she rubbed circles into the sweaty skin between Jennifer's shoulder blades. "But it scares me for *you*, Jen, not for me." She pulled back to look at her, to see her sad, conflicted gaze, and held it. "It's okay to be angry. It's okay to feel whatever you feel. It's even okay to throw and break things sometimes."

Surprise painted Jennifer's face. "Is it?"

"Of course it is. No one feels good or has control of themselves all the time, and they shouldn't have to. That's not realistic, especially when we know the kinds of terrible things that can happen. It's okay to be emotional as long as you're doing your best to be safe and healthy about it."

Jennifer's hands found Dosie's waist and gripped, drew her flush again. Neither spoke. Quiet and touch were perfect balms, and Dosie wouldn't push beyond them. This moment, this day, was about Jennifer. Whatever she needed, Dosie would abide it.

"What if he gets out?" Jennifer's whispered words came and went quickly. Like vapor, they were there one second and gone the next, a fear so delicately expressed that it barely reached Dosie's ears.

Dosie didn't know what to say. *Was* there anything to say? Anything that would soothe? She knew better than to say it wouldn't happen. People, even those who had committed terrible crimes, were paroled all the time. "I don't know," she admitted with a sigh, "but we will be okay either way. You will be okay."

Jennifer didn't answer, only held Dosie tighter and breathed as if attempting to quell new tears.

"Do you believe me?"

Her heart crumpled as, again, Jennifer said nothing, and the quiet that had only just been a balm became a black hole of doubt.

A shower was a good idea. The heat radiated through her muscles to force them loose. As the tension finally eased, she sighed into the gathering steam and tried not to think about her earlier behavior. Or her appearance. How broken and mad and *pathetic* she must have looked when Dosie walked in on her. She'd tried to work it off, the

Corrie MacKay

adrenaline, the fury. God, the anger; it was as if reading that notice had transported her back in time. She felt sick with the presence of it, like a second skin shrinking around her, suffocating her to death.

And then the ringing started. *Brrrrrrrrrnnng. Brrrrrrrrrnnnng.*

Jennifer could almost feel the phone at her ear again, her fingers curled around its neck. "Fuck," she grunted as she threw a hand forward to brace herself on the wall. Her stomach rolled as she shut her eyes and held her breath and let the shower's spray beat into her face like a hot slap of reality. It didn't work.

Brrrrrrrrrnnng. The robin-egg blue door. *Brrrrrrrrrnnng.*

"Give me a squish."

She couldn't do this. She had barely survived any of it the first time around. The loss of her sister. The investigation. The long, drawn-out criminal trial. The sentencing and the appeal. She'd had to claw her way back from it all like a wounded bird kicked from the nest too soon. *I can't do this.* Her gut gurgled as nausea struck. She felt like a fucking child again. Incompetent. Nobody. That shy idiot teenager who couldn't speak up for anything or anyone. Not even the one person who should have been able to count on her. *Brrrrrrrrrnnng.*

Jennifer's heart squeezed like a fist as all the world narrowed to the panicked pulse in her throat. To the ringing in her ears. To the murky, surrealist painting of her sister's sad, tired face in her head. To what was left of it in the courtroom photographs. *No! No.* Jennifer hadn't thought of those images in years. Her sister's empty eyes. And his expression. His fucking expression. *I'm going to be sick.* His blank, untouched, *stupid* expression, as if the mess he'd made of a young woman's body, of her life, of her spirit was little more than that of spilled milk. Like she didn't matter. Like she wasn't someone's big sister, someone's best friend, someone's whole world. Like she wasn't *someone.* *Brrrrrrrrnnng.*

"Fuck," Jennifer panted again. Her mouth watered and dripped. *I'm going to be sick. I'm going to be sick.* She needed to move, get to the toilet instead of vomiting on the shower floor, but she couldn't. She was frozen where she stood, bracing herself on the wall, desperate to both hold it in and have it out of her at once. But when she opened her mouth to free the sick, what came out instead was a scream.

It started like a rupture, like something breaking under pressure. A dam cracked somewhere in the deep of her, and all she had packed away came spewing and spilling through any crevice it could find until the pressure was too much. The dam gave with the force of Jennifer's guttural cry, and a lifetime of grief flooded through. She slapped both hands over her mouth and screamed until her chest hurt. She screamed until her throat was grated and could give her only shreds of sound. Whimpers. Groans. Pained gasps for air that gave her no relief.

The shower rings screeched over the rod as the curtain shifted, and a puff of cool air hit Jennifer's back. Then warmth. Dosie's arms slinked around her from behind, and their bodies connected like two puzzle pieces finding their match. No words interrupted the shower's roar. Dosie was quiet as she laid her cheek on Jennifer's shoulder blade and held her, but that was enough. New sound burst from her aching throat, a sob wrenching itself free, and Jennifer latched onto Dosie's arms to steady herself. Except she wasn't steady. She didn't even feel real, or she felt *too* real. She wasn't sure which she felt, or which was worse. All she *was* sure of was the searing, remarkable pain in her chest. It was as if she'd forgotten there was a hole there, a terrible absence that could never be filled, and now she was confronted with it again. She could feel the sting of its still-bloody edges, and all she could do was purge, so she did. She cried as if she'd never cried, as if she hadn't already survived this once before. As if she knew her own certain death lay just around the corner.

And Dosie held her. Held her still. Held her steady. Dosie held her until the purging stopped, and the streaks on her cheeks were nothing but lukewarm shower rain.

Corrie MacKay

The light pricked Jennifer's eyes as she finally left the bathroom and went in search of her girlfriend. Dosie had left her to her own devices once the crying stopped, slinking out of the shower as quickly and quietly as she'd slinked in. No washing. No lingering. She had only come to soothe, like a dose of medicine relieving the worst of Jennifer's pain, then she'd gone again without a word as if sensing Jennifer could only abide that kind of exposure for so long. After she left, Jennifer switched the shower to its harshest spray setting and dropped to the floor, sat until her ass hurt and the water became a chilly drumbeat at the back of her neck. She sat there and held her arms tight enough to leave indentations behind, because it kept her from scratching her skin off. She wanted out of her body and out of her head. She felt as if she'd been dropped into the past like a person in a carnival dunk tank. She wasn't ready. No amount of knowing, no amount of bracing, could have prepared her for the anger she felt, for how painful a decades-old wound could still be.

Jennifer hated herself for letting it get to her, for letting it break her down and in front of Dosie, no less. She hated that her eyes were swollen and red, and that she couldn't hide it. She hated that her throat hurt, and her head was throbbing. Most of all, she hated how wide open she felt. Something about it threatened her. Her senses screamed danger, terrified of what might escape the gaping chasm inside her where her family used to be, or worse, what might enter.

She found Dosie in the kitchen in nothing but a baggy T-shirt that fell to mid-thigh and her still-wet hair hanging down her back. "I forgot it was daytime," Jennifer said and winced at the gravel in her voice. "It's too bright."

"I know." Dosie glanced up from the kettle and dropped the spoon in her hand. It clattered on the countertop as she said, "Oh."

Jennifer stopped. "What?"

"Nothing." She smiled and flicked on the kettle. "It still shocks me sometimes when I see you naked."

"You were just in the shower with me."

"I know, but that's different. I knew you would be naked when I got in there. I was ready for it."

"I am frequently naked in the kitchen."

Dosie chuckled as she started rummaging through Jennifer's collection of teas. "Yes, and it's still surprising. You're the only person I've met who thinks the kitchen is naked territory."

Jennifer shrugged. "It's my house. I'll be naked where I choose."

"Sure, but you're naked in my kitchen a lot, too." Dosie stopped her rummaging to look up at her. "That's not a complaint, by the way. Please never stop being naked in my kitchen. I'm just saying, you think a lot more than your own house is naked territory."

Jennifer's gut tickled unexpectedly with a tiny urge to laugh. Nothing came of it, except *everything*. The minutest trickle of pleasure through her deepest pain. It hit her system like the fledgling sparks of a first high, and she wanted more. She wanted haze and euphoria. She wanted transcendence. And she wanted it now.

"Well," she said as she crossed the kitchen and rounded the counter, "in my defense, I wear it well."

"You aren't wearing *anything*," Dosie laughed out as Jennifer sidled up behind her.

"And I'm doing it very well," she murmured and pushed Dosie's damp hair aside to kiss the back of her neck. She smiled when a shiver spilled down her girlfriend's back. "Or do you not agree?"

"I think literally anyone who has ever seen you naked would agree with that," Dosie said and tilted her head to the side as if on autopilot—instinctual consent for Jennifer's mouth on her. It made Jennifer's blood hot. Dosie sighed and let her head fall back. Her body followed, weight giving against Jennifer's frame. "I know what you're doing."

Jennifer's smile grew. She turned it into an open-mouthed kiss just under Dosie's ear. "I know what *you're* doing," she countered, and Dosie's sudden laugh trumpeted through her body like a call to attention. A promise of rapture.

"I'm making *tea*!"

"No, you're not." Dosie's scent invaded and intoxicated. Her natural aroma was stronger after her brief soak, the way grass smelled so much more like grass in the moments after it rained. Jennifer wanted to coat herself in the scent, wanted to be so covered in it that she couldn't tell if she was breathing air anymore or just her, just Dosie. Could she live on that? *Fuck yes.*

"Okay, no, I'm not," Dosie agreed, "but only because you're apparently out of chamomile, which is what I was going to make to help you sleep." She turned in Jennifer's arms. "And now you're bragging about how hot you are naked and trying to seduce me."

Jennifer resumed her kisses along Dosie's neck, then up to her jaw. "Is it working?"

A slow exhale, then Dosie's chin dipped with her nod. Her voice scratched like a record when Jennifer pulled one of her hands down to her bare breast and encouraged it to massage. "It definitely is," she admitted. "But—"

Jennifer stopped her kisses to look at her. "But?"

For a moment, Dosie said nothing. She didn't need to. Her face twisted with the conflict she couldn't put to voice, and Jennifer's stomach dropped. She braced herself, waited for Dosie to get the words together. "I'm worried about you."

Jennifer's affection bowed to an influx of irritation, and she had to resist the impulse to scoff. It wasn't unwarranted, Dosie's worry, but that didn't make her hate it any less. She already felt gored and splayed; was there any purpose in calling further attention to it than they already had? Her reply sat just on the edge of frustration. "And?"

"I don't know," Dosie said as she moved her hand from Jennifer's breast to her side and squeezed. "Please try not to get angry. I'm just worried that you're vulnerable right now, and maybe that's not the best time to have sex."

"Or maybe it's the perfect time to have sex," Jennifer argued, her irritation growing despite Dosie's plea and her own efforts to tamp it down. "So that I don't have to feel so fucking vulnerable." She jerked herself away from Dosie and turned her back to her. Immediately, she loathed herself for doing it, but she couldn't not. She couldn't stop biting, stop hurting, stop *needing*. She itched. "I feel like my blood is on fire."

"I know," Dosie said, and Jennifer heard her move, then her hands were there, cuffing the backs of her arms. "And I want to be here for you however you need." Jennifer waited, tensed, then she felt Dosie's forehead ease down against her nape. Warm breath puffed against her skin. "But I don't want to have sex if you're just trying to use it like some kind of eraser because you feel vulnerable and embarrassed. I'd rather us talk—"

"Okay, stop. Stop." Jennifer yanked herself free of Dosie's hold again and spun on her. Her heart felt like a hammer, weighty and dangerous. *Don't hurt her*, she screamed at herself even as her head hazed beyond reason. *Don't hurt her*. "Don't do that. Don't analyze me. You're not my therapist or anyone's. Stop trying to be."

Dosie's eyes widened like a scolded child's. "I'm not."

"You *are*," Jennifer snapped, "and I can't fucking stand it right now!" *Stop. Stop. Fucking stop yourself! You don't mean this.* She didn't, not below the surface. As irritating as it could sometimes be to have a mirror held up to her own behavior or to have someone consider her motives beyond the surface, it had also been one of the most clarifying and liberating experiences of Jennifer's life. She had learned more about how to regulate and communicate her emotions from Dosie than she had in the entirety of her life before. But now? *No.* She couldn't do the work now. She couldn't be rational. She couldn't be calm. Her insides were melting. The mirror was shattered, and Jennifer couldn't bear the sight of her own jagged reflection. Tears stung sharply in her eyes, and her heart beat too hard. She felt sick and high and *desperate* all at once.

"Jen."

"No, Dosie, stop," Jennifer said, "and just be my girlfriend. Be my lover. Be my fucking partner and comfort me the way I need you to!"

The roar of boiling water overwhelmed as the words hit the air

Corrie MacKay

and died. The kettle clicked off behind them, then finally, only quiet and steam remained, the fragility of debris after detonation. The air grew heavy as Dosie gaped at her, lips hanging slightly open, eyes big and round. And wet. The sight made Jennifer ache.

Regret was a shard in her heart. She opened her mouth to apologize, but just as she did, Dosie unfroze. She licked her lips and cleared her throat, blinked as if returning from a dream. "You're right," she said, voice a breathless rasp, then she peeled off her baggy shirt and let it fall to the kitchen floor. In two steps, she had Jennifer by the back of the neck, tugging her into a fervent kiss.

The first cry was a whimper, a tiny bubble of hurt escaping its ruptured container. A hiccupped breath followed, and Dosie slowed her moving fingers to a gentle massage then stopped altogether. "Babe?" she whispered against the sweaty neck at her cheek.

"No, don't stop." Jennifer sat in Dosie's lap, wrapped around her like someone caught in a current, clinging to banked tree. Her thighs trapped Dosie's waist and hips, leaving just enough space for a hand to wedge between. One of her hands fisted in Dosie's hair while the other gripped her lower back. "I'm fine," she choked out. "Don't stop."

Dosie didn't. She wanted to; rather, the part of her that wasn't neck-deep in arousal thought it might be the best idea, or the healthiest one, to stop. She was still buzzing from the three potent orgasms Jennifer gave her after she picked Dosie up and carried her from the kitchen to the bedroom. She'd then licked and sucked her zealously, refusing any respite between climaxes. When she finally let up, it was only long enough to climb on top of Dosie and pull one of her hands between her legs. *Three fingers,* she'd commanded before Dosie had even caught her breath. *I want it fast and deep. Don't let up until I collapse.*

Dosie had heard every word of it like blunted music in her ears, commands pushed through a bulky filter that gave her little time to think or react. But she listened. Her body did. It heeded as if it was made to abide Jennifer Dupont, to pleasure her. It was instinct. It was pure, unadulterated desire, and it overrode everything else. The tickle in the back of Dosie's mind, the concern, the worry, seeped away like water through a sieve. Nothing remained after but want.

"Don't *stop*." Jennifer pushed the words through gritted teeth as she ground her hips down. Her pulsing inner muscles crushed around Dosie's three fingers as she threw her head back. Her long neck arched, breasts jutting forward, and Dosie's breath caught in her lungs until her chest grew tight.

The sun's brilliant afternoon rays, tossed to and fro between Bay Area cloud cover, danced in Jennifer's damp black hair and made it shimmer like an oil slick. Her skin became a golden-white kaleidoscope and her eyes a couplet of shadow and blue. She was sublime beauty in her wanton pleasure, in her boundless grief. If Dosie still believed in holy things, she might even call it divine, the way Jennifer appeared to her now.

The second cry was a sob. Or, it would have been, had Dosie not trapped it with a kiss. She swallowed the sound so Jennifer wouldn't have to hear herself cry again. Dosie didn't think she could bear it. She wasn't sure she could handle it herself. The immensity of Jennifer's grief, and how easily it overwhelmed her, was painful to witness when she knew that, ultimately, there was nothing she could do to ease it. Her bounty of experience with such darkness had taught her well that the only way out was through.

Jennifer shuddered as Dosie's fingers sank deeper and drew a messy circle inside her. But her eyes were closed too tightly, forehead scrunched. Her mouth frowned. Tears sat in her eyelashes, threatening to fall. Her hips rocked harder as she whined, "I *can't*," with her voice on the edge of a growl. "I keep losing it."

"Okay, hey," Dosie said as she used her free hand to slow Jennifer's movement. "Look at me. Is it something I'm doing? Or something I'm not doing?"

"No, it's not you." Her bottom lip quivered, and Dosie's heart shook as if attached. "I'm distracted."

"Do you want to stop?" She blew a cool breath over Jennifer's flushed cheeks as the woman shook her head from side to side. "Okay. Tell me how to help." She kissed Jennifer's neck, sucked the salt from her skin, and kissed her again. "What can I do to make it better?"

Her voice was a rumble against Jennifer's pulse, lower than intended and scratchy from her earlier breathlessness, and Dosie noticed right away that it had an effect. The more her voice vibrated against Jennifer's neck and ears, the harder her girlfriend gripped her. Her hips shifted as if of their own accord, and Dosie hid her smile in the crook of Jennifer's neck. The idea of her voice alone giving her lover pleasure never failed to excite her.

"Or is this it?" she asked, willing herself to speak without judging, without the constant worry of sounding dumb or awkward. "Do you want me to talk to you?" *Don't overthink it.* It wasn't an easy thing to avoid when said thing was her standard response to life, but Dosie had done it before. She had given herself over to nothing but desire and voice and the sublime experience that was Jennifer Marie Clementine Dupont in her element, and she could do it again.

Jennifer's reply was a moan as she enthusiastically reanimated her hips.

"So, if I keep talking, you'll come?" Dosie tugged Jennifer's ear lobe between her teeth. "Is that what you want, Jen? To come on my fingers with my voice in your ear, telling you how good you feel?"

"*Fuck,*" Jennifer groaned as she dropped her forehead onto Dosie's shoulder and rutted herself harder against her hand. "*Yes.* Tell me how good my pussy feels."

Pleasure zinged through Dosie's body, struck her clitoris like a clapper to a bell. How was she supposed to focus on her own talking when Jennifer could so easily say things like that? *Do it anyway,* she demanded of herself and did, even though she knew, could *feel,* how hot and red her cheeks were. "It feels perfect. You're so hot and wet for me. I love feeling you sliding up and down my fingers."

A strangled sound left Jennifer. Her vagina constricted around Dosie's hand like a vise, trapping it in place and rendering Dosie nearly immobile. Still, Jennifer continued her thrusting, her hips taking command of the work. Head tossed back again, she panted into the air as she fucked herself on Dosie's fingers to the sound of Dosie's voice.

"That's it," Dosie encouraged her, dizzy with the sensation of being gripped and rocked. Jennifer's naked heels dug into her lower back, one pushing at the top of her ass. Jennifer's naked breasts rubbed against her own. Jennifer's slick heat and mad need. It all overwhelmed. Loving her, making love to her, was and continued to be an intoxicating, incredible affair, and Dosie lived for it. "You're close. I can feel it."

Jennifer gasped when it hit but stayed otherwise silent, as if the force of it knocked the wind out of her. Her muscles clamped tighter. Dosie's knuckles screamed for the several seconds it lasted, then all the tension released, and Jennifer collapsed against her.

For a moment, they were only silence and breath and the *thump-thump* of Jennifer's heartbeat against Dosie's sheathed fingers. "I'm sorry," Jennifer whispered against Dosie's sweaty neck. "For raising my voice at you."

"Thank you," Dosie said and kissed her collarbone. With care, she pulled her buried hand free, stretched and flexed her sore fingers, then wrapped both her arms around her girlfriend. "I'm sorry, too. I shouldn't assume your needs are the same as mine when you're triggered or that you'll communicate them the same way I do. We're different people, and we've suffered differently. It's only natural that we deal with that suffering in different ways sometimes."

She felt Jennifer's nod, but no words followed. Stillness and silence crept in like a sandman's spell in the middle of the day, and they simply held one another until their limbs turned liquid and their eyes grew heavy. But it wasn't relaxing. The air felt tense and weighty around them, as if the atmosphere was holding its breath, and Dosie didn't care for it. She hadn't felt such tension since the early months of their relationship, before they became something, *them*. When they were just two strangers, drawn to one another and helpless to ignore it, each carrying weights and burdens and buried desires with them. It wasn't bad, just uneasy. For the first time in a long time, Dosie wasn't sure what Jennifer was thinking or how she was feeling, and it unsettled her.

"How do you make it stop?"

Dosie roused from her thoughts at the quiet pain in Jennifer's voice. She stroked down Jennifer's hair to let her know she was heard. "How do I make what stop, baby?"

A terrible sigh, one that had to have started in the darkest, most neglected depths of her, left Jennifer with an equally terrible ease. She disentangled their limbs and rolled off to Dosie's side, crawled up to her pillow, and lay down. They wordlessly reconnected, Dosie molding herself around Jennifer from behind and covering them with the duvet. In their rapidly warming nest, Jennifer held Dosie's hand, both resting over her navel, and said, "Since the moment I opened that letter, the memories.... Things I don't want to remember. That day. The last time I saw her. The way she sounded. The bruises on her neck." She shuddered and choked on her words. "The pictures they showed at his trial."

Dosie winced as if jabbed. Empathy coursed her body like a current. She knew those kinds of memories, possessed countless of her own, and knew just how violent they could feel. Like an attack from your own body, a mental form of self-mutilation. It was torture, to have such memories, to have seen such things and survived them, because they never left. All those countless precious memories to recall, and the ones that rose to the surface in the end, the ones that came most vividly and lingered the longest, were always the worst. Always the ugliest. Always the most painful.

"Oh," she said when no other words came, and Jennifer freed another sigh. Quieter. Softer. No less terrible.

"I keep trying to make it stop. I force myself to think about other things. Better things. You. Us. But they creep back in." She rolled in

Dosie's arms, and their sad eyes met. She lay a hand on Dosie's neck, thumbed along her jaw. "Your touch makes everything else disappear, but not this. I tried, and I'm trying, but I feel like I'm going crazy." She grunted her frustration and buried her face in Dosie's chest, spoke muffled words against the warm flesh of her right breast. "How do I make it stop? How do you do it?"

Dosie didn't have answers, only hopes and honest efforts and best tries. Nothing definitive. Nothing that would offer any immediate relief. It devastated her not to be able to provide that, that there was no right thing to say and no medicine but love that she could offer to ease the pain.

"I don't," she admitted as she ran her fingers over Jennifer's hair. "I just do my best to remind myself that I'm safe, and I'm okay now, and I wait for it to pass. I know that's probably not what you want to hear, but I don't have anything better. I do my mantras, and I write and talk about how I'm feeling, and I let others be there for me, and I just hope that I can keep myself from obsessing until it passes."

"And you're positive you don't know any magic spells to make that happen faster?"

"I did briefly have some success with a particularly dramatic Abra Kadabra once, but then I realized I was just holding my breath waiting for something to happen, and it made me feel kind of dizzy and high for a second."

She smiled when Jennifer snorted against her chest and said, "So, no?"

"I'm sorry." Dosie kissed wherever she could reach with her lips: Jennifer's temple, the top of her head, the corner of her eyebrow. "All I've got are kisses."

"Fine," Jennifer grumbled. "How much for your entire stock?"

Dosie chuckled. "Well, you're in luck, ma'am, because today they're all free."

When Dosie woke, the sun had dipped beyond the horizon and left them in darkness. Her. Left *her* in darkness. Her hand met empty space beside her. The sheet was cool to the touch, so she knew Jennifer had left the bed some time ago. She lay staring into the shadowy corners of the room a moment longer, breathing through her rising anxiety that she might find her love sobbing in the shower again or on her treadmill running herself ragged in a futile attempt to outpace her pain. Sitting amongst a pile of shards because she'd decided that her possessions should match her insides—broken and scattered. Dosie threw back the covers, the last thought enough to scare her into action, and left the last warm remnants of repose.

She found her in the living room, thankfully neither surrounded by debris nor sweating herself to death. Jennifer sat in her favorite spot—the cushioned lounge tucked under her large bay window—with a mug housed between her hands and her gaze set on the dark horizon. She wore a pair of sweatpants and a t-shirt, and her thick, long hair was still visibly damp in places from her earlier shower. A stained tea tag hung over the side of her mug, and no steam rose from the within. Dosie wondered how long she'd been sitting there, her tea cold or gone, her mind elsewhere. She knew where, of course. The papers resting on Jennifer's lap told her as much, not that she needed any clues. This haunting wasn't new. It had lasted Jennifer's lifetime, its dark hum an inconsistent frequency that grew louder and softer and louder again but never turned silent. Dosie knew because she had her own frequencies, some similar, some unique, buzzing about her brain and body like flies seeking somewhere to land. Sometimes, they were easy to ignore. At others, they demanded attention.

Dosie took one of Jennifer's soft, cashmere blankets from the back of the nearest chair and wrapped it around her naked body like a cape. It smelled like Jennifer—a rich scent, woodsy and layered, that Dosie had begun to associate with a sense of home. "Hey," she said as she approached, almost regretful. Jennifer seemed as close to peaceful as she could be, given everything, and Dosie hated to disturb that peace. But the immediate soft smile that greeted her as Jennifer turned her head, eyes tired and sad, sapped her regret away.

Jennifer wordlessly set her mug aside and extended a hand, waiting. Her cold fingers wrapped around Dosie's and tugged her closer, pulled her into her lap, right on top of that damning bit of mail that had turned the dial on the noise inside. The papers crinkled under Dosie's behind, and neither of them cared.

"Did you sleep at all?" Dosie asked, and Jennifer sighed and stuck her chilly nose against her neck.

"Not really."

Do you want to talk about it? Dosie thought but didn't ask. She knew what the answer would be. Instead, she ran her fingers through Jennifer's hair and said, "Let me make you some more tea."

"No, stay," Jennifer murmured against her skin and slinked her arms under the blanket to ring Dosie's nude frame. "You're so warm."

"I won't be if you keep putting your ice-cold hands on me." Her nerves jumped every time her lover's fingers slid to a new location, and goosebumps appeared along her arms. "How long have you been sitting here?"

"A decade or two, maybe. I feel like a corpse."

Dosie snorted. "Well, you look great for a decades-old corpse."

"I try."

"Jen?"

"Hm?"

"I love you."

"I know."

"Do you? Really?"

She pulled back to look at Dosie. When their eyes met, Dosie cupped her angled cheek, thumbing the point of her cheekbone. "Of course I do," Jennifer said and lay her own frozen hand atop Dosie's. "I'm okay, love. Stop worrying."

"Worrying is my default setting."

A tired smile pulled one corner of Jennifer's mouth. "You know that causes wrinkles, right?"

Dosie rolled her eyes. "Well then, it'll even out our age difference since you basically have none. You're like a vampire. How do I know you're not secretly 500?"

"Periods," Jennifer said. "If I was still having periods at 500 years old, I'd fucking stake myself."

Dosie laughed and kissed her. "I wouldn't blame you."

"Mm," Jennifer hummed. "One more."

Dosie kissed her again. "Happy?"

"Something like that," Jennifer sighed. "Thank you for being here."

"My pleasure."

They sat in silence for a while, Jennifer resting in the crook of her neck as Dosie stroked her hair and let her mind wander. And worry. She worried about Jennifer, about the parole hearing, about what it would mean for the safety of countless women to have someone who had committed such a heinous crime set free upon the world again, and at such a young and capable age. Dosie wasn't sure how old the man was, but she knew he couldn't be much older than Jennifer. Mid-forties, she assumed. She couldn't imagine the terror of knowing her own demons, her father especially, might be released into the wild again. The day he'd been condemned to spend the remainder of his years in a prison cell had been the greatest relief of her life, and if he hadn't been, Dosie had zero doubt that he'd have ended up right back where he started: turning people into puppets and children into ghosts. The thought made her shiver.

Dosie held Jennifer a bit tighter and closed her eyes. "I'm glad you canceled your work appointment."

"Me too," Jennifer mumbled. "But I'm not staying."

With a frown, Dosie put some space between them, caught Jennifer's eyes. "What do you mean?"

"I'm leaving tonight."

"It's almost nine," Dosie said, confused. "Where are you going to go?"

"I booked a red eye to Boston," Jennifer told her. "I have to go."

Dosie's heartrate increased. "But you can't wait until morning?"

"The sooner I get there, the better," Jennifer said. "I need to get my head on right, and I need to talk to my aunt. I don't know why she waited so long to send me the notice." She shook her head and closed her eyes. "I'm *furious* with her for not contacting me sooner, and now the hearing is in just a few days, and I have no time to, to—"

"To process," Dosie supplied, and Jennifer nodded and opened her eyes again.

"Or prepare." Her voice cracked, and she glanced away. Dosie watched the fear creep into her expression, tugging her lips down, coating her eyes in a sheen of unshed tears.

Understanding dawned, and Dosie felt her eyes go wide. "You're going to speak at the hearing?"

Jennifer shifted back against her cushion, retreating to cover her face with her hands. She breathed into her palms. Once. Twice. Then she lay her head against the windowpane and said, "There are things I have to make up for, things I, that I, things I'm ashamed of that I need to make right."

The words left her in forced puffs of air and sound, like something pushed through a grater and forced to function on the other side. She was a mess, just tatters trying to be whole as she spoke about the one thing that she had never been able to outside of short bursts of bravery and ruthless necessity. It tore Dosie in two just to witness it.

She wanted to ask. There were so many things about Jennifer's youth and family that she didn't know, so many details about that terrible event and all that came after that Jennifer hadn't told her and likely never would. Dosie knew why. It wasn't because Jennifer wanted to keep her in the dark or refused to share with her. It was because some experiences were just too terrible to revisit. Dosie had written and could now speak about many of her own, but there were still some experiences that made her voice shake. There were some that even the thought of sent her spiraling. Some traumas remained open, refusing to scar, and calling attention to them was like digging into an open, infected wound. The pain of it was overwhelming, and it could linger for days after. Months. *Years*. Dosie didn't want to ask Jennifer to do that for her, even if she believed it might ultimately be good. She had decided to let her curiosity go unanswered, just as she knew Jennifer had done with her own questions about Dosie's past. Even having read Dosie's memoir, there was still so much she didn't know, so much that *no one* knew apart from the people who'd lived it, most of whom were now dead, and the therapists who had collectively, over many years, saved Dosie's life. She was content, for now at least, to keep it that way. And this? This wasn't her story. She could not and would not demand it be told.

Instead, Dosie gathered herself. She blinked away tears and squeezed Jennifer's thigh. "Okay," she said as she turned her mind to the days ahead. She cycled rapidly through the tasks she had set for the week—appointments and supply deliveries and construction plans for the remaining renovations on her house—and determined they were all trivial in comparison. She could rebook. She could move things around. This was important. "Okay. I'll have to make some calls and change some stuff around, but I can do that when we get there. Was the flight fully booked? Do you think I could get on, too, or maybe standby? Red-eye flights aren't usually full, are they?" She laughed as she pressed a hand to her forehead, a bit dizzy with the sudden change in her plans. "At least I already have clothes here."

Wait. Dosie's breath caught in her chest as she realized that Jennifer had suddenly gone quite still. Blue eyes darted, avoided. *What's happening?* Jennifer cleared her throat, and Dosie knew without doubt that the next words that left her girlfriend's mouth would sting.

"Dosie, I... I don't think you should come."

It hit like a wind-sucking knock to her gut. For a moment, she couldn't breathe. "What?"

Jennifer exhaled heavily through her nose. "I'm sorry."

"I don't understand. You want to do this alone? I don't think that's a good idea, Jen."

"Well, it's what I've decided I'm doing," Jennifer said and rocked her legs up in a way that made it clear she wanted Dosie to move. The moment she did, Jennifer was up off the cushion and on her feet, already walking away. "And I'd like it if you would support that decision instead of challenging it."

Dosie snapped her mouth closed, and the challenge she'd been prepared to present died bitterly on her tongue. Her heart squeezed as if trapped. *What do I say? What do I say?* She knew, *knew*, that it wasn't a good idea, but she also knew, unfortunately, that trying to tell Jennifer Dupont what was good for her and what wasn't was like trying to tell a zebra it should consider being spotted instead of striped. It was possible, sure, if you were willing to be blinked at as if you'd grown an extra head, but whether it yielded any results depended entirely on whether the Director was willing to be directed. One needn't be an empath to sense Jennifer's current mood was decidedly *not* willing. *Crap.*

Frozen in place, Dosie waited until Jennifer's back disappeared through the open door to her bedroom. The second she was out of sight, she collapsed onto the window cushion and blew a loud, annoyed grumble of a breath into the air. How the hell was she going to convince her stubborn-as-an-ox girlfriend to stop being so private with her pain and let her *help*, for once.

The loud sound of a throat clearing startled her. Jennifer had reappeared; well, her upper half had. She leaned out of the bedroom doorway with a toothbrush stuck between her lips and popped it free just long enough to say, "My flight leaves at 11:40. Carolina will be along for me shortly." And then she was gone again, disappearing like a ghost into the dark of her bedroom.

Dosie turned her head to check the large clock on the wall and groaned. The convincing would be hard enough. Now she had to do it in less than two hours. *Jesus, take the wheel,* she thought as an anxious warmth spilled into her cheeks. She scolded herself as she blew a cold breath up over her face. *No, don't. I've got the wheel. I'm driving the damned car!*

She huffed and hopped off the cushion. Maybe she could subtly pack a bag without Jennifer ever noticing. Or contort herself enough to hide in Jennifer's luggage. No, she was too tall for that. Also, it was creepy. She headed for the bedroom to attempt to plead her case without ever actually pleading it. Puppy-dog eyes: check. Sweet voice: check. Dimple: check. Last resort, more sexy talk: kind-of check? *Just don't sound like a therapist. Oh, God damn it, this is never going to work.*

3

A thick tension, one that felt borderline alive, pervaded the crisp night air as Dosie followed Jennifer down the short walkway in front of her building. Almost an hour had passed since Jennifer dropped the bomb that she was leaving for Massachusetts on the world's shortest notice and that Dosie was not welcome to join her. The bitter film of failure sat on Dosie's tongue, further souring her mood, as she watched Jennifer's cool, unbothered steps toward Carolina's waiting car. The grinding sound of her suitcase rolling along the concrete grated on Dosie's nerves, but then, even the slight whistle of the breeze made her want to scream. All her senses had heightened with her anxiety. All her emotions felt as if they'd been cycled through a tumble dryer and come out hot, wrinkled, and riddled with static. Chief among them: her crackling disappointment.

She had not been able to convince Jennifer to let her accompany her. In truth, despite her intentions, she didn't apply much effort. Every time she had opened her mouth to try, it was as if Jennifer sensed what was coming, and she would either hurry her packing or leave the room in search of something she suddenly realized she needed. Dosie didn't want to needle her, and she didn't want to argue. She just wanted to be with Jennifer. She was terrified of *not* being with Jennifer, not because she didn't believe her girlfriend could handle the situation but because she knew, in every cell of her body, that she shouldn't be handling it alone. Not when she didn't have to. But Jennifer was nothing if not sure of herself, even when she wasn't. It was a trait Dosie had always found both deeply attractive and troubling.

At the curb, Carolina rounded the car looking half-asleep and grumpy. Suit traded for sweatpants and a hoodie, she appeared much less intimidating than usual. She was a brick house, to be sure, but she was also a teddy bear, and Dosie had grown to love her despite them having only spent short periods of time together. At least she knew Jennifer would make it to the airport safely; after that, anything was possible. She wasn't entirely convinced Jennifer would even answer her calls once she'd fled the state like a thief in the night.

"Why do you look like that?" Carolina asked as she took in Jennifer's chic navy dress pants, matching silk top, and high-heeled white leather booties.

Jennifer stopped, appearing so utterly lost by the question that Dosie almost laughed. "I don't know what you mean."

"Is there going to be a best-dressed competition on your middle-of-the-night flight? You know most people fly in their most comfortable clothes, not their most stylish."

Jennifer rolled her eyes. "These are far from my most stylish clothes, and I'll have you know, I'm quite comfortable."

"Sure you are." Carolina turned her attention to Dosie and held out her arms. Dosie barely stopped herself from shouldering Jennifer out of the way to get inside them. "Come here, you. It's been a while."

"I know," Dosie said as she sank into the embrace. "Squeeze me. I need this hug."

Carolina laughed. "You got it."

"At least you get a hug," Jennifer said as she opened the rear door to set her luggage inside.

"You forced me out of bed," Carolina countered, "*after* you'd already texted to say work was canceled and I didn't have to get out of bed."

Jennifer scoffed. "It's not like I'm not paying you to be here, and you know I hate leaving my car at the airport."

"You hate your car in general. You only have it for emergencies," Carolina said, then she nudged Dosie's arm. "Well, and for this one now."

"You also don't like hugs," Dosie said, just as punctuation, and Jennifer deflated like a plant in need of water.

"It would still be nice to be offered one."

"For God's sake." Carolina held her arms open again. "Come on then."

Jennifer wrinkled her nose and shuffled awkwardly in place. "No, thank you."

"Oh, will you just get in the damned car already?" Carolina said, and the three laughed as if the air wasn't still thick with tension.

It felt good, that laugh, like an instant balm. But it didn't last. Dosie's blistering anxiety returned a moment later when Carolina asked if she had a bag to load. "No, because I'm not invited."

Jennifer's sigh was monumental. "Dosie."

Ugh. Dosie hated feeling this way, like someone had scooped all her insides out, dunked them in hot glue, and tossed them back in. Everything was sticky and irritated, and she could do nothing to help it. "She likes to make decisions when she's underfed and hasn't slept."

Carolina smacked her lips as if she suddenly had a bad taste in her mouth. "Yeah, it's too late and too cold. I'm going to avoid whatever this is and return to my toasty car. Good to see you, D."

"You too," Dosie said as she wrapped her arms around herself to replace Carolina's warmth. When the car door shut with a reverberating snap, she was left alone with her irritation again. And Jennifer.

"You're angry," Jennifer said as she came to stand in front of her. Her hands moved restlessly at her sides for a moment then rose to Dosie's shoulders. "Please don't be angry."

"I'm not angry," Dosie told her and meant it. "I'm upset. There's a difference."

Jennifer glanced away as if she might find her next words in the bush nearby. When her gaze returned, her eyes were conflicted. Her lips dipped with a frown. "Can you really not understand that this is something I need to do on my own?"

"I can understand why you *think* you need to do it on your own," Dosie said, "because you're so used to facing the hard things in your life that way, *if* you face them at all." Jennifer winced as if Dosie had pinched her, her hands falling from Dosie's shoulders to dangle at her sides again. "What I don't understand is why you can't even consider that maybe you're wrong about that, and I'd like to be able to say that without you thinking I'm trying to therapize you, or whatever."

Silence invaded their awkward stand-off, growing like a hungry beast until Jennifer swallowed loud enough for Dosie to hear it and said, "I don't have time to argue with you, and I don't want to."

"I don't want to argue with you either."

"So, don't," Jennifer said and reached for her hands. "Please, love, I can't do this right now. Can you please just try to trust me when I say that this is what I need?"

"And if you realize that it's not?" Dosie challenged despite Jennifer's plea. Because this was the heart of it. This was her fear, the one that wouldn't stop pacing the edges of her heart, trying to find a way in. "What if you realize you're wrong, and you *do* need me, and I'm not there, Jen? And I can't get there in time? What if things go badly, and you're alone?"

For a moment, it was as if Jennifer actually considered her words and the weight they held, the possibility that she might need Dosie to help her, even if she didn't want her to. But the moment passed as quickly as it came. Jennifer's hand rose to Dosie's cheek, her cold fingers stroking. "Then that will be on me," she said and shuffled close enough for their noses to touch. "Not you."

Dosie sighed and gave in, put her arms around Jennifer and held her tight. "I don't care about who's to blame. I care about you."

"I'm okay," Jennifer promised, and Dosie hated that she didn't believe her. They looked at each other, and she could see Jennifer's exhaustion in her eyes, could she her unsurety, her anxiety, her pain. It was all right there on the surface despite her best efforts to mash everything down into something unrecognizable and powerless. "I'll do what I need to do, and I'll be okay. Okay?"

Dosie had no idea what would happen. Maybe Jennifer was right. Maybe she would go and face her past on her own, and she would be fine. She would come back better for having done it, stronger for having faced it alone, and with some sense of peace. But Dosie couldn't shake the feeling that that wouldn't be the case at all.

"Okay," she whispered.

Jennifer's shoulders dropped as visible relief spread through her, and Dosie both loved and hated the sight of it. She loved that she could offer her comfort, but she hated that it didn't feel genuine.

"Stay here, if you like," Jennifer said, nodding toward the building. She thumbed Dosie's cheek, pressing her dimple like it was a button she could use to activate a smile. Dosie tried for her, but all she managed was a grimace. "I will see you in a few days."

Dosie nodded, said nothing.

"You're really not going to tell me you love me?" Jennifer asked, and Dosie rolled her eyes.

"Stop trying to be cute," she grumbled as she grabbed Jennifer by the front of her fine silk shirt and reeled her into a kiss. "I love you. So much."

"See? Was that so hard?" Jennifer teased as she eased away, taking slow steps backward to the waiting car. At the open door, she smiled at Dosie. It was soft and tired but genuine, and it touched Dosie's soul like a delicate kiss. "Don't worry, darling."

And then she left Dosie in the cold with her featherlight, fragile comfort and the worry she wasn't supposed to have.

Corrie MacKay

When the partition dropped, Jennifer braced herself for yet another difficult conversation. Carolina's eyes found her in the rearview mirror. "You know if you keep canceling on Mr. Ben Dover, he's going to start paying someone else to bend him over."

The laugh bubbled in Jennifer's belly like a fizzy drink then floated up her throat. She covered her eyes as her shoulders began to shake with it and relief spilled through her system. "And here I was girding myself," she said. "I thought you were going to ask me about what happened back there."

"Oh, I am," Carolina assured. "Just thought I'd break the ice first."

"Great," Jennifer groaned as she lay her head back against the seat and closed her eyes. "Well, Mr. Dover is welcome to find someone else to bend him over any time he likes. I'm sure whomever he chooses will be far less effective at what comes after."

"Ah, la, la, no details, please," Carolina begged, "even if it's just you bragging about you."

"You started it."

"And now I'm ending it," Carolina laughed, "and segueing right into—"

"Please don't," Jennifer said, but Carolina breezed past the words like she did the other cars on the freeway.

"Sorry, but this is how friendship works, Jennifer. We ask each other about our bullshit and try to help. How many times do I have to tell you this?"

"At least a few dozen more," Jennifer grumbled. "What do you want me to say?"

"Whatever you feel comfortable saying," Carolina told her. "But really, I just want to make sure that you're alright and that Dosie is, too. I mean, I can only assume whatever's going on is something at least a little bit serious given the whole last-minute flight and that hella tragic goodbye back there. But you don't actually have to tell me anything if you don't want to, Jen. I'm just checking on you."

"And I adore you for it," Jennifer said, "truly, but I can't talk about it." She closed her eyes, convinced that if she couldn't see anything or anyone, it might make getting the words out easier. "It *is* something serious, yes, but not something that I speak about. Ever." She choked on her words, laughed off the break in her voice as if doing so might take the edge off her pain. It didn't. "I mean, you saw that, what happened between Dosie and me. We kissed like two cardboard fucking cutouts." Frustration trickled into her voice, only straining it further. She hated the sensation, hated the sound. Hated the world. "We never kiss that way. We never *are* that way. Even when we first met, when things were at their most awkward and unsure, we had an ease about us. It was natural. It's always been natural with us, but with this.... I'm sorry, Carolina. I'm just talking around it without saying anything, I know, but this is something I can barely even speak about with Dosie, who is literally the *only* person I've ever been able to talk to about anything. And it's an issue. I know it is, but I still just—"

"Can't," Carolina supplied. "I get it. You're not ready to talk about it. I'm sure Dosie understands that, too."

"She does. She understands everything, more than probably anyone else on earth. It's honestly annoying."

Carolina snorted. "Oh yeah, I'm sure it's super annoying to have someone in your life who understands you perfectly without you even having to say a word."

"You know what I mean."

"I do."

"She worries," Jennifer said. "About everything. About me. Even when I tell her not to."

"Well, not to be all Team Dosie or anything, but it seems like you've given her good reason to worry about you. You said yourself it's something serious, and you're clearly having trouble with it."

Jennifer let the words sink in, let them flit about inside her like leaves caught in the wind. When they finally fell to rest, she freed a weighty breath and nodded. "Yeah," she said, more to herself than her companion. "That's fair."

"Look, I don't want to push you to talk about it, and we're almost to the airport now anyway. But if you're good with telling me, I'd like to know you're okay. Like, it's nothing bad to do with your health or your safety or anything, right?"

"Yes, I'm okay," Jennifer assured, touched by Carolina's care. "It's a family thing."

"Ah," Carolina said and trilled her lips as she exhaled. "Family stuff can be tough."

"Yes, it can."

"I've got plenty of my own family crap, so I get it." The glow of the sprawling San Francisco International Airport loomed ahead as she steered them into the ever-steady traffic that surrounded it. "Maybe, someday, we can sit down together with a drink and talk about it all. Your family stuff and mine." She caught Jennifer's eyes in the mirror. "If you want."

The thought of baring it all a second time to a second person overwhelmed, and Jennifer's throat grew tight. Her tongue swelled as if in protest. Still, she opened her mouth and said, "Maybe. Someday."

Her T-shirt smelled like Jennifer. The sweater she grabbed from the hall closet did, too. The sheets and pillows were soaked with the scent. Dosie couldn't escape it as she trudged back through Jennifer's place and threw herself face-first onto the bed. It wasn't that she wanted it gone, the expensive-smelling aroma that invaded her senses; she just wanted it to stop reminding her that Jennifer had left. More importantly, she wanted it to stop reminding her that Jennifer had left *without her*.

Dosie's phone lay on Jennifer's bedside table. She grabbed it to check the time and had to resist the urge to text her girlfriend something along the lines of, *Wait. Come back. You forgot something important!* Just to see if Jennifer would come rushing back, so Dosie could leap out from behind the door and shout, "It's me! I'm the important thing!" *Not that I should have to remind her.* She tossed her phone aside again and rolled onto her back. With an annoyed huff, she demanded of the universe, "How am I supposed to survive a six-hour flight?!"

Normally, it wouldn't have been a problem. She and Jennifer had grown incredibly close since the start of their relationship. They were, she imagined, as inseparable as two people who lived hours apart and who maintained relatively busy schedules could be, but they weren't joined at the hip. It wasn't the distance that was eating her alive, infecting Jennifer's perfect scent with the stench of doubt. It wasn't that they were apart. It was Jennifer herself.

It was the way Dosie had learned her like an extension of her own body, knew her so intimately that she believed her worry was warranted. She didn't know everything, but she knew enough to understand Jennifer's strengths and weaknesses. She had seen her triggered, dealt with her fear, soothed her anxieties. Dosie knew where the cracks in Jennifer's defenses were and what types of pressure might have the power to rend them open. That, she was sure, was the reason she couldn't settle. No matter what Jennifer told her, no matter how many times she assured Dosie that she was fine and could handle the weight of what lay ahead, and no matter how much she might even be convinced that it was true, Dosie just didn't believe her. And she hated that she didn't.

She wanted to believe. She wanted to be just as convinced as Jennifer that the choice to go alone was the right one and that she would be okay. But Dosie knew grief, the deep kind that didn't visit but stayed, that sat in the body like a second soul and left precious little room outside it to breathe. She knew grief, and she knew that, even after so many years, Jennifer had barely even begun to process hers. Not when it came to her sister. And what a layered grief it was. A sister. A best friend. A confidante. Jennifer's safe place.

Lauren had been all that remained of Jennifer's core family, and then she, too, disappeared, her life taken while still in the breath of its beginning. Everything she might have become, every dream she could have had and talent she could have nurtured, every laugh that might have shaken her belly and every hope that might have been whispered from her lips, was snatched like a flame from a candle's wick. Dosie couldn't know, because Jennifer's talk of her only came in rare, meteoric bursts that fizzled before they struck, but she hoped that Jennifer allowed herself, every now and then, to imagine a long, beautiful life for her sister. As a painter. Or a pathologist. A forest conservationist with kids named after mushrooms. Or a mechanic who moonlit as a magician. Someone silly and serious and fascinating and *happy*. Someone loved. Someone safe.

She wished Jennifer could do that now, hoped she would try even if Dosie knew it would be in vain. Because the loss of her sister wasn't Jennifer's only ghost. It was also, and perhaps predominantly, the betrayal of her brother-in-law. The man she and her family had all welcomed and loved and trusted became the man who terrorized and tore them apart, and the possibility that that man could walk free wasn't something Jennifer was prepared for. It wasn't something she should be facing on her own, not because she couldn't survive it; she could, even if she came out the other side in pieces. It was because she didn't have to. As long as Dosie breathed, Jennifer would never have to be alone again if she didn't want to be.

Dosie wiped a few tears from her cheek with the back of her hand. Her phone begged her attention despite its blank, black screen, and she couldn't help herself. She tapped to see the time again and felt an urge to scream.

Barely ten minutes had passed.

The brisk air was a welcome reprieve as she passed through the boarding bridge. In a rare change of pace, the airport had been less tundra, more cozy winter cabin, and Jennifer's cheeks were flushed with warmth. Sweat beaded down the bumps of her spine like rain over a rocky riverbed. The heat hadn't been excessive; any other day, Jennifer would have been grateful for it. It was just *her*.

Her body was reacting to pressure, the crackling, climbing inferno inside that she had allowed to smolder untended for far too long. She knew it didn't show. Her heels tapped smoothly with even steps. Her back was upright, shoulders relaxed, and her face was a cool, well-practiced screen reflecting disinterest at whomever glanced her way. She knew her exterior appeared as it always did, the epitome of put together, but inside, she was a wreck. She was a sweaty, trembling finger rimming the pin of a grenade, so tightly wound that with the slightest tilt or tug, she, the world, *something* may very well detonate.

I can do hard things. The mantra floated into the chaos of her mind with Dosie's sure, sweet voice wrapped around it. *Even if I have anxiety or am emotional, I can still do what I need to do.*

Her next breath came easier, though it felt no lighter, and Jennifer repeated the mantra as she boarded the plane and handed her suit bag to a flight attendant to be hung. She hated them, the mantras. The idea that something that had consistently, for decades, made her feel so terrible could be cured by the steady repetition of a few reflective and encouraging words to herself seemed preposterous. How could that even be possible? She knew it was, knew the power of repetition on the brain, but every time she tried it, she felt stupid. She would think the words, mutter them under her breath, and feel so ridiculous. So childish. So *pointless.*

Just trust me and keep trying.

Dosie's voice in her head was just as persistent now as her doubts, it seemed, and Jennifer found herself soothed into obedience. She even opened her lips, just the tiniest gap, to mouth along with her next repetition. Then a whisper of sound as a she began to murmur. "I can do hard things." She raised her carry-on into the compartment above her second-row aisle seat. "Even if I have anxiety..." The seat beside her was, as yet, empty, a small relief. No one to stare at her, bewildered, as she spoke to herself like an exhausted teacher going over a lesson with the world's most recalcitrant class. "...even if I am emotional..." She sat and buckled her seatbelt. "...I can still do what I need to do."

"Something to drink, ma'am?"

The sudden reappearance of the flight attendant made Jennifer's skin crawl. Had she seen her talking to herself? *I can do hard things, even if I—Oh, for fuck's sake!* "Whisky. Neat, please."

"Of course."

She hadn't slept, and she knew she likely wouldn't. Her brain was a bully, prodding her every time she nodded off. Ripping her seat out from under her just before she sat. But maybe a bit of alcohol would take the edge off. *Or maybe it will make it worse.* Jennifer all but growled at her own thoughts.

"Actually," she said, catching the flight attendant before she could disappear into the tiny prep area ahead, "nix that. I'm fine. Thank you."

As the attendant nodded and carried on with her business, Jennifer lay her head back against the seat and squeezed her eyes too tightly closed to allow her any rest. It didn't matter. All she needed was for the world to go dark for a while, as dark as the growing pit in her belly. She exhaled heavily, and Dosie's voice filtered back in like a whisper from the depths of her soul.

I can do hard things.

"Even if I don't fucking want to," Jennifer grumbled to herself and wondered if dying in a plane crash would be the worst thing in the world. Didn't most people pass on impact? Quick and painless, minus the whole terrifying, reckless descent part. *Jesus Christ! Am I seriously wishing for a fucking plane crash?* No. If there was one thing she knew after all she'd been through, it was that she had no interest whatsoever in dying.

I can do hard things.

4

Jennifer inhaled until her lungs burned. In her held breath, the walkway ahead warped until it seemed miles long. The concrete felt like quicksand beneath her feet, lazily shifting as it sucked her down. Hot. It was so hot out. Sweat seeped through her shirt, making a streak down her back and two more beneath her breasts. Her hair lay heavy on her shoulders, too heavy. She should have pulled it up. She let the breath go in a *whoosh* and shook out her hands.

Go. She willed her feet to free themselves and do the damned thing they were made to do. *Just go already!*

It worked. Even with the ground wobbling before her like something out of a funhouse, she moved along the path until the toes of her tennis shoes met the first porch stair. Her tongue tasted dry. Was dry a taste? Her hand made a wet imprint on the railing as she climbed toward the robin-egg blue door.

Why am I so nervous? It's my *house!* Or, it *was* her house, so long ago now it seemed. It was her house when things were different, when spaces were fuller and lovelier for it, and there were quiet, safe places to spare. It was her house when she was still someone's daughter and when death was still an ending that came only at the end.

The door opened. Her sister's face was the sun. Jennifer blinked and blinked, adjusting to the bright sight after so long. Lauren never came home to their aunt's house anymore, not even for Jennifer's birthday, or her own.

"You're not going to say anything?" she managed to say between short breaths. "It's been months!"

Lauren's face was at odds with itself, her expression a strange blend of happy and…. Jennifer didn't know. *Not* happy. Disappointed, maybe? Or *scared?* Jennifer's worry blasted through her anger like a snap freeze. She barely heard the words that followed, Lauren's or her own, as she followed into her old house with her pulse in her head like a war drum.

There was a hole in the wall. *Holes.* Multiple. The butt end of a television remote stuck outward from one of them like an art exhibit waiting to be labeled. *Fragile Masculinity* by Orwell Glass. Price: Worthless.

The drum in her head beat harder, its pace igniting into something frantic as the rest of the living room came into view. The old TV was toppled, one bulky brown side smashed against the floor, and nothing but spiderwebbed glass shards remained of its face. Most of them speckled the carpet. A strong smokey odor hung in the air, then Jennifer saw scorch marks. Small, charred circles dotted the couch arm as if someone had taken the lit end of a cigarette to the leather.

"It's not as bad as it looks," Lauren said as she nervously adjusted the high neck of the thick sweater she wore, one that should have been in storage for the summer. Jennifer could see bruises peeking from beneath the material, fresh purple-black smudges in the shapes of fingertips.

Her mouth watered as if she might vomit. "It looks pretty bad."

"Well, it's not." Lauren's voice grew defensive only to dissolve into a titter of a laugh, something dismissive and far too casual for the scene. It was her lying voice, the obnoxious pitch she used when she felt insecure about the truth, and Jennifer hated the way it hit her ears like nails on a chalkboard. "We just had one of our tiffs, and things got a little out of hand. It was my fault, really. Honestly, it wasn't that bad, Jennifer. Don't make it into something it's not."

She didn't feel she was making it into anything. It was what it was, and what it was, was bad. But when she opened her mouth to say as much, nothing came out. No protest. No lecture. Her eyes stung as tears brewed and muddled her vision. She blinked them away and cleared her throat, and then she dropped to the floor and began collecting the scattered glass.

"What are you doing?"

"Helping you clean up." Jennifer didn't know what else to say or if her sister would even be able to hear her, to *listen*. What if she argued with her and made it worse? What if Lauren told her to leave? She barely saw her as it was. The thought of her being alone with this, with his mess, with *him*, made Jennifer's throat tight. The little hairs at the backs of her arms prickled.

Then the door opened.

When he appeared, it was like the slow approach of a storm cloud, its dark mass looming over the atmosphere until it engulfed everything. The room rippled like disturbed water in front of her, and suddenly, Jennifer was aware. *Something isn't right*. The thought licked at the back of her brain like a whisper. *He didn't come back this soon.*

She stood to face him with her bones all but rattling and braced herself for his frigid demeanor, for the chill she knew his enraged silence would bring. Instead, with near pep in his step, he crossed the room and stood in front of her. Close. Jennifer could smell the sour mint stench of his most recent menthol cigarette on his breath. His eyes swam in front of hers, blurred beyond any definition, and another thought floated through Jennifer's mind, still too quiet to be anything other than background color. *Is this a dream?*

A weight dropped into her hand. The room clarified as Jennifer looked down to see a large hunting knife balanced atop her outstretched palm. *No.*

"Thanks, kid," Orwell said, his voice as indistinct as his eyes as he took the knife.

Wait! Jennifer tried to shout but couldn't make a sound. She tried to move, tried to lunge for the knife again just to keep it out of that monster's hands, only to abruptly find herself on the porch again, staring at the blue front door. *This isn't real.*

A scream tore through the home's interior, blasting through Jennifer's logic like a rock through a window. She threw herself at the door, hammering one fist against the wood while the other jerked the handle in vain. Locked. She shouted her sister's name, her voice still silent, and threw her body harder against the door. Then she felt it.

Warm and wet, it seeped into her tennis shoes and turned them a dirty red. Jennifer gaped in horror at her feet as blood spilled from under the door to surround them. She screamed soundlessly again as terror stampeded through her body. *What do I do?!*

It didn't matter if she couldn't make a sound. She needed to find something, anything, *anyone*, who could help her. *The neighbors.* The nearest house was close. She could make it. She could get help. She turned to race down the porch and came face-to-face with Glass.

Jennifer was stunned still as he stared at her from only inches away, his eyes wide and wild. He raised a hand between them and put his blood-soaked index finger to his lips. "Shh," he said. "Don't make it worse than it is."

Pressure at her sides startled her, and Jennifer looked down to watch her sister's hands, just as bloody as Glass's, ease around her waist. Lauren's voice gurgled wetly at the back of her ear. "Give me a squish."

The jagged blade sank into Jennifer's gut with a visceral *squish*, and she gasped and coughed herself awake to the concerned expression of her first-class seatmate. The sixty-something year old man who had boarded at the last possible moment and ruined the magic of Jennifer's empty row had seemed pleased at the initial sight of her;

now, he looked at her as if he half-expected her to break out in boils from the plague. He angled his body a bit more away from hers and used his hand to make a barrier in front of his mouth.

"Are you sick?" he asked, but Jennifer didn't answer. She had barely begun to process her return to reality. She was exhausted despite having just woken, and her stomach began to churn, crunching in on itself until she was sure she would vomit. Jennifer fumbled her seatbelt open and stumbled out of her seat.

"Are you all right, ma'am?" the flight attendant at the front of the plane asked. "We'll be landing soon."

Jennifer ignored her the same as she had the older man and shut herself inside the small lavatory. Her breath came in little gasping bursts as she latched onto the sink and tried to breathe through her nausea. She wet a paper towel and slapped it over the back of her neck, instantly soothed by the cold. Her nausea quelled, but her pulse still soared. She hadn't had nightmares like that in over a decade. Her body screamed with stress, but she refused to let it incapacitate her. She had things to do, responsibilities, and she was determined not to fail.

She checked her watch, still set to Pacific Standard Time, and considered how long ago they'd left the airport. Little more than a half-hour remained before their Boston touchdown. She groaned and braced herself, then she exited the lavatory with her head high. No one needed to know that she wasn't as fine as she appeared. "I'll take that whisky now before we land, please," she said to the flight attendant, who nodded and headed for the refreshments. "Neat." She needed to take the edge off.

Her drink arrived a moment after she retook her seat, and the relief she felt from the first sip was enough to scare her. How was she going to survive the next week being neck-deep in her past when she couldn't even handle the trip over? *No.* She wasn't a child anymore. She didn't need baby steps or kid gloves or someone to see her through every difficult moment.

"I can do hard things," she told herself and nearly melted from

Corrie MacKay

embarrassment when her neighbor's confused response told her she'd spoken aloud.

"That's...good for you, I suppose."

"For fuck's sake," Jennifer whispered under her breath and closed her eyes. This flight couldn't be over soon enough.

Logan International Airport felt both strange and familiar. The light buzz tickling her brain bolstered Jennifer's mood as she rolled her carry-on luggage through the terminal. Morning traffic hadn't hit its stride, but the shops were open, and the smell of breakfast was in the air. Jennifer's stomach grumbled in response, but she ignored it and headed for baggage claim. Once there, she hoisted her largest and last bag off the conveyer belt and felt renewed gratitude for the invention of suitcases on wheels. With all her luggage in hand, she took off for the pick-up location.

As she exited the airport, the first gust of Boston chill hit her like a sharp slap to the cheek, and Jennifer's lungs tightened. Tears blurred her eyes. Above her, the sky was a cloud-scattered, grayed-over blend of pre-dawn periwinkle and peach. The air tasted crisp and cold, and it smelled like city and syrup and time. The feeling of home stirred, but Jennifer pushed it away. This wasn't her home anymore.

A black town car waited for her. Standing at the rear door, a fit elder man in a fine suit held a small dry-erase board in his hands. The name "Dupont" was scrawled across its face.

"Hello, I'm Jennifer Dupont," she said as she approached. "I believe you spoke with my assistant, Candace."

He gave her a warm, simple smile. "Ms. Dupont, ma'am," he said, "it's nice to meet you. I'm Ned. I'll be driving you this week. Can I load your luggage up for you?"

"Thank you." She passed her bags over. "And thank you for being available on such short notice."

"Oh, you bet," he said as he loaded her bags with surprising ease. "You bet."

Bags handled, he opened the door for her, and Jennifer settled herself inside. "Are you familiar with the area," she asked when he slid into the driver's seat, "or will you need an address?"

"I'll be just fine, ma'am," Ned told her as he clicked his seatbelt on and started the car. "Not from Boston originally but been here going on thirty years now, so I'm plenty familiar. Where to first? Hotel?"

Jennifer nodded and gave him the name. "And you can have the morning for yourself," she said. "Likely the early afternoon as well. I won't be going out again for a while." She needed sleep.

She checked her phone. One new notification. A text had arrived from her assistant informing her that one of her clients was annoyed with the last-minute cancellation. Jennifer's lack of care surprised her. She merely rolled her eyes at the notification and went to her text exchange with Dosie. Nothing. Disappointment bubbled in her gut. It was still quite early in San Francisco, but Dosie was worried about her and possibly also pissed at her, so she had been expecting *something*. Encouragement. Whining. Feelings she couldn't keep in. Tangents about food due to her frequent late-night cravings. Instead, she got nothing, and it took everything Jennifer had not to read into it and assume that Dosie was *furious* with her, that she wasn't even at her condo anymore. She'd left. She wouldn't come back.

Stop, Jennifer begged of her mind. She forced the thought instead that Dosie was simply asleep. Or she was trying to give her space. Hadn't Jennifer made it clear that's what she wanted? Didn't she tell Dosie to keep her distance? Hadn't she asked her to stay behind? Dosie was just trying to respect her wishes.

And succeeding, Jennifer thought, annoyed at having gotten exactly what she asked for. She wished she was asleep so she wouldn't have to think about such things at all. Quickly, she typed out a message and hit send before she could second-guess herself.

The door wrenched open, its hinges screeching like a horror-movie ghoul in need of exorcising. The man who filled the open frame wore track pants and a grimace and nothing else. His shoulder-length hair was unkempt, and so were his eyebrows as they scrunched over his squinting eyes.

"Uh, yeah?" He scratched his chest where he had a small tattoo of a fly hovering over his nipple. "Sorry, who are you? And, like, what time is it?"

Dosie was confused. Had she gone to the wrong apartment? She frowned and stepped back to check the number beside the door again. Yes, it was the right number. Was it the wrong building? Wait. Was she in the wrong town? Emeryville, right? She almost laughed at the ridiculous thought. Her anxiety was on the fritz, causing her to doubt even the things she *knew*. Of course she wasn't in the wrong town. She wasn't at the wrong building either. She'd been there before, *for God's sake*. She even remembered the annoyingly tight circular drive-in at the head of the complex, and the squatty fat palm tree beside the welcome sign.

"Um, hello?" the guy said, and Dosie realized she hadn't said a word. "Are you, like, lost or something?"

"I don't think so?" Dosie asked more than declared, and the two stared at one another, equally bewildered. "Sorry. I think my friend lives here, but I've met her roommates, and you aren't—"

"Oh, yeah, no. I just crashed here last night. Are you looking for—"

"Dose?" Natalie's voice drifted out from the dark of the apartment, and then her small frame squeezed past the man and into the morning light. Her hair was pineapple yellow with pink streaks, and she wore it up in two messy space knots. Her T-shirt had the name Blondie written across the chest in an electric blue that complemented her navy flannel button-down. Some of her nails were painted orange, and some of them weren't painted at all, and her eyeliner was smudged into two smoky clouds around her eyes. She was the epitome of herself, and the sight sent a soothing ripple of calm across Dosie's over-fried system. It must have been obvious, because Natalie's face immediately tightened with concern. "Did you just drive here? It's so early. Have you even slept? What's going on? Are you okay?"

Before Dosie could answer anything, Natalie stopped as if suddenly remembering something and turned to the man beside her. "Why would you answer the door at an apartment that's not even yours?"

He scratched his head, seemingly just as confused about his behavior as she was. "Bruh." Then he laughed. "I guess the knock just woke me up, and I forgot where I was."

For a moment, both Natalie and Dosie stared at him, and then a laugh tickled its way up, and within seconds, all three of them were practically in tears.

"Okay, I'm going back to bed," the guy said. "Or couch. Whatever. Cool?"

"Yeah, man," Natalie said. "Go ahead. Wait. Why do you have a fly on your tit?"

"Flies are cool," he said with a shrug, "and they always land on hot shit."

Natalie scrunched her nose in disgust. "Bro," she said, and he laughed and disappeared into the dark living room. She turned her attention back to Dosie. "Honestly, I don't even know that guy's name. He came home with Delaney last night. I think she's, like, passed out on the floor somewhere. I don't know." She shook her head as if realizing she was rambling, or that the explanation didn't really matter, even if she had one. Then she smiled. "Come here. What's going on?" She grabbed Dosie by the shoulders and pulled her into a hug. Her hair smelled like coconut and patchouli. "I was just getting ready to leave, but I can call the shelter and tell them I can't make it in today if you need me."

Right. It was still the weekend. In her emotional frenzy, Dosie had forgotten. Natalie worked full-time as a freelance *whatever*. Data entry and analysis. Website design and development. Coding. Logo creation. She did a bit of everything and made her own schedule. The weekends, though, she almost always dedicated to volunteering at a local animal shelter. Dosie couldn't remember the name of it, only that it was the place Natalie had gone to for solace in the immediate aftermath of the wildfire that claimed her childhood home and the lives of her two dogs. Seven months after that fire, Natalie walked into Dosie's grief group with a scowl and a dark sense of humor and took the empty seat beside her.

"I'm okay," Dosie said. "Well, mostly. I was at Jennifer's, and it's kind of a long story, but I couldn't stay there."

"Shit," Natalie said. "Did you guys have a fight?"

"No." Dosie frowned. "Maybe? Not really. It's...."

"A long story." Natalie nodded. "Right. I got you. Did you want to talk about it or eat about it?"

"Maybe both," Dosie said with a laugh. "I just really don't want to be alone right now, and if I don't have someone to talk to, I'm going to spiral into doing something impulsive like getting on a plane to Massachusetts when I know I'm not supposed to."

"Uh, okay. I definitely have questions about that, but first, how would you feel about meeting some dogs and cats?"

Dosie perked up. "Yes, please!"

"Good, because we need the help. We had a new litter yesterday, and it's the biggest one I've seen in a while. Mom's a stray we picked up last week, and she had like ninety kittens."

"Ninety?!"

"Obvs an exaggeration, Dose."

"Right. *Obvs*."

"Let me just grab my jacket, and we can go. It's cold as hell out here."

"I know. I'm the one standing out here."

Natalie pulled her inside to wait while she went in search of her jacket and keys. When she returned a moment later, she handed

Dosie a sweatshirt. "In case you need an extra," she said and led her out the door again. "Also, we're getting coffee on the way, and you can tell me all about your not-a-fight."

Dosie followed with a soft smile, already feeling better in Natalie's company. Until her phone chimed from her pocket. She braced herself and dug it out, saw a new text from Jennifer waiting to be read. She halted halfway to the car, her attention now glued to her screen. With a swipe, Jennifer's message opened: *I miss you already.*

"Guess you're not fighting anymore," Natalie said, seeing the message. She laughed as she grabbed Dosie's elbow to drag her toward the car.

Dosie's chest warmed. A pleasant buzz seated itself low in her belly. "I think we kind of still are, actually," she said. "It just doesn't matter right now."

Natalie shook her head, smile echoing hers. "You guys are annoying."

"I know. It's the best."

5

"I can't say anything, right? I shouldn't say anything. Not yet." Dosie dug a few fries from the squashed bag in the console and crunched them between her teeth as she spoke. "It would just be too much for her right now, right?" She smacked Natalie's hand away from the bag. "You finished yours already! And why am I even asking you about any of this? You're the whole reason I'm in this mess!"

"I don't know why you're mad at me. You're a grown woman, Dosie. You made a grown-woman decision."

"Yeah, with you in my ear cheering me on!"

Natalie shrugged. "I'm a supportive friend. I'm literally on my way to stay at your house so you don't have to be alone. Like right this moment. That's the definition of supportive. Speaking of supportive, please support us staying alive by keeping your eyes on the road, ma'am."

Dosie laughed and did as she was told. "You were supposed to support me by not letting me do something impulsive."

"Well, I thought you meant going to Massachusetts. That's what you said."

"I said something *like* going to Massachusetts." A pitchy whine trilled from the backseat, and Dosie hated how cute she found it. She whined, herself, and deflated. "Like adopting a cat."

Natalie turned to look back at the 9-year-old Bombay cat soaking in the afternoon sun atop a brand-new fluffy bed. "Aww, he's so comfy and sleepy." She poked Dosie's shoulder. "It's like he knows he's going to his *fur*-ever home, so he can finally let himself rest."

"Stop."

"You understand that feeling, don't you, Dose?" She pouted in Dosie's peripheral. "You know, black cats have a harder time getting adopted because of all the superstitions about them. I'll bet you understand that, too. Having a harder time because of religious bullshit you didn't even choose?"

"Oh, for goodness' sake! He's in the car already!" Dosie huffed and fanned her hot face as Natalie cackled. "I'm not going to drop him on the side of the road!"

"It'll be fine," she said and thieved the second-to-last fry. "You love him. You know you do. Jennifer will love him, too. I'm sure of it. But I meant what I said at the shelter. If it really isn't working out after a bit, I'll take him. I was planning on taking him or one of the other seniors home anyway. No big."

"I can take care of a cat, Natalie. I raised about a billion kids who weren't even mine, not to mention the livestock. I think I can handle a cat."

Natalie chuckled. "You're so happy."

Dosie rolled her eyes and grinned. "Fine. I love him," she admitted. "And Jennifer *might* love him, you're right, but what if she doesn't want to be a cat mom?"

"So, what? You're scared she's going to treat him like he's the ugly stepchild she never wanted and ship him off to a boarding house every chance she gets? Who is she? Meredith Blake? Is this the *The Parent Trap*?"

"What? I'm lost."

Natalie waved her off. "It's a movie, which we will now watch tonight. Look, Dose, I don't know why you're worried. He's perfect. He's shiny and classy and leggy and just a little bit scary. Like, are you kidding me? That's basically Jennifer. They're twins."

The description scattered Dosie's nerves, and she laughed. She let herself imagine her new cat and her girlfriend together. She pictured Jennifer curled up in her window seat with a book, the cat snoozing in her lap, the two of them happy as any pair could be.

"Yeah," she said, affection warming her chest. "Maybe you're right."

———

In her hotel suite's bathroom, Jennifer stood naked before the sink and mirror and stared at her reflection. She was fresh out of the shower, wet hair clinging like tar to her neck, back, and shoulders. Her exhaustion stuck, too. She could see it in her hunched posture and droopy eyes, the little lines around her face that, most days, she didn't notice. Today, it was as if someone had taken a red marker to all the places time had touched her. Jennifer felt her age. She felt older, which was odd given she felt no wiser; at least, not where her current situation was concerned. It had been so many years of *after*— after her parents, after her sister—and she'd made it work for herself. The unnatural order of things had restructured her world, but Jennifer found it still had space for her. She survived. She succeeded. She found confidence and agency and joy. She even found Dosie. But sometimes, in short bursts of moments, the losses caught up. The exhaustion crept in, and all the cracks and ruptures she had learned to ignore shifted just enough to make themselves noticeable again, to trip her up and knock her down. She felt old, yes. She also felt juvenile. Her legs wouldn't stop wobbling.

She still hadn't slept. An hour, maybe, was all she managed, and even that had been plagued by nightmares. It wasn't something she dealt with often, but Dosie did and often relied on routines before bed to calm her mind. She did slow, gentle stretches and played soothing frequencies on her phone, and when she got into bed, she would wrap herself around Jennifer and murmur restfulness mantras against her back until she finally drifted off. Jennifer always knew she was asleep by the way her muscles began to twitch. A flicked wrist. A jerk in her thigh. One finger tap-tapping over Jennifer's chest.

Fuck. Maybe she shouldn't have left Dosie in San Francisco. Maybe she shouldn't have come at all. *No. I have to be here.* And it was better that she was on her own. She felt less and less like the woman she had become and more like the girl she was before, and the vulnerability of such a state made her queasy. She hated the thought of Dosie seeing her that way, the way she *was*, timid and weak, and the way she saw herself in the mirror now, weathered and spent.

Her eyes were ghosts in the glass, dull and tormented as they gazed back at her. Jennifer wondered if she really looked that way or if it was just her perception, colored by stress and fear and *bullshit*. She wondered if anyone ever saw themselves the way they actually were. The chime of her phone alerted her, and she left her reflection with a sigh.

Jennifer felt strangely guilty as she picked up her phone, as if she had knowingly lied about something and now regretted it. What her body thought she was lying about, she didn't know. Ill at ease, she opened the message hoping it was something she could be angry about, something she could use to pull the focus off of herself. It wouldn't be. The message was from Dosie, and that wasn't her way. She didn't pick fights, and she was never mean. She was never rude. It just wasn't her, and it wasn't *them*, and as grateful as Jennifer was for that, the darker, uglier parts of her grief still desperately wanted something to set her off.

The message was long, as Dosie's texts often were, especially when she was anxious. Jennifer read through the paragraph too quickly to retain any of it, exhaled the breath she'd been holding, then read it again. *Hey. I'm back at the house. Natalie is with me. She's going to stay a few days and help me with the wall panels for the corner room upstairs. I know you want to be left alone, so I'm doing my best to give you space. That's really hard to do when I know what you're going through, but I want you to know that I respect whatever it is you tell me you need. I just wanted to update you on where I am and tell you that I love you. I know you know that, but I think it's important right now that you see me say it. I love you. Even when you're mad. Even when you want to be alone. Whatever you're feeling is okay. Just be safe and take care of yourself, please. And check in a couple of times a day, if you can, so I know you're okay. I will too.*

Jennifer let go her hope of being riled. Dosie wanted to give her exactly what she wanted, even if Jennifer wasn't sure she wanted it anymore. It was infuriating in its own way but also too sweet to spark any ire. She dropped her phone on the bed and focused instead on getting dressed. She was proud of the outfit she'd earlier assembled, the perfect somber-chic look for a morose reunion with her solitary aunt. *Possible* reunion. Jennifer had yet to inform her aunt that she was in town, or that she would be dropping by within the next hour or so. How could she do that when every time she thought about the woman, she wanted to scream her throat raw? She would never get the words out. *How* could she have waited so long to send Jennifer the notice and never even say anything?

Let her be surprised the way I was surprised, Jennifer thought as she donned her underwear and snatched her wool pants off the bed as if from a thief. *See how she likes it.* She clipped her bra into place then made for the bathroom to get the blow dryer for her hair. Two steps, and her phone sounded again with another message.

You're okay, Dosie had written, *aren't you, Jen?*

The slimy sensation of guilt swam in her gut again at the first thought that came to mind. *No.* She wasn't okay, and she hated that. But she loved Dosie.

I'm okay, she typed back and realized her body had been right; she was lying about something. *I love you.*

"How do we make him drink from it?"

"Eh," Natalie said and stuck the plug into the outlet. "He'll drink when he gets thirsty."

Dosie squealed as the tiny fountain came to life, cycling fresh water like a miniature waterfall. "It's so *cute.*" She curled her hands into fists and gritted her teeth. "I can't take it."

"Calm down before you break a tooth," Natalie said. "It is super cute though, for real."

"I want him to drink from it now."

"Yeah, good luck with that. He's already claimed the sunny spot on your couch. Dude's fully comatose."

"Maybe we can train him to use it before Jennifer gets back, and then he'll be that much cuter."

Natalie hummed as if considering a brilliant idea. "And she'll be unable to look away."

"Yes, entranced by his adorableness."

"And then she, too, will become one of his willing servants." In her best movie villain voice, Natalie unleashed a classic evil laugh and shouted, "It's the perfect plan!"

They set up the automatic litterbox next, and as they were pouring in the litter, Dosie's phone dinged with Jennifer's reply. She read it—*I'm okay. I love you.*—and immediately felt uncomfortable. Her mind threw out projections faster than solutions, always, and she had to tell herself not to pull tones and intentions from her own imagination and paint them over Jennifer's words. Instead, she had to hope that when Jennifer said she was okay, she meant it. The 'I love you', she didn't doubt. There had never been any lingering 'buts' at the end of Jennifer's rare love confessions, and Dosie trusted the feeling in her heart that told her Jennifer always meant every word.

But didn't she also have to trust her gut? Wasn't it telling her that something was off? That Jennifer wasn't okay, because *nobody* would be okay in her situation? Or was that just Dosie's fear? Was it just her mind? *Thoughts and feelings are not facts. Don't project them onto other people.*

"Dosie?"

"Hm?"

"Everything good?"

Dosie sighed and set her phone on the countertop. "Do you think it's ever okay to tell your girlfriend you think she's full of crap about her own feelings?"

"Uh," Natalie chuckled. "I think when your girlfriend is Jennifer Dupont, you should probably never tell her you think she's full of crap about anything, unless you want to get your ass beat." She raised her eyebrows as if suddenly considering new information. "Then again...."

"Stop," Dosie groaned. "I'm serious. I can't tell if it's just me or if it's real. I'm worried about her, so maybe I'm convincing myself things are one way when they're not? But if they actually *are* that way, then maybe I need to do something?"

"Something like going to Massachusetts?" Natalie asked and pinned Dosie with a look that could pass for a lecture.

"Don't look at me like that. It makes me nervous." Dosie shook out her suddenly sweaty hands. "I'm so worried about her. I can't stop."

"Okay, so just be worried about her," Natalie said and took her by the shoulders to still her anxious fidgeting. "That's what we do for the people we love. It's normal. But also accept that it's *her* choice, Dose, and she gets to deal with whatever she's going through in whatever way she thinks she needs to, even—"

"But—"

"Hey," Natalie said, and Dosie forced herself quiet, "*even* if she's wrong." Their eyes met. Defeat cooled Dosie's burning blood. "Right?"

Dosie cuffed her hands around Natalie's forearms to let her know she'd been heard.

"And you know, she might *not* be. Wrong, I mean," Natalie said, and Dosie hated the way it sounded, hated the way it felt. She hated that it was the truth. "You don't always do what I think is best when you're struggling, but what I think is best for you and what actually *is* best for you, aren't always the same. You know? She might be doing exactly what's best for her. Who's to say until it's done?"

Dosie's mouth twitched, and her throat swelled. She didn't want to cry. She wouldn't. Natalie was right. There was no reason to assume the worst. Worrying made her fragile, and she couldn't be fragile when Jennifer might need her at any moment.

"Good?" Natalie dropped her hands from Dosie's shoulders. "You want a snack?"

Dosie grumbled away her doubt and flopped into a seat at the kitchen island. "I always want a snack. You know this."

"You're right. I don't even know why I asked." She opened the refrigerator. "Grapes? Cheese? Yogurt?"

"Yes."

"Which?"

"Just yes," Dosie said with a pitiful laugh, and Natalie began unloading the refrigerator.

"Oh, dude, speaking of snacks, did Kaylia send you a pic of Spanish guy yet?"

Intrigue struck Dosie's anxiety like a wrecking ball. She gasped. "So there *is* a guy in Spain! Since when? She told me she was going to visit her parents. I didn't even know she'd met anyone after New York guy until she called me last night. Wait, no. Last night? Or was that the night before? I don't even know what day it is anymore. Anyway, I want to see! I can't believe you got a picture, and I didn't."

"She always sends me pictures of the guys she meets just in case she ever goes missing."

Dosie frowned. "That's so depressing."

"I know, right?" She stopped and dug her phone from her pocket, opened her texts with Kaylia and the photo she'd received, and passed it over. "There he is."

It was a three-quarter shot of a man, late twenties or early thirties maybe, though Dosie had never been great at those estimates. He had short, wavy hair the color of wet beach sand and a nice shy smile. His wire-frame glasses sat crookedly on his nose, giving him a sweet, nerdy appeal that screamed of Kaylia's type. If Dosie had to guess, he was probably some kind of artist, too.

Natalie snickered. "Did you see what she said below the pic? That she kind of hates his little mustache but wants to 'deliberate further' before deciding if she hates it for real? She fucking kills me."

"Mustaches do kind of make me uncomfortable."

"Word."

"I haven't even talked to Kaylia since she left. Well, I said hello when she called me, but that was it, because she didn't even want to talk to me. She wanted Jennifer."

"What? Why?"

"Sex stuff, I think," Dosie said and stuck a cube of cheese in her mouth. "I mean, I know. Jen said something about condoms, but then they just hung up like that was normal, so that's all I got."

"Jennifer didn't tell you after?"

"Well, no, because we were—" Dosie choked on her words. Or her cheese. Both, maybe. She coughed her throat clear and said, "— distracted. We were distracted with, um, other things. Around the house."

Natalie's eyes narrowed. Her shoulders trembled with silent humor, a smile glinting in her eyes. "Other things," she said. "Around the house. Right."

"Don't," Dosie said as she got up to grab a glass from the cabinet and filled it at the sink. "You'll turn me into a tomato."

"Fine. I'm don't-ing."

"Thank you. Ah!" Dosie jumped, spilling some of her water back into the sink, as a warm, furry body slid like living water around her leg. "Oh, God. You scared me! Hi!" She set her glass down and scooped up her surprise cuddler. "Did you come to say hi to me? That makes me so happy. Are you so happy in your new home? Are you a happy baby?"

"He's not clawing your face off, so probably."

Dosie stroked his head and squeezed him as much as he would

allow, already addicted to his squeaky trills and his broken top fang and the tiny bald patch on his tail. "You're so pretty. You're the prettiest boy. I can't wait for you to meet Jennifer. She's moody and broody, but she's also very pretty. So, you already have something in common."

"You'll be mad if he picks her as his favorite."

"Yes, I will," Dosie said in her baby voice, still looking at the cat, "but I'll forgive him, because she's *my* favorite, too."

Dosie shifted the cat's weight so she could grab her glass again. As she brought it to her lips, her gaze passed over the window and out. Then she froze. The heavy glass clunked into the sink as her hand spasmed, and her entire world narrowed to a ripple in the tall grass past the gate.

"Whoa, hey." Natalie was at her side in an instant. "What is it?" She followed Dosie's gaze out the window. "You see something?"

Dosie blinked and stared. Nothing moved. Nothing emerged. "I thought I did. Out by the gate."

"I don't see anything. You sure it wasn't an animal?"

"No. I'm not sure it was anything." The light was playing tricks on her. Her stress had turned shadows into shapes to scare her. Still, she stared a moment longer, a sense of dread tugging at her gut.

"Coyote maybe?" Natalie offered, and Dosie nodded.

"Yeah, maybe." She told herself, again, not to worry and put it out of her mind. She put on a smile and nodded toward the cat's flowing fountain. "Let's see if he'll get a drink."

The town car's rumble at her back eased Jennifer's nerves as she stood outside her aunt's old colonial style home for the first time in years. The walk to the front door felt both old and new, an odd warring sensation that simultaneously comforted and disconcerted her. It was always the same. The more time she spent away, the more challenging her return, and while her aunt did, for a time, raise her, seeing her again had never felt to Jennifer like coming home to a parent.

She rang the doorbell and closed her eyes, listening until her ears found the thrum of the car engine again. Ned was waiting for her. If she became overwhelmed, if things grew strained or heated between her and her aunt, she could make a quick exit. She could flee and *feel* and then return calmer, more clear-headed, and she and her aunt could try again. *Or,* she could skip the return and focus on doing what she came to do, so that she could get back to her *actual* home and the only person in the world with whom she always felt she belonged. Then things with her aunt and her past could return to the way they were. A boil to a simmer to a nicely predictable stillness.

I hate this. She was already assuming things would go awry, that this visit wouldn't or couldn't be beneficial or even civil, let alone pleasant. She was already planning how to react, how to recover, as if she needed an exit strategy just to have a hard conversation. *Fuck,* she felt weak.

The interior curtain on the door's window shifted, and a woman appeared. Jennifer met her aunt's eyes through the glass, and instead of shock, she saw somber acceptance. *Was she expecting me?*

"Jennifer," her aunt said as she opened the door, and they got their first true look at one another.

Jennifer couldn't explain it, but the woman seemed less frazzled than she used to be. Her shoulders weren't tense, and neither were the here-and-there age lines around her mouth and eyes. A calming energy wafted out from her like a slow draft of incense smoke. Jennifer inhaled it and felt her own shoulders drop.

"I'm sorry I didn't call first." *So much for righteous fury.*

Her aunt wore the hint of a smile. "You want to come in?"

The house smelled like oven-fresh bread and citrus. It made Jennifer's stomach rumble. It also gave her something to focus on. "How's the baking going?"

"Oh, it's fine. I have my regular customers, and I picked up a partnership with a local café for some of my pastries this year."

"That's great. Which one?"

"A new place near the park. Harriet's."

"Ah." Jennifer felt like she had a board strapped to her spine as she took a seat at the kitchen table. Ease came and went like the memory of a dream, a wisp then nothing, a wisp then nothing. The longer they spoke, the more awkward she felt, as if she couldn't stand to sustain small talk with her own family anymore. "Well, congratulations on that. I'm happy for you."

"Thank you." Her aunt took a small jar from the refrigerator and held it up. "I have marmalade if you want a croissant. I've just finished a batch."

Jennifer scolded herself for being dramatic. This wasn't hard. It was conversation. It was her aunt, a woman she'd known all her life and who had seen her at her highest and lowest, best and worst. She needed to get over herself. "That sounds amazing, actually," she said and stood again to serve herself as her aunt pointed out where everything now resided in the kitchen.

They moved around one another in quiet conjunction, and Jennifer's wisp of ease took a more permanent form. Perhaps they *could* have a visit rather than a confrontation. If she was willing to try.

Change was a constant throughout her former home. As she was given a short tour, Jennifer realized she had often thought of her aunt strictly in terms of the past, as if she existed in only one time, only one way, and was never meant to be anywhere or anyone else. Carine was a person, a woman, outside of being Jennifer's aunt and former guardian, and much like Jennifer, loss and time had turned her new shades and taught her new ways of being. She was different. They both were.

There were cookbooks and advice books, memoirs and biographies, and fiction books of all kinds where Carine's favorite artworks used to be. Plants she once would have struggled to keep alive thrived on bookshelves left and right. They dangled from pots on hooks above the windows and trailed along the walls, held aloft by strategically placed clips and décor.

"I'm glad you started watering your plants," Jennifer said, and her aunt gave her a tired smile that reminded her so much of her father that she felt a sudden urge to look away. She didn't. She wanted to see.

"Arrête de me charrier," Carine said as she poked Jennifer's side.

Jennifer's French had corroded after years of disuse. Her comprehension was still good, fluent even, but her conversational skill was rusty. She hadn't had cause to speak French since her last trip to Toulouse over a decade earlier to visit her grandmother and, before that, had only used it sparingly since her father's and sister's deaths. Even with her aunt, it was rarely required.

"I would reply," Jennifer told her, "but I'm afraid my French these days would give you nightmares."

Carine's laugh was loud and genuine, so familiar it made Jennifer's chest ache. "It's my secret to keeping the plants alive. I speak with them in French, and they grow more beautiful." She waved for Jennifer to follow her down the hall. "And yes, I also water them now, too."

What appeared to be a small yoga studio or meditation room occupied the space Jennifer once called her own. "The guest bedroom is where the den used to be now," Carine said with some urgency in her tone, as if she wanted Jennifer to know that there was still a bed available for her, should she ever need one. "Do you want to stay the night?"

No. It wasn't where it happened, but the place still felt haunted. "I got a room in the city," she said, "but thank you."

Carine nodded in quiet acceptance and led Jennifer back toward the sitting room to settle down. She *had* changed, but in some ways, she was just the same as Jennifer remembered. Carine no longer moved through spaces as if she expected them to collapse around her, but she still kept her hands close to her chest as if warding off a chill. Jennifer wondered if she was calmed by the thud of her own heartbeat, the constant reminder that she was alive.

"How long will you be in the area?" Carine asked as they sat opposite one another on matching wool-blend couches.

Jennifer braced herself. This was the entry point, the open window into the conversation she had gone there to have despite not wanting to have it. "Until it's over."

Quiet.

Another of her aunt's unchanged habits: she was slow to react. Instead, she reflected. She considered. It had always been a marked change from her brother, Jennifer's father, who often had his reply ready before he knew what he was replying to. In Jennifer's grief and anger, Carine's long pauses irritated and sparked arguments, but since, she had developed an appreciation of that kind of active listening and deliberation. She had even worked such elements into her own communication habits and found them especially effective with her clients, and later, her relationship.

"You're mad," Carine finally said, no hint of a question in her tone. "I wasn't going to send it at all."

Jennifer's frustration was quick to spark. "Yes, I guessed as much from the state of the envelope, as if you'd thrown it away then dug it back out again. What I haven't been able to guess is why. How could you even think about not telling me? You didn't think I would want to know? That I would want to be here?"

Carine folded her arms around her middle. "Does it matter now, Jennifer?" Her tone wasn't defensive, just resigned. She cast her eyes to the floor. "I sent it. You're here."

"Yes," Jennifer snapped and launched off the couch. She needed to move. Her legs ached with restlessness. "I'm here, and with no time to get my head on straight. I feel like I've been hit by a fucking truck. Did you not consider that I might want an actual chance to prepare for this?"

"I'm sorry."

Jennifer spun to face her again. "Are you? Because you sure as hell don't sound it."

"How should I sound?" Carine countered, quicker than Jennifer expected. "Should I beg forgiveness for not having a guidebook for this type of thing?"

Jennifer scoffed. "Oh, what does that even mean?"

For a moment, her aunt seemed to deliberate, but when she spoke again, she did so as if she had practiced every word. As if she expected she might someday have occasion to say them. "Jennifer, you have never given me the grace of not knowing."

"What? What is that supposed to—"

"Laissez-moi finir. Please."

Jennifer hated that she felt so defensive. She sighed and apologized, waved for her aunt to continue.

"You were so young when your parents had their accident. You were teenagers, so you were old enough to know what was happening and why, but you were still too young to understand just how young you really were. Which meant you certainly couldn't understand how young *I* was."

The words sent Jennifer's stomach to her knees. Her mind shot straight to the past, trying to picture her aunt from before again. Trying to picture anything, *everything*. Given how infrequently she allowed herself to do so, the images were hazy, and Jennifer wasn't sure anymore if the memories she had of that time were true or just outline images of her reality colored in by emotions and *pain* and time.

"I know you blame me for what happened," Carine said, and Jennifer's eyes began to water against her will. "Or you did. I'm sure some part of you must still. For not being more involved in your lives. Yours and your sister's. Or in your grief. For not seeing the signs that were there, or that boy for what he really was. For not protecting her from him." Her aunt's voice thinned as if her throat had shrunk. She twitched her nose the way she had always done when warding off tears and turned her head away. "Or you from losing her."

Jennifer felt as if her chest would cave in. "Tata," she said as she moved to sit beside her. She hadn't used the affectionate name in longer than she could recall, and she hadn't meant to again. It came on its own, and Jennifer didn't hate it. She found it comforting.

The war inside fizzled. Her dizzying anger dissipated like a bad scent in the air. The burden of growing up again left her drained as her aunt took her hands and said, "I was thirty years old the day I found out my big brother died, and that I had inherited his teenage daughters."

Jennifer felt chilled to the bone. *Thirty.* That was barely older than Dosie. She thought of herself at that age, imagined being solely responsible for two grieving, hormonal teenagers at the height of their pain and the depth of their vulnerability. Trying to be a parent when she wasn't one to kids she didn't ask for and who never asked for her. The thought alone induced stress.

"I know you don't remember," Carine said, patting her hands, "but I was only eleven when Lauren was born."

Jesus. Jennifer hadn't thought about it before, but now she couldn't stop. Vague recollections flickered on in the back of her brain like glitching lights. She had memories of her aunt as a teenager. She could *almost* recall her face then, untouched by time and obligation, and the more she tried, the more uncomfortable she felt.

"I loved being your tata," Carine said, "especially the older I got, but I was never meant to be your mother, never mind both your mother and your father. I wasn't ready, and I wasn't equipped for it, and neither were the two of you. And we struggled. I know we struggled. But I...."

"You didn't know what you were doing," Jennifer said, *realized,* as she wiped a tear from her chin and cheek. How strange it was to see something, someone, so familiar from a new angle, in a new light, through a different lens. The complexity Jennifer had never afforded her aunt made her breathless.

"There are so many things I would have done differently had I known better," Carine told her. "And that isn't an excuse for anything. It is only the truth. There was so much to consider in those early days, and I wasn't prepared to consider any of it. Lauren was angry all the time, and you were so quiet, and it only seemed worse when I was around, so I let you two take care of each other, and I dealt with the rest as best I could. And I didn't see...."

Her voice hiccupped, and she stopped herself with a hand over her mouth. When she looked at Jennifer again, her eyes were glossy and wide and hauntingly sincere. Carine's devastating whisper stirred Jennifer's soul.

"I know what you must think. I have thought it myself so many times. How could I not have seen? How could I not have known? My brother left his children in my care, and I let a monster destroy one of them." Her hand lingered over her mouth, tapping between her pained words as if attempting over and over to stop herself from speaking. Her breath stuttered as if every syllable hurt. "And I can never go back. I can never fix it. I can never.... I can't go back and know better. I can't go back and see red flags where I thought I saw relief. I can't ask more questions or insist on more visits or be a mother for her when she needed one most. When *you* needed one most. And I am sorry." She sniffled as tears raced her cheeks. The hand at her mouth moved to cup Jennifer's face instead. "I'm sorry, Jennifer. I'm sorry. Je suis profondément désolé."

Jennifer wasn't sure when her last breath was. Her chest burned. Her eyes did, too. She gripped her aunt's forearm as if she might drift off to sea or into space without it anchoring her to the room and to this perfect, awful conversation that she had neither expected nor prepared for. "I need a minute," she said, voice tight, and stood on wobbly legs. She had no destination in mind when she walked away, only the need to be gone.

Carine's fenced backyard had not changed. It was dark out now, but the same well-worn path that Jennifer had walked countless times unwound before her between two rows of solar lamps. She walked it mindlessly, knowing where it led. The same rotting stick fences bordered the bare, chaotic remains of her aunt's seasonal garden to her left, and the old, browned willow tree still stood at the northern corner. Jennifer followed the path to its trunk and sat on the stone bench hidden among its untrimmed tendrils.

Cool nature coated her nose with every breath as she lay her back against the willow trunk and ran her bare fingers over the bench seat. The stone stung her fingertips, cold to the touch, but she didn't care. She followed the pattern, tracing each letter of the name engraved beside her thigh. L-A-U-R-E-N. Then she started over again.

The air was a mixture of fire and laundry soap, traces of neighborhood dinners and evenings that were winding down. L-A-U-R-E-N.

Jennifer wasn't having a panic attack. L-A-U-R-E-N. She was sure she was in control of herself. Her jaw wouldn't stop shaking. *Mostly* in control of herself. L-A-U-R-E-N.

"*My brother left his children in my care, and I let a monster destroy one of them.*" Jennifer winced. L-A-U-R-E-N.

"*Give me a squish.*" Her mouth watered. Her hand didn't stop. L-A-U— "*I can't go back and know better.*" —R-E-N. "*Je suis profondément désolé.*"

A hiccup of a cry escaped, and Jennifer growled at herself, at everything. Her aunt's apology whispered around her head, and she pressed harder into the gutters of her sister's name. She hadn't even known she wanted an apology, or that she had, on some subconscious level, thought all the things Carine said she had. She didn't know until she heard it all aloud, and now the truth burned in her like a fresh wound.

"*I was only eleven when Lauren was born.*" Grief had stolen her aunt's life, too.

Jennifer did not have the stomach for this, any of it. She didn't have it then, and she didn't have it now. L-A-U-R—Her phone buzzed in her pocket.

She dug the device out and saw an incoming call from Dosie. "Hey," she answered and cleared the weakness from her throat. "I was going to call you when I got back to the hotel."

"You just called me," Dosie laughed. "It took me a minute to figure out you didn't mean to. I couldn't hear anything but swishing and maybe a cricket? But I wanted to call you back just in case."

"Oh. No, I didn't realize. I'm sorry."

"Don't be," Dosie said. "It's really nice to hear your voice."

"It's good to hear yours, too." So good that it somehow made Jennifer feel worse. She *ached* for that voice at her neck, touching her ear a second before Dosie's lips.

"Are you outside?"

"Mhm."

"Oh, okay. That must be where the cricket came from." She giggled, and it heightened Jennifer's ache for her. "Is it cold there?"

"Mhm."

"Do you have a coat?"

"I'm fine."

Dosie was quiet a moment. "You sound so sad, baby."

Pain lanced through her, and Jennifer had to tuck her phone against her chest to keep Dosie from hearing the breath that shuddered in and out of her like possession. When she brought the phone back to her ear, she was met with silence but for a clicking sound she soon realized was Dosie's pearls against her teeth. Jennifer pictured her gently gnawing them as she did her best to keep quiet and give Jennifer time.

"I'm at my aunt's," Jennifer finally said, "and we've been talking."

"Oh, talking. Your favorite."

Jennifer tried to laugh. It fizzled before it began. "Yeah."

"Good talking?"

She pushed her hair back from her face, wiped her cheeks, and stared up at the dark branches above her. "Uh, I don't know. Yes. Both maybe."

Another short silence, then Dosie asked, "Are you okay, Jen?"

The impulse to tell her old lie struck with urgency. *Don't make her worry any more than she already does. Don't pity yourself. Don't wallow in this. Just tell her you're fine and let her go on with her night.* Jennifer ignored all of it and whispered into the phone. "No."

Dosie's next silence seemed to go on for ages. Or maybe it was seconds. Jennifer didn't know. Time seemed both speeding and still. "I'm just going to sit with you for a bit then, okay?" she finally said, and all the tension leaked from Jennifer's body. "We don't have to talk about it. You don't have to say anything. Just breathe, and I'll be here, and you can hang up when you're ready."

Jennifer closed her eyes, causing a flood of built-up tears to spill down her cheeks. Not for the first time, she wished she could pull her girlfriend through the phone. "Okay."

———

Little was said between them as Carine followed her to the front door. Every step seemed difficult, as if there were ropes around Jennifer's ankles trying to pull her back. Her body screamed for her to escape. She was at her limit, and she wanted to be alone. She wanted to shove her head under the cool side of a pillow and forget the world existed for a while. She wanted to go home.

She pulled the door open, and the silence popped like a bubble. "You don't have to go to the hearing."

Jennifer stopped. "Yes, I do," she said. "And you should, too. He doesn't deserve the chance to be free again. He doesn't even deserve the chance to *ask* to be free again, but since I can't stop him from getting that, then I will stop him from getting out."

"Jennifer, you cannot stop anything," Carine said, then sighed. The sound grated at Jennifer's nerves. How could her aunt be so resigned about this? This of all things? "We can write letters, and we can make calls, and we can speak our piece, but whatever happens will happen. We have no control, and that man does not deserve any more of our family's pain. He doesn't deserve to see it."

"I owe it to her."

"You don't owe her anything."

The words struck Jennifer like lightning, scattered through her body in crackling waves of heat and pain. "How can you say that?"

"Jennifer, you did not fail her."

Jennifer felt as if she could tear the knob off the door. "That's *not* true."

"It *is* true," Carine said and took Jennifer's arm. "My love, please, you have struggled with this every day since you were seventeen. You have grieved your sister a lifetime over, and you deserve to let go. That's why I didn't want to send the notice. How could I bring this pain and ugliness back to the fore of your life when all I want is for you to be free of it and happy?" She drew Jennifer closer, just inside the cool embrace of the open door, and gripped her shoulders as if she intended to embrace her. Instead, she matched her gaze and said, "I love you, Jennifer. I know I never said that enough. We are not those people, I know. But I do love you. You are mine, even if you never were, and you and your sister were never burdens. I should have said that to you both a long time ago."

Jennifer's body was screaming. Or the world was. She couldn't tell anymore. Everything seemed so loud. Everything touched so deeply. The air burned in her nose. The taste in her mouth turned sour. Crickets and frogs sang in warped melodies at her back. "I'm going to the hearing," she said and felt the words in her mouth like chewy rubber. "I have to."

Carine didn't argue again. She looked away, hands still gripping Jennifer's arms, then let go. She nodded, her only answer.

"I have to speak for her," Jennifer said as she crossed the threshold into the night. She stopped, could feel her aunt lingering just behind her in the open frame. "Like I should have done before."

She left without a backward glance, treading the path to Ned's waiting car with her pride in her throat. "So many fucking times."

She slammed the car door when she got inside and felt like an angry child. Her eyes watered as Ned pulled from the curb, and Jennifer wondered if, the moment she stepped back inside, her aunt would cry, too. Each hidden from the other, unable to be together with the most prominent thing they had ever shared: the loss of someone they both deeply loved and deeply failed.

6

Dosie woke with the sun when a small sable paw rose from the dawn-blue shadows to bat at her nose like it was a bug on the wall. She opened her eyes to find a whiskered midnight face floating mere inches above hers and almost gasped. A sleepy laugh left her instead. *I have a cat*, she reminded herself and reached up to scratch behind his ears.

"Hi, sweetheart," she cooed as she adjusted to being awake before she was ready to be. "It's so early. What's wrong? Are you cold? Do you want in the bed with me?"

He chirped at her then smacked her nose again. A second later, he hopped off the mattress and made a soft *thud* on the floor. Before Dosie could sit up, he had taken off into the dark of the room like a dream disappearing the moment after waking. Then he was out the open bedroom door and gone.

Dosie whined. Her bed was so *warm*, which meant every inch of space outside of it wouldn't be. But she was a mom now, and her child who didn't speak the same language as her had woken her up with violence, which must have meant he needed something. So, she had to get up.

He's probably hungry, she thought, and her stomach reacted as if it was her second child, reminding her that it had needs as well. Dosie whined again, just because it felt appropriate, then threw her blankets off and got out of bed.

The cold leapt on her like a trillion little fleas finding a new target, biting at her exposed skin. She grabbed her fluffy robe from the back of the door and stuck her feet in a pair of fur-lined slippers that felt a touch big, so they had to be Jennifer's. Then she crept into the hallway, eyes glued to the floor for signs of a cat that too easily blended with the shadows. If he was nearby, waiting for her, she didn't want to step on him.

She made it down the stairs without issue and sneaked past the living room with a quick peek in. Natalie was passed out on the air mattress they'd set up by the fireplace, one foot sticking out toward the few glowing spots of orange left among the gray ash. The smell of bacon—*ooh, and pancakes!*—would wake her, but until then, Dosie would let her sleep.

She found the cat in the kitchen. *I really need to give him a name already.* Of course, he technically already had a name, but Dosie hated it and refused to use it. Even calling him "the cat" seemed a better option, so that's what she decided to do until a better name came along, a name that felt right.

The cat had been in her house all of one day and night, yet he had the layout down. He knew where everything was, including the cabinet where Dosie had stored his food. It was in an airtight container, and the cabinet door was closed, but he sat right outside it like he expected it might open any minute and auto-dispense a tray with the day's selection.

Dosie giggled at him. "I guess you have something in common with me, too, huh? I'm always hungry. Just wait. Jennifer will tell you." She bent and let him butt his head into her hand. "Okay, let's get you fed, sweetheart."

Preparing his meal was much quicker work than her own. His bowl was full and on the floor in seconds. As he quietly went about eating, Dosie gathered some eggs and a package of bacon from the refrigerator, some bowls and the pancake mix from the pantry, and a few utensils from the drawer beside the stove. With everything laid out, she began her work.

Once she had the bacon in the oven, she started on the pancakes since she would be working on them the whole time she was cooking the eggs. She shook some mix into a bowl then went to the sink for the water that would transform it into batter. As she measured it out, she glanced out the kitchen window and jolted. A gasp tore from her lips as she dropped the measuring cup with a metallic clatter. The sink splattered on, unbothered, and Dosie left it. Her whole body had gone cold, and she was frozen in place.

There was a person standing in her backyard.

It wasn't *early* early, but it was early enough. Jennifer felt how early it was in her bones as she walked through the city with the wet morning cold at her cheeks. She wasn't much of a morning person, but on occasion, she found them strangely magical. There was something about a chilly morning walk that made her feel new, as if she could restart her week, her month, her life, and face new challenges, find new opportunities. It often proved invigorating when she felt listless.

In the heart of the city, she passed by a cemetery that was stuck between two old brick buildings and surrounded by a wrought-iron fence. Something about it called her to stop and go back. The headstones were devoured by uneven ground, and time and weather had worn most of their words down to faint scratches of history. She could pick out a few of the dates, though. *1793. 1813. 1804.* An odd sensation hit her, the way one might feel when standing in the shadow of a mountain. A pleasant sort of shrinking in the presence of something immense. The expansiveness of grief and life. Jennifer wondered if, hundreds of years in the future, her family's headstones would still be standing for someone to gaze upon. She wondered why it had been so long since she had visited them herself.

Guilt pooled in her stomach, and Jennifer had to move. She left the cemetery where it had stood for centuries and took her fleeting life further into the city.

Dosie heard Natalie behind her, clearing her throat as she stumbled into the kitchen. She didn't turn from the window, too afraid that the person she was looking at might disappear if she did, terrified that he wasn't even real. She needed Natalie to see him, needed her to confirm that it wasn't nothing. It wasn't a trick of the wind or a coyote out by the gate, hiding in the grass. It was a man.

"Hey, what's going on? Why'd you shout?"

Did I shout? Dosie's eyes watered. She was afraid to blink. She couldn't remember shouting. She couldn't remember what she was doing even a minute before. Her mind felt as if it had stumbled off a cliff into freefall. She wasn't quite sure of anything—what was up or down, left or right or backwards. Nothing had definition, except the terrible sensation of falling.

"Dosie?" Natalie's arm rubbed against hers as she stepped into the space beside her. "What is it?"

Do you see him? Dosie licked her lips and blinked away tears. *Is he real?* She loathed that she had to ask her next question, but sometimes, she just couldn't trust herself. She opened her mouth to ask, but the answer came before she could.

"Who the fuck is that?"

"Oh, God," Dosie said, choking out the words as relief washed over her. She wasn't having an episode. He was really there. Her respite sapped from her body like syrup from a tree as the thought came again, crawling across her mind like a sickness, and filled her with dread. *He's really there.*

"Hey, what's going on?" Natalie asked, grabbing Dosie's shoulder to steady her. "Should we call the cops? Do you want me to call the cops?"

"No," Dosie said, but when she closed her eyes, a flash of a memory spilled across her eyelids and made her tremble. "I don't know."

"What do you mean?" Natalie turned Dosie to face her and said, "Look at me. Tell me what's going on. I can't help if you don't talk to me. Do you know that guy? Is he dangerous?"

You're safe, Dosie told herself despite the unsteadiness taking residence in her limbs, the sickly boil bubbling to life in her gut. *You're safe.* She needed to focus, needed to be *here*, not there, not then. *You're safe.*

"His name is Ira," she quietly admitted as she turned back to the window. Her gaze made the journey from his fluffy copper-blonde hair to his dimpled chin and back. Her tongue stuck to her teeth, to the roof of her mouth. Everything felt dry and raw and *wrong*, and she was sure her heart was going to burst from the force of its beat. Her knees were going to give out. "He's my little brother."

The coffee shop was a steam room compared to outside. Jennifer felt like a car exiting a carwash as she stepped over the threshold and warmth blasted over her. She shivered with the sudden change and scanned the place for her aunt.

Carine sat at a high-top table by an east-facing window, fingers toying mindlessly with a paper coffee cup. Her head was tilted back, eyes closed, and cloud-scattered sunshine speckled her nose and cheeks. How young she seemed in that moment, relaxed and seemingly unthinking as she waited.

Jennifer removed her scarf and tucked it under her arm. She stopped by the open counter to order a cortado then made for her aunt's table. "Carine."

Now that she was close, Jennifer could see she was wrong about

Carine's relaxed state. She noted the bleariness in her aunt's eyes and the heaviness that sagged beneath. "Oh, Jennifer," she said as she sat up and blinked a bit of sleep from her eyes. She reached for Jennifer's hand, a quick connection to say hello.

"Your text surprised me," Jennifer said as she took a seat. Her cortado appeared a moment later, and Jennifer nodded her thanks to the barista. "Why the early meeting?"

Carine's tired voice had gravel in it. "I couldn't sleep. I thought about what you said all night." She rotated her coffee cup this way and that. "That you feel you need to go to the hearing and speak, because you owe it to Lauren."

"Yes."

"I believe what I told you, that you don't owe her or anyone anything. You weren't perfect, but you did your best, Jennifer, and you deserve to be free from all this pain. I believe that with all my heart, but I realized last night that it isn't my place to decide that for you. If you feel you need to do this, then I should be there for you the way *I* should have been years ago." She took Jennifer's hand and held it. "I want to do what is right for you, but you are a grown woman now and have been for longer than I've been willing to accept. The best person to decide what is right for you, is you."

Jennifer couldn't speak. Her throat felt stuffed full of feelings. Instead, she tightened her grip on Carine's hand. In truth, and as much as she appreciated her aunt's words, Jennifer wasn't convinced she *did* know what was right for her. She was following her gut, because she didn't before. She didn't before, and it cost her everything. It cost her aunt everything. It cost her sister *everything*. And she had still been too afraid to do anything about it. Now, she was afraid *not* to, so afraid that she could feel it in her bones. Everything hurt.

"I don't think you will find anything in here to help," Carine said as she reached under the table for a briefcase Jennifer hadn't noticed until now. "His records show he's been a 'model prisoner,' as they say." She pulled a thick, worn-out folder from the briefcase and set it on the table. "But everything I've amassed is here. Everything that's public record, which isn't much, and everything I could pull through various contacts I've made over the years."

"Contacts? What contacts?"

"Mostly people in law enforcement, but I have connected with a few friends of his family as well."

Jennifer's eyebrows shot up. "Tante Carine!"

"I know," Carine said with a dramatic slump. "I hate socializing. But sacrifices must be made at times." Jennifer was still too surprised to do much more than gape, and Carine took it as a sign to continue. "I haven't been able to find anything for an edge. Other than his parents, his family has little contact with him."

"How long have you been keeping this file?"

"Since the year before he became eligible for parole," Carine confessed and patted the folder. "Seven years ago."

Jennifer's thoughts spiraled. *Seven years? Glass has been eligible for parole for seven fucking years?* How had she not realized how much time had passed?

"This isn't the first time he's applied," Carine told her, "only the first time he's been granted a hearing. He applied once before, and I wrote letters. I made calls. I thought they must have worked, because he was never given a hearing. But...." She sighed. "It doesn't matter. It is happening now, and we must accept it. So, I brought this for you." She nudged the file toward Jennifer. "I know you will probably find nothing here to help but knowing that I have given you everything I have is enough." She reached for Jennifer's hand again. "And I will be there with you. I would have been anyway, but I had hoped you wouldn't need to be. I had hoped you would let me take the entirety of this burden from you after so long, but since you won't, I want you to know you won't be alone. I will be there, right at your side, if you need." She patted Jennifer's hand, rubbed her thumb lovingly over her knuckles. "Oui?"

Jennifer felt bolstered and when she least expected to be, by someone she never expected it from, and it felt good. Her body buzzed with renewed energy and hope. She would speak at the hearing. She would speak because there was no one to speak over. There was no one to worry about upsetting. There was no precarious balance to tip or fury to provoke. There was no one to tell her she was overreacting or causing trouble or that she had gotten it wrong. Lauren lost her voice before Jennifer had found hers, but now that she had it, she would speak for her big sister, because she owed it. Because it was right. It was necessary. Even if it broke her, she would speak.

The chair's wooden legs screeched over the tile floor as Jennifer pushed back from the table and stood. They weren't huggers, had never been, but her aunt needed no requests or warnings. She saw the move for what it was and immediately opened her arms, and when Jennifer buried her face in her neck and hair and let herself be held, she felt connected to Carine again for the first time in decades. Since before the loss of her sister and her parents. When she was just Tata Carine, a bright-smiling, fun-loving, stylish woman who brought Jennifer books to read and taught Lauren how to do her makeup because their mother rarely wore any, and who always stayed over on their birthdays to make chocolatine with them for breakfast. Jennifer had almost forgotten *that* Carine ever existed.

"Oui," she said as her heart burned with affection and hope. "Thank you."

"Dosie, stop! Wait!" Natalie grabbed her arm to keep her from opening the back door. "You didn't answer my question." She put herself between Dosie and the doorknob, and while her hair was a ridiculous, sleep-tangled mess, her face was serious. Scared, even. It forced Dosie to collect herself. "Is he dangerous?"

Dosie's impulse was to say he wasn't. The truth was more complex. The truth was that she didn't know. The truth was: he *had* been. But there were layers to that reality that Dosie didn't know how to explain or even, necessarily, to understand. And how could she know if he was dangerous after years of separation? He was her brother, but she didn't know him anymore, and he didn't know her. They were strangers, which ultimately meant very little to Dosie. Strangers, as it turned out, had never been a danger to her. Family, on the other hand....

"Dose?"

"I don't know," Dosie admitted and shook her head. "I don't think so, not anymore, but I don't know."

"Not anymore?" Natalie asked, voice tinged with worry. "Okay, that sounds like a yes to me. So, I don't know. I don't know what to do here. I mean, are you sure it's okay? Are you sure *you're* okay? Like, am I supposed to support an impromptu reunion with the used-to-be-dangerous guy lurking in your backyard? I don't know what to do."

"I don't either," Dosie said, then she moved around Natalie to grab a hoodie from the hook by the door. She yanked it on and took a deep breath, steadied herself as she stood at the back door and stared out at the man still lingering there, the man now looking back at her. "There are only four of us left."

The words left her in a whisper, and then she was out the door.

Natalie followed her as they silently crossed the large back yard and watched Ira do the same. He stopped a distance from them, fifteen feet or so, maybe less, and Dosie felt her feet glue themselves to the earth. As if they had walked right into the past, they stood nearly the same distance apart as they had that day. It wasn't the same location, but it was close, and though the grass hadn't been tall then, Dosie felt the weeds around her shins and calves now like something pulling her down. The dead latching onto her just to drag her back to the place, to the morning, to the very moment she should have joined them.

For the first time in almost a decade, Dosie stood face-to-face with one of her siblings. Her chest was hot and tight, and she already felt like she was going to cry. *What do I say? I don't know what to say!*

"Hi," she blurted weakly, and her chest burned hotter. The heat crawled up her neck into her cheeks.

"I didn't know anyone lived here anymore," he said as he looked at her oddly, like he wasn't sure who he was looking at. It made Dosie question herself.

Is this not even Ira?! Her skin felt two sizes too small all of a sudden. *Am I having a panic attack for no reason?*

"You look more like Father than I remembered."

Oh. The words, both confirming Ira's identity and calling to mind the man who had abused and exploited them both, rattled Dosie. She wasn't sure what to say. She knew she looked like her father. She didn't favor him as strongly as some of her other siblings, like Janice, but she did resemble him. So did Ira. When Dosie last saw him, he was nine years old and resembled his mother, Nicole. Now, at twenty, he had their father's hair, though lighter, and had grown to have his nose and brow, too. His voice was much deeper, but there was still something recognizable there. Dosie wondered if that was because his voice, too, had notes of their father in it. His soft timbre, especially—a sweet voice, one that could convince you of nearly anything.

"Yeah," she said and hugged her arms around herself in a vain attempt to soothe. "You, too."

An uncomfortable silence took hold until Natalie stepped a little closer to Dosie and introduced herself. "So, uh, hi," she said with an awkward half-wave. "I'm Natalie, by the way, one of Dosie's friends. You're Ira, right? Dosie's younger brother."

Ira, even more awkwardly, said nothing in response. He only nodded in acknowledgement, one corner of his mouth twitching toward a smile. It never fully formed.

"Alrighty," Natalie said, and turned toward Dosie, lowered her voice. "Should we go inside to talk? It's kind of cold."

She couldn't. Her body screamed its resounding disapproval as she considered it. *No.* She couldn't have him inside her home, even if it was once his home, too. It wasn't anymore. It couldn't be again.

Dosie couldn't put voice to the reasons, but she felt them, pricking and prodding at her to ensure they were noticed. She couldn't let him in, but she also couldn't tell him he wasn't welcome. The thought of doing so made her sick.

So, she pivoted. "You were here last night," she said, putting all her focus on the man in front of her. She knew Natalie would go along whatever path Dosie led them, that she would let her set the pace and take the wheel. And she did, nodding so subtly that Dosie almost missed it. "By the gate."

Ira stared at her, unflinching. "Yes."

"Why? Are you looking for something?"

"Are you?"

Dosie frowned. "What do you mean?"

"You're here."

"I live here," Dosie said, and heard herself, realized that she wasn't saying anything different. It didn't matter that she lived there. She lived there *because* she had gone there looking for something. Just a few years prior, at the face of this very property, she had stood like a moth drawn to flame, hoping to find something she couldn't name. The admission stuttered out of her. "Yes. I was, yes."

"Yes," Ira echoed, his own answer to the question.

Dosie's pulse became a thunderous roar in her head. "Are you okay?" she asked when he said nothing more. "Have you been okay?"

Still, he didn't answer. He stood with his hands shoved in his pockets, elbows tucked against his sides, and stared at her silently like she was an exhibit to be analyzed. The longer he looked, the more unsteady she felt. A prickling sensation popped and fizzled along the backs of her arms and neck. Fear coiled in her belly like a snake sensing danger. Guilt followed. She hated how intolerable she felt toward her brother even as some small, buried part of her yearned to reach out to him and tousle his hair, draw him into an embrace, tell him he mattered; it was as if he was some living representation of an old version of herself, one she couldn't make herself love despite a sincere effort. It wasn't Ira's fault any more than it was her own that they were born into the family they were or that they were conditioned the way they were, or that ultimately, he was made to do the things he did, but Dosie felt sick just seeing him. It was like seeing the dead rise up from their graves in real time, still decaying as they cracked through the surface. She could not reconcile the thrill of knowing her brother was alive and seemingly well with the horrors that his mere existence brought back into her life. It broke her heart in ways she couldn't swallow and couldn't speak.

She started to tell him, felt compelled to—*I need you to go. I can't have you here. I don't want you here. I'm sorry. I'm not sorry. I'm so sorry. Please.*—before he spoke again.

"It's strange," he said, and Dosie choked down her impulse, closed her mouth. *Too late.* "The last time I saw you, you were standing just like that. Stiff like one of those big dolls they put in store windows. What are those called?"

Dosie barely managed the answer. "Mannequins."

He nodded, shoulders bunched up toward his ears. So much quieter, so much more reserved than he had ever been when Dosie knew him. He held his body as if he had to make space for everything and everyone else, even if it meant contorting himself. It stirred a deep sadness in Dosie, who couldn't help but wonder how different he might appear if he'd had a better childhood. She had wondered the same of herself. How differently would she carry herself through the world? She imagined she would be nothing like herself. She imagined neither would Ira.

He swayed from side to side as he looked out over the property. Out past the gate, where she had first seen him the night before, and where she had last seen him, all those years ago. He chewed his bottom lip in the same way Dosie often did herself. Their father had done it, too, poring over the bible with his lip between his teeth, chicken-scratching notes in the margins. "Dosie?"

"Yeah?"

He kept his eyes on the expansive, overgrown field, as if picturing

Corrie MacKay

the structures that once stood there and the people who once kept it neat. Dosie pictured them sometimes, too. "Are you afraid of me?"

Natalie shifted in her peripheral, leaning from foot to foot as discomfort worked its way through her body. Dosie knew because she felt it, too, worming around like something seeking and insidious. The urge to move, to leave, to *run* was like a steady breeze at her back, whispering over her ears. *Go. Just go. Just go and don't look back. You're done with this.* She reached for her pearls, but her collarbone was bare under the fluff of her hoodie. She wasn't wearing her necklace, because she had only woken twenty minutes ago. She wasn't prepared for this. She wasn't armored. She felt exposed.

"I don't want to be," she quietly stated, and watched those words paint her brother's face with a subtle frown. She thought to say she was sorry, that she felt bad for feeling the way she did, for not being able to tell her little brother that she wasn't afraid of him or that she wanted him around. She thought to say she was sorry for all his wretched life and for whatever ways it haunted and would continue to haunt him. But she didn't. She didn't say anything, and he seemed to hear that just as clearly as he'd heard her actual response.

"I thought I would feel different." He grimaced and met her eyes again. "Coming back here."

The way he looked at Dosie pained her, like he was seeing things in her eyes, in her face, in her body that shouldn't be there. Dosie knew. There were film frame negatives painted over her presence, warped horrors splashed over sweetness, burned into tender places. She saw the same awful imprints on him, hazing his image into a nauseating smear of then and now.

"Different how?"

He shrugged and looked older than he was, like that one simple motion had tired him out. "Less scattered."

Dosie breathed deep as her eyes began to tingle and burn. "I feel that way too sometimes. There are a lot of memories here."

"I think of you," he said. "It's okay if you don't care. I just wanted you to know. I think of you."

Dosie glanced toward the sky as tears flooded her lower lashes. She blinked them down her cheeks and said, "I think of you too, Ira."

"I read your book." He chewed his lip again. "I like reading now."

With those words, he sounded so like he once did that Dosie briefly lost her breath. Memories spilled through her head as if a dam had broken, and the man in front of her shrank until he was four feet tall. He softened around his cheeks and jaw. His hair grew blonder and wilder. She could almost hear his mischievous little giggle as he tried to sneak out of reading sessions. Contrary to what most of the world assumed, their father never discouraged education. He carefully selected the materials within it, of course, but kept an impressive library on the compound and required all his children to spend an hour reading every day, starting at age seven. Dosie loved it, but Ira had, with every cell in his small body, *hated* it.

"You married Zebadiah."

Dosie blinked herself back to reality. "Um, yes." She forgot that was in the book. "I did."

"You didn't love him," he said as if it was a simple fact that anyone who had known them would know. Looking back, Dosie knew it was. It still struck her, even after years of unpacking it in therapy, how blind she had been to how little she and Zeb cared for one another; just two traumatized, isolated kids clinging to each other as they were flung ruthlessly into a new world. It wasn't love. It wasn't a marriage. It was a desperate attempt at normalcy that only further robbed them of a childhood and brought them pain, and Dosie had never stopped wishing they had known better. She had never stopped wondering if that might have changed things. Or saved him.

"No," she admitted. "But I knew him."

Ira seemed to understand, his expression softened by the words. "I did things, too," he said, "that didn't make any sense."

"Yeah."

She couldn't imagine the kind of chaos Ira must have held in his body over the years, the desperation he would have had to escape it, release it, soothe it. She figured, in some ways, it was fortunate that he was institutionalized for so long. Dosie had so much trauma that she still often felt disoriented by it, but she had been released into the free world at fifteen as if she needed no transition period, and despite others' attempts at guidance, she made tremendous mistakes and set her recovery back years. There were nights she was sure she wouldn't survive the pain or the memories, the fear and adrenaline that still woke her up at times. There were nights she was sure she *shouldn't* have survived, and she knew that those same nights plagued her siblings. Only nine of the Prophet's children lived through that final day, and in the years that followed, five of them, along with several others outside the primary family, took their lives. One of those others was the troubled young man that Dosie had married, Zebadiah Carson.

"I'm sorry he died," Ira said.

Dosie's exhale was a fog of pain. "So am I." *God, so am I.*

"Do you have somebody now? A new husband?"

"No. I mean, not a husband, no." She sputtered her words. "But I do have someone."

"Oh." He gazed out over the property again, shivered off a chill. "He nice?" He gnawed at one corner of his bottom lip.

Instead of being touched by his concern, Dosie was distracted by her fear. Her heart rate elevated again, the muscle squeezing hard enough to hurt. *He.* She could simply correct him; except, no, *I can't*, and the fact that she couldn't ate her alive. Old shames wrapped around her like a retired outfit and squeezed her breath away. She couldn't tell the truth, not all of it. All she could bring herself to say was, "I'm happy," with a voice so strained that it sounded more like a cry for help than a confession of contentment. She was hiding Jennifer, the love of her life, because she was a woman. Because they both were. Guilt was not a lump in her throat; it was a goddamned fist. But she did not know this man, her brother. She only knew where he came from, and that was enough.

Thankfully, Ira accepted the answer and didn't prod. The silence that followed almost made Dosie wish he had. It seemed like an hour went by before he spoke again.

"'Looking back, it was like seeing innocence altered right in front of me, an angel transformed into a demon.'"

Dosie longed for silence again. The recitation chilled her. How many times had Ira read her words that he could recite them now verbatim? As he read, she wondered, did he try to picture himself through her eyes? And if he did, did he have her paint him as a victim or a monster? Tremors raked Dosie's soul, unearthing buried pains that she had long since put to rest, and a fresh torrent of tears rose and refused to quell no matter how quickly she blinked.

"'A little boy who, in minutes...'" Ira's voice dropped to a near-whisper. "'...became a ghost of who he was.'"

He morphed right in front of her again. Through Dosie's tear-mottled eyes, he was three years old, squealing as he ran naked through the house, having escaped the terrible confines of his clothes. He was five and seated on Father's lap, saying grace at Christmas dinner for the first time with his hands clasped together and his eyes squeezed so tightly shut that he complained of a "headache in his face" for the next two days. He was eight and in cowboy boots too big for his feet, laughing and hollering as he sprinted through the field to herd the startled goats back to the barn. He was nine years old, and his little hands were shaking. His face was streaked with dirt and smoke, and his pajama pants were dark from a flood of urine. *I had to.* His voice was so small, so terrified, so *determined.* *"I have to, okay?"*

Dosie sucked in a cold breath and forced the image away, refused the weight of obligations that never should have been hers. Ira wasn't her son. None of her siblings were her children, and she wasn't responsible for what became of them. She wasn't responsible for what happened. She wasn't responsible for any of it.

"I'm sorry," she said, because she felt responsible anyway.

Ira shook his head. "You don't need to apologize. You wrote the truth." He surprised her then by turning as if to leave, as if to walk out across the property until he disappeared on the horizon, like a dream of the past that she would soon wake from. But then he stopped again and said, "I don't have anyone."

Dosie wasn't sure what he meant. A partner. A friend. Family. *Anyone.* It didn't matter. It pained her. "Oh."

His gaze bounced around as if searching for his next words. Or the courage to say them. "I haven't been to see him again, not since I first got out of the hospital."

Dosie frowned, confused, then it dawned on her. Her stomach clenched as if in protest, and she wanted to say something but didn't know what. She wasn't sure what, if anything, Ira was asking her yet.

"Sometimes, I wish I didn't go then," he continued, "but it wasn't bad. He was nice to me."

"He doesn't deserve to see you," Dosie told him. "He doesn't deserve to see any of us."

"I guess."

Dosie's cheeks burned. Anger coiled in her chest. "I *know.*"

"You haven't gone?"

"No," she all but spat at him, as if even considering doing so left a bad taste in her mouth. It did. "And I *never* will."

He nodded, said nothing, and Dosie felt compelled to move closer.

"Ira, don't," she said—a suggestion, a command, a *plea.* "I don't want to tell you what to do. You're grown up now, and it's your life. You should make your own choices. But if you're thinking about going to see him again, please reconsider. Nothing good will come of it."

"He's my father," Ira said weakly. "He's *your* father."

Dosie's anger flared into fury. "He is my abuser," she snapped, and he flinched. Natalie sucked in a breath behind her. "And he's yours, too."

Ira's nostrils flared, and his eyes glossed over. "Does that mean he can't love us?"

Dosie's knees shook, and she was gritting her teeth so hard that she was afraid they would crack. God, the number of times she had asked herself that question. *Did he ever really love me? Did he care about any of us? Did he want us? Did we matter?* The number of times she had lain in her bed at night surrounded by the immensity of absence and believed she would never have a family again. That maybe she never did. *Oh, this is torture.*

"It doesn't matter," she told him, softening at the pain in his eyes. *He was so young.* "Love isn't supposed to be the way that it was with him, Ira. Okay? That's not real love."

"How do you know? You married someone you didn't love."

"Because I have real love *now*, and it doesn't hurt me," Dosie said with conviction. "It doesn't ask me to hurt myself." She waited for him to look at her. When he finally did, she added, "Or anyone else."

Ira blinked and tears dripped down his cheeks, catching the morning sun. "Yeah," he said but his shoulders shrugged, and his body shrank further in on itself, and Dosie knew he didn't believe her. They lingered, again, in the quiet that followed, and though the chill in the air had long ago infiltrated her hoodie and stung her skin, she didn't move. He was a stranger, but he was her brother, and she would stand there as long as he needed her to, to convince him that abuse was not love.

"Sooner or later, he will find a way to use you," Dosie said. "You know he will. He is a rapist. Even if he never lays a hand on you, he will rape you of everything you have until you have nothing."

"I don't have anything."

"You *do*," Dosie assured him. "Intangible things. Things you would never even think of until you're stuck with their absence."

"Like what?"

"Like your dignity. Like your ability to have or understand boundaries. Your sense of security. Being able to touch your own body and speak about parts of yourself without feeling sick to your stomach and wanting to die. Ira, you know as well as I do that abuse doesn't always leave visible marks. Please, *please*, do not go back to him. You deserve better. Please, try to believe that you deserve better."

Dosie felt brittle, seconds from crumbling, as Ira kicked at the dirt like a kid too upset to lift his head, too guilty to defend himself. "Well," he said as he cleared his throat, "I should go, I think." He scratched the back of his neck as if trying to find some way to extend the conversation. "I don't want to bother you."

"You haven't bothered me," Dosie told him and meant it. "You just surprised me."

He nodded but still walked away, without another word or a backward glance. Back the way he came, over the expansive property to the southern end. There, a gravel road waited to lead him back to civilization.

"Ira, wait!" *What am I doing?* Her heart beat fast as he stopped and looked back, as she closed the gap between them again. "Do you have a phone?" *What am I doing?*

"Dosie," she heard Natalie call from a few feet back, her voice a warning, but she ignored it. Her instincts simmered under her skin, flared at the back of her brain. She ignored those, too.

Ira pulled a prepaid flip phone from his pocket, and Dosie held her hand out. When he placed the device in her palm, her stomach rolled. She flipped open the screen and entered a new contact. "If you need me, you can call me," she said, and her voice sounded strange to her ears, like it wasn't her own. Like someone else had borrowed it and was speaking for her.

"Really?" His eyes opened wide with his surprise. "Do you mean that?"

Dosie swallowed her anxiety. It was done. *Too late.* "You're my little brother. I want you to be okay. I want you to have someone. I don't want what he did to you to define the rest of your life." She summoned what bit of courage she still had in the face of her past and added, "But Ira, listen, I cannot have him in my life. Okay? I won't. And I mean that. If you go back to Father, if you want him in your life, you cannot be in mine. Please understand."

The Depth of You

Ira didn't agree or try to argue. He didn't say anything as he took his phone and returned it to his jeans pocket. Then he grabbed her hand and held it.

Dosie froze, their connected fingers dangling in the space between them, and couldn't look away from him. It was like being touched by a ghost. All her body went cold.

"I'm sorry," he said. "For Faith."

Dosie shut her eyes as an image of their sister spirited across her mind.

"And Mother Wendy."

Then another, the kind, older face of her father's third wife. A sinking feeling yawned inside her, a chasm of grief reopening. Dosie opened her eyes again and saw only sun splotches where her brother's expression should have been.

"And for being the boy outside the barn," he said, and then he let go. As her hand dropped back to her side, he turned and shuffled out into the weeds, back out of her life.

Dosie watched him for what felt like forever, her hands in tight fists and her gut in her throat. She wanted to stand there until she collapsed, and she wanted to go to bed, and she wanted to change her mind and redo it all and *cry*. She wanted Jennifer.

God, she wanted Jennifer. She wanted to sink her face into Jennifer's neck and forget the rest of the world existed. Forget she had a past or that anyone did. Forget there was anything but Jennifer's scent in her nose and Jennifer's arms securely around her back and Jennifer's voice in her ear, telling her everything was okay.

A hand at the back of her arm startled her.

"Sorry," Natalie said but didn't let go. She stepped closer, ran her hands up and down Dosie's arms, trying to warm her through her hoodie. "Are you okay? That was intense."

She couldn't see him anymore. He was a spot in the distance with no shape, no significance. A spot that had shaken Dosie down to her soul.

"Dosie?"

When she finally let herself look away, she found Natalie's eyes, and everything seemed to speed up. The world kicked back into gear, and whatever adrenaline had been holding her there, rigid and enduring, spilled out of her like air from a blown tire. She swayed in place, unable to feel her feet on the ground.

"Hey, I got you," Natalie said and caught some of her weight, slung one of Dosie's arms around her shoulders. "You're shaking. Let's get inside."

As they neared the back door, the smoke alarm screeched to life, and Dosie remembered the bacon. Inside, the oven was smoking. "Shit," Natalie said and ran to shut it off. She yanked open the door, and a black cloud billowed off a selection of charred crisps, the bacon burned to nearly nothing, and Dosie *just couldn't take it.*

"I'm sorry," she wailed as tears poured into her eyes.

"Oh hell," she heard Natalie say, and then she was being drawn into a tight hug. "Hey, come on. It's just bacon."

"It's not just bacon," Dosie cried and ripped herself away. "It's my whole ridiculous life!" She would never be free of it, and neither would anyone who loved her. She left the room as they found it, a smoking mess, just like her past. Just like her heart.

7

Despite what nearly every news station claimed at the time, the Hand of God was not a death cult. Many unspeakable things happened on the compound, and many people, both within and outside our community, played a part in allowing for those things to happen, uninterrupted, for years. But apart from himself, the only Hand of God children who knew anything about my father's insidious plan for "exodus" were his own, specifically his sons. The rest of us found out the day it was executed, when we were thrust into the ghastly midst of it and made to scramble for our lives.

That day comes back to me in flashes now and is sometimes so vivid that I feel like I am there again. I remember everything and have recounted the events numerous times over in police interviews, court testimonies, and therapy sessions, but with time and healing, some moments have faded and lost their edges. Others, however, refuse to soften or obscure and always do harm. Those are the moments that still crack behind my eyes like the piercing sound of a gunshot across the dawn. Those are the moments that keep me up at night.

The first scream, *screams*. The warm wetness gushing over my feet and ankles as I dropped the milking pail and ran hard enough to tear the muscles in my knees. The scent on the breeze as the wind shifted, pleasant at first, then acrid, and the way it stung my nostrils. The charred taste in the air that made my mouth dry. Everything happening all at once.

Thanks to the testimony of Meera Hines, a girl I grew up with who ran from the compound earlier that year, the FBI had begun a slow and quiet infiltration of the far east side of our property. In the pre-dawn dark, they seized our silos and storage facilities, then our equipment bays, emergency root cellars, and livestock barns. Three illegal weapons caches were uncovered in the process, and five men working the east end were taken into custody. All five of those men survived the day because of it. One of them had managed a radio call to my father before they were found.

On the other end of the property, over 100 acres away, eleven structures housed the sleeping majority of the Hand of God's 200-plus members. There, my father, a man who always had to be in control, reacted furiously to the news and quickly enacted what he believed to be the ultimate countermeasure. "Immaculate Exodus." Just as he'd secretly planned, he unleashed my brothers like a pack of well-trained, bloodthirsty hunting hounds, and within minutes, the only place I had ever called home transformed into a nightmare from which many would never wake.

They stalked the property like predators, my brothers, guided solely by instinct. They were no longer steering their own bodies, no longer in control of their own limbs; they were just *doing*. The family was under attack, and they had a divine obligation as the sons of the Prophet to ensure that no one—man, woman, or child—was taken from the compound. *That*, my father had convinced them, would have been a fate far worse than any other, even death. So, they became his faithful instruments and carried out his orders as if they'd come from God himself.

Bunkhouses were locked and barricaded and set on fire. Those still in their beds would never leave them. Glass shattered left and right as my brothers threw bottles of gasoline through the windows to hasten the damage. It was so chaotic, so savage and sadistic as to be incomprehensible. I stood on the edge of it with the heat of the growing blaze pulsing at my face, chest, and arms, and nothing felt real. How could any of it possibly be real? But then someone, their face so sooty that I couldn't recognize them, attempted to escape from one of the broken bunkhouse windows. The back of their shirt was on fire, and their mouth was a gray gap of pain, and I watched in horror as my eldest brother Othniel—Ottie—stuck the barrel of a shotgun right inside it and calmly pulled the trigger.

That was the moment that jarred me awake and convinced me that it wasn't a bad dream. All of it was really happening. My brothers were killing people. They were *killing people*, our family, our friends, and amidst it all, my father's voice rang clear. "Do not run!" he commanded from somewhere in the smog, his voice so chilling and awesome that it raked like a frozen claw down my back. "Do not be afraid. 'The Lord will fight for you; you need only to be still.'"

I couldn't be still. I ran. I had a million thoughts, too many to isolate them all, but two in particular seemed to drive my feet: *Get the kids. Get away.* For the first time in my life, it didn't matter what my father commanded. My body didn't care. I ran. *Get the kids. Get away.* The Big House seemed miles away even as I hit my full stride with thick black smoke choking the air around me and turning the morning to night. Firecracker gunshots speckled the dark haze from every direction, and my heart jumped so hard with each one that I was sure it would rip right through my chest. *Get the kids. Get away.* I kept running.

I rammed into someone and fell. I still don't know who. I remember their breathing, as ragged and panicked as mine, and then I was running again. I fell again, too, tripping over debris that I was afraid to look back at or reach for. What if it was someone I knew? What if it was someone I loved? What if it was someone? *Get the kids. Get away.* I kept running.

Corrie MacKay

The hens screeched from inside their small coops as I passed, startled awake by gunfire and smoke. I couldn't see much, but I knew the compound like I knew my father's moods, like I knew my mother's recipes, like I knew all my sisters' favorite colors and how much extra food I could squirrel away without getting caught. I was almost to the gate. *Keep running. Keep going. Get the kids. Get away.*

Fires roared louder and turned the air hotter as I raced along the side of the barn closest to the Big House, where we kept our chicken feed and gardening equipment. My eyes stung so badly that they became a constant blur of tears, but I was too afraid to close them. More and more gunshots echoed around me. I could hear bullets hitting wood and metal and dirt, ricocheting and embedding and slaughtering, and then I rounded the front of the barn and came face-to-face with the smoking tip of a pistol.

I have had many out-of-body experiences in my life, but that moment was like having my soul cleaved from its physical form. At once, I was sinking into the ground and floating into an abyss as I met my nine-year-old brother's eyes over the barrel of a gun. He was still in his pajamas and socks, and every inch of him vibrated as if plugged into a socket. His chest rocked, every breath heavy, as he glanced between me and the ground. At his feet, at *my* feet, lay our sister, Faith. Her eyes were still open over the hole he'd just put in her face.

I tried to say his name or anything, but I could only cough, and something about the jarring sound seemed to anger him. His small face hardened. "I had to," he said, and I knew he believed it. "I have to, okay?" Looking back, it was like seeing innocence altered right in front of me, an angel transformed into a demon; a little boy who, in minutes, became a ghost of who he was.

As he steadied the gun, I became certain of one thing: I was going to die. Any minute, I would be shot just like my poor sister and left to crumple atop her in a lifeless heap. The sweet boy I had been helping raise since I was six years old would be the violent, instant end of me, and there was nothing I could do about it.

Dosie shoved the open pages of her memoir toward Natalie and stood. "I told you." She shook her hands as if she could fling away her anxiety and paced the foot of her bed. "The exact words."

"I believed you," Natalie said as she traced a few of the words with her finger then met Dosie's eyes. "Dosie. I'm sorry. I don't know what to say. I can't even imagine." She sighed as Dosie increased the force of her pacing, every step heavy enough to *thunk, thunk, thunk* against the floor. "It was brave of you to face him again and talk to him."

The room seemed to pulse around her in agitated time with her heart. "I don't feel brave."

"Doesn't mean you aren't. You gave him your number. That was definitely brave."

"You mean stupid."

"That's not what I said."

"I can't think about it." Dosie gagged and fanned her face, feeling everything all at once. "I don't want to be brave."

"Okay. Well, what do you want? Do you want to call your therapist?"

"No. I have a session next week. It can wait."

"Can it?"

"I think so. I think I'm okay. I mean, I'm *not* okay, but I'm... I'm okay, and I'm not alone, so, you know, that's good."

Natalie nodded as if she understood, though how, Dosie wasn't sure. Her thoughts and feelings were all jumbled. "Do you want to call Jennifer?"

"Yes, but I'm not going to."

"Why not?"

"Because she's dealing with her own stuff right now."

"You're dealing with a lot too, and you'd still be there for her if she called and asked you to talk."

"She'll be worried, and I don't want her to worry about me while she's trying to take care of things. And I'm okay." If she said it enough, it would surely be true. *Right?* "Mostly. I'm better than I thought I would be if I ever encountered one of my siblings again." Her skin itched. *Why am I itchy?* "I'm fine. Or I will be. Yeah."

"So, do you want to—"

"I don't know!"

"People who are fine don't shout, Dosie."

"I'm sorry. I don't know what I want. I feel like...."

Her head swam with pictures and sounds. She could hear a voice as if someone had switched a recording on in her brain. Clarion as a bell, Mother Wendy's words rang like salvation as she appeared from the smoke to place her body in front of Dosie's so that Ira's gun was instead trained on her. *"Run, Dosie. Just run and don't stop."* Faster and faster the images arose, as Dosie ran, as she disobeyed, as she stopped again when she shouldn't have, until they were so mangled and matted together that she couldn't separate them anymore.

"I want it to be over." There was smoke in her nose from the kitchen, and it may as well have been from that day. "I want it to be done."

"I hear that," Natalie said as she patted the bed for Dosie to stop her pacing and sit again. "But we both know that's just not going to happen."

Dosie's bottom lip quivered as she sat. It would never be over.

"As much as I wish we could, we can't suck our memories out of our heads and bodies and un-feel them."

"Yeah." It would never be done.

"You know that doesn't mean you can't be happy," Natalie said as she pulled Dosie down so that they lay side by side on their backs with their shoulders bumped together, staring up at the ceiling. "You *are* happy, Dose. If you're triggered, that's okay. We'll deal. But don't let yourself forget about the life you have now. You have a great life."

"Yeah," Dosie whispered again and told herself to believe it. To *know* it. Her chest felt raw and achy, like she'd lain in the sun too long and let her skin burn. Despite how badly she wanted to be held and squeezed until she felt safe again, the thought of being touched any more than she already was made the pain worse. She was a fresh bruise, and she couldn't bear the idea of being pressed.

"So," Natalie said with a deep breath, "since you can't yeet your memories into the sun, what else do you want?" She laughed, hollow but endearing, and Dosie tried to meet her where she was but only managed a quarter of the journey. "Seriously, if there's anything that I can do, anything that will help, just tell me. Like, anything. A long talk. A hug. A game of Mario Kart just to be mad at something else. I don't know. Pizza? You want pizza for breakfast? Can we get pizza this early? Should I even be asking, or should I just be ordering the pizza?"

Dosie more whimpered than laughed, but it was something. She skirted the edges of steadiness as she turned her head and felt a tear leak from the corner of her eye to soak into the bedspread. "I feel like a monster."

"What?" Natalie's bewildered voice pitched higher. She rolled onto her side to face her. "Why?"

Dosie's chin quivered. Her heart did, too. She couldn't bring herself to speak any louder than it took to be heard. "Because."

"Hey, talk to me. Because why? How could you possibly be a monster?"

"Because I was scared of him."

"Oh, Dosie, come on," Natalie said softly. "He killed two people, one of them right in front of you. I think having some fear related to that is natural. It definitely doesn't make you a monster."

"He was a victim," Dosie said, frustrated with herself and with everything. She pulled her shirt up over her face to wipe her eyes and cheeks then yanked it back down again. "He was a child. He's my brother!"

"I know, but that doesn't change the facts. He did it."

"Yeah." Dosie breathed. *It's natural to be afraid. You're not a monster.* "He did."

"Be fair to yourself, Dosie. You were a child, too. Not as young as

Corrie MacKay

Ira, for sure, but still just a kid. The kinds of things you saw that day would scare anyone, and it's not your fault that he's connected to that fear. You didn't make him a nightmare, you know? His actions did that, whether or not he was responsible for them."

New tears welled, and Dosie's frustration grew. She told herself to be calm. *It's natural to be afraid. You're not a monster.* "I feel like I have to be there for him. I have to... I have all this." She waved her hand to indicate the room, the house, everything. "And all this money, all this money I've got, because I survived the same things that he did, and what does he have?"

"Hey," Natalie said and sat up, turned to look at Dosie properly. "Don't do that. First of all, no, you did not survive the same things. The boys weren't abused the way the girls were, and you know it. Not saying they didn't have it bad, but it wasn't like *that*, and you were subject to your father's bullshit for a lot longer than Ira was. Second, it's not your fault that he or any of them did what they did, so their part of the settlement being forfeited to you and the other surviving kids isn't your fault either. And lastly, and this is the most important part so listen up, you did not ask for any of this shit, Dosie, not the civil trial or the settlement or any of it. The state decided that you and the others, and not your brothers, deserved the money."

Dosie knew Natalie was right. It wasn't her fault that her father's despicable deals with social workers and even a few cops over the years had won her a fortune, nor was it her fault that her sisters were dead at the hands of her brothers. She hadn't asked for any of it, hadn't wanted any of it. That didn't change how hard it was on her sometimes to know that the primary reason she had so much was because she was the only one left to have it. Thanks to her foolish young marriage, even Zeb's share went to her. She hadn't touched it. The sum still sat in the bank collecting interest, waiting for her to choose which organization—or two, or four—should receive it. She couldn't keep it, but she wasn't sure what he would want or if he would want her making the decision at all, and that haunted her almost as much as the fact that she had his money to begin with or that she'd felt the most terrible sense of relief when he died before she could tell him that she needed it to be over. Her mouth tasted like guilt, bitter and thick.

"It's not on you, Dosie," Natalie said, "and it's definitely not on you to rectify it. Ira is your brother, and he's a victim, and he's a killer, and you don't owe him a fucking thing. All those things can be true at the same time. Yeah?"

All those things can be true at the same time. Dosie breathed through the thought and nodded. "I need to talk about something else," she said and got to her feet.

Natalie hopped up after her. "Right. Let's talk about what kind of pizza to get. Come on." She put her hand on Dosie's back to guide her toward the hallway. "Or we could go out. You want to go out for pizza?"

It's natural. "I would rather be slapped across the face than seen by other people right now." *I'm not a monster.*

"Got it," Natalie said with a laugh. "No people. Just pick-up."

Dosie huffed and accepted that her day was just going to suck. *I'm not a monster.* "Extra pepperoni."

"Dude, it's like you know me."

Jennifer sat in a dimly lit booth at an Irish pub in Cambridge, half-consciously picking at her late lunch. The fat and crispy steak fries she'd ordered paired well with the two fingers of Redbreast 27 that she was letting them charge her an arm and a leg for, and that was just about the only thing keeping her mood in check. Everything she read in Carine's collected file made her want to throw something at the wall. Or at someone's head, one head in particular. Her aunt was right; Orwell Glass had done little of note throughout his time in prison, and the available information suggested he was active in prison extracurriculars like woodshop and track, worked well with others, and was rarely cause for attention. The few disciplinary issues that Carine had managed to uncover were so minor that Jennifer rolled her eyes as she read them.

Tardy to work assignment.

Running in the breezeway.

Poor hygiene.

Most of the infractions occurred in the early months and years of Glass's sentence; once he settled in, or so it seemed, he became the exemplar good boy serving his time. Nothing on his record would make him seem unworthy to a parole board, which made Jennifer's blood boil. The nature of the crime that landed him in prison in the first place should have made him unworthy from the start, but the prosecutorial team proved unsuccessful at convincing a grand jury that Glass had pre-meditated the murder. That took a first-degree charge off the table, and he was instead tried and convicted for the crime of murder in the second degree, which in the state of Massachusetts, meant he could be granted parole after serving a minimum of fifteen years in prison. Two decades later, it still bothered Jennifer. It still sat in the pit of her stomach like a red-hot coal that refused to cool. The man *slaughtered* her sister. He shouldn't be allowed freedom; the fact that he could even ask for it offended her.

She hardly recognized him in the few included photographs. He no longer wore glasses and had developed a more athletic build, along with bags under his eyes and a prominent receding hairline, emphasized by the long, ratty ponytail he wore at the back. Prison appeared to have been both beneficial and detrimental to his appearance; he was more physically fit, sure, but he also appeared to have slept only a month or two of his twenty-odd years behind bars. *Good.* Jennifer hoped he had the same kinds of nightmares she did; she hoped his were worse. She hoped they needed no trigger. She hoped they came often and lingered long after he woke.

Jennifer sighed and flipped another page. She hated this. As important as every word she said at the parole hearing would be, spending so much time marinating on what happened was an incredible energy drain. It wasn't good for her to be immersed in the worst event of her life again; her body told her as much with the sickly itch of irritation working its way across her skin and the weight of exhaustion pulling at her shoulders and eyelids. She was so irritable that every thought she had pissed her off, even the mundane ones. The two seconds of consideration that she gave the Lads and Lasses bathroom signs made her feel like her head might catch fire. Everything was bullshit, and she *did not want to do this.*

Much to her surprise, a fresh Glencairn glass appeared on her table, two fingers of golden-brown whisky glittering inside. She raised an eyebrow at the waiter.

"Another Redbreast for ya."

Jennifer's other eyebrow joined the first. "Which I did not order."

"Gift," said the waiter, as if no further explanation was needed.

Jennifer glanced at the bar and noticed a man looking over. She did not smile or indulge him in any fashion, certain he would consider it an invitation, but she could admit to herself that it was a nice reminder of this one way in which she not only had power but *a lot* of it. She turned her attention back to the server. "Does he know the price?"

The waiter followed her line of sight and said, "Oh, no, it's not from him. It was from a woman."

"A woman?" It wasn't unheard of, but it happened rarely when compared with how often she was complimented or propositioned by men, so it always surprised her.

"Yeah, uh...." He searched the bar, then his gaze bounced over the various booths. After a moment, he gave up. "I don't see her anymore actually. Maybe she went to the bathroom. Or left." He shrugged. "But yeah, she paid, so it won't be on your bill or anything. Enjoy."

As he walked away, Jennifer sat bewildered with her new drink. She could not fathom someone buying her what amounted to a $90 refill with no expectations. This mystery woman with either deep or reckless pockets wanted no exchange? No greeting or flirting? No empty small talk or obvious hints for a hook-up? Was that really possible?

She looked over the bar again then around the booths and tables that she had a clear shot of. Surely, if the woman still lingered nearby, Jennifer would find her eyes on her, watching, waiting for that satisfying moment when the woman she'd purchased a drink for finally took her first sip. Nothing.

What the hell? She narrowed her eyes at the whisky as if she suspected it to be poison. *Who does that?*

Her phone dinged with a new message, and Jennifer welcomed the distraction. She left the surprise whisky untouched as she dug her phone out from under a mess of papers and napkins and saw the message was from Dosie. At once, the heaviness lifted from her bones, and she felt sweet relief. Until she swiped to read.

Hey, sorry but I need to talk to you when you get a minute. No rush if you're super busy but, like, also call soon if you can. Thanks.

It sounded weird in Jennifer's mind, choppy and absent affection. Alarm bells rang through her head. *Something happened. Something's happening.* "I need to talk to you" was what girlfriends said right before they broke up with someone, right? Hadn't she seen that in a movie? Hadn't she read it in a book or two or ten? *Fuck. Fuck!* Jennifer closed her eyes, told herself to get a grip. *She loves you. Stop.*

Another text whooshed in. Jennifer's eyes went straight to it, read: *Don't panic or anything. I'm fine.*

Somehow, those words made everything worse. The instruction not to panic seemed the perfect trigger for panic, and in seconds, Jennifer's nerves were out-of-tune piano keys being smashed at random. No harmony. No peace.

She gathered up her things, then fired off a text for Ned to pick her up. She would call Dosie from the hotel; that way, if her world was flipped any harder, she'd have somewhere safe and private to melt into a puddle of despair. *Oh, fuck off,* she told herself, frustrated with her recent lack of cool or calm, let alone collected. The only things Jennifer had collected of late were dehydration headaches and a propensity for emotional instability. *Everything's fine. Stop assuming the worst.*

She headed for the door with a lump in her throat and left the mystery woman's whisky untouched on the table.

When the call connected, a rushed breath hit the speaker and crackled in Jennifer's ear like static. Then a voice that wasn't Dosie's said, "Uh, hey, Jennifer, thanks for calling."

Natalie. Jennifer was relieved she recognized the voice. She had spent little time with Dosie's friends outside a couple dinner dates, but she knew their faces, their voices. Her attention to detail had always been excellent. "Is Dosie okay?"

"Yeah," Natalie replied in a hushed voice. "She's good. Like I said, I don't want you to panic or anything."

No wonder Dosie's texts seemed off. "Why are you whispering?"

"Oh, uh, Dosie's asleep on the couch. Sorry. Let me go to another room."

Jennifer shook her sleeve down and checked her watch. Dosie was a napper, but it was only half-past noon on the west coast. When Dosie did nap, it was rarely before five. Prior to that, she tended to be a ball of energy. "So, Dosie is asleep, and you are sending me texts from her phone telling me to call you. Why? And don't tell me everything's fine. You are clearly hiding this call from her, or you wouldn't have waited until she was asleep. So, whatever's happened, kindly spit it out already, because my patience today is about as thin as a fucking wafer, and I'm worried."

"Right." To Jennifer's relief, she didn't sound offended. "She did say you were dealing with stuff. Sorry. So, uh, I'm just going to blurt it all out then, and you can, like, do with it what you will. Good?"

"Natalie."

"Okay, yeah, so, I know you read Dosie's book, and it wasn't all that long ago, so I'm just going to hope you know who I'm talking about when I say her half-brother Ira showed up at the house today, and they had a super fucking intense talk in the backyard."

Jennifer sat straight up in her hotel bed. *Ira*. Which one was Ira? It didn't matter. All of Dosie's brothers, all but the youngest, who was barely two, had killed people the day of the raid. That made them dangerous. Then again, anyone from Dosie's nocuous past showing up out of the blue was dangerous. If nothing else, the sheer weight of the memories they brought with them could inflict damage. It made Jennifer uncomfortable just to think about. *Ira. Which brother is Ira?*

"And he apologized for the people he killed and said he didn't have anyone and that he was thinking about, like, going to the prison to visit their dad, and it really upset Dosie. And she ended up...."

The hung sentence halted Jennifer's breath. "She ended up what?"

Natalie sighed. "She gave him her number."

Fuck. Then it came back to her. *Ira*. The boy outside the barn, the youngest one involved that day. *The one who held a gun in Dosie's face.*

"I'm sorry. I know she probably shouldn't have, but I didn't really know how to intervene," Natalie said, clearly having heard disappointment in Jennifer's silent response.

It was true; she was disappointed but not with what happened. There was no right way to confront a situation like that, and as she had been learning of late, when emotion whittled away reason, people often reverted to what was most natural to them. For herself, she realized, that was isolation and masking; for Dosie, it was yielding and self-sacrifice. She was never going to hear her sibling say he had no one and not try to fill that void herself, even if she shouldn't. It wasn't who she was. Jennifer wasn't disappointed in Dosie's decision to give her phone number or in Natalie's not to intervene, even if both later became a point of regret. The decision that disappointed Jennifer was her own.

If she hadn't left Dosie behind, then the confrontation wouldn't have happened; at least, it wouldn't have happened when and how it did. It was possible, had it been delayed, that Jennifer could have been there herself with Dosie when it did eventually occur. As much as she believed in Natalie's ability to support Dosie through anything, she preferred—she *needed*—to be the one who was there for her through the most difficult moments of her life, and she was devastated that she hadn't been.

Which is just so fucking rich, since you had to shut her out of yours. Heat scorched across Jennifer's cheeks and forehead, down the sides and back of her neck. *Why did I do that?* Every time she had come near to being overwhelmed, it was Dosie's voice in her head drawing her back to calm. It was Dosie's measured breathing over the phone. It was the thought of crawling into her arms where nothing else existed.

Fuck.

Dosie shouldn't have been there. She should've been in Boston with Jennifer, curled up beside her in her hotel bed, untouched by anything but Jennifer's hands and testy moods. Surely, that would have been better than being touched by the past. Jennifer knew she would take Dosie's anxiety and over-explaining over her own past any day. In an instant. Happily. Oh, she felt like such an asshole.

"Um, Jennifer?"

She cleared her throat. "I'm here, just processing."

"Oh, yeah. It's a lot."

"Why are you telling me this? Why isn't Dosie telling me herself?" She knew why, but for some reason, she needed to hear it.

"Uh, well, she wanted to, but she was afraid that it would be too much to add to your plate with whatever you've got going on over there."

Jennifer wanted to kiss Dosie for respecting her privacy, and she wanted to shout at her for thinking that any reason was a good enough reason not to share what happened with her. She didn't want to be kept in the dark, not for her own comfort, convenience, or otherwise.

"I wouldn't have reached out if I didn't know she wanted to do it herself and was just coming up with excuses not to."

"I understand," Jennifer said. "Could you wake her and put her on the phone, please?"

"Uh, yeah. One sec."

Jennifer imagined Dosie passed out on the couch from being overstimulated and emotional, and she hated that she wasn't there to wake her herself. She wanted to be the one gently jostling her. She wanted to be on the couch with her, pressed in at every inch between the cushions they'd made love on so many times since the first. She wanted to be the one holding her, whispering in her ear that everything would be okay.

"Hey, Natalie?"

"Yeah?"

"I mean no offense when I say this, and I'm glad you reached out to me, but should there be a next time, don't go against her decision not to tell me something, okay?" It was important that Dosie share what she wanted to share when she wanted to share it, even if not knowing occasionally drove Jennifer mad. "Even if you know she wants to and just isn't for some reason or even if you think she's wrong. Unless her life is literally in danger, I think it's better if you just tell her why you disagree and then let her deliberate instead of making the call for her."

Natalie's silence lasted only a second or two, barely enough to notice. "Yeah, for sure. You're right. Sorry."

"No need. I'm glad I know, and I'm glad you're there with her, for her."

"No doubt. I appreciate you telling me what you think."

"Rest assured I always will."

Natalie chuckled. "Right. *Director.*" The line filled with the sounds of shuffling. "I'm waking her up now." She set the phone aside, Jennifer assumed, as when her voice came through again, it sounded far away, muffled by distance and some surface or other.

"Hey, Dosie, wake up. Hey, sorry, but Jennifer's on the phone."

Jennifer warmed at the sleepy, crackly voice that had her heart. *"What? Jen? Jen's on the phone?"* More shuffling ensued, and then she came through loud and clear. "Jen?"

It was restorative, the way Dosie said her name, the way it touched every part of her and turned her easy, pliant, and love-drunk, no matter the circumstances. No matter how terrible the day or the dark looming ahead. Dosie said her name, and nothing hurt. She was home. "Hi, darling."

Dosie took the call in her bedroom, shutting the door behind her and letting her back slide down the wood. She sat herself on the floor despite the bed right in front of her, concerned that if she lay back down before she was properly awake, she would fall asleep again. "How are you?" she asked as she stretched her legs out in front of her and wiggled her cold toes to life. "How's your day going? Are you okay? Do you miss me?"

"I do," Jennifer said, "and it's good. Or fine, anyway. It's as expected."

"That was a lot of different ways to say you don't want to talk about you."

"Bingo," Jennifer said, then she paused as if considering something. "Do you know what Bingo is?"

Dosie smiled to only herself and shook her head. She felt silly and weightless all of a sudden. With a performative clearing of her throat, she said, "Well, thank you for asking, ma'am. Allow me to tell you all about Sister Brenda's Bi-Monthly Bingo Bouts."

"Oh, my," Jennifer said, and Dosie could hear the amusement seeping in like slow-flowing paint to add some color to her tired voice. "Kudos on the alliteration."

"She was super proud of that."

"If only she had been a man, then she could have been a Brother instead of a Sister. A perfect set of b's."

"If only."

"Did you play?"

"Bingo?"

"Already? I haven't even set all my cards out."

Dosie snorted. "I love you."

"I love you. So, did you play?"

"No way. The so-called prize was getting to perform an act of service for the Prophet, as if we didn't all do that basically every minute of every day anyway." She rolled her eyes then remembered they were speaking over the phone. "You didn't see it, but I rolled my eyes just now."

"You didn't see it, but I rolled mine, too," Jennifer said, "and I can't see it now, but I'm certain you're smiling."

This woman. Dosie was dizzy for her. "Bingo."

Jennifer exhaled into the phone, long and slow, and Dosie heard it for what it was: a shift in the conversation. "Are you okay? I can't imagine what you must be thinking and feeling."

"Yeah." Dosie let the words sink in and summon new thoughts, fresh memories. And old ones. "It's a lot."

"Dosie, I need you to know it doesn't matter what I'm dealing with here, or ever. You can always count on me to be there for you, and you can always talk to me. About anything." She sighed and added, "*If* you want to, obviously. I *guess.*"

Even her begrudging grumble of acceptance to potentially being shut out sent a flutter through Dosie's stomach, a scattering of butterflies to and fro until she felt a little like she could fly herself. She laughed. *God, I love you.*

"I do want to," she said, "but I was going to wait."

"You don't need to—"

"I know. I know. I don't have to protect you. I wasn't. I'm not. I just didn't want to tell you until you got back."

"Because you were afraid that I would freak out?"

"No." Dosie frowned. "Why would I be afraid of that? You hardly ever freak out about anything, and when you do, your version of freaking out is basically just pretending that you're not freaking out."

"I threw a fucking lamp at a wall and shattered it." The shift in Jennifer's voice pained her, a sharp disappointment that she'd clearly been whittling to a fine point since the moment the lamp left her hand.

Oh, Jen. Dosie wouldn't have guessed that the action would weigh on Jennifer this much, but it clearly had. "Honey, you were angry and shocked, and you hadn't slept."

"And that makes it okay? You could've been hurt, Dosie. A shard could've hit you."

"It didn't."

"It could have!"

Then Dosie remembered. Anger. Violence. Jennifer associated both, especially when expressed inside the home, with the man who murdered her sister, the man who had been at the forefront of her mind now for days. *Oh.* "Jen."

"Fuck." Jennifer's breath came through heavy and frustrated. "I'm sorry. I don't know what I'm doing. I wanted to tell you everything would be okay. I wanted to tell you that you could tell me anything, and now listen to me. I'm... I'm sorry, Dosie."

Dosie wished they were face-to-face. She wished she could hold Jennifer's hands and look her in the eyes when she told her, "You're upset. A lot is happening, and neither one of us has had any time to process, but baby, I promise you these thoughts you're having, this fear—none of it is necessary. It's just your trauma and everything you're dealing with putting crap in your head. You are not dangerous, and you do not have an anger problem. You are nothing like *him*, and you never will be. You thought you were alone, and you never had any intention of me or anyone getting hurt. Please don't think the worst of yourself. It's just your brain being mean. Okay?"

She waited for Jennifer's response, but it never came. So, Dosie kept talking. "I didn't call you right away after Ira, because I didn't need to, not because I didn't think you could handle it. Of course I *want* to talk to you about it, but I don't really want to have that talk over the phone, and even if I did, it's not a talk that needs to happen right now while you're dealing with stuff there. I'm okay. I'm shaken, and I'm definitely a little triggered, but I'm okay. Natalie worries— you all do—and I know I give you good reason sometimes, but I promise I am okay, and if that changes, I promise I will tell you. But unless that happens, I'd really rather us wait until you're back to talk about it."

Again, she received no response, and Dosie's mind started to race. The second it took off, she was incapable of certainty. "Um, did that make sense?"

"Yes." Jennifer's deep breath came through, and as if resigning herself to something both terrible and wonderful, she said, "You always make sense to me."

The flutter re-emerged, the rapid beat of wings in Dosie's gut enough to generate heat. She felt the blush creep over her skin, rising from her chest. "Well, considering how weird I am, that might make you a weirdo, too, you know. I hope that's okay."

"I am the definition of taboo, darling," Jennifer said. "If you can happily accept that brand by association, then I'll gladly be your weirdo."

Dosie's smile expanded until the corners of her mouth ached. Her face felt like fire as she buried it in one hand and tried not to judge herself for being so ridiculously beside herself in love. Her certainty was back. Jennifer Dupont had her whole heart. She had never been more certain of anything.

"I *hate* it when you say things like that," she teased and squeezed her thighs together at the throaty sound of Jennifer's quiet laugh.

"Oh? Are you devastated with me?"

Dosie resisted the urge to put a hand between her legs just to alleviate the sudden delicious ache she had there. "Just devastated."

"How can I make it up to you?"

"Say more," Dosie told her.

"A masochist now, are you?"

"*Jennifer.*" Dosie bit her bottom lip and pulled the neck of her shirt open so she could yank it up over her face. As if she could hide from the keen effect of Jennifer's voice or from anyone seeing how it turned her into goo. "This conversation is going in a completely different direction than I thought it would."

Jennifer's belly laugh exploded through the phone, and Dosie wished she could catch it on recording just so she could hear it whenever she wanted. It was her favorite of Jennifer's five distinct laughs. She loved them all—Jennifer's quiet and rough-hewn seductive laugh, her airy surprised laugh, her thin-lipped courtesy laugh, and the half-hearted laugh she did when she thought something was funny but not really funny enough to *actually* laugh at—but this laugh was the best. Dosie considered it her true laugh, as it was always unabated and lacked any control. It was louder than Jennifer ever was outside the bedroom and filled her entire face and body with glee. Her nose wrinkled up, and her eyes squinted until they were almost closed, and every time, she threw her head back as if the chaotic sound had to be tossed into the air, because the sheer force of it would knock someone out should it hit them head on. It even caused her to snort, on occasion, just to catch her breath. That laugh had no master, not even the person it belonged to. It was just joy, and Dosie lived for it.

"And to think it started with Bingo," Jennifer said.

Dosie felt too much at once. She was hot all over despite her freezing hands and feet, and she couldn't stop smiling despite her nerves feeling a bit like agitated bees. She cooled her face with a few rapid waves of her hand and said, "You wouldn't believe how much I want to kiss you right now."

The soft groan that answered her made her want that kiss even more. "Do it."

"Ugh. Don't tempt me, or I'll get on a plane."

"Do it."

Dosie sat up straighter. *That sounded serious. Had Jennifer changed her mind?* She gnawed her bottom lip for a moment then decided not to risk asking in case she was wrong. She didn't want

Corrie MacKay

Jennifer interpreting it as pressure to invite her when she didn't want to. Instead, Dosie pushed another joke and hoped it would reveal more. "Stop. You're just fantasizing about my kisses, and it's making you horny."

"I love that you whispered the word 'horny'."

"I still said it," Dosie said with a delirious smile.

"You did. Well done."

"Thank you."

"Dosie?"

"Yeah?"

"I was wrong."

A nervous sort of excitement purred to life in the pit of her stomach. "What about?"

"You staying behind," Jennifer said. "I think I need you here, and I made the wrong choice. It wasn't because I—I don't know. I'm sorry. I feel stupid, and I'm sorry."

"Don't be," Dosie said, her sudden excitement quelled by the guilty tremors in Jennifer's voice. "You don't have anything to apologize for or feel stupid about. It's always okay to change your mind."

"But you knew it was the wrong choice," Jennifer said, and Dosie could hear her continued apology like a sad, heavy rhythm behind every new word. "That's why you were so upset when I left. So, all of this could have been avoided, and I could have had you here to—"

She cut herself off again, and Dosie knew it was because she hated the thickness in her voice. She hated feeling so much, despite the fact that she *always* did, and she hated even more the idea that anyone might be aware of it. Where Dosie was concerned, she'd become much less resistant, even eager at times; with the rest of the world, however, she was still just a hair shy of hissing at a tear-stained face in her vicinity, even if she secretly hoped the person crying was okay.

"Please stop, Jen," Dosie told her. "You're just looking for reasons to be angry at yourself. We disagreed about it, but that doesn't mean you were wrong. And even if it did, does that matter?

Not everything has to be right or wrong. Sometimes, things just are what they are, you know? You chose what you thought was best, and then you realized later that a different choice might be better. I don't think that's anything to be sorry for. I think that's just being human."

"I hate it when you know everything."

"Me too," Dosie said and smiled at the relief she heard in Jennifer's voice. "It's such a burden to be so wise."

Jennifer's soft laugh trickled through her like cool water after a heatwave. "Poor you."

"I can still come if you want me to," Dosie offered. "There's no pressure either way. But if you do, just tell me, and I will make it happen."

"I feel like such an idiot."

Dosie hated when Jennifer spoke ill of herself. It happened rarely, usually only in times of stress, but when it did, her scathing self-reviews could be relentless. "Why? For loving me so much that you can't stand to be away from me for even a few days?" she asked, gladly seizing any opportunity to interrupt that pattern before it was established. "Honestly, I think it's one of your most attractive traits."

"Well, as long as you find it attractive," Jennifer said. "I will take care of your flight and have Candace send you the boarding information when she has it. I don't want to rush you, so I'll have her get one for the morning instead of tonight. Will that work?"

"Wait, Jen," Dosie said. "I just want to be sure. This *is* because it's what you really want, right? And not because my brother showed up out of the blue, and you're worried about me?"

"It's both," Jennifer admitted, "and that has to be okay, love. I can't force away my concern for you, and I wouldn't want to, so I don't want to apologize for it."

"You don't need to. It's okay if it's part of the reason you want me there. I just didn't want it to be the only reason."

"I think you know it's not. You knew from the start."

"Okay. I'll pack some things."

"Enough for a few days," Jennifer told her. "And it's a bit bitter here, so pack for cold."

"So, no short or sleeveless dresses."

"Mm, I don't think I said that," Jennifer replied, causing Dosie to giggle. "But if you must hide your gorgeous legs, I suppose I can settle for unwrapping them like a present at the hotel instead."

"Don't start," Dosie said, hearing the dip in Jennifer's voice. "I can't be dirty with you when I have a guest downstairs."

"Oh really?" Jennifer's voice dipped further, went raw around the edges, a clear challenge. "What happened to the girl who had sex in a fitting room?"

Dosie's jaw dropped open. "I'm hanging up. That was one time! I have to pack."

"Go on then," Jennifer said, and her sexy little laugh made Dosie feel high.

With a fresh spring to her step, Dosie bounded down the stairs in search of Natalie. "Best friend!" she called as she entered the living room to find her lounging on the air mattress, watching baking videos on her phone. She looked at Dosie with narrowed eyes.

"Hark," she droned, "I hear the call of a woman who wants something."

"You don't even bake."

"Um, do I have to bake to love bread and delicious desserts?" Natalie asked. "I haven't seen you throwing a ball of dough around any time recently, but you still happily stuffed your face with those four slices of pizza someone *baked* for you today."

Dosie got so tickled her ears hurt and threw herself onto the air mattress so that Natalie went rolling off the other side and onto the floor. "That's what you get!"

Natalie's laugh morphed into a silent shoulder dance, punctuated only by the whistling sound of her air escaping. When she collected herself, she crawled back onto the mattress and shoved Dosie over. "What is this mood?" she asked. "Why so buoyant after, like, the world's most intense not-breakfast?" Then she narrowed her eyes again. "Wait. Did you and Jennifer have phone sex?"

"No, I'd be asleep again if we did," Dosie said, and Natalie grinned.

"After one orgasm? Pathetic."

"*You're* pathetic," Dosie teased as she poked Natalie's shoulder. Then she remembered she needed a favor. "No, I'm just kidding. You're not pathetic. You're my best friend."

"Uh huh. What do you want?"

Dosie rushed through the words in one long exhale. "I want to go to Boston, but I've got deliveries coming in for the renovation that someone has to be here to sign for, and I think it's probably too late to reschedule with the company, so I was hoping you would stay here and sign for me." She gasped her next breath then chirped, "Please."

Blink. Blink. Natalie's eyes were like a window into her brain's processing time. A few more blinks, and she said, "I thought I was supposed to be stopping you from going to Boston?"

"Yeah, that was before Jennifer told me she wanted me to come."

Natalie's lips tightened as if she'd been hit with the sudden urge to smile but couldn't for some reason. It sent an alarm bell through Dosie's mind, and she quickly went back over her words. Her face burned.

"That's not what I meant," she said. "You are an actual demon."

"A demon you trust to sign for your deliveries and watch your house."

Dosie's new pet took that moment to remind everyone of his presence, or rather his *needs*, lest they be forgotten. He leapt onto the mattress from somewhere ridiculous and landed right in her lap. *Oh yeah. Oops.* "And my cat, too?" she asked as she curled in on herself like a scorned dog asking forgiveness. "Please?"

"God, you're *so* needy," Natalie groaned, but then she smiled and pulled the cat into her own lap. "Of course, I'll look after Doody

Butt." She scratched behind his ears, grinning at Dosie's grimace. "Hell, I'll be happy to. If I stay here, I get all this quiet and space to myself. If I go home, I have to try to get some work done with my roommates and whoever they bring over milling around every, like, twenty minutes."

"Are you sure?"

"Totally sure."

"Okay, good. Yay! Thank you!" Dosie clapped her hands. "I'm going to run up and get packed then. Do you want to help me pick outfits?"

"Sure."

They rolled off the air mattress, the cat vaulting the minute they moved, and made for the stairs. "And while we're doing that," Dosie said with Natalie on her heels, "we can talk about how you're not allowed to call him that while I'm gone. Or ever again."

"Are you still on about that? Dude, it's his name. I don't know what to tell you."

"It is *not* his name anymore," Dosie said as they hit the landing and turned down the hall. "I adopted him, so he's my son, and I refuse to call my son that."

"So, you just want me to call him Cat until you pick another name?"

"How is that worse than what you're already calling him?!"

"You just don't want the other cats to call you Doody Butt's Mom when he brings them over for playdates," Natalie said, and Dosie laughed so hard that she cried.

8

"Do you think Kaylia knows anything about parole hearings?"

"Parole hearings?" Natalie glanced over her shoulder to make sure she had clearance, then she merged into the lane that would take her to the drop-off zone for departing flights. "Probably not. She's said herself she doesn't really have any experience with criminal law, but she has a lot of other lawyer friends, so maybe she could find something out from one of them, or maybe she learned something in school. I don't know. Why?"

Dosie shrugged a shoulder.

"Someone in your family?"

"No."

"Don't want to talk about it," Natalie said with a nod. "All good. Yeah, I don't know about Kaylia, but I wouldn't bet on her knowing anything that you couldn't just find on the internet in about five minutes."

"Yeah. You're probably right. I don't want to interrupt her sexy Spain time anyway."

"Why not? She interrupted your sexy time, didn't she?"

"Oh, you're right. Good point. I *should* interrupt."

"Always."

They edged out of the main flow of traffic and into the unloading lane outside Terminal A where several others were being hugged goodbye. As the car rolled to a stop, Dosie released her seatbelt and shook out her hands. Anxiety started to worm under her skin.

"Hey, it's all good," Natalie said and squeezed her shoulder.

Dosie nodded, and they stepped out of the car. She'd flown a few times, four in all, and every time, it went perfectly well. It wasn't disaster that scared her. It was just that feeling she got when the plane went up and when it came back down, that feeling of being tilted, in defiance of gravity or sacrificed to it. But she had survived that feeling every time she'd had it, even when she statistically shouldn't have, so she could face and survive it again.

"Got everything?" Natalie asked as she pulled Dosie's suitcase out of the trunk. "Phone? ID? Money? Boarding pass?"

Dosie patted the front right pocket of her currant-colored corduroy pants. "I have my phone, and the other stuff is in my phone."

"Excellent. Get the hell out of here then."

Dosie pulled her into a tight hug. "Thank you for everything."

"Welcome for everything," Natalie said and patted her back. "See you in a few days."

"See you then."

She jogged back around Dosie's car and opened the driver's side door. With one last wave over the top of the car, she said, "Tell Jennifer I said hey."

"I will," Dosie promised. "Hey, wait." She moved closer until there was only the car between them. "If he comes back while I'm gone..." She knew she didn't need to say Ira's name for Natalie to know who she meant. "...I want you to do whatever you need to do to feel safe. Okay? I don't think he'll come back, but if he does, and you don't feel okay with it, that's okay. Tell him to leave. Lock the doors. Call the police if you think that's right. Just think of you first, okay?"

They looked at each other for a long moment, both silent under the sudden heavy shift in conversation. Then Natalie nodded and dropped down into the car to leave. Dosie stood at the curb, waving until she was out of sight.

As she headed into the airport and shook off the morning chill, she dug her phone from her pocket and sent a quick text. *At the airport.* Jennifer's response was a single heart-eyes emoji, nothing more, but suddenly, Dosie was eager to get her butt on that plane. The sooner her childhood home and state were in the rearview, or whatever the airplane equivalent of a rearview was, the better. If she could leave behind all her wretched childhood for once and for all, she would, but she knew better. Its disorganized pieces and straggler souls would always be there, clinging like raindrops to her skin and tar to her brain no matter where she went, or lived, or who she loved or was loved by. She could not escape who she was, but she did not have to be owned by it.

A text arrived before she could stow her phone again, and Dosie was surprised to see that it wasn't from Jennifer, but from Kaylia. It was a picture of a glass of red wine, Kaylia's fingers poised around the stem. Dosie smiled, grateful for the welcome distraction. She didn't bother replying, just smacked the button to call and waited for the ring in her ear.

When Kaylia's voice came over the line, Dosie launched the question that had been at the back of her mind since their last call. "Why in the world did you need super thick condoms?" She blushed as a passing woman who overheard rubbernecked to gawk at her, but Kaylia's loud laugh at the end of the line made her feel light as a feather.

Jennifer woke five minutes after nodding off; at least, that's how it felt. Her body was a million pounds heavier than it had ever been, and her eyelids were glued together. Her mouth was dry. She forced her eyes open with a few hard blinks and lifted off her stomach onto

Corrie MacKay

her elbows, searching for her phone. It was only a foot or so away on the mattress, and she grabbed it to check the time. *Fuck.* Only an hour and a half had passed since Dosie's plane took off, which meant it had been five hours since she first lay down to sleep only to wake up every thirty minutes for some reason or other. Discomfort. A noise. A dream. An itch. A notification that her favorite person was on the way. She didn't begrudge that last one. Still, Jennifer shoved her face into her pillow and growled, "I need to fucking sleep!"

Her brain didn't care. Every little obsession that had kept her up until four in the morning still flitted around her head like a panicked bird trapped in someone's kitchen. What would she say? How would she say it? Who would she look at? Would she look at him? *Could* she look at him? Should Carine be standing with her? Did she need her to? Should Dosie be there? Did she want Dosie there? What if she started crying while she was speaking? What if her throat closed up and her voice cracked, and she couldn't get through it? What if she let Lauren down? What if she failed?

The chime of a new text message briefly halted her spiral. Jennifer grabbed the phone again and checked. It was from Dosie: *I paid for wi-fi. The movie I'm watching is boring. The lady beside me smells like soap. Not in a bad way though. It's a nice soap. Are you still in bed? I wish I could crawl into bed with you. This plane is freezing.*

Jennifer grabbed one of her spare pillows and stuffed it against her chest, wrapped her arms around it. She imagined Dosie's lazy-day scent and the way she colored Jennifer's body with her fingertips like crayons making messy, perfect art. She imagined Dosie's ridiculous laugh as she did something silly like pull a tendril of Jennifer's hair around her chin and ask, "How do you like my beard?" The thought of being with her now made Jennifer relax, like a drug seeping through her system, bidding her muscles to let go of their tension, her mind to ease its obsessive ruminating. It wasn't enough to stop it altogether, but every bit of calm was welcome. If Dosie was really there, Jennifer knew the effect would be total. She would press herself against Dosie's warmth and bury her face in Dosie's hair, and the world would quiet and right itself, and she would drift into a rare peace.

The only other way she knew to achieve such bliss, though much more fleeting, involved a bit more energy than she was willing to expend at the moment. Then again.... She looked at Dosie's text. *She is bored,* she thought as an idea began to root, a fantastic, terrible idea. Definitely worth a try.

What are you wearing?

Dosie glanced down at herself, suddenly incapable of remembering her outfit once she'd been asked about it. She typed her answer and hit send. *Dark red corduroy pants and a cream sweater.* Her brow knitted together, and she quickly sent another. *Why? Should I have gotten dressy? Are we going somewhere?*

She supposed she could change in the airport bathroom if she really needed to, but her clothes would be wrinkled. Would that be appropriate for wherever Jennifer was taking her? *Was* Jennifer taking her somewhere?

No. Jennifer's response brought swift relief, but then she kept going. *I'm imagining.*

Imagining my outfit? Dosie asked, just to clarify.

Yes. Cords and a sweater. Cute but inappropriate for bed.

Dosie's breath halted as three dots appeared. Jennifer was typing again without waiting for a response, and suddenly, Dosie felt on the edge of her seat.

If you're crawling in with me, you had better take it all off, Jennifer messaged. *Then we'll match.*

Dosie's halted breath rushed free with a wretched squeak as, not a moment later, a picture came through. Her chest, neck, and face flushed with heat as her hands seemed to have an electric reaction to Jennifer's surprise gift. The phone bopped between her hands like a cursed hacky sack as she fumbled and failed to get a grip again. It flopped into her lap after a second, and Dosie yanked it up to hide it in her bosom.

Quickly, she looked to her aisle mates, certain she would find them staring at her in bewilderment. Or judgment. What if the lady who smelled like soap saw Jennifer's nipples before Dosie managed to hide them? Fortunately, she was fast asleep beside her. The man across the aisle was, too. One of them was snoring, and Dosie wasn't sure which. Regardless, neither was conscious enough to notice her girlfriend's nakedness nor her own flustered reaction to it.

Dosie scooted around in her seat, positioning and repositioning her phone until she felt it was mostly hidden from anyone's sight but hers. Then she peeked at Jennifer's message again just to make sure she hadn't imagined seeing nipples. As soon as she looked, she smacked the phone's screen back against her chest and *burned*. She had not imagined them.

It took a glance, microseconds of looking, to memorize every bit of the shot. Jennifer lay on her stomach, propped up on an elbow. Her breasts were bare and hanging down, just shy of brushing the white sheet below, and the tops of her soft, rose quartz-colored nipples were visible. Her mess of sable hair tendrilled around her makeup-free face and made her hooded blue eyes seem brighter, as if lit from behind. She didn't smile but looked directly into the camera as if in need, lips just parted, and Dosie had never wanted to climb inside a photograph before, but she did now. It was art. *Art!* She would proclaim it to the world if asked.

Another text coming in made her jump. She checked her aisle mates again. Both were still sleeping, so she read the message. *Does this make you wish the flight was shorter?*

Dosie breathed cool air up over her cheeks and, despite having just done so, checked her surroundings again. She felt like she was under a microscope, like every text and every *thought* about every text could be seen by everyone around her. It made her paranoid, but it also excited her. If anyone saw, what would happen? They would frown at her? Judge her? Not give a damn? There was no reason to feel guilty or afraid, Dosie told herself. There was no reason to lean into the paranoia when she could veer into thrill instead.

Yes, she typed back as she tried to think of something to add. Something witty. Something sexy. But nothing came to mind. Her brain was short-circuiting. One second, she was laser focused. The next, she was a blink away from shutdown. The perils of dating a woman who looked like she could suck your soul out with a kiss, and you would thank her for doing it.

But Jennifer's reply didn't indicate she cared. It did, however, result in the furious return of Dosie's blush. *I'd ask you for a picture, but I'm really enjoying the one in my head. You have very little on in it.*

Dosie's knee bounced as she typed. *What am I wearing?*

The airplane's freezing air did nothing to dissipate the heat reddening her cheeks or spilling down her spine like a lava flow. It didn't soothe. It clashed, too cold against her too-hot skin.

Your pearls.

Dosie's fingers crept toward her necklace as if triggered by some hidden command in the text. She fingered one pearl, then another, waiting for the rest of Jennifer's answer. When none came, she realized that was it. In Jennifer's mind, Dosie was wearing her pearls and *only* her pearls.

A new message came through. *Do you have them on now? Are you touching them?*

Twin shivers raced up Dosie's thighs and scattered to every sensitive spot they could find. Her lower back prickled and bowed. She told herself to relax even as her grip on the pearls tightened. They were talking about a necklace, *for God's sake, Dosie!* But there was something intoxicating about the idea of Jennifer picturing her so distinctly, imagining Dosie in nothing but her pearls, knowing her well enough to know she would be touching them when she asked.

Yes, she replied, and before she could even think to type anything else, another picture *whooshed* onto the screen.

Corrie MacKay

"O-oh," Dosie choked out unbidden. She covered with a quick cough and even cleared her throat for good measure. No one stirred beyond a passing flight attendant who didn't even look her way. Still, Dosie felt too exposed. No matter how she twisted or hunched in her seat, she wasn't convinced any image she might open would be safe from prying eyes.

Her heart hammered like she was about to commit a crime as she unclipped her seatbelt and got to her feet. She kept a death grip on her phone as she traversed the short main aisle to the first-class lavatory and shut herself inside. As soon as she slid the lock into place, her eyes were back on her phone.

In the tiny bathroom, she opened Jennifer's latest picture and nearly moaned. Her mouth went dry. Jennifer was on her back now, the phone held aloft for an angled shot of her torso and thighs. Her bare breasts were exposed in full, and one hand lay over her lower abdomen, the tip of her long middle finger buried in the black triangle of hair between her thighs. The only part of Jennifer's face that was visible in the shot was her chin and mouth, her lips set in a confident smirk that drove Dosie wild.

She shook one sweaty hand out, then wiped it on her cords. The other hand followed. She didn't know what to say, but she wanted to say something. She wanted to say *everything*, certain now that Jennifer was trying to have phone sex with her while she was 37,000 feet in the air and surrounded by strangers. Was she *trying* to mortify Dosie to death? And why did Dosie want her to?

A picture for every time you make my hand move.

Dosie's jaw dropped open around a silent whine. Squeezing her thighs together wasn't enough. She put a hand between her legs and cupped herself through her pants, desperate for pressure. Her clitoris felt as if it had been plugged into a socket.

She glanced at the time on her phone, trying to calculate how long she had been in the bathroom. A minute or two? Maybe less. She couldn't stay in there forever; someone would come knocking eventually. But she couldn't have this conversation at her seat either, and she *needed* to have this conversation. She needed to make Jennifer's hand move.

It would have to be quick, which meant she was going to have to get over herself, get over her anxiety, and just *do*. She told herself to listen to her body even if it was just long enough to paint a picture, and an idea began to form, a fantastic, terrible idea. Definitely worth a try.

You're making this flight difficult for me.

Jennifer grinned at the text, feeling devilish. She knew she was pushing Dosie out of her comfort zone, but she also knew the conversation wouldn't still be going if they didn't both want it to be. Her static hand tingled, waiting to be moved by the three little dots that showed her Dosie was typing again.

Your pictures made it impossible to sit still, so now I'm in the bathroom.

Jennifer held her breath and waited. Would she, or wouldn't she? Would they, or wouldn't they?

With a *whoosh*, Dosie did. *I'm unbuttoning my pants to give you room. Can you fit your hand in?*

Arousal and adrenaline flooded Jennifer's body in equal measure. "Fuck, *yes*," she moaned as she rolled over and up onto her knees for a position that would give her more depth and leverage when she was ready for it. She sent her fingers straight to her clit and imagined it was Dosie's touch instead.

Sex via text was a bit messy, and Jennifer didn't care for the mechanics of it all, particularly the need to have a hand available for typing. But it was what they had, and admittedly, at the moment, it was getting damned good. Jennifer snapped a picture and sent it, a close-up of her spreading her herself open, two fingers vising her clit with vicious pressure. She thought of Dosie receiving the image, thought of her losing her breath and trying not to moan Jennifer's name. She thought of her trying to quietly finger-fuck herself in an airplane bathroom just to take the terrible edge off, and Jennifer had to stop herself from shoving her own fingers inside herself and finishing too quickly.

She wasn't going inside until Dosie asked her to. *Please fucking ask me to,* she thought and rocked her hips down to trap her hand between her cunt and the bed. She wanted more pressure. She wanted to be full.

Dosie's three typing dots appeared then disappeared again and again. Was she too flustered to type? Too shy or anxious to decide what to say? Too busy riding her own hand to the thought of Jennifer doing the same? *Fuck. Fuck. Fuuuuck.* Jennifer needed to see the message already, damn it!

Lower, said the text when it finally came through, and Jennifer felt her one rebellious eyebrow jump. One word? That was all she got after all that back and forth? Maybe Dosie really was distracted with her own needs.

As much as Jennifer wanted to dip lower and push inside herself, she also wanted to resist, just to be obstinate, just to drag the whole thing out as long as possible. Dosie, of course, would never let her. Her boldness had a timer attached to it, and she was likely already a fit of nerves given her location. Jennifer gave in and opened her camera. She was just about to snap a new picture of her pressing her fingertip inside her vagina when another message appeared.

Send me a video? I have earbuds. At the end, Dosie added an emoji with wide eyes and blushing cheeks, and the sight made Jennifer laugh. It also made her wet. *I love the sound of you inside me.*

Jennifer moaned and shoved her fingers in her pussy, two with little more than a wince and a third on the back stroke. She thrust against her trapped palm, wiggling her fingers inside herself every time her hips shot forward. Nothing turned her on more than those moments when Dosie was unfettered and audacious with her sexuality. Her exhausted morning had taken a real swing for the better and was on its way to great. She was going to come, and then she was going to sleep, and Dosie would be there, bright as a star in her mental image, the entire time. And later, when she woke again, Jennifer would have her there for real.

Quickly, she worked herself up with the image Dosie had set in her mind. They were squeezed in an airport bathroom with little time. Someone would knock eventually. Someone would ask. Someone would kick them out. They had to hurry. Dosie's corduroy pants had been hastily unbuttoned for Jennifer's hand to be shoved inside. She was toying with Dosie's clitoris with one hand and held a finger to her lips with the other.

"*Shh,*" she imagined herself saying as she circled Dosie's entrance with her middle finger, collecting moisture, then back up to her clit. Once. Twice.

When she was nice and soaked and breathless, she whispered, "*Good girl,*" and plunged inside her to take on an immediate and brutal rhythm. There was no time, and Jennifer wanted that orgasm. She needed to make Dosie, *make herself,* come. Her imagination already had her halfway.

Jennifer leaned back so her strokes would rake her vagina's ridged anterior wall and shuddered with the ecstasy of the first long swipe. "Oh, fuck," she moaned and drew a circle inside herself. She imagined every sound she made was Dosie's, every tremor hers as well, and found herself at the edge of orgasm within a few short minutes.

She grabbed her phone and brought it close, clicked on the front-facing camera and pressed to record. With the lens aimed between her legs, she stared down at the image on the screen and hit record, watched her own glistening pussy swallowing three fingers like it was a starved animal presented with a treat. She was so ready to come that every time her hips went back, her cunt made a wet, sucking sound around her fingers. Jennifer imagined Dosie listening to the sound in the video, and that made her wetter, made the sound louder, made her orgasm unwilling to be staved off any longer.

She came on camera, the lens tilted back enough that it caught a full shot of her from between her legs, up the length of her belly and over her breasts. In her mind, Dosie's teeth were in her neck, in her shoulder, wherever the girl could find to bite her as she endured a forceful orgasm in necessary silence. In reality, Jennifer herself wasn't silent at all.

Her moan was less woman and more animal. A harsh grunt and growl rumbled out of her as her muscles clamped around her fingers like they wanted to bite them off, and every bit of breath in her body left her like someone had slammed their fist into her gut. It was a brutal, quick orgasm that ripped through her and demanded she shout for it, and she caught every bit of it but the collapse on camera.

She sent the video to Dosie then faceplanted into the mattress, eyes closed, panting against the sheet. "Sleep," she moaned, fingers still half-buried in her cunt. She wanted to drift right then, right there, exactly as she was, but she needed to go to the bathroom.

It would be quick, she told herself, and then she could return to that exact spot and that exact position with the smell of her orgasm still lingering in the air to keep her sleepy. As she got herself up and shuffled to the bathroom, her phone alerted with a new message. Jennifer finished as fast as she could and raced back to the bed, desperate to be in her perfect position again.

The bed was still warm when she dropped back onto her belly and smashed her cheek against the mattress. It felt so good she nearly cried, and her eyelids grew thick and heavy in seconds. Sleep tugged at her mind and body like a blanket that had been tucked too tight. She fought it just long enough to read Dosie's last message.

Thank you.

Jennifer's gritty, tired laugh ruffled the sheet. She imagined Dosie's cheeks as she'd typed those words. Red as a setting sun, no doubt. Her eyes closed as her fingers loosened around the phone. *Thank you,* she thought as sleep finally took her away.

9

"Hi," Dosie said as she approached the hotel's front desk. "I need to pick up a key for room 2102, please. The name is Dupont."

The man working the desk was older and had a bushy head of short gray hair that melded into his matching beard. He smiled without teeth, and his cheeks plumped under his eyes, giving him a sweet Santa Claus vibe. "Oh, yeah," he said, "I just spoke with Ms. Dupont a bit ago. She said to expect you. I've got a key for you right here."

He grabbed a plastic keycard from the desk and ran it through some kind of machine. After a beep and a green light, he stuck the card in a little paper envelope and slid it across to Dosie. "There you are, Mrs. Dupont."

His voice became a muffled blur as a fluttering sensation erupted in Dosie's gut like a flock of birds all suddenly taking flight at once and demanding she take notice. *Mrs. Dupont.* "Thank you," she said when he finished rattling off directions, then she took the key and left.

The hair on the back of her neck rose to attention as she rounded the corner to the elevators and stepped inside an open carriage. In just a few short moments, she would see Jennifer and touch her. Dosie closed her eyes and breathed through the image of the hard, slow kiss she'd been anticipating for hours. Now that she was so close to having it, the prevision made her squirm with need.

They always met as if returning from somewhere far away, that feeling of crossing a familiar threshold after too long elsewhere. Whether it was days or hours, they touched as if it sated something vital, as if they'd been doing it for a lifetime and would do it for another and another after that. Dosie thought they sometimes loved one another like it was a necessity, like hunger. The intensity of it waxed and waned but rarely subsided for long and never disappeared. Even when it grew rabid and impatient, its presence was a natural comfort, a reminder to stay alive. To moderate. To indulge. To tease. To sate. To care.

The elevator ticked up another floor, and the front-desk encounter came back to her.

Mrs. Dupont. Dosie's body groaned like an empty stomach, her hunger for Jennifer making itself known. "Faster, please," she hummed to the empty car as tingles ran her thighs and crept up her hips. She smashed her finger to the lit button on the panel again as if it might signal that a more emergent pace was needed. *Just in case.*

Dosie keyed herself into Jennifer's hotel room and was greeted by a small, chic lounge area with a couch, a television, a desk, and a mini bar. Past a brief threshold behind the couch, she could see the foot of a large bed. Once Dosie focused on it, she became aware of the ambient sound drifting from that direction to blend seamlessly into the background. It was the sound of fast, heavy rain. Jennifer was in the shower.

She left her luggage at the door and had taken no more than two steps when the steady sound squeaked to silence. Dosie crossed into the bedroom to see a cloud of heat billowing from the open door of the adjacent bathroom. Beyond that, there was no tub that Dosie could see, just a walk-in shower encased in glass from top to bottom. The shower walls that should have been clear were fogged with steam and murky white, blurring the view beyond. But in that blur, Dosie could see a tempting smear of color and motion.

She stood still outside the bathroom, staring in, observing her girl-friend through the glass like she was a surrealist painting brought to life. She knew she needed to say something. She needed to announce herself rather than let Jennifer finish toweling off and step out of the shower to find a person standing there, watching her. But she was mesmerized. Maybe it was the heat and humidity in the room making her lightheaded. Or maybe it was just Jennifer having the same effect on her that she'd always had.

"Jen?" she called, and the blurry figure inside the shower went still. "I'm here."

The shower door opened to unleash a fresh haze, and Jennifer's dew-dropped naked form stepped into the eye of it like a sea goddess at the center of a hurricane. Her wet hair was inky black against her skin and seemed even darker when she smiled and showed her teeth. As if she wasn't without a stitch and damp as the day she was born, Jennifer tossed her towel aside and crossed the distance between them in four long strides. Then her hand was in Dosie's hair. The floral scent of her shampoo was in Dosie's nose. Her bare hips were a puzzle piece slotting into the shape of Dosie's own, and then finally, she got her kiss.

Dosie's insides went gooey. Her body turned rubber. Jennifer kissed as if she was parched, as if Dosie had drunk the last of the water, and she had to suck the remnant drops off her tongue just to sate herself. *Wow. Wow. Wow.* Dosie's knees wobbled as her hand flopped against Jennifer's chest, fingers curling into nothing but warm, gummy flesh. She moaned drunkenly as Jennifer held her up and kissed away her identity and made her a nameless, faceless, wordless puddle.

When they parted, Jennifer stayed close, her mouth hovering an

Corrie MacKay

inch or two away. "You taste like coffee," she said and licked her lips, and Dosie suddenly had form again. She had needs and desires and a girlfriend who knew just how to provide for them both.

"Do you have any idea how awkward it is..." Dosie slid her hand lower to cup Jennifer's breast. It fit perfectly in her hand, swelling out from around her palm like a stress ball as she gently squeezed. "...to sit on a plane for hours with sticky underwear that won't dry because you can't stop thinking about your girlfriend *doing things* to herself?"

Jennifer grinned like a cheeky cat who expected a treat for doing something bad, because she was cute while doing it. "I believe you thanked me for that."

"And then you sent a sweet old man to the airport to pick me up."

"Ned is lovely."

Dosie circled Jennifer's nipple with her thumb. Her muscles twitched under her clothes, like a little reminder that she was over-dressed. "I can't believe you sent me that video."

"You asked for it!"

"I know!" Dosie's cheeks burned, and she knew it was visible, because Jennifer kissed each one as if to ward the red away. "I feel so bad." Jennifer frowned, and she quickly elaborated. "No, not bad, but *bad*, you know? Like, naughty bad."

"Oh," Jennifer said and slid her hands down Dosie's sides, heat-seeking fingers curling under her sweater to find her skin. "Well then you've come to the right place."

Dosie laughed and kissed her and said, "I want you so much, I'm in actual pain."

Jennifer's body language shifted. Her energy turned quiet and collected, an intensity about her that made Dosie tremble. That body language was wholly the Director's, but when she spoke, her voice was soft and every bit *Jen*. She cupped Dosie's neck like a collar, palm just over her pulse, and said, "That sounds like a terrible dilemma, Ms. Fisher."

Dosie's bones felt like they might start rattling at any minute. Ms. Fisher. *Mrs. Dupont.* God, the way she liked that, the way she liked

Jennifer, loved her, wanted her, felt dangerous. Like it could arrest her heart or stop her breath. Fry her brain. And something about that made it all the more thrilling.

"May I offer some assistance?" Jennifer asked, and Dosie shuddered.

A spark of boldness ignited in her gut, or perhaps farther south, she wasn't sure. "Do or don't," she said, "It's getting taken care of either way."

Jennifer stared at her, breathless. Then she dropped her hands to Dosie's waist and dug in, tugged her forward. Their next kiss felt like ignition, like a button being pushed, a key being cranked. With a rumbling moan in her chest, Jennifer took the first step. Her one foot forward pushed one of Dosie's back, and a quick rhythm followed. In five steps, Jennifer had her at the bed. With a shove and a laugh, she was on it.

"Babe?"

Jennifer stirred from her quasi-sleep, having been lulled by the loud whir of the hotel fan and Dosie's fingers mindlessly scratching through her pubic hair. She craned her neck to looked down the mattress where Dosie lay perpendicular to her, naked but for the sheet she'd tossed over her legs when she got cold. Her cheek was squashed against Jennifer's thigh, brown eyes staring back, waiting for a response.

"You okay?" Jennifer ran her hand over Dosie's head. A few cinnamon strands tumbled from her temple with gentle urging, and Jennifer chased, stroking along to Dosie's ear just to follow the curve of it.

"I'm okay." Dosie kissed her thigh. "I want you to know that just because I'm here now doesn't mean I have to be at the hearing, too. I don't want you to feel obligated to take me with you. I've never been to Boston before, and I can keep myself busy. You can have as much space as you need so that you don't feel like I'm right on top of you."

"But I love when you're right on top of me," Jennifer said, and the sweet laugh it earned her made her feel pounds lighter and years younger. When she was utterly weightless and timeless, nothing mattered but the girl in her lap who loved her.

"I'm trying to say that if you want space," Dosie said, "if you still want to do this on your own or think you need to, I don't have a problem with that. I never did. I just wanted—I *want*—to be close. In case you need a safe place."

Jennifer breathed deeper and deeper, as if filling a balloon. Her chest seemed to expand to twice its usual size just to house her swelling heart as she ran her fingertip down the bridge of Dosie's nose and said, "A safe place."

"Like you are for me." Dosie took Jennifer's hand and wove their fingers together, let the precious knot fall to the mattress. "You've become my safest place."

"Come here," Jennifer said, her voice thick with effort, and tugged their tangled hands to urge movement.

Dosie crawled up the mattress and coated the full length of Jennifer's body with hers. They wound their arms around one another, slid their legs together in an easy link, and held each other close. Breasts mashed together, Jennifer could feel both their heartbeats, still elevated, and found it made her want to shimmy herself closer despite having nowhere to go. They were touching at every point they possibly could, and it felt infuriatingly shy of enough.

A kiss landed on Jennifer's cheek. Another sank into the corner of her mouth. The last sucked at the hard line of her jaw. Then Dosie rested her forehead against Jennifer's lips and said, "I want to be your sanctuary." She leaned back again, enough for their eyes to meet, and Jennifer felt spellbound, stuck in honey. "I don't care if you're a mess. If you're going through something, anything, the hardest thing, let me be the place where you catch your breath."

As if triggered by the words, Jennifer inhaled a rush of cool air and capped it with Dosie's lips. She couldn't say what she wanted to say, wasn't sure the words existed, so she felt it instead. She felt it with every cell in her body, and she kissed and kissed Dosie and hoped she felt it, too.

Walking together had become a favorite pastime since their first walk around San Francisco, hours after Dosie slept through what was supposed to be their first date. They walked Dosie's property sometimes, the parts that weren't too overgrown or littered with ghosts, or in the neighborhoods near Jennifer's building and out along the bay. They explored sections of Sacramento, drove down to venture Ojai, and walked the beaches in Monterey, just observing the world around them with their hands linked by a finger or two, swinging between their hips. They would talk about what they saw or about anything, usually the random thoughts that popped into Dosie's head, and sometimes, they wouldn't talk at all. A sigh here. A hum of interest there. A perfect, quiet kiss mid-stroll said more than words often could. It seemed only right that they would experience Boston together in similar fashion; at least, for as long as they could stand to before the chill dug too deep and forced them inside.

They clutched hot cups of coffee and wandered the old cobblestone streets, discussed the red-brick architecture and how it looked like a painting under the blue-white sky. They rode Boston's subway rail, which Jennifer called "the T," and meandered through the shops on Newbury Street without buying anything. When Dosie asked if they should share some clam chowder to warm up, Jennifer said, "Phlegm shouldn't be eaten," and got them two more hot coffees instead, plus an extra-large slice of Boston cream pie. Jennifer took her to the Common where they followed the Freedom Trail and read every plaque at every monument they found. They discussed their mutual disinterest in sports, debated whether travel by horseback or carriage was bumpier, and tried to imagine what

Boston must have looked and smelled and sounded like before. Before there were cars and trollies and trains. Before skyscrapers and Harvard and electricity and revolution. Before Boston bore that name or any foreigners and was instead a seasonal home to the indigenous Massachusett people. There were so many iterations of the city to picture, and so many ways of life that had come and gone.

Dosie was content to walk and talk with Jennifer for hours, but the more they ventured, the quieter Jennifer became. She had never been as loose-lipped as Dosie, but most days, Jennifer was an engaged conversationalist. She spoke with care, as if she'd spent a lot of time practicing how to avoid saying the first thing that popped into her brain, so when she wasn't being a tease, everything she said sounded considered and felt given. Every topic had investment simply because Dosie had brought it up or cared to hear Jennifer's take. But Jennifer wasn't her usual self, and her replies grew short and half-hearted. The conversation lost its easy flow, and eventually, Dosie was the only one talking.

Jennifer's eyes had glazed over. Her feet seemed on autopilot, and her shoulders hung heavily beneath the weight of all that was on her mind. They'd spoken about none of it in person, neither Jennifer's reunion with her aunt nor the fact that Glass's parole hearing was the day after next. Dosie sensed it all hovering around Jennifer like a gnat swarm she couldn't shake, but she didn't want to push her to talk about it or risk upsetting her by suggesting she should. The mere consideration must have been plain on her face, however, because the moment she and Jennifer locked eyes, Jennifer looked away and said, "Tell me a story."

Dosie heard the unspoken request. *Please don't ask. Distract me instead.* "A story?" They turned onto a street lined with red maple trees that stood bare against their background. Scattered piles of discarded leaves still lingered around their trunks and along the curb-side gutters. "About what?"

"Anything."

"But a true story, right? Not a made-up one? Because there's a reason I wrote a memoir and not a fantasy."

"A true one, definitely."

"Hm. Okay, um. I'll tell you one about Peg."

"The woman who turned you into a Hepburn."

Dosie grinned. "She would take that as a compliment."

"I meant it as one."

"Yes, her," Dosie said and swung the ball of their held hands between them like a pendulum. "You know, her name is actually Margaret, but for some reason, she always went by Peg. I never understood why."

"I don't think it's uncommon for the name Margaret, actually, but I also have no idea why."

"Well, that's weird."

"Agreed," Jennifer said and let go of Dosie's hand to put an arm around her shoulders instead. "Get closer. It's cold."

It was harder to walk with their hips bumping every other step, but Dosie wouldn't trade it for anything, certainly not ease. She looped one arm around Jennifer's back and lay the other over her waist to hide her fingers in the warmth of Jennifer's wool-blend twill peacoat. Then she did her best to match her girlfriend's step. Most of the time, it was easy. They were close to the same height and had a similar long stride; every once in a while, though, one of them—usually Dosie—would lose the rhythm and trip them both up.

"You don't talk about her much," Jennifer said and tucked her gloved fingers under Dosie's scarf in the same fashion that Dosie had used her coat.

"Who? Peg?"

Jennifer nodded. "You've only told me a few stories about her."

"I know," Dosie said. "I don't know why." She loved Peg and, for a brief period of her life, spent more time around her than anyone. "I think it's been a little painful to talk about her since her Alzheimer's diagnosis. It's like she's here, but she's not really here anymore, so... I don't know. I don't know how to talk about her anymore—past tense, present tense—and it confuses me and upsets me, so I just don't."

Jennifer hummed, her usual response when she understood but had nothing to add.

"But you know, Peg didn't talk much herself. Maybe that's part of it, too. She mostly communicated with activities, a few instructions here and there. Sewing. Board games and game shows." Dosie shrugged, felt Jennifer's arm bounce atop her shoulder then settle into place again. "Soap operas."

"*The Young and the Restless?*"

"And *As the World Turns*, and *Guiding Light*, and *Days of Our Lives*, and whatever else she could record or buy on a DVD boxset. Sometimes, she watched them with the volume turned all the way down. I don't know why. The motion maybe, or just the familiarity of seeing it on the TV screen. But it must have really made a mark on me, because when I think about Peg, my head gets quiet like that, and then I'm just drifting with no sound, no interruptions. I think that's why I feel brave when I wear her old clothes or her pearls, or even just her style."

Jennifer looked over Dosie's whole face as if trying to remember the way it looked in just that moment. "I love the way you describe things."

The backs of Dosie's ears tingled. "Really? What do you mean?"

"I'm not sure how to explain it."

"But, not weird, right?"

"Not at all." Jennifer squeezed her shoulder. "Or yes, in the sense of it being uncommon, I think, but not bad. There's something artistic about it. It's like you're seeing something no one else is even though we're all looking at the same thing." She rolled her eyes at herself. "Clearly, I don't have the same talent."

"You have a lot of talents."

"True." Jennifer kissed her temple, wobbling their steady steps but only for a moment. "Tell me your Peg story."

"Oh, right. Okay, so, uh, you know Zeb and I were both placed with her after everything, right? I told you that? Anyway, so, a few months after we got there, we'd just been kind of going through the motions: therapy sessions, school sessions, and then whatever needed doing around the house. My favorite was always the film stuff. I think I told you Peg's dad worked in Hollywood in the 40s and 50s, right?"

"Yes."

"Right, so she had a bunch of his collectibles in this one room in her house that she would have us sort through and clean every week, even if nothing was dusty or out of place. And I just loved looking at all the old pictures and props and imagining what it must be like to work on a movie set."

"I think I would have liked that, too."

"She had a *lot* of stuff," Dosie said, and even the added emphasis didn't seem to rise to the level of stuff Peg had. "She ended up selling most of it before she moved into the nursing home. She never acted like it was a problem, but I always wondered if it broke her heart to do that." She waved her hand and sighed. "Anyway. Me and my tangents. So, a few months after we got there, this lady showed up at the door and offered Peg money in exchange for a few pictures of me and Zeb."

"A reporter? Seriously?"

"Oh yeah. Reporters were a real problem for a long time. So, Peg invites the woman in and pours her a glass of lemonade."

"And where were you?"

"In the den," Dosie said. "It was on the other side of the kitchen, down a couple steps in a kind of sunken part of the house, so we weren't really visible, but we could still hear everything that was going on." They passed between a parallel row of trees and past a statue of a man Dosie didn't recognize.

"What happened?" Jennifer asked and pointed toward a metal bench a short distance ahead. The moment Dosie laid eyes on it, her feet throbbed as if to confirm that a break from walking was worth the potential sting of cold metal through her pants.

"Peg waited for her to drink the lemonade," Dosie said as they settled on the bench with their knees turned together and their shoulders huddled close. "And then she asked her how it was, and when she said it was good, Peg said, 'Oh, good. I was afraid the poison would make it bitter.'"

Jennifer's jaw sprang open, and Dosie burst with laughter. "She didn't actually poison her," she said, "but she didn't admit that until the lady had jumped out of her seat and started coughing and gagging like she couldn't breathe. And then Peg said, 'But I want you to remember how easily I *could have* the next time you think it's a good idea to treat some traumatized kids like a business opportunity.'"

"A woman with moxie," Jennifer said. "I like it."

"Yeah. She hardly ever showed it, but she definitely had it. I think I decided to trust her that day, even if I didn't realize it for a while."

"How did you end up married?" Jennifer asked. "You've never said other than that it was a trauma bond. But if you were at Peg's, how did the two of you end up—"

"Ugh." Dosie groaned until Jennifer laughed. "I've thought about it a lot actually, and I'm sure it was a lot of things. Too many things all smashed together and happening at the same time."

"Did you two know each other well before everything happened?"

"No," Dosie said. "The girls didn't spend much time around the boys on the compound. Honestly, I didn't think I'd see anyone from that life ever again once the trials were over, so getting placed in the same house as him was a shock. And it probably shouldn't have happened. We didn't really know each other, but we knew the same way of life, so it was easy for us to find things to talk about and ways to comfort each other with little pieces of home. We kept up our prayers together and tried to talk about the compound like it hadn't exploded around us or was anything worth dreaming about even before it did. I don't know. But it didn't take long, really, for us to start talking about running away together. He brought it up first, and I think in the beginning it was just because he was scared to be on his own, but after a while, he started noticing me in a way that made it pretty clear he had remembered he was a teenage boy with functioning hormones."

"Ah, the worst kind of teenage boy."

A hard snort caused Dosie's nose to burn. She pinched it to soothe the sting. "Anyway, the more we talked and tried to keep that life with us, the easier it became to convince ourselves that we ended up where we were because we were meant to carry things on for Father."

"You can convince yourself of anything when the only person talking back to you always echoes what you say."

Dosie nodded. "Exactly."

"So, you decided to run away and get married and, what, live out your lives the way you did on the compound?"

"Yeah. I guess." Dosie lay her cheek on Jennifer's shoulder, the tip of her nose nudging her neck. "I didn't think I could have anything else or deserved anything else. Most days, I went back and forth between thinking that I deserved to be damned for testifying against my father and thinking that what I did was right. I would lay in bed at night and be consumed with guilt for having turned my back on God, and then I'd wake up in the morning, and Zeb would be there, the only thing left of my life before, and he would say it was meant to be, that it was what God wanted, and I was so desperate to make it right that I would believe him just like I always believed my father."

Jennifer rested her cheek atop Dosie's head. The weight was a comfort. Dosie sank into the warmth of her shoulder and chest and went on with her story.

"Peg confronted us before we could go anywhere. She'd heard us planning and didn't want us to end up hurting ourselves trying to run off on our own."

"Ooh. A thwarted plan. The suspense is killing me. And?"

"And she didn't try to stop us or anything."

"What?!"

"I know," Dosie said. "We were shocked, too. She just asked us if we were set on doing it no matter what, and when we said we were, she agreed to sign for it. We didn't even know we needed consent. Zeb was almost eighteen, but I was only sixteen. But Peg said she would do it if we agreed not to run away and moved into her back-yard studio instead. Even the ring Zeb gave me was hers. It's why I still wear it sometimes."

Jennifer scoffed. "You were underage. She could have nipped that in the bud immediately. You didn't even have the legal ability to get married."

"Yeah. And you know, I never asked her why. But I've thought about it a lot over the years, and I think she was just trying to keep us from running off and getting hurt or taken advantage of, drawn into drugs or something else that could get us killed. I guess she figured if we really wanted to run off, we would, but if she could let us have this one big thing, then maybe we would be placated enough to stick around and keep things mostly as they were, and probably for a lot longer than we would have had to legally if we'd just stayed her foster kids."

"What do you mean?"

"Well, we were right there, so she was able to keep an eye on us pretty much all the time, and since she covered the bills and provided everything from our clothes to our food, we agreed to her conditions."

"Which were?"

"There were four," Dosie said and counted them off on her fingers as she spoke. "The first was that we had to keep up with the chore schedule around her house and have dinner with her every night. Silent dinner, by the way. She hardly said a word, but she always wanted us at the table."

"Peg sounds like an interesting woman."

"You mean weird?"

"You said it."

Dosie giggled. "She was a bit, yeah, but I think that's what made her good for us, too. Or for me, anyway."

"Fine. Go on."

"So, the second condition was that we keep up with our schooling. We both completed a GED thanks to that."

"Well, that's a positive, I guess."

"The third was that we had to stay in therapy, which I'm pretty sure is the only reason I ever woke up and started to see things for how they'd really been. It saved my life."

She only wished it could have done the same for Zeb. Maybe it would have if he hadn't been so resistant to it, to any of it, but unlike Dosie, he never went through his trauma, only into it, and for a while, she'd been resigned, even content at times, to stay there with him, playing house as if nothing had changed. But then one day, she met a pretty girl at a doctor's office and felt alive, and suddenly, all the pieces she'd been holding together with fear and denial and ignorance and pain started to chip apart like old, rotted wood, and Dosie *wanted* a new life for herself. She started to listen in her therapy sessions and *think*. She opened up about things that were not just hard but excruciating to talk about. She triggered herself over and over to heal, and did her best to trust that the strange new adults in her life who had promised she was safe wouldn't take advantage of her pain. That they wouldn't hurt her like all those who had come before. And for once in her young life, that trust panned out, and the new life she wanted began.

"What was the last condition?" Jennifer asked as she twirled a strand of Dosie's hair over her shoulder.

"No pregnancies."

Jennifer's twirling stopped. "Wow."

"Yeah," Dosie said. "That saved my life, too, I'm sure. She actually took me to my first ever gynecologist appointment. It was...not great."

"The speculum isn't great for anyone," Jennifer said, and Dosie chuckled. "So, did you want kids?" Her voice thinned a bit, and she cleared her throat to no effect. "*Do you?*"

Dosie couldn't help her smile as she lay her hand over Jennifer's chest and traced the soft designs in her cable-knit sweater. "No."

Corrie MacKay

"Oh." Jennifer's exhale rivaled the breeze. "Are you sure?"

"Definitely," Dosie told her. "I was a mom my entire childhood." *And the worst things imaginable happened to every single kid that I loved and looked after and raised.* "I don't want to be one again."

Jennifer nodded. "Mothering is not for me."

"Really?" Dosie tried to sound genuine in her surprise, but she couldn't hold her laugh. "Your bulging eyes and squeaky voice didn't give that away at all."

Pale rose dusted the high points of Jennifer's cheeks as she chuckled at herself. "Yeah, yeah," she said and poked Dosie's side, then her middle, then her cheek. Right in the heart of the dimple that appeared the moment Dosie smiled. The fact that Jennifer always did that, as if compelled to, did something to Dosie. She wasn't sure what, only that she felt it everywhere, and she loved it.

Jennifer ran her thumb over one of Dosie's eyebrows then around her cheek and down the short bridge of her nose, her eyes following along. Then they locked onto Dosie's as her voice dropped to a whisper, and she said, "I'm sorry."

Dosie rubbed the space over Jennifer's heart until it was warm and staticky. "What for, baby?"

"All of it," Jennifer said. "Nothing happened for you the way it should have."

"Oh." Dosie sat up to face her again and was surprised to find Jennifer's eyes were glassy. She looked one touch, word, or sigh away from crying. It pained Dosie. "Well," she said, "what a thing to have in common with the love of your life, hm?"

There they went, the tears, dropping as Jennifer barked out a laugh and pulled Dosie into a tight hug. "The love of your life," she mouthed against Dosie's neck, and suddenly, Boston wasn't cold at all.

It didn't take long for Ned to arrive after Jennifer's call. When the car pulled to the curb, he stepped out to get the door for them only for Dosie to dart forward and wave him off. "I've got it, Ned. Thank you."

He stalled a moment, clearly as confused as Jennifer, then shrugged and returned to the driver's seat. When he was settled inside again, Dosie went to the rear door and pulled it open. She leaned her hip against it, causing her jeans to tighten around her thighs, and with the most relaxed smile said, "After you."

Jennifer's lower back tingled. She cocked one eyebrow as she approached. "What's all this?"

Dosie wore a faint blush as she casually shrugged one shoulder and said, "Just wanted to get the door for my girl."

Warmth spilled through Jennifer's belly like guttered summer rain, and for a moment, she forgot to breathe. She didn't need to. All the world narrowed to the beat of her heart and the lazy, lovesick smile of the woman in front of her.

"You *are* my girl, aren't you?" Dosie asked and took Jennifer's hand as she reached the door, drew her in so that their chests pressed together.

That dangerously sweet smile that Jennifer had fallen in love with was so close to her now that she could almost taste it. Her heart felt like confetti fanned around a hot room, and for some fucking reason, she wanted to cry again. She pulled Dosie in by the chin and murmured against her lips, "I am so completely your girl."

For a moment, they simply looked at one another and existed together. Dosie shivered as they hovered, lips touching but never pressing, just outside of a kiss. Then Dosie nudged Jennifer's nose with hers and guided her by the hip toward the waiting backseat. They settled side by side, hands finding their way together as if implanted with magnets. Dosie snuggled up to Jennifer's arm like it could easily stand in for her bed, and Jennifer felt an incredible thrill. Why that still happened after months of being cuddled by the same woman, she didn't know, and she didn't care. She wanted Dosie to lay on her like that and make her feel that way forever.

"Where to then?"

Jennifer startled at Ned's voice, having somehow forgotten the man was there. "Hotel, please."

"Can do."

He turned his attention to the road, and Jennifer turned hers back to Dosie just in time to see a massive yawn hit her. As if she'd inhaled it, Jennifer felt it infect her immediately. Her eyes burned and the back of her mouth ached with the need to stretch. When she couldn't fight it any longer, she let herself yawn, and as soon as she did, Dosie's mouth popped open around another, bigger yawn. Jennifer felt it building in her jaw before the other had even finished.

"Stop," she said as they ended up in an airy fit of laughter.

Dosie wiped away tears. "I'm trying. You stop. I suddenly feel like I haven't slept in days." She turned and lay her legs over Jennifer's, leaned her cheek against the seat, and looked at her. "Feelings are exhausting."

"Feelings are the fucking worst," Jennifer said and watched Dosie's last yawn turn into a sleepy smile.

The waning light outside the car window caught her dark honey-drop eyes and turned her dimple to a shadow. *The love of your life.* She played with Jennifer's fingers atop her denim-clad thighs. "Except this one," she said with a dreamy air that made Jennifer feel like she could do impossible things.

"Yeah," Jennifer said, voice creaking through her sandpaper throat. When she slid her hand under Dosie's hair and cupped the back of her neck, she didn't care that the car's windows weren't as tinted as Carolina's or that they had no partition to bar them from Ned's gaze. She kissed the girl senseless.

They stayed close on parting, breathing against each other's lips in shallow huffs that felt like conversation. *"Jen,"* Dosie said, as if Jennifer had told a dirty joke or tried to wriggle a hand down her pants. She peeked around like she expected Ned to suddenly be in the backseat with them, filming. "What are you doing?"

Jennifer chuckled and lay her forehead against Dosie's cheek. *Being head over stupid heels in love with you.* "Just feeling it."

She felt Dosie's smile. "Oh."

As the hotel room door clicked shut behind her, Jennifer leaned against it and stuffed her hands in her coat pockets. She watched Dosie continue ahead, doffing her warmer layers along the way. "I know you want me to talk."

Dosie stopped beside the sitting room couch and looked back. "Only if you want to," she said as she tossed her scarf, coat, and gloves onto a small table beside the couch.

"I don't know what to say."

"Just say how you feel. If you want." She returned, holding her hands out for Jennifer's, and when Jennifer gave them, began removing her gloves as well. "But if you don't, then that's okay, too." She unbuttoned Jennifer's coat next. "You don't ever have to talk to me about anything before you're ready to."

"You don't have to do this either, you know," Jennifer said as Dosie tugged the coat off her shoulders.

"I know." She hung the coat and set the gloves aside then wriggled her arms around Jennifer's back and squashed their chests together. "What are you thinking?"

Jennifer sighed. "I'm thinking, what good will it do?"

"Talking?" When Jennifer nodded, Dosie said, "I don't know. Maybe more than you expect. I think maybe some part of you wants to or you wouldn't have brought it up at all."

Jennifer considered then hummed her acceptance. "And what if the reason I'm not talking about it is because I'm afraid of what you'll say."

"What if I say something wonderful?" She smiled and shook her head as if to say that it was hopeless. "We can go back and forth like this all night."

She was right, of course. Jennifer fought the impulse to roll her eyes. She didn't hate when Dosie was right. She just hated when *she* was wrong. She wanted them both to be right, in consensus rather than at odds. But she still felt the urge to push back.

"I'm not saying it'll fix anything," Dosie said, before she could, "but you can talk, and I can listen, and sometimes, that's all that's needed. And I know that, because you do it for me all the time. You can't take away my triggers or fix my anxiety, but you hear it all. You observe it. You keep it. You don't judge me for it, and it just makes everything so much easier and less lonely to bear."

Well, fuck. There went her resistance. "Dosie."

"Oh, baby, please give me a chance. If I can give you even just a bit of the relief that you give me, and you know I want to, why not let me?"

Jennifer stuck her face in her hands and blew a loud, annoyed breath through the cracks. Her chest felt like it had been emptied of her vital organs and replaced with boiling water. Humiliation. She fucking *hated* it. Her eyes prickled the way they did when they were dry, but she could feel that they weren't. Tears welled as she dropped her hands from her cheeks and looked into Dosie's earnest eyes and whispered, "I am terrified of being unattractive to you."

Dosie blinked like a computer rebooting, and the first of Jennifer's tears fell. She didn't give Dosie a chance to respond. With the floodgate open, the words spilled as if compelled by gravity. "And I feel stupid saying it. I feel stupid *feeling* it, because it's not something I've ever been worried about, but now I'm obsessing over it."

"Over me not being attracted to you?" Dosie looked at her as if she'd grown a second head. "*Honey*."

"I don't mean physically," Jennifer said. "I mean *me*. This me that you keep having to see. The me who falls apart every time the goddamned wind changes." She shuddered with her next breath, and her voice began to shake. "The me who throws things and doesn't

sleep and makes irrational decisions and can't stop *fucking crying.*"
Jennifer furiously wiped her cheeks and refused to meet Dosie's eyes.
She felt disgusted with herself. "Don't say you find this attractive."

"I don't think I'm supposed to find it attractive when you're triggered and heartbroken," Dosie said, and Jennifer half-laughed, half-
scoffed. She collapsed forward onto Dosie's shoulder, and let her
weight be theirs for a moment. Dosie lazily swayed them from side to
side, a slow dance that lulled Jennifer's nerves. "When we have to
take things slowly in the bedroom, do you feel less attracted to me?"

Jennifer stood back to look at her, confused. "What?"

Dosie took her hands. "You think I don't know this fear? That I
don't feel it every time you have to slow down for me? Every time
we've had to take a break or stop altogether or not even start because
I've gotten triggered by something that's basic or natural or even
exciting for you? You think I don't feel terrified that you'll get tired of
all my needs before I grow past the point of needing them? That
you'll decide you want someone more exciting and experienced or
even just that you want to be single again?"

"I want *you*," Jennifer said and pulled Dosie's hands closer. She
placed one over her heart and the other around her cheek, found
comfort in the warmth of both. "I'm not going anywhere." *I'm in this.*
"I promise." *For as long as you'll have me, I'm in this.*

"But I don't know that," Dosie said, and Jennifer felt a terrible,
defensive ache in her chest. A kind of panic for her to prove herself
erupted from her soul like a hidden security system.

"Dosie, I'm committed to you." She squeezed her hands.
"Entirely."

An almost playful smile touched one corner of Dosie's mouth,
and Jennifer felt confused again. "Okay," Dosie said, "but I don't
know that for sure, and there is no way for me to know it except to
experience it, so I just have to trust you when you say that you're
committed to me."

Jennifer's eyebrows tilted together. Her thoughts swam dizzily.
"Don't you?"

"With all my heart, yes," Dosie said with such ease that Jennifer suddenly felt a bit drunk. "But that doesn't make the fear go away."

Oh. Jennifer freed a half-hearted laugh and placed a hand to her forehead. "Okay," she said. "I see what you're saying."

Dosie kissed the center of Jennifer's left palm and said, "I've told you before, but I'll tell you again. I didn't fall in love with the Director. I fell in love with you, and *you're* who I'm with, whether you're being a seductress or a mess. And just to be clear, I never expected you not to be both."

"You thought I would be a mess?"

"Just human."

"So, yes?" Jennifer sighed and leaned into her touch, and the tumult inside fizzled to an irritable, but not all-consuming, static. Something manageable, ignorable even. She closed her eyes. "I never wanted to need anyone this much."

"You don't need me, baby," Dosie said and kissed her cheek. "You just want me."

God, the way I want you. "Yes," Jennifer whispered and grabbed Dosie's chin to direct her sweet, little kisses to where she wanted them.

"Mm," Dosie hummed into Jennifer's slow, closemouthed kiss. She exhaled through her nose and melted into Jennifer's chest as if a drug had taken over her system, and suddenly, she was liquid. Limp in Jennifer's arms. When it was over, her eyes remained closed and her lips slightly parted, hand curled into the front of Jennifer's sweater.

Jennifer committed the sight to memory. "I do want you."

"I want you, too," Dosie said and kissed Jennifer once more before opening her eyes. "And I know I can't make your fear go away, but please trust me when I tell you that I'm with you." Her fingers, still fisting Jennifer's sweater, unfurled and lay gently over her heart. "All of you. I'm so freaking with you that I can barely even be with just myself anymore."

"Yeah," Jennifer huffed, drawing a lazy laugh from Dosie that made her insides feel like warm butter. "I know the feeling."

"And I'm so attracted to you that I freak myself out sometimes."

A halcyon energy settled over them, and Jennifer breathed easy. "I know that feeling too."

"And I mean *you*, Jen, not just the you that you are when you *know* you're being hot, but the you that you are when you think you aren't hot, or better, when you don't even care."

All the tiny, undetectable hairs along the backs of Jennifer's arms and neck floated off her skin as if she was about to be struck by lightning. "What do you mean?"

"I don't know. Little things, I guess." She closed her eyes, and Jennifer could see them moving behind her eyelids as if scanning through a visual collection of her memories. "When you're using instructions, like when you cook with a recipe, you do this little half-squat-dance thing. You'll just be holding your phone, squatting from side to side while you read the directions."

The moment it was said, Jennifer realized it was true. She could almost feel the bend and bounce in her knees as she thought of herself in the kitchen cooking. How ridiculous.

"You look like a happy little cricket just making her dinner." Jennifer snorted as Dosie turned and led her to the couch. She toed off her shoes and sat, and Dosie crawled into her lap, straddling her thighs. She cupped both sides of Jennifer's neck and smiled as she looked her right in the eyes. "It's so cute, and it's so dumb, and every time you do it, I want you so much, it makes me feel dizzy."

"Yeah?"

"Yeah."

Jennifer felt dizzy herself, dizzy and full. Her heart was inflatable and swollen. She hooked her fingers behind Dosie's head and reeled her in. "Come here."

They kissed. An unhurried series of slow connections took them from one deep press to a peck to a light brush of Dosie's tongue against hers, and Jennifer felt every one of them like a pulse feeding a low electric current across her body. Once, twice, Dosie bucked her hips, her pelvis knocking against Jennifer's as if seeking pressure, but then she calmed to stillness again, and Jennifer didn't try to urge her back into a rhythm. She wasn't in the mood for sex. She just wanted to be close. She wanted to be held. And she did, after all, want to talk.

Jennifer kissed her way across Dosie's cheek, then hugged her close and lay her forehead against her shoulder. She closed her eyes as Dosie's fingers landed in her hair and began scratching along her scalp. Quickly, it became rhythmic, ambient. Jennifer might have fallen asleep had it not been for the thoughts in her head, the same ones that had kept her awake for days. Years.

"It's just you and me," Dosie whispered as she kissed Jennifer's temple then along her hairline to her ear. "Talk to me."

"I didn't speak for her." The confession was so airy that, were they outside, it could have passed for a misheard sound in the wind. But she'd said it, and in the still, quiet hotel room, Dosie must have heard it. Jennifer hid herself in Dosie's chest and in the rhythm of Dosie's hands in her hair and her sporadic, fleeting kisses, and maybe none of it gave her courage, but it gave her refuge, and they felt the same. "I testified at the trial, because I had no choice, but when he was sentenced, the judge gave us an opportunity to make impact statements, and I just couldn't."

She's judging me, Jennifer thought when Dosie said nothing. Every instinct she had told her it wasn't true, but the thought came and stayed anyway. She didn't voice it, and it turned out she didn't need to, since Dosie seemed capable of reading her mind.

"You were a kid, Jen. And you were shy and anxious. And traumatized."

"Please don't," Jennifer said and squeezed Dosie tighter. "I had a responsibility to speak up for her, to protect her, and I failed. Twice. Twice, I failed when she needed me."

Dosie was quiet for a long moment, then she leaned back and urged Jennifer's face out of its hiding place to look at her. "Tell me why you think that was your responsibility."

"Because she was my sister."

"But not your child," Dosie said. "Or your ward. She wasn't even littler than you. She was your big sister."

"That doesn't matter," Jennifer said with a huff. She didn't want Dosie making excuses for her. There were no excuses to be made. She knew her reasons—her anxieties, her fears, her age, everything—and they would never be enough. "I should have said something. And I had time. Nearly two years before his trial even started, and months after it was over before he was sentenced. I wrote so many fucking drafts, I can't even...." She laughed at herself, and her chest grew tight. "I knew exactly, *exactly*, what I wanted to say to him, what I wanted to say *about* him, and then, it came time, and I remember the lawyers looking at me and my aunt looking at me and her voice in my ear, saying my name, asking me if I was ready, but...."

"But?"

Jennifer's memory of her days in court were hazy, at best, but she remembered every time their eyes had met. "He was looking at me, too, and I couldn't move."

"Oh, baby," Dosie said and wiped through a streak of tears on Jennifer's cheek that she hadn't felt fall. "That happens sometimes. That's not your fault. That's just your body trying to protect you."

"I should have protected Lauren," Jennifer said, and her voice crackled like static. Then it broke entirely, and every word became wreckage for Dosie to sift through. "I should have gotten over my fucking self and *said something*. If I had said something, if I had called the cops, if I had told my aunt—"

"Shh, shh, shh. Stop. Stop." Dosie wrapped her arms around Jennifer's shoulders and head and held her close to her chest. "Just stop, and listen to me for a minute, okay? You don't *know* any of that. You're assuming that you could have saved her or helped her some-how, but you don't know."

Jennifer's heart lurched. "Yes, I do."

"No, you don't," Dosie said, her voice soft but sincere. She had no doubt in what she said. "You *think* that if you had called the cops that day or told your aunt, that your sister would have survived, but you don't *know* that, and you can never know that. What if your aunt didn't believe you or told you not to mettle? What if the cops didn't get there in time, or what if they did get there, but they didn't do anything? As terrible as that is to even imagine, we both know it happens. You think, in all those years, that none of us on the compound ever tried to tell anyone about what was happening to us?"

Jennifer looked up at Dosie through tears, cupped her cheek and felt her lean into it.

"I will always advocate for speaking up," Dosie said and placed her hand over Jennifer's, "but I know, and I think you know, too, that it doesn't guarantee anything. Evil things happen all the time, and everyone knows it, and they just keep happening. You could have told everyone you saw that day and still lost your sister. So, what good does it do to dwell on it like this?" She turned her face to kiss Jennifer's palm. "No amount of you obsessing over what you did or didn't do is ever going to turn back time for you to change things. It will only make you feel terrible and stop you from living your life."

Until Dosie, Jennifer hadn't experienced the kind of care that came with being loved in a very long time. Even after half a year together, she hadn't fully reacclimated and still often felt overwhelmed by how well Dosie understood her and all the things she had been through. How readily she offered support and how eagerly she gave affection. How easily she accepted all the things that Jennifer had once convinced herself no one ever could or would.

She closed her eyes and sank her face into Dosie's chest again. She kissed her there, right between her breasts through her sweater, then back up her neck to her chin, her mouth. "You always know what to say."

"Only for you," Dosie said between kisses. "If I could talk to myself the way I talk to you, my self-care work would probably be much more effective."

"I will happily care for yourself if you need a break."

Dosie's tired laugh was sweet and sexy, and every time Jennifer drew it out, she felt she'd manifested art. Or something like it. Some living, breathing wonder, inducing desire and a subtle sense of awe.

"Jennifer," she said with a lazy, flirty smile. Her name had never sounded better. She looked into Jennifer's eyes and nuzzled their noses together. "Take me to bed?"

Her answer drifted out of her as if lured, an easy, "Yes," as Dosie peeled herself off of her and stood. She pulled Jennifer up next, and they made their way to the bed, hand in hand in silence. They undressed each other just as quietly, one piece of clothing after another, Jennifer then Dosie and back. Jennifer let every touch linger, her fingertips skimming over Dosie's skin as it was bared. The goosebumps that rose in their wake sent a spike of adrenaline through Jennifer's system, fleeting but exhilarating.

When they were naked, they crawled into bed, and Jennifer let herself be spooned. Dosie slid one arm under her neck and slotted Jennifer's hips into hers so that her short, soft pubic hair tickled the top of Jennifer's ass. The other arm, Dosie wrapped around her waist, and then she stuck her nose in Jennifer's wily hair and sniffed the loudest, most obnoxious sniff. "Oh yeah. That's the stuff."

"You're ridiculous."

"Can't help it," Dosie said and squeezed her. "You smell like my favorite person."

Jennifer's chest warmed. A smile stretched her lips as she felt Dosie's teeth between her shoulder blades, gently nibbling in the way she sometimes did when she felt particularly affectionate. Jennifer lay her hand over Dosie's and rubbed along her fingers and wrist. "Did you speak at your father's sentencing hearing?"

"Yeah."

"Did you feel like you had to?"

Quiet. It lasted a tense moment, then Dosie answered, "Yes." She swiped her thumb back and forth over Jennifer's stomach, like a slow-moving windshield wiper. "But not because I thought I owed it to anyone else. I felt like I owed it to myself and like I had to say how I felt, because I'd never done that before. I'd never told him how much he hurt me. I just endured it."

"Do you think it helped you?"

"I don't know," Dosie said as if she'd never considered it before. "Honestly, I think about it sometimes, and I wish I knew everything then that I know now, so that I could have said all the things I've since learned how to articulate. But for who I was at the time and for what he'd just put me through, I think I said what I needed to, and I'm okay with it. The rest, I don't need to say to his face. I just need to know it and believe it for myself."

Jennifer let the words sink in as she played with Dosie's fingers, tracing down one, then onto the next and the next and back.

"I think, if you speak at the hearing, you should do it for yourself," Dosie said. "Not because you think you owe it to anyone or because you think it's your duty or responsibility, but because you're hurting and you've been hurting for a long time, and you likely always will be to some degree. You need to say it, and he needs to hear it, and so do the people making the decision."

Jennifer swallowed, but the growing lump in her throat didn't budge. "What if I can't do it?" She asked the question so quietly that she was surprised when Dosie answered.

"You can."

"What if I see him again, and the same thing happens, and I choke?"

"You won't."

Jennifer rolled in Dosie's arms so she could see her sincerity, feel their heartbeats right up against each other. "How do you know?"

Dosie combed Jennifer's hair back from her face. "Because he was my own father, and I was more afraid of him than of any demon or devil or monster someone could dream up, and I still did it. I got through it, and you can get through this." She kissed Jennifer's lips and pulled her into a hug. "I promise you can. You just need to believe it."

In the quiet that followed, Jennifer let her mind inch toward the hearing. She let herself imagine standing, walking to a podium, and opening her mouth to speak. She tried to imagine his eyes on her, his gaze barely a bother as she spoke in spite of it. No freezing. No choking. Just nausea.

Fuck. Jennifer breathed in through her nose to quell it and slowly exhaled through her mouth. Dosie was the strongest person she'd ever met. Just because she could do something didn't at all mean that Jennifer could. *Fuuuuck.*

"Try to rest," Dosie said, rubbing a hand down Jennifer's arm. "The more you think about it, the more you'll freak yourself out."

"Yeah," Jennifer said and thought about it anyway. *What if I choke again?* She closed her eyes and tried to do as Dosie suggested, but rest didn't come. Sleep seemed far away. Even when Dosie began to subtly twitch in her arms, having fallen asleep herself, Jennifer remained wide awake, consumed by the thought that had become larger than life in her mind. *What if I choke again, and he gets out of prison?*

Frustrated, Jennifer slid out of bed. *What if choke again, and he gets out of prison, and he kills another girl? Someone else's Lauren.* She wasn't going to sleep, no matter how tired she was. She needed something to focus on. *What if I choke again? What if I choke again? What if I fucking choke again?*

10

"I am going to lose my mind," Jennifer muttered under her breath as she finished the page and flipped to the next. Her eyes scanned quickly, excitement doubling her processing speed. "No. What? It was him the whole time?!"

"Jennifer!"

Her father's voice drifting in from elsewhere did nothing to break Jennifer's concentration. Her eyes remained glued to her book as she lay in bed, clutching her pillows like supports as the story she read got more and more intense. She was yanked back to reality, however, when another pillow came flying from the doorway to knock the book from her hands.

"Lauren!"

"What?" Lauren stood outside Jennifer's bedroom, a mischievous smile on her lips. "Do you not hear Dad calling you?"

"You made me lose my place."

"You'll find it again."

Jennifer rolled out of bed and dodged her sister's tickling hands on the way out the door. "Stop it!"

"Geez." Lauren followed her down the hall. "Why are you so moody this weekend? Are you on your period?"

"Where is he?" Jennifer asked, ignoring her.

Lauren shrugged and broke off toward the kitchen. "Front yard, I think," she called over her shoulder before disappearing around the corner. Her disembodied voice followed Jennifer to the living room. "Take some Midol!"

"Jennifer!" her father called again, and she picked up her pace.

She opened the front door to find him standing just ahead of her at the foot of the porch. "Oui, Papa?" She frowned at the oversized clear protective jumpsuit that he wore atop his slacks and button-up. "What are you wearing?"

"Donne moi un coup de main," he said and waved Jennifer down to him. Four open cans of paint sat at his feet. "Come, come."

She laughed, confused, and went barefoot down the steps. "What do you want me to give you a hand with? An art project?"

He put his hands on his hips and smiled. "Oui."

Jennifer snorted. "Since when are you an artist, Papa?"

"Your mother wants the fresh look," he told her with a playful roll of his eyes, "so we paint the door for her. Maybe the post box, too."

"Why are *we* painting the door and the mailbox? Lauren isn't doing anything."

"Please, ma puce, you need the sun," her father teased. "You look like the adorable snowman. Come."

"That would be the abominable snowman, Papa, and too much sun is bad for the skin."

"There is a distance, Jennifer, between no sun and too much sun. Oui?"

Jennifer laughed as he tugged her into a strong side hug and waved a hand over his selection of paints. "Her favorites, of course," he said as Jennifer's eyes dropped to the first. It was a pale shade of yellow that she didn't dislike but immediately cut from the running because the name on the side of the can bothered her. Whoever thought calling the color Winter Yolk was a good idea needed firing.

Nobody wanted their front door covered in winter yolk, or any yolk, for that matter.

"I like this one," her father said and pointed to the third can.

Jennifer turned her gaze to the bright pastel blue bearing the name Robin's Egg. The air warped, everything shivering as if suddenly chilled, then returned to normal, and Jennifer got the distinct sensation that something was wrong. "Papa?" she said and realized his arm wasn't around her shoulders anymore. His plastic jumpsuit wasn't crinkling against her side.

Panic woke like a sleeping giant in Jennifer's heart as she whirled in place to find nothing as it was. Her father was gone. The paint cans, too. The sun had fled, and the day was cold and covered in clouds.

"Jennifer."

She gasped and looked up. She was still there, still home, standing at the base of the front porch stairs, listening to the voice of someone who shouldn't be there. Calling her name.

"Jennifer."

At the top of the stairs, where the front door should have been, stood Dosie Fisher in a 50s halter swing dress the color of a robin's egg. Her hair had been drawn into an updo and tied with a scarf, just like Rosie the Riveter's. "There you are," she said as Jennifer stepped toward her. "Come here. Give me a squish."

Jennifer frowned at the words. "What?"

"What?" Dosie asked innocently as her cinnamon hair began to change, turning redder and redder until it wasn't cinnamon but sanguine. Her lips too, red pooling around the corners of her mouth like spittle she couldn't control. The pearls around her neck turned pink then red then began to drip down her chest and into the blue of her dress, and all Jennifer could do was watch. Horrified, she stood frozen as Dosie began to bleed from nothing, from *everything*. "Oh, Jen. It's okay."

She hyperventilated as she followed Dosie's sad, bloody gaze to her own hands. There, she found a massive hunting knife, clutched firmly and coated scarlet. *No.* Her fingers trembled around the grip. *No.* A scream raced up Jennifer's throat.

The first pained moan barely registered, just enough to stir her from the depths of sleep but not quite enough to wake her. The second tore through her haze like an alarm, and Dosie opened her eyes to a bedside clock blinking 4:21 like a beacon in the dark. She sat up and took a moment to orient herself.

She was in a bed, a big bed but not her bed. Not Jennifer's bed. A hotel bed. An empty hotel bed. Her eyebrows scrunched together as she looked over the large, vacant expanse of mattress beside her. Where was her girlfriend?

Then she heard the moan again.

Dosie was on her feet in an instant, following the sound to the sitting room where Jennifer lay on the couch in a hotel robe and a fitful sleep. The files her aunt had given her lay in a messy heap over her chest, half-spilled onto the floor, and Dosie wondered how long ago she'd gotten up to go through them. She had no memory of her even leaving the bed.

As her eyes adjusted more to the dark, Dosie could make out Jennifer's facial features and noticed the strain. Tension pulled at her cheeks and tightened her jaw. She groaned a low and almost constant note as her chest bounced shallowly with each short breath. Whatever she was dreaming, it wasn't pleasant.

Carefully, Dosie removed the files from Jennifer's chest and kicked aside the ones on the floor. She rubbed warm strokes along the soft skin of Jennifer's elbow and shushed her, back and forth, back and forth, not trying to wake her, just soothe her. Jennifer needed the rest.

The tension eased from her love's face, and the pained note dwindled to a sporadic hiccup, then nothing at all. Dosie sat herself on the floor beside the couch and lay her head on Jennifer's arm, near meditative as she watched her in the dark and wished her kinder dreams. "I hope you know," she whispered as her fingers skated along Jennifer's arm, "how loved you are."

When Jennifer woke, it was still early. Her eyes felt like throbbing balls of fire as she blinked them open to see the ceiling streaked with dawn. She sat up, every muscle in her back pulling and aching in protest, and swung her legs off the side of the couch. Papers crinkled under her feet. The files she'd spent the night rereading—*fucking pointlessly*—lay scattered over the floor as if tossed.

"Fuck." Her voice was a wreck. She pushed her hair out of her face and rubbed her sore eyes and tried to determine if she was awake enough to get up and stay up or just enough to shuffle herself back to the bed.

A shower or bed. Both sounded good, but the bed had the added bonus of having her girlfriend in it. Jennifer dismissed the advantage. The shower could have her girlfriend in it too if she asked nicely enough. She smiled at the thought, but then her chest grew tight, and her stomach dropped. Her breath caught at the back of her throat as a terrible feeling of dread sank through her. Fleeting, it passed nearly as soon as it began, and Jennifer sat bewildered in the wake of it. She rubbed her chest over and over until she felt soothed and shook off the feeling as a side effect of too little sleep and too much stress. In a day, she'd be before a parole board, pleading for them not to be idiots. What *wasn't* there to be stressed about?

Fuck today. Fuck tomorrow. She was going back to bed. She was going to shove her face in her girlfriend's hair and forget the rest of the world existed.

Jennifer moved to the bedroom and saw the near-horizontal lump of blankets waiting. A healing warmth seeped through her, just the knowledge of Dosie's presence like a balm to her overworked nervous system. She was there. She was safe. They were together.

From the foot of the bed, she watched the first bits of morning light creep over the mattress and speckle Dosie's half-covered face. She remembered the feeling she had the night of their first date, when Dosie accidentally stood her up and Jennifer had gone into her hotel room to find her sound asleep, curled up just as she was now. Such incredible relief.

Jennifer dropped her robe to the floor and crawled up the bed. Words itched in her throat, slinking up her tongue, but she had no idea what they were. She'd had no intention of waking Dosie, yet the moment she reached her, she couldn't stop herself. She eased herself under the covers and down beside her lover. Dosie's mouth hung slightly agape, and a tiny crease pulled her brows together. Jennifer smiled and smoothed the crease with her thumb, whispered Dosie's name until her lovely dark eyes fluttered open.

For a moment, Dosie only looked at her, as if she hadn't yet processed that she was awake. But then she hummed a soft, sweet note that sounded much the way Jennifer felt inside. "Are you okay?" she whispered and took Jennifer's hand.

Jennifer kissed her fingers. "I never feel at peace anymore," she confessed, "except when I'm with you."

Dosie's eyes turned sad, but she hummed the same sweet note, and somehow that was all Jennifer needed. "Come here," she said and pulled Jennifer into a lazy kiss. Over and over, she kissed Jennifer, until they were breathy and flush against one another, and nothing else in the world existed. Jennifer's thoughts dwindled to one, the one getting her through the worst of her days. The one of which she was most certain.

"I'm so fucking in love with you," she whispered, and felt Dosie shiver. Her heart jumped into overdrive when Dosie's hand found hers again under the covers and pulled it to her abdomen. She flattened Jennifer's palm over her belly, looked her in the eye as she slowly began to urge it down.

As Jennifer's fingertips slid into the hair between her legs, Dosie took a shaky breath and said, "Show me."

Want spilled through Jennifer's system as if through a ruptured dam. In seconds, she was flooded with it. She moaned and licked up the length of Dosie's neck, sucked her pulse until it throbbed between her lips. She cupped Dosie's cunt, massaging with her palm until she felt a throb there as well, then Jennifer brought her hand to her mouth.

As Dosie watched, she slid her two middle fingers between her teeth and licked them wet. When she returned them to Dosie's heat, she realized she needn't have bothered. Jennifer spread her open and found her dewy and flexing around nothing. She drew slow circles with her fingertips, gathering moisture, then a line back up to Dosie's tender, twitching clit and drew circles there as well.

Dosie's breath shallowed, chest bobbing with each quick gasp. Little hums of pleasure became full-bodied moans, higher in pitch and whinier in nature the longer Jennifer toyed with her. Her hips jumped, and her hands grabbed at Jennifer wherever they could. She sucked hungrily at Jennifer's lips, jaw, and shoulder, and when Jennifer told her to bite her, she sank her teeth into the tender spot at the base of Jennifer's neck until it stung.

"*Dosie*," Jennifer moaned and slid her fingers back down. "Do you want me inside you?"

Her lover's "yes" was a fractured plea, and as it trembled out of her, Jennifer teased one tip in and then thrust smoothly down to the knuckle. As she retreated, she sucked one of Dosie's nipples into her mouth until it was pinched between her teeth and caused her girl to gasp. Jennifer soothed the sting with her tongue and added another finger. In an easy stroke, she was two fingers deep in Dosie's perfect heat, and all but humming with energy. Were someone to press a light bulb against her skin, Jennifer was convinced it would glow.

Dosie pulled Jennifer's face back up to hers, kissed along her jaw to her earlobe. "Go slow, Jen," she half-whispered, half-moaned. "I want it to last."

Something about the way she said it made Jennifer think it wasn't just about the sex or the orgasm, or even the moment. Perhaps she meant the love, too. Jennifer slowed her strokes to a glacial place, a lazy pattern like homegrown magic at the tip of her deep-buried fingers, and just as before, she promised Dosie, "I'm not going anywhere."

"Okay," Dosie said and stuck her hand forward for the hair tie. "It's not too tight, right?"

"No, it's good, love. Thank you." Jennifer pulled the elastic band off her wrist and strung it around Dosie's fingers.

"You're welcome," Dosie said as she thrice wrapped the band around the end of the finished braid. She gave it a tug to make sure it was secure, then nodded, satisfied with her work. It was loose and fat but still had structure, just the way Jennifer liked it. "Go look."

Jennifer stood from the foot of the bed and stretched her neck from side to side. She smoothed the front of her indigo button-down then the barely wrinkled seat of her charcoal pleated trousers. Lastly, she skated her hand over the braid as if she needed to smooth a third thing in order to make her feet move, then she crossed into the bathroom to inspect it again with her eyes.

"I think I want oatmeal now instead of a muffin," Dosie called after her.

"I'm sure they will have both," Jennifer said and peeped around the corner, now popping one gunmetal gray hoop through her earlobe. A sexy hint of a grin touched her lips. "I think I could even secure a breakfast burrito, should the lady desire one."

Dosie laughed at Jennifer's waggling eyebrows and threw a pillow at her. Still in her underwear, she slid off the bed where she'd already lain out her hideously wrinkled outfit, and went to the small closet. The hotel's provided ironing board screeched when she pulled it into position, but it wasn't stained, at least, and the iron began heating up as soon as she plugged it in.

"Are you having Ned take you?" she asked as she threw her pants onto the board first.

"No need."

Dosie turned at the sudden nearness of Jennifer's voice and found her just a few feet away. She leaned against the wall with her loose braid over her shoulder, her hands in her pockets, silver watch glinting from her left wrist, and her still socked feet crossed over one another. Her body held no tension, visibly relaxed for the first time in days, and her blue eyes, dreamy and dazed, watched Dosie as if expecting to see something awe-worthy, rather than a mostly naked girl ironing some pants.

"What?"

Jennifer's eyebrow popped up as if Dosie had pressed a button and commanded it to. "What?" she replied with a silky, not-at-all innocent voice that made Dosie's skin tingle. "Just looking at you."

The tingles turned prickly, and Dosie felt her lower back bow inward. She quickly glanced at the iron to ensure she'd set it down, then she giggled at herself. "Keep looking at me like that, and I'm going to burn a hole through my pants."

Jennifer eased off the wall. "Well, we wouldn't want that," she said and closed the distance between them. She molded herself to Dosie's back and ran the tip of her nose along the line of her neck from shoulder to jaw. "I'll just go..." One warm hand palmed the arch of her hip then crept around to her belly. Jennifer's thumb dipped into Dosie's navel, while the tip of her middle finger inched under the band of her underwear. "...so I don't distract you."

Dosie felt like she was made of air. She reached back for an anchor and found it in Jennifer's thigh, fingers curling into the soft wool of her pants pocket.

"Though really," Jennifer said as she brushed Dosie's hair aside. She ran her finger over one of the long scars between her shoulders and kissed the knobby base of her neck. "Who is the distraction here?"

Dosie's stomach took that moment to interrupt. It rumbled and sloshed like a washing machine as if to say it wouldn't abide any further delays, and Jennifer laughed and said, "Fine. I'm going." She kissed the back of Dosie's neck again then went to don her shoes and coat.

"So, you're walking there and back?" Dosie asked, her focus returning to task. She laid one pant leg out and smoothed it with her hands, then she let a bit of steam off the iron and set the hot metal to the material. A smooth, rhythmic glide turned her wrinkles to a flat plane of navy in seconds.

"Yes." Jennifer reappeared, now in her low-heel black leather Ralph Lauren boots and in the process of pulling on her peacoat. "It shouldn't take long. Oh, and—" She went to the dresser, a dark blur of color in Dosie's peripheral, and then she was a divinely-scented shadow at Dosie's back again. "Wear these today," she said, and Dosie felt the cold weight of her pearls against her skin as Jennifer slid them into place around her neck. Her warm fingers fiddled the clasp at the back, then a tender kiss whispered across Dosie's ear. "You might want them."

"Oh?" Dosie set down the iron again and lay her hand over the pearls. Then she turned and looped her arms around Jennifer's waist. "Should I be nervous?"

"I want to take you somewhere."

"Somewhere that will make me nervous?"

"Maybe."

"Oh no," Dosie laughed. "Now you have to tell me, or I'll expire before we even get there."

Jennifer kissed Dosie slow and deep until she was almost limp. "That would be a terrible way for you to meet my aunt," she said, and every process in Dosie's body screeched to a halt and held. One second. Two. A pulse of energy, and everything reanimated, kicked into high gear.

"Really?" Dosie asked as she straightened, eyes widening. Jennifer wanted her to meet her family. *Her*. Dosie Fisher, the girl with the whacky, wounded past and the minefield of triggers who had never imagined that anyone who didn't think she was a Prophet's daughter would want to bring her home. "You want me to meet your aunt?"

Jennifer held her securely in one arm and brought the other hand to Dosie's hot cheek. "If you're willing."

"Yes." Dosie's body crackled with energy. Her eyes watered as she smiled and bounced on her toes. "I'm willing."

Time seemed held in place for a second or two. Her heart was twice its usual size. Then her lover exhaled a slow, subtle sigh and said, "Good."

"Good."

Once more ensnared, they remained in place, gazes locked, mouths hovering at a hint of a kiss. Jennifer tilted, breaking the stillness, and touched the tip of Dosie's nose with hers in a little zap of static. "I'd better go," she said but didn't move beyond that.

Dosie's pulse picked up as she watched Jennifer's gaze drop then rise then drop again, unable to tear itself away from Dosie's mouth for long. "I guess you'd better."

"You're hungry," Jennifer whispered, and her hands snaked down Dosie's naked sides to the arches of her hipbones.

Dosie shuddered as Jennifer's thumbs slipped under her waistband to make prints at the bends of her thighs. "So hungry."

"You could starve," Jennifer said and flicked her tongue over the center point of Dosie's top lip.

Dosie's breath thinned as she fisted Jennifer's fresh shirt. "I'll starve," she panted and kissed Jennifer as if it might be her only source of oxygen. She hiked a leg around Jennifer's hip, and Jennifer's hand found her ass immediately, her long fingers curling around the curve of one glute and squeezing. Two frantic heartbeats and one eager growl later, Jennifer had her off the floor entirely, whirling her toward the bed.

After a forty-minute drive, the town car eased onto a skinny asphalt road that led into an expansive cemetery. If Dosie had to guess, the place was likely older than most of the country it stood in. Its sea of dull green grass and moss-mottled granite was well-maintained and speckled with trees, some naked and some needled, and gray squirrels flitted between them as if unbothered by the cold.

"I hope you don't mind a short stop," Jennifer said and waved Ned on, further amongst the rows of headstones and the few mausoleums.

Dosie held her hand atop the seat between them. Jennifer hadn't told her why they were there, but she could guess. It was the place where her family was buried. "I don't mind."

Ned parked where directed and let the engine idle. "Just let me know when you're ready to head out again."

Jennifer looked at Dosie with a melancholy smile. "Come with me?"

In the sunlit cold, they tread softly over dewy grass and dropped leaves. Jennifer swung their clutched hands between them, a gentle sway that bumped between their hips like a slow-rolling pinball, and neither said a word. The right spot was four lanes over and consisted of two simple headstones, both flat to the ground rather than standing, with ornate metal framing and carefully engraved text.

Centered across the top of the larger of the two was the surname DUPONT, and beneath it, the names HENRI-CLEMENT and MARY ROSE, along with the dates of their respective births and deaths. The latter was the same for both. *Nov. 21, 1997*, the day of their car accident. No other words marked the stone, just an engraved and somewhat weathered laurel leaf.

The second, smaller headstone bore only one name, its entirety etched into a single line: LAUREN ROSE RENEÉ DUPONT. Under that, there were the simple and succinct dates spanning her short life—*1981-2000*—and on the third and final line, one word engraved in script. *Free.*

An incredible, familiar ache burned in Dosie's chest as she stared at the word and felt both elated and heartbroken by it. She hadn't expected to feel a connection with Jennifer's sister given her inability to ever meet her, but standing there at her grave, she did. She, too, had once been trapped in something abusive, yearning for a way out even before she knew there was one, and she, too, had eventually gained her freedom. Dosie had come quite close, but in the most incredible stroke of luck, hadn't died for hers. It broke her heart that she couldn't say the same for Lauren Dupont.

Jennifer's grip on her hand threatened Dosie's blood flow, so tight that her fingertips were numb. She looked over, eyes glistening with tears she held at bay. "I've never brought anyone here before."

Dosie brought their clasped hands to her mouth and kissed the back of Jennifer's. "Do you talk to them?" she asked. "I don't have graves to visit. All my family was cremated. But I think some people find it therapeutic to have a place like this to go and talk."

"No. I rarely visit. Even before I left, I didn't come here often. It always felt too final, I think; like if I stayed away, I could imagine they weren't gone, only off on some adventure somewhere. Or working. Out getting groceries. Something normal, boring, and then they'd be back." She breathed a heavy breath. "Sounds stupid."

"It sounds nice," Dosie said and kissed her shoulder through her coat. She ached for Jennifer, for the pain left festering at the heart of her for decades, never letting her rest. "Like they'll be home soon, if you just wait long enough."

"Yeah." Jennifer's voice creaked, and she closed her eyes for a moment. A rogue tear broke from the watery line of her lashes and fell. Dosie reached up and wiped it away as Jennifer looked at her again, eyes heartache blue and beautiful. "I can never introduce you to my parents or my sister," she said, "and I've never been spiritual. I don't think they're lingering here, waiting for me, but I thought, maybe, if you and I could just stand here for a while, it would be like...."

"Like we're all here together," Dosie guessed, hoping she was right.

In the quiet atmosphere, punctured by only the occasional bird and the breeze through bare branches, Jennifer's thick swallow was like thunder. She dipped her chin in a nod, and Dosie let go of her hand to loop an arm around her waist instead. She pulled Jennifer flush against her and lay their heads together, temples rubbing.

The urge to give a blessing, to say a little prayer, to talk of better places and streets of gold fizzled to life in the back of Dosie's mind like the flame of a match. She blew it dark again and held her tongue, and they stood in the tranquil cold for what felt like ages. Dosie didn't know if the souls of Jennifer's family were around or if something like that was even possible, but it didn't matter. In that moment, they were together, all, whether it was real or not.

"It's good we came," Jennifer said as they returned, hand-in-hand, to the car. "Thank you."

"Of course." Dosie watched remnant leaves squish under her boots with each step between the stones. Her eyes scanned the legible names they passed along the way. *Michael. Theresa. Franklin and Adele. Faith.* She sighed a puff of fog and bumped her shoulder against Jennifer's. "Thank you for bringing me."

"I wouldn't have anyone else."

Dosie smiled and looked up. The smile stuttered away as her eyes caught beyond Jennifer, across the cemetery's crisp, sunlit expanse. A figure she knew stood in the distance, the red in his hair catching the sun. Her steps faltered, but Jennifer caught her by the arm before she could take them both down.

"Whoa, love." Jennifer stepped in front of her, and the view became her amused eyes and moving lips. "Did you trip over something?" Her gaze turned worried when Dosie tried and failed, for a moment, to answer. "What is it?"

"I thought I saw...." Dosie looked past her, heart thumping madly, and Jennifer followed her gaze. *There's nothing there.* No movement.

No figure. It was just her and Jennifer and the parked car waiting for them. Dosie frowned and felt queasy. "Nothing." She closed her eyes, lay a hand over her chest, and breathed. *There's nothing there. I'm in Massachusetts. No one I know is here except Jennifer. There's nothing there. Nothing.*

"Talk to me." Jennifer's voice was softer now. She drew Dosie close and put an arm around her shoulders. "What did you see?"

Dosie leaned into Jennifer's body and braced herself. When she opened her eyes again, there was nothing. *Still nothing. See? There's no one there. There never was. You're fine.*

"Nothing," she said again and turned her face to hide in Jennifer's neck. She huffed against the warm skin there. "Just my mind playing tricks on me."

Jennifer was quiet a moment, then she whispered, "Your brother?"

"Or my father. I don't know." Another slow breath with Jennifer's rich, woodsy scent in her nose, and her heart began to calm again. "It was so quick I...." She stood back and shook her hands out. "I'm sorry. I didn't mean to startle you." She laughed at herself as her eyes began to water. "I haven't had a lot of time to process, and our sleep schedule has been so random. I think I'm just a little fried."

Jennifer swept her back into a tight, encompassing hug. She didn't hurry her toward the car or ask if Dosie wanted to go anywhere else. She simply held her and breathed warm air over her cheek and ear and waited.

Years earlier, Dosie had learned not to rush herself. Nothing good had ever come of it. Things got brushed aside or mashed down, snap-processed for the kind of quick and lousy healing that had never healed a thing. So, she ignored the chill and the waiting car and the day ahead and sank into Jennifer's arms like a small stone to a riverbed, and let all the thoughts and the feelings come as they willed.

"Can I tell you a secret?" she asked as Jennifer swayed them from side to side, a slow dance just shy of a stand-still.

"Mm." She nuzzled Dosie's neck. "Always."

"I don't think I want him." She shivered and felt sick to her stomach; at the same time, it was as if she could suddenly catch her breath. Cold, sharp, and incredible, she sucked in a lungful and pushed the words out again like a prayer she never intended to voice. "I don't want him."

Jennifer eased Dosie back to look at her. "Ira?"

"I'm glad he's alive," she said. "I am. There are so few of us left."

"I know."

Who *didn't* know? More people than Dosie could ever count had read all about the immediate aftermath of the raid. There were trials and imprisonments, hospitalizations, and later, a rash of suicides. It was a brutal reality that she knew Jennifer understood, because she was the sole survivor of her family and was more than familiar with what a burden it could be. The kind of shift in reality that they had both experienced as children, like a violent chasm opening across the middle of one's entire identity, was just too much for some people, and even if they were otherwise healthy, they couldn't move on. They couldn't adapt. She and Jennifer had talked before about the kind of dark thoughts that came after such suffering. *What was the point of life? Why did they deserve to survive? Maybe they didn't.* The cycle was vicious.

"But there's a part of me that feels like I need to be there for him," Dosie said, "and I just resent it so much, and I'm so ashamed of myself."

"No, baby," Jennifer said and drew her in again. "Don't be." She swiped her thumb back and forth over Dosie's cheek as their cold foreheads pressed together. "You have nothing to be ashamed of."

Dosie's chest was a lava pit, scorching Jennifer's reassurance to a crisp before it could soothe. *Stop,* she pleaded with her own mind and body. *Please.* She didn't want to feel this way. Just moments ago, she'd been calming down, and now she felt on the verge of tears again. Guilt wrecked her gut, and she couldn't bear Jennifer's affection. She turned, put her back to her. Jennifer's hands landed on her shoulders,

Corrie MacKay

a comfort she didn't feel she deserved, and she had to fight the impulse to shrug her off.

"You would give nearly anything to have your sister back," Dosie said when she could bring herself to form the words, to confess her ugliness, "and here I am, with the potential to have a sibling back in my life, and I don't want him." Her voice trembled, and Dosie let it fall to a whisper. Let no one but the dead and Jennifer hear her shame. "I don't think I'd want any of them back." She palmed her forehead and forced a breath, forced herself to just feel what she felt and accept it, even if it made her want to dig herself a grave.

"I loved them all." She turned back, faced her girlfriend, who looked at her not with judgment but empathy. "But I can't stomach the thought of being responsible for any of them again, and I just know that's what would happen if I let Ira back into my life. I will fall right back into those patterns, my sibling like my child, my own needs tossed aside, and I just can't. I can't. I don't think I could ever even be myself again. I couldn't even tell him about you. And he asked. He asked if I had someone, a husband, and I couldn't say the truth, because I was afraid of how he would react, of how he would judge me, and it made me *sick*, Jen. It made me sick, because I've never been prouder of anything than I am of loving you, and I still couldn't say it. I could feel myself shrinking back into that terrible little box I used to be in, and I just couldn't stand it."

The words poured out of her now, shaky but true. She was purging, and she couldn't stop herself. "And I feel like the worst person in the world, because the idea of *that* makes me feel so much more afraid than the fact that he is a killer." Jennifer flinched, and Dosie cast her eyes to the ground, felt the first of several tears fall. "And I feel even worse for admitting that to you when the whole reason we're here is because you're fighting to keep a killer in prison."

"It's not the same." Jennifer raised Dosie's face with a finger under her chin, and her sad eyes were so accepting that it was difficult for Dosie to hold her gaze. "Your brother was a baby, and your father turned him into a weapon. He killed because he thought he had to. Glass is and was a grown man who killed because he wanted to. It is not the same."

"You're right." She let Jennifer take her hands and rub some warmth back into her fingers. "You're right. I know." She whimpered. "But I feel—"

"Awful," Jennifer said, and Dosie nodded. "I know. It's complicated, all of it, more than any life experience has any right to be."

"Yeah."

"But whatever you feel, it's okay." Jennifer gave a soft, sad smile and poked Dosie's dimple. "Right? Isn't that what you're always telling me? That no matter what you feel, it's okay?"

For a moment, Dosie stared at her, breath caught in her throat, tears caught in her gaze. The burning in her chest ceased, and a new kind of pressure began, like her heart had spread against her ribcage and started pushing, trying to make more space for itself. "You really listen to me, don't you?"

Jennifer hummed in answer, drew the pad of her thumb along Dosie's top lip then back along the bottom. "You're in my head," she whispered, and whatever darkness had consumed Dosie scattered as if stricken by a brilliant beam. "Your voice. Your advice. It drives me crazy." She placed a tender, chaste kiss on Dosie's lips. "And it gets me through the day."

Dosie curled her fingers around the open edges of Jennifer's coat and said, "I never would have imagined when I met you that the Director was secretly such a lovesick sweetheart."

"Ha!" Jennifer's laugh was bold and turned the air white. "Darling, I am not lovesick," she said as she bumped their noses together and kissed her again. "Loving you is the healthiest thing I have ever done."

"*God.*" Dosie shook her head, baffled by how easily Jennifer had always been able to turn her from anguish to ecstasy. "And you said *I* say the worst, best things." She tugged at Jennifer's coat until she was kissed again, deep and slow, as if, while surrounded by all those whose time had run out, she and Jennifer had all the time in the world.

When they finally made themselves move again, Dosie's fingers and toes were near frozen, and she didn't care at all. "Is this where you want to be?" she asked as they approached the warm, running car still waiting for them. "When you go, I mean. Do you want to be buried here with your family?"

"I don't know," Jennifer said and opened the door for her. "I've rarely given my own death any thought, let alone what I want done with my body."

Dosie climbed in. "Well, I'm sure an art museum would buy you," she said, and Jennifer's soft, sexy laugh followed her into the backseat.

"Flatterer."

11

"There's no reason to be nervous," Jennifer said, and even to her own ears, it sounded like a lie. She wasn't sure why. There truly was no reason to be nervous. It wasn't as if her aunt would treat Dosie poorly or turn her away. That wasn't Carine, and if it was, Jennifer wouldn't bother visiting at all, let alone bringing someone she loved.

"You look like there's a reason," Dosie told her with a grimace. She peered out the window as the car turned onto a residential block. "Is there something you're not telling me? Does she not know you like girls?"

"She knew before I did."

"Oh, well, is it because of how we met then?" Dosie asked. "Does she not know you're a—" She glanced toward the driver's seat and cleared her throat. "Does she know about your job? Because we could just avoid it, or we could make up a story if you want."

It was so endearing that Jennifer's muscles relaxed. Her nerves stopped twitching. She pursed her lips to hold a laugh then said, "She knows." The laugh escaped anyway when Dosie's mouth opened in a surprised 'o'.

"Really?"

"Really," Jennifer said. "My aunt is European and not at all religious. She isn't a prude about these things the way most Americans are."

"Oh, well then why are you so nervous?" She gently poked Jennifer's side. "It's not like we have to tell her I was in a cult."

A choking sound erupted from the front of the car. Ned coughed his throat clear of the ill-timed drink he'd just taken. "Sorry," he said, voice garbled, and tried to wave off their attention.

Jennifer turned to Dosie and found her already looking at her. She shook her head, just the tiniest side-to-side, and their next breath erupted like an oil spill catching a match. They laughed like hyenas, Dosie's head tossed back and Jennifer's sides aching, until Ned was rose-cheeked in the mirror and chuckling, too.

"Sorry," he said again as he pulled the car around one last corner and rolled it to a stop. "I try not to listen, but..." He held his hands up atop the steering wheel as if to say he'd been caught red-handed. "...I can't turn my ears off."

"I'm just glad you weren't drinking something hot," Dosie told him. She looked out the window at the place they'd stopped. "Is this it?"

"This is it," Jennifer said and opened the door, her anxiety returning as the humor waned and reality set in again. She stepped out and held the door for Dosie. "No need to stay close, Ned. We will likely be a while. I'll call you when we're ready. Thank you."

"You got it. Have a good one."

With a rumble and puff of exhaust, the car rolled away and left them standing on the sidewalk, staring up at the stately old colonial with its tall columns and grand front porch. "I think I'm nervous because I've never done any of this before," Jennifer said as Dosie's hand curled around her wrist then slid down to lock with her own. "I never got to bring someone home to meet my parents. I never had any of those moments, really, the ones that are supposed to make you feel more like a grown-up, I think." She looked at Dosie, at her soft hair curling around her face and the tilt at the corner of her mouth, the golden glint in her honey brown eyes. *God, she's beautiful.* "And now, I'm a grown-up, and I feel like a teenager with the most insane crush, and we're about to go to prom or something."

Dosie rubbed her pearl necklace as if it might produce a genie, as if she could wish them somewhere far away should things prove too awkward to endure. "I have no idea what that feels like."

"Me neither," Jennifer said. "I never went to prom." She snickered, feeling like an airhead, and that was all it took for them to lose themselves again. They laughed hard enough to make themselves cry before the creak of a door opening drew their attention to the house.

"Jennifer," Carine called as she stepped onto the ornate porch in a sapphire pantsuit and a flour-spotted apron. She propped her hands on her hips and wore an unexpected bright smile on her face. "What is so hysterical out here?"

Well, Jennifer thought and took a breath, *I guess we're really doing this.* She looked at Dosie again. "Ready?" When she nodded, Jennifer led them to the porch and up. "Hi."

"Hello again," Carine said and reached for Jennifer's cheek, pulled her in to kiss one and then the other. "Who is this?"

Jennifer suddenly felt like she didn't know what to do with herself. She was awkward and excited, and her top lip was sweating. *Oh, get over yourself.* "Right," she said and drew Dosie closer. "Tante Carine, this is Theodosia Fisher. She's..." She didn't know why, but suddenly, the word girlfriend felt wrong, as if, for this occasion at least, it wasn't enough. "...my love."

Dosie looked at her as if she'd just made the stars visible in the middle of the day. Face splotched with heat, she turned back to Carine with a silly, girly smile that made Jennifer's heart race. "Hi," she said with a small wave. "You can call me Dosie. It's so, so nice to meet you."

Carine seemed frozen, temporarily struck silent by the lot of it, and Jennifer couldn't blame her. Nothing like this had ever happened before, and Jennifer was likely the last person she ever expected to fall in love. Jennifer was the last person *Jennifer* ever expected to fall in love. Naturally, the moment called for a bit of shock.

"And you," Carine finally managed.

"I hope it's okay," Jennifer said, squeezing Dosie's hand, "that I brought someone home with me."

There was something immense in the way her aunt looked at her then, as if Jennifer had just given her a gift of great value. Her eyes glossed with tears that she quickly blinked away. "Bien sûr," she said, thin as a whisper, then smiled and began ushering them both toward the door. "Of course. Come in. Come in, both of you."

As they passed through the door, Carine took hold of Jennifer's forearm. It was a brief touch, a barely felt pulse of her hand, but it seemed like an entire conversation. It felt like a new beginning.

Carine Dupont's old home was beautiful and filled to the brim with things. It smelled like oven-fresh bread and melted butter and warm, gooey chocolate no matter the room Dosie wandered into. Or perhaps that was the hot, half-eaten chocolate croissant in her hand. Every bite melted in her mouth and sent her eyes rolling back.

Currently, she occupied a small room that looked to be the place where Carine preferred to read. There were book stacks and loaded shelves, little art pieces and scattered candles, and plants wherever they fit under small, halo-like grow lights. An oversized, cushy armchair filled one corner of the room with a table at its side where Dosie spied a glass jar of cookies that seemed to call her name the longer she looked at it. Could a cookie be the perfect companion to a croissant?

"Snooping?"

Dosie jumped and spun around, found Jennifer fresh from the bathroom, leaning against the door frame like some kind of frizzy-braided winter goddess. "Oh my God, Jen," she said, "I don't think we can ever leave here."

"What?" Jennifer sauntered forward and took Dosie's hand, bit the top off her croissant to even out the last bite. "Why?" Then she started chewing and closed her eyes, *mmm'd* until Dosie giggled.

"That's why," she said. "Your aunt keeps giving me warm bread. I think I love her."

Jennifer took another bite before she'd even swallowed the first. "Where is she?"

"Kitchen. She had to take something out of the oven and box something else up."

Jennifer nodded and tapped the small remaining tip of the croissant. "She sells all this stuff. Bread and pastries and what-not." She licked her lips and kissed Dosie's cheek. "You okay? Having a good time so far?"

Dosie felt high. On sugar. On carbs. On love. "I'm having the best time," she said. "Your aunt looks just like you." She had taken one look at the woman and seen all the little ways that she and Jennifer matched. Their faces wrinkled in the same places, though Carine's were pronounced, and they had the same strong jaw and sharp cheekbones. The same dark, wild hair. "Or you look like her, I guess."

"She and my father favored each other," Jennifer said. "And everyone always said I looked like him."

"What about your sister?" Dosie asked and glanced around, scoping for photographs. She saw none in the room. "Does your aunt have any pictures?"

"Mm, come on," Jennifer said and took her hand, led her out of the room.

Down a short hallway, in a wee alcove that seemed to punctuate the corridor, an antique wooden display cabinet stood on gold cabriole legs. Jennifer carefully opened its old French-style doors to reveal a collection of framed photographs and various trinkets that Dosie couldn't begin to guess the value of, sentimental or otherwise.

Her eyes found the picture the moment Jennifer touched it and brought it out of the cabinet.

"Here," she said and handed it over, an image of two teenage girls outside on a sunny day. One leaned against the base of a large tree trunk, arms crossed over her chest and dark hair hanging freely as she stared up into the thick branches above. Jennifer. Dosie was sure. She looked the same, even in profile, only much younger and a touch fuller in the face. Which meant, Dosie realized, that the other girl, the one sitting in the u-bend of the fat bough above Jennifer's head, had to be Lauren.

She favored Jennifer, too, though not as much as Dosie had expected her to for some reason. She had the same high cheekbones and blue eyes, bright in the photograph's natural light, but her hair was much lighter, almost a dark blonde, and only about chin-length. She wasn't as lean and tall as Jennifer but clearly wasn't short. Her long legs dangled from the branch until her feet were nearly level with Jennifer's head. Unlike Jennifer's, Lauren's smile was toothy and undiluted, almost goofy, and infectious even in still form.

"I hated those jeans," Jennifer said, and Dosie blinked and blurted a laugh.

"Whose jeans? Yours or hers?"

"How dare you?" Jennifer said, looking offended. "Obviously hers."

"Right." Dosie snickered. "I knew that."

Jennifer eased herself around Dosie and encompassed her, arms looping her waist, chest warming to her back. She set her chin atop Dosie's shoulder and gazed down at the photograph alongside her. "I forgot she used to smile that way," she said, voice gentle and awed. "She hardly smiled at all toward the end."

Dosie lay a hand over the arms ringing her waist. "Let's think of her like this then."

"I'm sorry I haven't shown you a picture of her before," Jennifer said. "I'm ashamed to say I never even thought to. I rarely look at pictures of her myself."

"Time goes on," Dosie said with a small shrug that bounced Jennifer's chin. "Life does. Things get pulled into the shuffle. You know?"

Jennifer hummed her agreement as Dosie returned the picture to the cabinet and pointed at another. It showed a man seated on the floor in front of a Christmas tree. He had a short black beard and matching hair that stuck up on one side as if he'd just crawled out of bed. A little girl, no more than three or four, sat beside him with her mouth stretched open in surprise. In front of them, from an open present, the man held up a purple T-shirt with white text printed across the front: Best Big Sister.

"Your sister got you for a present," Dosie said, and Jennifer chuckled beside her ear.

"Whether she wanted me or not."

"I'm sure she did. Your dad was handsome."

"Yeah. If only he didn't wear so many turtlenecks."

Dosie smiled at Jennifer's teasing, at her tranquility. She'd expected, had even prepared herself for, nerves and tension, perhaps even a little heartache. But it hadn't been that way at all. For a night, at least, they'd been able to step into Jennifer's past without it pinching her into her old, ill-fitted shapes and were simply observing, in idle bliss, the things that had never given her cause to hurt.

"I can definitely see the resemblance."

Jennifer's voice turned playful at her ear. "Are you calling me handsome, Ms. Fisher?"

"You know you're handsome."

"Yes, but it's nice to be told."

Dosie crooked her neck to kiss Jennifer's cheek. "You are very handsome," she murmured into the kiss and felt aflutter at the sweet little grin it earned her. "And beautiful. And sexy. And adorable."

"Okay, okay, rein it in," Jennifer laughed and turned Dosie's attention back to the cabinet by grabbing one of the frames. She pointed to the edge of the photograph where Dosie saw a blurry partial outline of a woman from behind. Nothing much about her was distinguishable besides the light brown shade of her long, curly hair, and she was so smeared across the edge of the picture that it seemed she'd been running from the shot in the moment that it was taken. "My mom."

"What?" Dosie gaped at it. "That's it?"

Jennifer seemed amused, smiling as she mindlessly rocked them from side to side. "Yeah, she hated having her picture taken and never let anyone put them on display. It drove my dad nuts."

"Was she shy?"

"Oh, brutally, yes. I'm sure she's who I got it from."

"I still can't imagine you like that."

"Good," Jennifer teased. "Stop trying." She sighed and held Dosie a bit tighter. "That's part of it for me, too, you know. What you said in the cemetery about your old self not being who you are anymore."

"Yeah?" Dosie told her swelling heart to deflate and relax. She told her lips to stay even and her feet not to bounce. Anytime Jennifer opened up to her and really talked about how she was feeling, it made her feel like a soda bottle someone had shaken up. She had to keep a lid on herself, so she wouldn't spew her bubbling excitement and send Jennifer scurrying off in a panic like a spooked rabbit in the woods. "Tell me what you mean."

Jennifer continued their gentle swaying, quiet for a moment. "I would love to have my sister in my life again, my parents, too, but part of me thinks if I could go back and change things, fix things.... I don't know. If things had played out differently, would I even be this person that I am now? Or would I still be how I was? Because that isn't me. I like who I am now. I love my life. I love *you*, Dosie. And I don't think I ever would have met you if things hadn't happened as they did."

Dosie turned in Jennifer's strong hold, overwhelmed with the feeling of being so completely understood. She wrapped her arms around her neck and buried her face in the hollow, breathed in Jennifer's scent, and felt at home standing in a stranger's hallway.

"Are we terrible people?" she whispered, only half-serious, and Jennifer blew a long, slow raspberry between her lips.

"Probably," she said, making Dosie shake with laughter. "Who fucking knows?"

A throat gently clearing called their attention to the end of the hall. Carine stood watching them, a small smirk on her lips. She opened her mouth and spoke, and Dosie blinked as if someone had suddenly started flicking the lights off and on. Or the sound. The understanding? Carine's words were like a song Dosie didn't know the lyrics to. The only thing she did know was that the song was in French.

As they slinked from their tight embrace, Jennifer said, "Yes, please," as if the song made perfect sense to her, and Dosie's head spun a bit. "This one never says no to more sweets."

"You speak French?!"

"Spoke, more like. I can't even remember the last time."

"She once spoke it beautifully," Carine said and motioned for them to follow her back to the kitchen where there were supposedly more sweets waiting. God, Dosie loved this magical place. "But she apparently has no cause to practice while whipping men into retirement."

"Not just men," Jennifer said and winked Dosie's way.

That one little look made Dosie's whole face feel hot. She fanned it quickly and mouthed for Jennifer to behave herself, knowing she never would. "So, what sweet thing are we having?" she asked and saw her girlfriend's expression turn downright devilish.

Jennifer said nothing as her eyes turned blue fire and burned a hole through Dosie's face. Her wicked grin sat subtle and sexy at one corner of her mouth as she smoothed down the front of her shirt then turned her eyes ahead, toward the last few steps to the kitchen. *Dear Father in Heaven, have mercy on your sinful child, for I am weak and —Oh, get a grip!* Dosie blew an exasperated breath at herself and then shoved her girlfriend just hard enough to make her miss the kitchen door. As Jennifer tumbled into the other room, laughing, Dosie followed Carine to the kitchen counter and the incredible scents of yeast and citrus and cinnamon.

The day passed into night around the large kitchen island. Its surface sat covered in pastries and a few chocolates, a small variety of cheeses, and an old wooden version of Scrabble that they played as they chatted. As it turned out, Dosie was quite good at Scrabble, and Carine was a talker, though if Jennifer's bewildered expression every time the woman launched into a new story was anything to go by, that particular trait was new.

She told Dosie a few stories about growing up in Toulouse, one which featured Jennifer as a toddler getting altitude sickness at a ski resort. Dosie learned that Carine had a degree in architecture but hated it and preferred baking and that Jennifer had a brief blonde phase in high school that made her look like a completely different person. The latter came with photo proof that Jennifer bid Carine burn like a sacrifice. She refused, of course.

Carine talked about Jennifer's father, Henri: his two left feet and his knack for strategy games and his perpetual good mood. She told Dosie about Jennifer's childhood fear of the tooth fairy, which Jennifer swore she couldn't remember, and about the time Lauren's appendix ruptured when she was just seven years old, and Carine was fresh off the plane from France. She'd gone straight from the airport to the hospital and stayed there, luggage and all, until the surgery was finished.

The more Carine spoke, the more similarities Dosie noticed. Like Jennifer, Carine preferred more subtle smiles and body language. She wasn't over-animated with her hands when she spoke like Dosie could sometimes be, and she often said more with her eyes and her expression than she did with words. Dosie wondered if she was like Jennifer in other ways too. Icky about feelings. Quick to create walls. After all, she'd had the same losses, different but the same. Dosie wondered if she carried her grief the way Jennifer did, not like a weight on her back but like a chain around her heart. Any time it swelled, when she became a bit too happy, a little too attached, such pain.

The night went on without a hitch, all easy conversation and scattered laughter and too many snacks, and as it wound toward its end, Jennifer seemed to become more and more aware of her. Dosie felt her eyes on her, and her skin prickled every time she looked up to find her staring. Then Jennifer would glance away, a smile teasing, and carry on some conversation, like she was oblivious to the havoc she was wreaking on Dosie's system. She wasn't. She never had been.

When they finally shuffled to the foyer and back out into the cold, Carine kissed each of Dosie's cheeks and thanked her for visiting. She squeezed Jennifer's arm in place of a hug, something Jennifer often did herself, and said, "This has been a treat for me." She briefly cupped Jennifer's cheek, swiping her thumb as if to wipe away some nonexistent spot of something, then let her hand drift back to her side. "You're happy."

Dosie felt ten feet tall when Jennifer looked at her as if she was the reason and said, "Yes, I am."

In the muggy warmth of Ned's backseat, with the road thrumming beneath her feet and the radio playing wordless piano, Dosie's hand resting easily on her thigh, Jennifer felt more relaxed than she had in years. She was near meditative and high on the feeling, not an ounce of tension pulling or stressing or tearing her apart. When the sun rose tomorrow, all that had ebbed would come rushing back, but she could deal with it then. For the moment, she was loose and happy and a little head over heels, and she wasn't going to waste it.

She couldn't stop staring at Dosie's hand on her thigh, skinny fingers massaging every so often. At Dosie's slender neck, pale against the raw cinnamon splash of her hair, as she stared out the window at the passing cars and night. At the slope of her cheek and the curve of her soft jaw and the one little freckle she had at the edge of her hairline. Jennifer couldn't stop staring at Dosie, because everything about the girl made her feel hot and effervescent. And safe. And wide awake. And terrified. And *free*. She couldn't stop staring, because she had never wanted anyone or anything the way she wanted Dosie Fisher, and it was as true then as it had been the first time she realized it some six months before.

What a fucking feeling, she thought, a little breathless, a little intoxicated. The latter could have been the wine she consumed at her aunt's house. *No, it's her*. She drank in every inch of the woman beside her again. *It's always her*. Jennifer's body felt like a lightning storm.

An idea struck as they entered the city. "Ned, would you mind making a stop along the way?"

"Not at all," he said. "Where to?"

Jennifer gave him a quick and simple set of directions and hoped it would lead them to a still functioning business. She hadn't been since she last lived in Massachusetts, and a lot could change when counting in decades rather than days. Businesses came and went.

Dosie's eyes found her. Her usual honey brown irises appeared black in the dark backseat with the city and the night pulsing by the window behind her. "Where are we going?"

"Wouldn't you like to know?" Jennifer softly teased and watched Dosie's eyes drop to her lips. It sent a ripple of energy crackling across her lower back.

In what felt like no time, the car slowed to a crawl outside a concrete building with two display windows featuring scantily clad mannequins. One wore a pair of assless leather underwear and another a ball gag, awkwardly sitting atop the closed plastic mouth. The third mannequin had on a naughty policeman's uniform with aviator sunglasses and held a bright red flogger as if ready to use it.

Jennifer watched Dosie gape out the window at the displays and the bright neon sign of a jewel-encrusted chest branded with the words The Treasure Trove. Her wide eyes jumped to Jennifer. "Is this a—"

"Yes," Jennifer said before she could speak the words and blush herself into a dead faint. She chuckled at Dosie's visible relief. "I'll just be a moment."

"What? You're leaving me out here?"

"Darling, if I hope to make it through the door, yes."

Dosie chewed her bottom lip and freed a nervous laugh. "Yeah. Okay. Good idea." She stacked her hands in her lap and fiddled with her fingers. "I'll just be here then."

Jennifer tamed her smile as she patted Dosie's knee then stepped out of the car. She imagined Dosie watching the sway of her ass as she walked away from the car toward the building and added a little extra for her benefit. It was the least she could do. With her back to Dosie, Jennifer let her smile widen until it felt unhinged, and a devious little laugh slithered across her lips. Leaving the two the way she had was diabolical, she knew. Poor Ned, no doubt trying desperately to mind his own business, and Dosie, Jennifer's sweet and innocent love, stuck in the backseat avoiding his eyes, mortified and nervous and, more than likely, a little turned on.

"God, I'm terrible," she said gleefully and opened the Treasure Trove's door.

She made quick work of her shopping. After years of trials with countless sex toys, Jennifer knew both what she preferred and what would work best for her particular purposes. She also knew her girl-friend's body and her pleasure like she knew her own, and she was sure Dosie would find her choice satisfactory.

Jennifer swiped her credit card and was handed her purchase in a black velvet bag with glittery red lettering on the side. *Get your Treasure at the Trove,* it read, glinting under the sporadic lights overhead as she walked back through the parking lot. Inside the car, silence was like a cloak choking the air. Jennifer, mischievous to her core, settled in as if returning from a more respectable place, one that didn't have silicone dicks in its windows, and placed the little black bag between her thigh and Dosie's. And she didn't say a single word about it.

"Thank you, Ned. We can go on to the hotel now."

The car wobbled as the gear was shifted, and then they lurched into motion again, and Jennifer relaxed into her seat. Beside her, to her amusement, sat the opposite of relaxed. Wide, dark eyes flicked from the velvet bag to Jennifer's face and back again as Dosie pinned her hands between her knees and gnawed on her bottom lip as if she could mine it for nutrients with her teeth.

"What'd you get?" she finally asked, and Jennifer raised an eyebrow in challenge.

"Wouldn't you like to know?" she said again, and their eyes locked hard. The silence stretched and grew taut. Tighter and tighter until the look between them felt as if it might trigger an explosion if one of them were to glance away or move too quickly.

Dosie risked it, letting loose a slow breath as her hand slid over her pearl necklace and brought it to her mouth. She rubbed it over her lips once, twice. "Fine," she said as a shy, sexy smile touched her lips and turned away to put her attention out the window again. Jennifer watched her thighs squeeze together as if to soothe an ache and felt like she was on top of the world.

"Oh." Dosie's neck reddened as she pulled the simple harness and dildo that Jennifer had selected from the bag. The red crept up over her jawline and painted her cheeks the way it always did when she was quickly overwhelmed.

"Oh?" Jennifer stood leaning against the wall only a few feet away. She watched Dosie's hand curl around the dildo's lightly curved shaft and felt a little spark between her legs as if the thing was attached. *Fuck,* she was excited. "Good 'oh' or bad 'oh'?"

Dosie looked up from her place on the couch, and her mouth hung open a bit. "Huh?" she said, and Jennifer couldn't help laughing.

She crossed to the couch and sat, took the dildo from Dosie's grip.

"I was hoping we could try again," she said as she set it aside and refilled Dosie's hands with her own.

They hadn't had sex with a strap-on since the first time. Jennifer still sometimes felt a bit sick at the thought, when the memory crept into her mind, and she could see Dosie underneath her as if it was happening all over again. Her tear-filled, vacant eyes staring up at nothing. Her frozen body. Her wordless mouth hanging open.

It took a while for Dosie to finally tell her what the trigger was, both difficult for her to say and for Jennifer to hear. But knowledge was power. It gave Jennifer the power to avoid and to protect and to pleasure without turning that pleasure into pain.

"I don't want that first time to be the one that lives in our heads," Jennifer said and rubbed Dosie's sweaty palms. "And I don't want it to scare us away from this kind of sex any more than it already has, because I know how pleasurable it has the potential to be for you, for both of us, if we get it right."

Dosie's back bowed forward, and she exhaled in a loud huff, laughing at herself. "I'm going to melt," she said and brought one of Jennifer's hands to her throat where the skin was hot to the touch. Then she pulled Jennifer in by her open shirt and pressed their foreheads together. "What if it happens again?"

Jennifer had asked herself the same question for months, every time she thought about strapping on for Dosie. Every time, she chose not to. She never even brought it up. But then she realized something. It could happen anyway. Dosie didn't even know she had that trigger until Jennifer had already pulled it, which meant there was no way around it, and that could happen any time with anything, not just sex. They could avoid where appropriate, and they did, but they couldn't live their lives not doing the things they wanted to do just in case something bad happened when they did them. Could they? Hadn't Jennifer been learning that lesson for the last year, since the moment she'd taken that booking and stepped onto that old Victorian porch, met the pretty girl with the honey eyes and the pearls? She'd spent her life avoiding connection to protect herself, terrified of love just because it could end. And then Dosie. Now Dosie. Always Dosie.

"Then it happens," Jennifer said, "and we will deal with it, and it will be okay." She made slow circles over Dosie's lower back, enjoying the odd static from her sweater with every other swipe. "Tonight feels, has felt, good. It's been healing, I think, for me."

Dosie's hand found Jennifer's shoulder then her neck, then it slid into the loose body of her braid and cradled the back of her head. "I saw that," she whispered. "I see it."

"I want us to heal this, too. I want to make a better memory, and I want you to feel as good as I do right now. I want you to...." She shrugged, unable to find the words. "I just want you, Dosie." She sat back and looked at her love. The red in her skin was retreating, ebbing like a tide, but her eyes were still as hot as a hearth, staring right back at her. "And I want this. But there's no pressure. If you don't want to, that's okay, or if you don't want to have sex at all tonight, then that's—"

"I do," Dosie blurted, surprising her, and turned the conversation into a kiss. A second later, she was in Jennifer's lap, straddling her hips. "I really do."

"Mmm." Jennifer licked the taste of her off her lips and dipped back in for more. "You know what eagerness does to me."

Dosie's hands shot to Jennifer's buttons. She fiddled open the collar of her shirt then made her way down in quick succession. "You know what healthy communication does to me."

Jennifer snorted and said, "Fuck's sake," as she was sucked into another kiss and Dosie's hands spilled into her open shirt and across her belly like warm water. Her own hands disappeared under Dosie's sweater and splayed across her hot lower back. "God, you feel good."

"*You* feel good," Dosie said and wriggled her fingers under Jennifer's bra. Her sweaty palm swiped over one nipple, and Jennifer drew a sharp breath that made Dosie moan and rock her hips forward. The crotch of her pants wrinkled against Jennifer's belt buckle. "Should we go to the bed?"

Jennifer kissed up the length of Dosie's throat. "Not until you tell me what you want," she rasped and felt a tremor shake through Dosie's body. She raked her hands up Dosie's sides, dragging her sweater in the process until it urged Dosie's arms up, and then the garment was on the floor. "Do you want my fingers inside you, Dosie?" With a quick pinch between forefinger and thumb, Jennifer unclasped Dosie's bra with one hand while the other drew a strap down Dosie's arm. "My tongue?"

Dosie moaned and bucked her hips again. "*Jen.*"

"Hm? Tell me, love," Jennifer said and sucked Dosie's pulse as she pulled the second strap free and dropped Dosie's bra on top of her sweater. "Do you want me to lie down, so you can ride my face?" She yanked viciously at the button on Dosie's pants and sucked the tender spot below her ear. The zipper groaned in the breathy quiet. "Or my cock?"

Sound gurgled in Dosie's throat, then a rush of breath. "Yes," she said as she collapsed against Jennifer's chest like her body had gone liquid.

"Yes, what?" Jennifer buzzed with the sensation of Dosie's naked flesh under her fingertips. Her hands danced in opposite directions. One knuckled up Dosie's spine to fist in her hair while the other skated to her loose waistband, fingers splayed, one dipping into the top of her ass crack. "Which one?"

"All of it," Dosie said, voice bordering on a whine as she pushed Jennifer's shirt off her shoulder and sucked the newly exposed skin. "I want everything." She kissed her way back up Jennifer's throat and over her jaw, sucked her bottom lip and pulled until it hurt. "God, Jennifer, I want everything with you."

Fuck. Jennifer moaned into Dosie's kiss. *It's yours.* Her nipples hardened until they tingled, and every muscle in her abdomen grew taut. Her thighs flexed and twitched under Dosie's perfect ass. "Let's go to bed," she whispered. *I'm yours.*

Oxygen ceased to exist when Jennifer stepped out of the bathroom with nothing on but her new appendage and a small bottle of lubricant in hand. Dosie sat naked on the bed, soaking a wet spot into a towel Jennifer had thrown at her after she stripped off Dosie's pants, spread her open like a flower, and licked her until she leaked. Jennifer sauntered toward her, and the appendage bobbed with every step. It was flesh-toned, only a little darker than Jennifer's skin, and curved proudly toward the sky. Dosie imagined it sliding inside her, Jennifer's hips pushing it deeper until their bodies met like two puzzle pieces snapping into place. The thought made her mouth dry.

Jennifer was stunning as she crawled up the bed on her hands and knees, her braid destroyed in favor of chaos and her lips set in a confident smile. "Nervous?" she asked as she nudged Dosie onto her back and lay herself over her, let the weight of her new addition fall upon Dosie's thigh.

Dosie shuddered, breath returning in a gasp, as Jennifer kissed her deep and shifted her hips so that the swollen head of the dildo prodded Dosie's vulva. "No." She looked into Jennifer's eyes, two indigo haloes around dilated black. "I'm excited."

"Good." With catlike grace, Jennifer eased off her again and sat back on her knees. "That's what I love to hear." She popped open the little bottle in her hand, squeezed a generous drop onto the tip of her middle finger, then capped it again and tossed it aside. Slowly, she drew a wet circle around the tip of her appendage, and suddenly, as if bewitched, Dosie couldn't look away.

She had not been prepared for how sensually Jennifer Dupont could lubricate a silicone cock. Her vagina, throbbing with her pulse, flexed around nothing as she watched Jennifer go from one circling finger to a gripping palm sliding the length of her shaft. Dosie felt Jennifer's eyes on her like a hot spotlight as she languidly stroked and pumped herself for the benefit of show, every inch of the dildo long since lubricated.

"Touch me," she said, and Dosie knew what she meant. Touch *it*. She wanted to. When her fingertips slid over the head, Jennifer closed her eyes and moaned as if it was her actual flesh, and Dosie's excitement compounded. Jennifer took Dosie's hand and molded it around her girth in a tight cuff. "Feel how hard you make me?"

"Oh my God." The words stuttered out of Dosie's mouth, guttural and intoxicated. She *wanted*, so much, so intensely, that it made her feel dizzy. The room hazed as Jennifer kissed her and pumped into her hand as if about to come, and Dosie's want turned to an all-consuming need. "Jen, I'm ready."

Jennifer's fingers slid through and spread her labia, sank smoothly into her vagina then right back out again. "Yes you are," she said, and the brief tease made Dosie shake for more. "Come here." She shifted to Dosie's side to sit herself up against the headboard and urged Dosie into her lap. "I want you to try being on top. It can be a lot at first, but once you're comfortable, it might help you feel more in control."

Dosie straddled her, and Jennifer's glistening length pressed against her pelvis, the tip poking up toward her bellybutton. Her breath left her in a slow tremble as she lifted herself up on Jennifer's command and let her slide the bulbous tip of the dildo along her sex. When it pushed into her opening, Dosie gasped. The thick, unyielding head met the resistance of muscle and stalled, burning, but then it slid right past, raking along the ridged flesh of her upper wall, and sent Dosie's eyes rolling back in her head. She sank halfway down then retreated again. Three-quarters then retreat. She took the entirety on her next downward thrust and shocked herself into stillness.

"Take a moment," Jennifer said and held her there, hands gripping her hips. "Breathe, and let yourself adjust."

Dosie held onto Jennifer's shoulders like the wall around a skate rink. She had never had sex in this position with anything bigger than Jennifer's fingers inside her, which were long but not six inches long and another full inch around. "It feels like a lot," she said through gritted teeth. "It's too much."

"Hold on," Jennifer said and adjusted her hips until the angle inside shifted, and the intense pressure eased. "How's that?"

As if triggered by the change, Dosie's hips jerked, and pleasure zinged through her. "*Oh*," she moaned and did it again.

"That's it," Jennifer said, and Dosie could hear the excitement in her voice. It fed her own. Jennifer dug her fingers in, pads leaving prints in Dosie's hips, and began to guide her into a lazy rhythm. "Better? Does it feel good?"

"Yes." Suddenly, that word wasn't enough, but it was all she had. "*Yes*."

"Good," Jennifer said. "Now, take control, and fuck me."

A whine left her unbidden as Jennifer's words alone brought Dosie halfway to orgasm. Her body took the command and ran with it, heedless of her thoughts or nerves or fears, and changed the rhythm instinctually. It started slow, a gentle forward and back as her knees pushed into the bed and her thighs squeezed Jennifer's hips. Then faster as Jennifer began to work on the rest of her, kissing whatever bare, sweat-slicked flesh passed in front of her face. She sucked Dosie's collarbone and her pulse, her bottom lip and her earlobe and the hard, bumpy peaks of her nipples. She dropped a hand between Dosie's thighs and tugged and massaged her pubic hair, pressed her thumb to clit and moaned when Dosie shouted and thrust forward.

"Oh God," Dosie groaned and increased her pace again. Somehow, what had only just been too much now barely felt like enough as she ground herself down to pull Jennifer in as deep as she could get her. She slung her arms around Jennifer's shoulders and back and pulled her as close as she could so that their breasts smashed together and the barest of gaps existed between their bellies. "Oh, *God*, Jen." They didn't kiss, instead panting into one another's mouths as Dosie thrust with abandon and pressed her forehead so hard against Jennifer's that she was sure there would be a red mark later. "Does it feel good for you? Can you feel it?"

"Yes, baby, it feels so fucking good," Jennifer said and slid her hands under Dosie's ass and thighs. "I love being so deep inside you."

Dosie's breath stuttered across her lips. She felt on fire as she whispered, "I want you to come."

Jennifer let loose a raspy laugh, and just like that, Dosie was a breath from orgasm. Or a dead faint. Were bodies meant to experience this much pleasure? Surely, it was a health hazard. "Already?"

God, can this woman be any sexier? It wasn't fair. Jennifer was so hot that it almost hurt Dosie's feelings. Or something. Some part of her body was definitely aching. Her pleasure had grown so immense as she barreled toward climax that it nearly passed for pain.

With a burst of courage and need, Dosie roughly pinched one of Jennifer's nipples and said, "Who's in charge?"

She felt her face go red, but her pussy gushed around Jennifer's firm length when a full-body moan tore from her lover's throat as if exorcised. Jennifer's forehead drunkenly dropped to Dosie's collarbone, and her arms tightened around Dosie's waist. Her hips began a merciless upward thrusting to meet Dosie's downward tilt, and her hands, still gripping Dosie's ass began to lift her over and over so that her cock pulled out an inch and sank back in with each thrust.

"Jen, please, I want you to--

"Fuck!" Jennifer shouted as her eyes shut and her mouth shot open. Her body went still and rigid and her grip grew punishing. "*Fuck*, I'm coming."

Dosie's heart felt like an abused drum. Her pulse hammered in her ears and between her legs as she slammed her hips down hard and rode Jennifer's orgasm right into her own. Her vagina squeezed around Jennifer's girth like a vise, and Dosie cried her pleasure until her voice cracked and fell apart, and every last little tremor had run its course from head to heel.

Oh, wow. Dosie felt drunk as all the tension left her body, and she and Jennifer melted against one another. *Wow. Wow. Wow.* A puddle of quivering breath and shaky hands, they sat in the thick-aired silence and held each other. An incredible feeling swelled inside Dosie. She knew what it was, had felt it over and over every minute since she first let it in. Love. Its immensity still stunned her.

The urge to laugh or cry struck. She wasn't sure which, but she held them both and let herself float serenely in her lover's pleasure-drunk gaze and loose arms, the full of Jennifer still buried between her legs.

A chill fell over Dosie's skin as the calm set in. Her knees began to ache. Her thighs trembled as she carefully lifted herself up and watched the dildo slide out of her still throbbing vagina with a wet sound that Dosie found almost maddeningly erotic. She settled into the cool space beside Jennifer and stretched her legs out, grabbed her cup of water from the bedside table. She drank greedily as Jennifer watched.

"You are so fucking sexy," she whispered, and Dosie's nerves jumped as if they hadn't just strained and twitched and flickered to their death. How it was possible that Jennifer could reanimate her over and over and over no matter how spent she was, she didn't know, but she loved it. "You make me so hot."

"Stop," Dosie said and grinned around the rim of her cup. "You're making *me* hot, and I don't think I can do it again."

"No?" Jennifer asked with a soft little pout to her bottom lip. She took the water Dosie offered and drank it, then set the cup aside again. "Are you sure?" She held Dosie's gaze as her hand curled around her slick shaft, still standing proudly between her legs, and let her eyes flutter as she squeezed it. Her thumb ran a ring around the base of the prominent head where a milky white film had collected. Jennifer held up her thumb, the evidence of Dosie's pleasure coating the tip. "But you enjoyed it so much." Then she stuck that thumb in her mouth and sucked Dosie's orgasm off her skin like a bit of jam that had fallen off her spoon.

"Well," Dosie squeaked, throat suddenly dry as a desert.

"Well," Jennifer repeated, already rolling atop her, hands braced on both sides of her shoulders and a cocky little grin set across her perfect lips.

"I suppose I could give it another go," Dosie said, and Jennifer's grin became an honest-to-God giggle that ignited Dosie's soul like a holiday light display. She pulled her in and tasted her joy and gave herself over to more and more. More pleasure. More love. More Jennifer. More everything. She deserved some abundance. They both did.

The gibbous moon sat high in the sky outside the window as the night neared its peak. Jennifer's back was sore from sitting for too long, and her eyes were sticky from overuse. Her own handwriting appeared like a foreign script to her after writing, scribbling, scratching out, and re-writing a dozen times over.

The sound of soft footsteps over carpet reached her just a moment before two soft hands appeared, slinking down her chest from behind. Jennifer hummed a note of approval as Dosie leaned over the back of the couch and kissed her cheek. "Hi."

"Hi," Dosie said through a yawn then let her chin rest on Jennifer's shoulder. "Waking up to an empty bed is a lot less fun than it used to be."

Jennifer chuckled and lay her temple against Dosie's. "You're telling me."

"How's it going?" She rubbed the space over Jennifer's heart. "It's been a few hours since you got up."

"Has it?" Jennifer knuckled her eyes and reached for her phone to check the time. Almost midnight. *Fuck.* "I didn't realize it was so late. I'm sorry, love."

"Don't be," Dosie said. "Can I help with anything?"

"No," Jennifer sighed. "I don't know."

"Do you want to talk about it, or do you want to be alone some more?"

"Come with me tomorrow."

"Really? To the hearing?"

Jennifer moved all her papers and notes and patted the cushion beside her. Instead of walking around, Dosie rolled herself over the

Corrie MacKay

back of the couch and into place. "Are you sure that's what you want?" she asked. "And you're not just tired and high on sex still?"

"I'm sure," Jennifer said and pulled Dosie onto her chest, wrapped in her arms. "I've been trying to think of the perfect thing to say at the hearing, the perfect way to express the impact his actions have had on my life, and I *wanted* to find a way to approach it so that I could, I don't know, keep my power, I guess."

"What do you mean?"

Jennifer pushed a hand through her hair and blew a heavy breath. "I wanted to feel superior to him, and I think I convinced myself that in order to do that, I needed him not to see me. I needed to appear unbothered and unemotional, because the idea of giving him any little bit of vulnerability felt...."

"Like a violation," Dosie whispered.

Jennifer closed her eyes, momentarily overwhelmed with the way Dosie always understood her, even with the most minimal explanation. Or none at all. "Yeah," she breathed as her eyes began to sting. "When I think about what happened, when I let myself remember, I feel like I can't breathe. Like I can't move. Like I don't know how to work my own body anymore. And I realized, *that's* the way it's supposed to be. How can I stand up there and be unbothered by my sister's murder just because I'm afraid to show how much it hurts me?"

Dosie said nothing, but her continued slow-rubbing hand over Jennifer's heart told her she was still listening.

"I've been telling myself that I have to be brave, but I realized, over the last few days, that I always feel bravest when I'm with you. No armor. No mask. No persona to hide behind and embolden me. Just me being brave enough to let you see and love all of me and to see and love all of you the same."

Dosie took a deep breath through her nose as her hand curled into Jennifer's T-shirt, bunching it under her fist. A sweet smile began to play over her lips, and she quickly turned her face into Jennifer's chest to hide it.

"I don't want to speak tomorrow because I hate Orwell Glass," Jennifer said. "I want to speak because I loved my sister, and her life mattered. It matters. Does that make sense?"

Dosie kissed her chest. "It makes perfect sense."

"I don't know if I'll say everything I've written down." She grabbed her notepad from the table, glanced at it for only a moment. Her words were gibberish to her dry eyes. She tossed the pad back onto the table. "Or any of it."

"You'll say what you need to say."

"I'm a little afraid I'll get up there and turn into a statue, or do something juvenile like flip him off and run."

"Well, that could be a little fun," Dosie teased. "Do you want to practice? Your speech, I mean, not the flipping off. You've got that down, I'm sure."

Jennifer laughed and said, "No, I'm okay. I don't even want to think about it anymore." She drew Dosie closer to her chest, held her tighter. "I just want to be here with you. No more past. No tomorrow. Just us right now, please."

Dosie *mmm'd* and ran her index finger down the bridge of Jennifer's nose. She freed a little sigh. "I love it so much when you talk to me like this."

The gentle stinging returned to Jennifer's eyes, and she blinked it away. "I know." She pressed Dosie's cheek where her dimple would be if she smiled. It appeared, puckering around her thumb when she said, "I'm beginning to see the merit in it."

"I knew you would."

"Will you come with me?"

Dosie leaned up and nuzzled her. "As it happens, I *did* bring a pretty dress."

Jennifer's heart flitted about her chest. "As it happens, hm?"

"Just in case," Dosie said and snuggled herself back into place.

"You're a good girlfriend," Jennifer said, laughing when Dosie squeezed her until she grunted.

"So are you."

Jennifer raked Dosie's hair back and played with the edge of her ear. She let herself relax into the feeling those words gave her. Aflutter and afloat, disappearing into the starless sky. "I'm glad. It's my first time, you know."

"Jen? You're a good sister, too," Dosie whispered unexpectedly, and the stinging returned in a mad rush. Tears flooded Jennifer's lashes. "Nothing that happens tomorrow will change that."

Jennifer squeezed Dosie until she was sure it hurt a bit, but Dosie didn't complain. She let herself be held and gave back as good as she got and asked, "Do you believe me?"

I want to. "I'm trying." *I will.*

12

Theodosia Fisher may as well have been the name of a classic movie star, as Dosie appeared to have just stepped off a screen. She wore a royal blue long-sleeved pleated swing dress with a notched lapel and round-toe baby doll heels in pearl white to match her necklace. Her red hair lay in lustrous waves around her neck but was pulled back from her face and secured in a single swooping victory roll that somehow made her appear both older and more darling. A carmine lip added a pop of color to her otherwise subtle makeup. She stepped into the room with a whisper of a smile and crossed to Jennifer's side before the full-length mirror beside the closet.

Jennifer wasn't sure she needed air anymore as she slinked her arm around Dosie's waist and brought her closer. "What an entrance," she murmured into a gentle kiss.

They looked at themselves in the mirror, side by side, Dosie in her pretty dress and Jennifer in a two-piece pinstriped pewter pantsuit with an Egyptian blue cashmere sweater and black Bottega Veneta loafers. She wore her hair back in a French twist that exposed and accentuated the sharp angles of her face, and two small pearl earrings dangled from her ears, courtesy of Dosie's suitcase.

"Well," Dosie said and propped a hand on her hip. She caught Jennifer's gaze in the mirror. "I think we look just dashing, don't you?"

Jennifer eyed them up and down, an incredible energy rolling through her. A sense of rightness. It made her forget she ever had anything to fear or that fear even existed. "I would say, if parole hearings had best-dressed competitions, there would be no competition."

Dosie turned in her arms, stroked her cheek. "How are you feeling? Are you okay?"

"I'm okay."

"Ready?"

Jennifer wanted to laugh. The idea that she could ever be ready for something like this seemed like a joke. "The thought of seeing him again makes me feel sick."

"I know the feeling."

"But I'm okay." *I am.* "Surprisingly." *I can do hard things.*

"It's okay if you aren't, you know," Dosie said as she slung her arms around Jennifer's waist and rocked their bodies in an easy dance. "It's going to go well, I'm sure of it, but it's absolutely okay if it isn't exactly what you imagined. And it's okay if you struggle. It's okay if you cry. It's okay if you panic. Whatever you feel, it's okay. Okay?"

"Okay," Jennifer said and cupped her cheek, "I hate all of those things."

"I know, but it's still okay if they happen."

Jennifer kissed her. "Thank you."

"For what?"

"Everything."

"Oh." Dosie let loose a dreamy sigh and brought Jennifer's hand to her mouth. She planted a short, sweet kiss atop her knuckles and asked, "Are we ready to go then?"

"I believe so," Jennifer said but made no attempt to leave their little bubble of connection. She leaned into the rhythm of their lazy sway. "Breakfast along the way?"

Dosie pulled a face that made Jennifer snort, then she led her by the hand to the door. "Who are you talking to?"

"Any requests then?"

"Can we get French toast?" Dosie asked as she turned to let Jennifer help her into her coat. "I feel like something sweet is a good idea."

"You would say that," Jennifer said and pulled on her own coat. She held out her wrists, and Dosie secured each of her sleeves so that the material beneath wasn't bunched and uncomfortable. "Since you are so very sweet yourself."

She peacocked a bit at Dosie's bright smile and pulled her in by the nape. She needed to kiss her. One last, lingering kiss before they left the blissful little bubble that always formed when it was just the two of them. Then, she would be ready.

Dosie hummed a pleasant note into the kiss and, when it was over, whispered, "Is it just called toast in France?"

The laugh that filled Jennifer's lungs felt like medicine. She let it go, all her anxieties unsticking themselves to go with it. Another feeling took its place. *I can do this.* It wasn't confidence, but it wasn't far off. Jennifer, on some level, might have even called it optimism. *I can do hard things.* She tucked her phone into her pocket and pulled the door open, waved for Dosie to go ahead. "French toast isn't actually French, darling."

"What?!"

The prison atmosphere unnerved. A hard lump formed in Jennifer's throat as she stared out the window at the massive concrete complex ahead. An electrified fence topped with barbed wire surrounded the place and met in two looming guard towers at a secure checkpoint for incoming and outgoing vehicles. The whole effect was bleak. It was exactly what she desired for Inmate #15275-210 and, without question, what she believed he deserved.

"I had no idea they had parole hearings at the actual prisons," Dosie said, and her voice sounded thin, as if she'd suddenly become quite nervous.

Jennifer found her hand atop the seat between them and threaded their fingers together. "Neither did I," she said and glanced to the rearview mirror. To his credit, Ned seemed to be having no reaction. At this point, he had to think they were baiting him to be nosy.

They cleared the entrance without fuss and were given a designated area to park and building to enter. Ned dropped them at the building's front door and left to wait in the lot. As the car pulled away, exhaust clouding in the cold air behind, an eerie chill coursed the length of Jennifer's body. It was happening. They were about to enter a maximum-security prison, and she was going to see him. She was going to stand face-to-face with Orwell Glass more than twenty years after he murdered her sister and finally say all the things she wanted to say, should have said, *needed* to say. *Fuck.* It was happening.

Dosie's hand locked with hers again. She pressed into Jennifer's side and said, "Ready?"

In answer, Jennifer made her feet move, and they walked the last few steps to the door and let themselves inside. A rush of warmth washed over them as the doors suction-sealed behind them again, and they were closed inside a sterile, metal box of a lobby with a secretarial desk on one side and a large set of walk-through metal detectors on the other. Everything from that point seemed to happen in a strangely slow blur.

They checked in at the desk and were directed to the metal detectors. Jennifer set her phone, money clip, and hotel room key in a plastic tray alongside Dosie's small purse, then followed her through the detector. Cleared, they were sent with their belongings and a mammoth-sized corrections officer to an assigned locker and made to leave everything inside, plus the skinny leather belt that Jennifer wore. It was a good thing her pants fit. The belt was just for style.

Their jewelry had to go as well, and the sight of Dosie's bare neck, sans pearls, made Jennifer feel as if she had a knot in her chest, like a breath she couldn't catch or an ache she couldn't stretch around. It wasn't even her armor, yet she felt utterly exposed the moment it was gone.

A foghorn-loud buzzer sounded from somewhere across the complex, and Jennifer's nerves twitched. The fine hairs at the back of her neck stood on end. But the CO had no reaction to the sound, so Jennifer assumed it was normal and told herself to relax. Surely, if a mad man had escaped, there would be at least a modicum of panic to clue them in.

"This way." The CO took them down a short hall and into a small room that looked, remarkably, like a courtroom. "It shouldn't be too long of a wait."

He left them there, standing just inside the doorway, and Jennifer suddenly felt like a child lost in a store. The space was morning chilly, as if someone had only just come in and flicked on the lights, but within seconds, she was sweating. Only two other people were present at the moment. Another corrections officer stood near a heavy metal door, opposite the one they entered, and a man who Jennifer assumed must be part of the parole board, sat to his right at an expanded judicial bench that headed the room. He was hunched over, so engrossed in a file that he didn't even glance up at them as they made their way down the aisle between the two small seating sections.

Dosie let her pick the row, and Jennifer sat in the second. She didn't know why, only that it wasn't the first, and that somehow made her feel better about it. In the quiet wait that followed, with Dosie's hand tucked between hers in her lap, Jennifer's senses heightened. The fluorescent lights burned brighter than seemed normal, hitting her eyes like a thousand microscopic needles, and the buzzing sound they made became an angry swarm of bees in her ears. The CO cleared his throat in ominous thunder. The board representative flipped a page, and lightning struck. The cool air grew cold, so cold that it hurt, and she could feel her toes turning black with frostbite. Her jaw clenched with her teeth's sudden need to chatter. She could taste her breakfast again, hints of sweet syrup and peppery egg, bitter coffee, then before to her winter mint toothpaste. She may as well have swallowed a bar of soap as each flavor twinged on her tongue and at the back of her throat and threatened to gag her until she left it all on the floor.

The door they came in opened again with a metallic clang, and a few more people filed in. Jennifer didn't look back, but she heard them coming down the aisle. There were at least two people, their footsteps offset against one another, but then the door opened again, and more steps joined the din. A woman came into view, passing by Jennifer's peripheral to the front row. But then she passed it, too, and crossed into the procedural portion of the room where she veered to the left and set her stuffed briefcase on the table there.

Jennifer could only see her from behind and didn't want to judge, but the moment she saw her destination, it was as if her mind couldn't *not* be a bully. As the room roared and buzzed and glared and froze around her, she homed in on the woman's simple brown bun and simple brown skirt suit to match, her simple beige heels that did not, and thought unhappy thoughts. Her suit was cheap and ill-fitting. Her hair was tacky. Her shoes were the wrong shade and the wrong style and, if the angry red splotches on the backs of her ankles were anything to go by, also the wrong size.

Jennifer's lip curled in disgust. It wasn't the lawyer's fault that even shit stains like Glass were entitled to representation, but she kind of hated her anyway and couldn't make herself stop. She had done a lot of questionable and even bizarre things for the sake of kink over the years. Her profession, her entire empire, was technically criminal in nature thanks to what she thought of as bogus and unnatural laws that targeted the wrong people. Jennifer did not have the inclination to judge others for what they did to make money or get by. But she could not imagine being able to sleep at night if she spent her days in prison courtrooms saying, *"He's been a good boy since he slaughtered that girl for fun, Your Honor. He deserves another chance."*

With a deep breath through her nose, Jennifer closed her eyes and bid herself to relax. *Get it together.* She bid herself not to be a judgmental asshole just because she had pain. She bid herself to stop bouncing her fucking knees before her feet started making tapping sounds on the tile floor and drawing everyone's attention her way. *Fuck's sake.*

When she opened her eyes again, the world stopped.

The woman, the lawyer, was looking right at her, and Jennifer couldn't move. Her body was a block of ice, breath frozen halfway down her throat. Even after a decade and some weight loss, the woman's face was recognizable. When their eyes met, she smiled without teeth, a smarmy sort of sneer that turned the buzzing in Jennifer's ears up to a scream. The woman then raised her hand and, as if holding a drink, subtly toasted in mid-air.

Jennifer could not believe it. The truth sank like a bomb in the ocean, sending a flurry of impact up in its wake. *It was her.* The bar. The mysterious whisky refill. The woman who disappeared before she could be seen.

The room rocked like a boat caught in a storm. The buzzing scream became crashing waves, and Jennifer's mouth flooded with saliva the way it always did right before she vomited. *Oh, fuck.* She needed to get up. She needed to leave. She needed it to be over. She needed to wake up.

"Jennifer." Dosie's voice called her back. Her hand on Jennifer's forearm jostled her aware. "Baby, ease up."

Jennifer's gasp felt like her first breath in minutes. Her gaze dropped to Dosie's hand trying to massage her own calm, because her grip on Dosie's other hand was so tight that it was hurting her. She jerked her hands off of Dosie and looked at her. She couldn't say she was sorry, because if she opened her mouth, she might puke. Or burst into tears. *Fuck.* She did not feel like herself at all anymore.

Dosie lay a hand on Jennifer's thigh and quietly said, "Tell me what's wrong."

Harsh breaths left Jennifer's nose as she kept her lips sealed tight and subtly shook her head.

Dosie leaned in closer. "Can you calm down?"

Fuck. Fuck. FUUUCK! Jennifer wanted to tear her own skin off just to get away from the insufferable feeling crawling through every inch of her. She felt like an idiot and a child, like the girl who used to have such terrible anxiety that she would rather be in pain than draw attention to herself. She felt as if she was being tortured into a shape that she was never meant to fit again.

"Let's step out."

Jennifer shook her head harder and closed her eyes until they stung. *No. We can't. It's about to start.*

"We have time," Dosie said as if she had read her mind. "Come on."

She stood and pulled Jennifer up by the arm, and all Jennifer could do was pretend no one else was there. No one sat in any of the rows. No one stood at the head of the room. No one existed. Jennifer stifled a sob and the sick that pulsed around it and followed Dosie through the door.

I fucking can't do hard things.

"Oh, sorry," Dosie said as she nearly barreled right into— "Oh, Carine. Hi."

"Fuck," Jennifer murmured under her breath and turned herself away from the unexpected trio of people at the door.

Carine was with two other people, the corrections officer who led them to the room before and a sharp-dressed man with a neat gray beard and a leather briefcase. Dosie didn't know him, but she did know a lawyer when she saw one. He squeezed by them and through the door as the CO returned to his primary station at check-in.

Carine hardly took notice of Dosie at all as her attention went straight to Jennifer, and her brow stitched itself into a worried line.

"Mon cœur," she said and reached for her, but Dosie caught her arm and gently guided it away. She didn't want to seem rude, but she also didn't want to give Jennifer's system any extra chances at overload. It wasn't thrilled with physical affection on the best of days; toss some in while it was already on turbo cycle, and she was likely to start violently vibrating across the room like an overstuffed washing machine. Dosie, much to her own delight, seemed to be the one steady exception to the rule, and even she made a point of avoiding too much touch from time to time so that her girlfriend could have a break.

"We just need a minute," she said and let her hand slide down to Carine's. She squeezed her fingers and gave her a warm, reassuring smile. "And then we'll be back in."

Carine lingered as if to object, but then she nodded and patted Dosie's hand in a sweet fashion that reminded Dosie a little of Peg. She left them to themselves, then, and Dosie pulled Jennifer a little farther from the door. "Okay," she said. "We have a few minutes."

Jennifer finally turned to face her again, eyes red-rimmed and glassy, tormented. Her mouth opened and closed like that of a fish on dry land.

"Oh, baby." She hated seeing Jennifer struggle so much. It was jarring and unlike her and devastating, and Dosie wanted to be there for every second of it, but she also wanted it to be over. She wanted Jennifer to feel better, to have closure if such a thing really existed, and peace. "What is it? Talk to me. You went stiff as a board in there."

"The lawyer," Jennifer finally managed to say. Then she breathed as if she'd just purged. "His lawyer. I know her."

Dosie frowned. "Is it not his same lawyer from before?"

"No. No, his trial lawyer was a man, a much, much older man. This woman, when I knew her, she was still in law school."

"Were you friends?" Dosie asked, and then another possibility came to mind, and she felt an odd tickle in her gut. It wasn't something she had experienced often in her life as she had no natural inclination toward it, but she recognized the slimy grip of it the second it took hold. Jealousy. "Or more than friends?"

"Absolutely not," Jennifer all but growled. "She was my client."

Oh. Dosie had not grown up around monogamy and had never cared that Jennifer engaged in sex acts with other people for her work. It rarely even crossed her mind outside of moments of curiosity about people's weird fantasies and habits. But she had also never had to be in a room with another person she knew had had sex with her girlfriend before. Clearly, her body felt a bit strange about it.

"Do you remember I told you I had a client once who I crossed a line with?"

The feeling amplified, and Dosie's chest tightened. "Yeah."

"That's her." Jennifer grabbed the collar of her shirt and pulled it back and forth to let some air down the front of her chest. "I can't believe she would do this."

"Do what?" Dosie asked, because she still wasn't quite understanding why the situation was so terrible outside of just general awkwardness.

"Be here," Jennifer hissed at her and threw her arm toward the courtroom door. "Fucking representing him."

If Dosie thought the feeling was bad before, it tripled in a heartbeat. Was Jennifer really implying what she thought she was? "Are you saying you think she's representing him to get back at you for something?"

"Unless this is the world's most heinous coincidence," Jennifer said and her eyes looked wild, "yes! Yes, I fucking am."

"But why? Why would you think that? Why would she *do* that? What happened between you two?"

The CO reappeared with another person, and Jennifer looked as if she wanted to scream. Or run. Maybe both.

"We don't have time," she said, and Dosie knew she was right. They needed to go back inside if they hoped to actually attend the hearing. So, whatever questions Dosie had would have to wait. She had to get Jennifer in that room and through the next however many hours it took to convince a panel of strangers that some people's second chances were that they got to live, even if they had to do it behind bars.

"Okay," Dosie said and held out her hands. "Hey, it's okay. Come here."

Jennifer set her hands in Dosie's and closed her eyes. "I'm sorry."

"Don't be," Dosie told her. "Don't even think about it right now, because it doesn't matter. Okay? She doesn't matter. What matters is that we are here for a reason, and that hasn't changed. Right?"

Jennifer breathed slow and nodded. "Right."

"Tell me the reason."

"Lauren." Her voice strained, but she held it together.

"Lauren," Dosie repeated and squeezed her hands. "You can still do this, baby. I promise you can. And no matter who else is here, *I'm* here, and I'll be here the whole time."

Jennifer opened her eyes again. "Kiss me," she said, and Dosie did, brief but firm. "Okay. I'm ready."

They returned to the room as the last of the seven parole board representatives took her place at the bench. There were five men and only two women, which irked Jennifer, and all seven were designated by a small name card set out in front of their skinny, mounted microphones. Before them, at two tables set apart from one another, stood the two lawyers—the woman who had thrown Jennifer into a tailspin and the man who would stand for the state in opposition to Glass's parole. Jennifer recognized him, too. *Hugh Rainey. Junior,* she supposed. He had attended the original trial as well but only as a paralegal, sitting quietly to the side of the prosecutor, who happened to be his father. Jennifer recalled reading that Rainey Sr. had passed a few years ago.

The civilian seating sections were mostly empty. Three young men with notepads and pens occupied the row nearest the exit, but otherwise, there was only Carine. She sat in the third row, dead center of the room, and close to the aisle as if she hoped to make a quick getaway. Jennifer was sure she did.

"Tata," she said as she slid into place beside her aunt. They didn't reach for each other or hold hands, but Jennifer pressed her shoulder against Carine's and stayed there. She could hardly look at her, terrified that whether she spoke to the board or not, something she had done years ago might actually result in Glass getting paroled. She supposed it depended on how good of a lawyer the woman was and how convincing she could be. Clearly, being unhinged from reality didn't prevent her from passing the Bar, so anything was possible.

Dosie squeezed past Jennifer's tucked knees to sit on her other side and had just settled into place when the CO at the front of the room opened the door he guarded. Another officer stepped through, and the sounds of clinking, scraping metal and shuffling feet echoed in from behind him. A blink of the eye later, and he was there, Glass, standing in the frame like a nightmare silhouette slowly clarifying.

Carine's shoulder tensed against hers. Dosie's hand curled around her thigh and flexed. Jennifer felt as if her insides were made of glue as she watched her former brother-in-law waddle into the room in a beige jumpsuit and chained ankle cuffs. Another chain secured his wrists together then looped them to his waist so that every movement was minimized, not just his steps. He looked so very different. Defined muscle was clear under the sleeves of his jumpsuit, and his face appeared fuller. He had a short, bushy beard that was speckled gray and, paired with his long, salt-and-pepper ponytail, made him appear much older than he was.

It bothered Jennifer that he no longer looked the same to her. There was satisfaction in seeing that he had aged poorly, but Jennifer wanted to look into the face she remembered. She wanted to know she was facing her demons when she told him how she felt.

Glass was led to his lawyer's table and unshackled, the sounds deafening in the otherwise silent room, and then he looked up. And suddenly Jennifer realized she'd had no idea what silence was, not until his empty eyes found hers and plunged her into a frozen void. Beyond the barest spark of recognition at the sight of her, there was nothing. No sorrow. No pain. No remorse or avoidance. No love or connection or care. There was nothing left of the charming jokester she had once gotten to know, only the intolerable revelation lurking underneath.

Once his restraints were removed, he sat at the table alongside Jennifer's former client, and the two leaned in close for a quiet conversation. She watched as the woman—her name was Kim, if Jennifer correctly recalled—touched Glass's arm as she spoke with him, as if they were old friends. It made her blood boil.

Kim Pritchard. It came back to her. She had been calling the woman a variety of *other* names in her head for so long that she'd almost forgotten the real thing.

A throat cleared, and the room's minimal conversation ground to a halt. Every head turned toward the judicial bench, where the seven parole board representatives appeared ready to begin the proceeding. As they introduced themselves and allowed the attorneys to do the same, sweat beaded along Jennifer's spine and ran. Her mouth went dry. When she tried to swallow, an itchy pain seared at the back of her throat.

"So, we are here today," said the board member who had been in the room from the start, "to consider a petition for parole on behalf of Inmate #15275-210, Orwell Blythe Glass, incarcerated since the year 2002, for the crime of murder in the second degree."

Every breath felt like a prelude to a gag as Jennifer turned to look at Dosie. She wasn't surprised to see that she, too, appeared pale and uncomfortable. Still, she gave Jennifer the closest thing she could to a smile and mouthed, *"It's okay,"* and somehow, despite it all, Jennifer believed her.

The prosecutor, a Mr. Hugh Rainey, opened the hearing, and while Dosie was glad of his presence and his impassioned plea for continued incarceration, the bulk of his persuasion hinged on the hideous nature of Glass's crime. It needed to be said. The board *needed* to hear it, so that they could feel in their bodies with every twinge, recoil, and wince, just how vile the man's actions had been. But knowing that made it no easier to endure Mr. Rainey's graphic and protracted recounting of Lauren Dupont's final hours alive.

But for the subtle tremble Dosie felt at every point where Jennifer's body pressed against hers, the two women to her left appeared made of stone. Their faces, similar in both appearance and expression, stared ahead in perpetual pain as the prosecutor recounted each of the twenty-two times Lauren was stabbed and how none had been fatal on their own, because Orwell Glass hadn't wanted them to be.

"He wanted her alive," Mr. Rainey said, voice harsh with disgust, "and he wanted her conscious, so that she would feel every last little thing he did to her until he decided he had had enough."

Glass had done things to her. Dosie blocked out the details, sang songs in her head at a scream so that she wouldn't have to know. She couldn't afford to be triggered. Jennifer needed her. When Mr. Rainey held up photographs and panned their way, Dosie jerked her head the opposite direction. She'd caught a flash of blood—*God, so much blood*—and knew she shouldn't see any more. Her hands were starting to shake.

"And *then*," Mr. Rainey said, "after all that, after he forces her to endure all of that—she's in horrific pain, laying in a massive pool of her own blood, *knowing* she'll die if she doesn't get help soon—he makes her beg for her life."

Dosie shuddered at the words and heard both Jennifer and Carine breathe sharply beside her.

"Something we only know thanks to Mr. Glass's own diary." The prosecutor shuffled through a few papers on his table then held up a printed copy of a picture. In it, a lined diary page with loopy handwriting. "In which he absolutely *gushed* about what he'd done, saying, and I quote, 'There was so much blood, the carpet looked like it had always been red, and Lauren's face was so covered in it that she was basically featureless, and I liked her better that way. She could barely talk but kept trying when I told her to beg for her life like I was her god. It was too late at that point. She had lost too much blood and was going to die either way. I just wanted to hear it.'"

Silence blew through the room like a hard wind, and for a moment, nobody moved. No pens scratched. No throats cleared. No one adjusted in their seat, and Mr. Rainey held that devastated quiet in his piercing gaze as he looked at each of the board members and then around the room. Everything braced until the tension turned taut and painful. Then he dropped his voice to a soft and solemn note and repeated, "'I just wanted to hear it.' In the final moments of his young wife's life, Mr. Glass *just wanted to hear* her beg him not to kill her before he slid his knife across her neck and killed her anyway."

Bile burned up Dosie's throat, and she swallowed it back with a grimace. Her eyes found the man in question. She could only see his profile, but it was enough. Orwell sat with more ease than seemed appropriate, a slight hunch to his posture and one elbow leaning on the table, chin resting in his palm. He stared blankly ahead as the prosecutor spoke. No reaction. No remorse. Not that she saw, anyway, and it amplified the effect of the details. The less he seemed to care, the more bothered she became. By the time Mr. Rainey rested his case, Dosie had the urge to launch herself across the room and punch Orwell Glass in his unbothered face. She wouldn't, of course, but it felt good to curl her hand into a fist even if she never intended to use it.

When the floor was passed, the odd sensation from the hallway returned. Dosie had almost forgotten the whole controversy of Glass's lawyer being Jennifer's former client until the woman began to speak. Her name was Kim Pritchard, and her nasal voice made Dosie's eye twitch. Whether it was the sound that truly bothered her or the woman's past with her girlfriend, she wasn't sure. What she *was* sure of were the words leaving Ms. Pritchard's own mouth, and they were more than enough to earn her a little disdain.

As likely any defense lawyer would do, she leaned heavily into his history of depression and presented his prison record like it was a badge of honor or a good deed that should have earned him one. Why focus on the one beastly crime he committed when there were years that followed in which he committed no crimes at all? Despite the threat of violence from other inmates, he never engaged in violent activities himself and even joined in-house group counseling sessions to address his issues with anger and melancholy. He worked daily in the prison library and taught illiterate fellow inmates how to read, became a devoted Christian who attended weekly services, and was an annual participant in the prison's scared-straight program for at-risk youth in the greater Boston area.

Dosie didn't care about his religious affiliation and knew better than anyone that devotion to spiritual *anything* didn't make one a saint. The rest, however, she could admit sounded compelling. Glass had been in counseling. He was active and communicative and non-confrontational and spent a fair chunk of his time helping his fellow inmates. It seemed, from his lawyer's depiction, that he was a rare example of incarceration yielding just the result it was meant to: a rehabilitated man where once there was a monster.

But when Ms. Pritchard segued into the last leg of her defense, Dosie no longer cared to wonder at Glass's state of mind. If he allowed his lawyer to say such things on his behalf, how could he possibly have remorse? And if it had been his idea, and Kim Pritchard didn't find it distasteful enough to refuse him, then, in Dosie's view, she deserved a few nights in a cell alongside him.

"That is the sad but simple fact of the matter," she said, and Dosie felt Jennifer's grip begin to tighten again. She heard Carine mutter something under her breath in French, and while she couldn't translate it, she could tell from the inflection that it wasn't nice. "Did a young woman lose her life? Tragically, yes, but my client has now served more time in prison than the length of the life that was lost.

He sacrificed more than twenty years of his own life to pay his debt, and he has earned a chance to start again."

Dosie used her free hand to massage Jennifer's wrist and calm her, but then the man himself was asked if he would like to speak on his own behalf, and Jennifer's grip became a clamp. A tourniquet. Had Dosie not been able to see her hand on the other side of Jennifer's fingers, she might have wondered if it was even there anymore.

Orwell Glass stood with a bit of a lean to his left and clasped his loose hands together at his waist as if he expected them to be cuffed. He cleared his throat, and the sound was softer than Dosie expected. When he spoke, his voice was even more-so. "Thank you," he said, "for giving me this opportunity today to speak for how much I've changed."

Jennifer's breath left her in a slow rush as she closed her eyes and whispered, "He sounds exactly the same."

The words sent a chill down Dosie's back. She imagined some of the things she'd heard earlier, words Glass had uttered to Lauren in her final moments. She had a voice to wrap around those words now, and it was too much. Dosie pushed the thought away and focused again on calming Jennifer. Massage didn't work, so she subtly latched onto the meaty pressure point between Jennifer's forefinger and thumb and began to squeeze with all she had. Jennifer's grip relaxed after a moment, and she glanced at Dosie, nodded her thanks. A moment later, the pressure returned.

"I am truly remorseful for what happened that day," Glass said, "and for how it affected the victim's family and friends. I wish it had never happened and regret that I cannot change it."

The words sounded practiced but not deceitful. But Dosie remembered Jennifer telling her how charming he had once been. Stoic only a moment before, he now seemed passionate and genuine and terribly soft-hearted, and despite her tendency toward optimism, Dosie couldn't help but suspect that it was all just a well-played act.

"But I *have* changed myself over the last twenty years, and I believe I have earned a second chance. I believe, as my lawyer laid out, that my record while incarcerated speaks to this. And if I am granted parole, I am fully prepared to be an asset to our society instead of a burden. I have family who is ready to provide temporary housing and start-up employment."

Dosie glanced back but saw no one new. The men scribbling notes at the rear of the room remained in their seats, and the rest of the pews were empty. Whoever the family supposedly willing to support Glass was, they weren't present for him now.

"And a church congregation ready to accept me as their own," he said, and Carine's under-breath muttering started up again. "I know I made a mistake, but I'm not that person anymore."

A mistake? Dosie cringed at the word. *That's what we're calling torture now?*

Jennifer reached for her aunt for the first time since she sat down beside her and slid a hand over hers. When Carine latched on, the two looked at each other, and Dosie saw tears in Carine's eyes that clashed with the furious sneer of her lip. She tamed it as she brought Jennifer's hand to her lips and kissed her knuckles, then held them to her cheek. They stayed there until it was over, until the last dubious promise left Glass's lips.

"If you all were to grant me this chance," he told the board, "I promise you I would not waste it."

"Thank you, Mr. Glass," said one of the women on the board and directed him to sit. When he did, she added, "Now, just a few questions."

The board members took turns and covered everything from the size, financial status, and wellbeing of the family and home he would live in if released, to the details of the job he claimed to have lined up and the location of and pastor associated with the church he intended to join. They asked him if he still had anger issues, which he denied, and if he had a plan for securing health insurance and continuing drug therapy for his depression. He reiterated his remorse when they asked him if he *truly* regretted his actions, and Dosie noticed something in the way he spoke about the crime.

I'm sorry for what happened. I wish it had never happened. What happened to her was terrible, and it shouldn't have happened.

It was all so removed, as if *what happened* hadn't happened specifically because he caused it to. As if someone else had committed the crime, and he was just a person who'd heard about it. A bystander to a life that was "lost" instead of taken. That, and the fact that he repeatedly referred to Lauren, the girl he married and supposedly loved at some point, as "the victim" or simply *"her"*, made Dosie grind her teeth.

"Now, it's our understanding that we have someone in attendance who wishes to make an impact statement," said the board member at the center of the bench, and Jennifer sat up straighter, one hand gripping Dosie and the other Carine. The board member checked a sheet in front of him. "A Jennifer Dupont. Is Ms. Dupont present today?"

Jennifer raised her hand, fingers visibly sweaty, and all the eyes in the room shot straight to where they sat. Dosie kept her own eyes on Jennifer but could feel them all like heat lamps, baking her from every angle. She couldn't begin to imagine how magnified the feeling must be for the women beside her, especially Jennifer.

"Right," the man said. "Good morning, Ms. Dupont. I see here that you are the sister of the victim, Lauren Dupont. Is that right, ma'am?"

Jennifer's mouth flexed around air, no words, no sound, and Dosie felt a momentary spark of panic. But then, with a gentle adjustment of her throat, Jennifer's lovely, deep, heartbroken voice floated through the room. "Yes. She was my sister."

"I'm sorry for your loss, ma'am," the man said, and Jennifer gave a swift nod. Her chin wobbled as if she might cry, but she didn't. "Do you still wish to speak on your sister's and family's behalf today, Ms. Dupont?"

"Yes."

Dosie's panic gave way to pride. Jennifer felt like a timebomb beside her, vibrating its way down to detonation, but she was upright and attentive. Her strong chin jutted forward as she held her head up, and her voice was clear. She spoke when she'd feared she couldn't. She spoke when she'd believed she never would. Dosie wanted to kiss her and hold her, cry with her and tell her how incredibly brave she was for facing her fears and how much it meant to her to be there while she did. She would. Later. *Soon.*

"Are you prepared to give that statement now?"

Jennifer turned toward her, gaze seeking Dosie's like a beacon in the dark, some reassurance that she would make it safely through to the other side of the storm. She nodded as she looked into Dosie's eyes and squeezed her hand. "Yes, I am."

13

The cold started at the back of her head. Like a brain-freeze from eating ice cream too quickly, a vicious ache bounced around her skull. Then the ice melted, and cold spilled down her back, tensing every muscle and turning her spine into a spike. Jennifer didn't know if it was a welcome change from the constant nausea she'd felt over the course of the hearing or if it was worse. She could not remember what relief was.

She made herself breathe through the feeling. *It will pass.* Even if it didn't, she had to keep going. She had to make herself move. Her hand lingered on the wooden gate separating the civilian and procedural portions of the room. *Even if I have anxiety, even if I'm scared, I can still do what I have to do.* Dosie's fucking mantras were going to save her life or, at the least, her sanity. *I can do this.*

Jennifer briefly closed her eyes. She imagined herself somewhere else. The back of Carolina's town car, a cozy leather seat, a snifter of Signet in her hand and mocha notes on her tongue. She could almost feel her compact in the other hand, popping open so she could stare into her own hooded eyes and watch a confident smile form on her lips. *Go get 'em, gorgeous,* she told herself as the mental compact snapped shut. It was time for her to work.

Through the small gate, the room felt like a different place. It was a stage, spotlit and hot, and the cold ceased to matter. Every part of her that could sweat did. Without her coat, left in Dosie's lap, it was only a matter of time before small wet spots began to appear on her clothes. *Fuck. Shut up,* she told herself. *You're freaking yourself out.*

There was no dais, platform, or microphone, no central point to approach until the man who had invited her up, held out a hand to direct her. She placed herself in front of the bench, midway between both lawyers' tables, and made herself make eye contact with each of the board's representatives. They were polite, nodding or smiling as she did, and it eased some of Jennifer's fear. The awful height of anticipation revealed a gentle slope on its other side rather than a violent drop to her end. *I can do this.* All she had to do was take another step, and she'd already taken so many. *I can do this.*

"Whenever you're ready, Ms. Dupont," said one of the board members.

Jennifer reached into her suit's breast pocket and retrieved the speech she'd spent hours writing and rewriting. The crinkling, shifting sound of the papers unfolding was amplified in the silence. She took a breath and let it go, that sound, too, like a siren in the night. *You've already done the hard part. Just open your mouth and read.*

She opened her mouth, every millimeter of it as dry as sunbaked sand, and she began to read. "When I first met Orwell Glass, my family was still in the early stages of grief following a fatal car accident in which both my parents died. My sister Lauren, who was both my best friend and my polar opposite, was an extroverted, energetic optimist and jokester, but in the months after the accident, became withdrawn and moody and unlike herself. She hardly spoke and never smiled and no longer seemed interested in any of her hobbies. Then we started a new school, and she met a young man. My first impression of Orwell Glass was that he was vain and superior with a false sense of sophistication and a bad sense of style."

God, that felt good to say.

"But my sister was smiling for the first time in months, so I promised her I would give him a chance. A month or so after that, I was glad that I did. Or I believed I was. Mr. Glass and my sister had become virtually inseparable, so he was around a lot. He helped out around the house, even if he wasn't asked, and had a sense of humor that grew on me until I found myself laughing most of the time that he was there. It made it so much easier to ignore the little things he said or did that bothered me, like his occasional rants about immigrants in front of my immigrant aunt or the way he would put his hand around the back of my sister's neck like a vise or a collar. I forgave him every flaw and ignored every red flag, because we were all laughing together like a family again, and after a while, Mr. Glass seemed less smarmy and more the type who simply didn't know how to be himself around people until he got to know them a bit better. In the worst of ways, I learned I was right."

Jennifer took a breath. Even with all she had already said, she had barely begun. Her chest felt as if it had caved in, and her heart was now struggling to pump under the pressure. As long as it didn't stop, she had no intention of doing so either.

"The charming traits Mr. Glass exhibited in those early days and months were an act, and when he married my sister and moved into our former home, he dropped that act and revealed himself. He no longer needed it to be invited in. He was in. He was anchored. He had such a hold on my sister that she trusted him over her own family and heeded him over us as well. Within a matter of months, he was her master, controlling everything she did, everywhere she went, and everyone she spoke to. He convinced her to quit her job and drop out of her first year of college. She stopped seeing her friends and stayed away from her family. She would hardly even take our calls, and on those rare occasions when we did get to hear her voice again, it was always overshadowed by Mr. Glass in the background saying that we were suffocating them. That we couldn't mind our own business or give them any space. That we had never liked or approved of him and wanted to pry her away. His complaints were endless and spoken as if true, and with enough time and repetition, they worked. They worked so incredibly well that even when he began to physically abuse her, she stayed with him, and she never spoke a word of it to me or our aunt or anyone. And if we had the chance to see her and noticed, she always had an excuse ready. A 'silly fall' caused the handprint-shaped bruise around her neck. A cabinet door blackened her eye. It was never him, never his fault. He wasn't a monster. We just didn't understand him. We weren't giving him a chance. Even the day she died, the day that he killed her, my sister made excuses for him. She forgave him. She saw hope where I saw hatred and heartbreak and abuse, because that's who she was. An optimist. A lover. A funny, sweet, smart young woman who just wanted to feel happy again and chose to believe the young man who promised her he would make that happen. Who promised her that he would love her and honor her, and then tortured her to death simply because he could."

Jennifer gripped the papers so hard that they wrinkled around her fingers. The edge tore when she pulled the top sheet to move to the next, and tears spilled into her eyes. She blinked them away and cleared her throat. *Keep going. Just keep fucking going.*

"I did not speak for my big sister when Mr. Glass was first sentenced. I didn't speak for my family or our loss. I didn't even speak for myself, for what it felt like to have the last member of my core family taken from me by someone we all trusted. I didn't speak, because I couldn't. I was not a person with a backbone then. I wasn't brave or confident. I wasn't even an adult. I had no idea who I was or how to talk about the kind of pain that I was in. Thankfully, justice was served despite this, and Mr. Glass received a rightful life sentence for murdering my sister. But today, he is asking you to give him a life outside of that sentence and allow him to reintegrate into society as if he never violated, abused, and slaughtered a person, and

I cannot and will not stand by in silence while he makes that plea. I am not a child anymore. I'm a woman. I have a voice that I know how to use, and I will use it until I run out of breath if it means keeping this violent megalomaniac behind bars where he belongs."

Over the days she'd spent preparing herself for this moment, revisiting Lauren's murder and all that had followed, Jennifer realized how limited she had been. How restricted. As free and privileged as she was, and as satisfied as she became with the life she built for herself, a large part of her had spent the last two-plus decades in a kind of prison of her own. A prison of grief, yes, but it was more than that. Grief came from any loss. Loss from violence created a particular kind of agony. It took so much more than a life, and it left Jennifer with so much chaos and so little joy that the only way she could survive was to compartmentalize so severely that all the tender parts of her may as well have been imprisoned. She could not even remember, before Dosie, the last time she let herself *feel* for a person the kind of connection that made her want to volunteer vulnerability. She wasn't sure she had ever felt that way about anyone she wasn't related to, and there were so few of those people left.

"For years," she told the board, "I could not connect with others because of Mr. Glass's violence and betrayal. I couldn't let myself trust anyone. I resisted friendships. Even the idea of romance or partnership made my heart race, not out of desire or excitement but out of fear. Genuine, down-to-my-bones fear that I have only now, in my forties, begun to conquer. I spent years alone, *deeply* alone, because someone my family welcomed, trusted, and loved chose to betray and violate us. Orwell Glass's crime was so thorough and deviant that it forced a life sentence on me and on my aunt as well. One in which we isolate and disconnect ourselves just to avoid the possibility of ever experiencing again the horror he inflicted on our family. Still, we suffer because of him, so I ask why his suffering should end."

Jennifer paused to quell her fury. She wanted to feel it. She wanted to expel it even. But she wanted to do it properly. She wanted it controlled and measured, so that he felt each word like a blade sinking slowly and deliberately into his body and into any possibility of his ever seeing the light of day outside the filter of an electrified chain-link fence again.

"It sickens me to have to stand here today, because this man has the audacity to ask for a second chance and a new life. I challenge him: What second chance does my sister get? What new life can she begin? The answer is none. There are no do-overs for the dead. I'm appalled that Mr. Glass, and his lawyer, are claiming he should be free because he has 'sacrificed' and served more years in prison than the length of my sister's life. They are implying that justice has been served, but Mr. Glass did not take nineteen years from my sister. Those were the years that she *lived*, the years he could not strip away or beat or stab out of her. What he stole were all the years that should have followed, and that is what he owes in payment. A *full*, long life."

And his face ground into a bloody pulp. But she would settle for him rotting behind bars until he was an old, crusty man with nothing to leave behind except a pair of prison-issue slides and a pack of instant noodles.

"I *am* a believer in second chances, and I *do* believe that many people can be rehabilitated and saved from a life of future crime. But I have also learned to listen beyond the face value of what people say when they tell you who they are, and Mr. Glass, despite his solemn words and pretty promises, has told you today that he is a man without remorse. He did not sacrifice his life to pay for his crime. He has life. He breathes. His heart beats, and for the last two decades, he has enjoyed three meals a day, regular showers, and clean clothes. He has continued his education and earned a degree, has access to a gym and track if he wishes to exercise, and it is my understanding that inmates at this prison even have their own baseball field and handball courts. Mr. Glass has enjoyed access to therapeutic, medical, religious, and social services and events, and if he likes, he can listen to music, watch television, and read books. He can make phone and video calls, send emails, and even have in-person visits with anyone willing."

The more she said aloud, the more Jennifer's blood burned. She definitely had sweat spots under her arms and breasts. She could feel them. Her clothes were too tight and were starting to make her itch, and Jennifer knew she was fast approaching her limit for the whole wretched affair. But it wouldn't be over until she made herself clear, until she pounded home every last word she had agonized over and every last word that had spilled into her brain as she sat in that pew and listened to Orwell Glass and Kim Pritchard push audacity to its limit. *Every last fucking word.*

"My sister isn't clean and cared for. She's not getting her degree or playing sports or being entertained. She isn't going to the doctor or finding God or making friends or teaching anyone how to read or even reading herself. She doesn't eat or breathe, and her heart doesn't beat. And she isn't standing here today asking you to consider *her* suffering, because she is dead."

Jennifer's stomach rolled. Her throat bobbed around nothing but bitter dryness. *Keep going.*

"She takes her visitors at the cemetery, where she is bones in the ground beneath a stone. No! I do *not* accept that Mr. Glass has sacrificed his life, and frankly, I have no care or patience for the disgusting implication that his record of being a 'model prisoner' is in any way indicative of how he would behave in society if set free. It is not hard to behave when under a watchful eye. It is not difficult to avoid committing a violent act, when the violent act you prefer to commit requires a type of victim, like young women, that you have no access to. What matters is what he did while he was not imprisoned. When he was free, he slaughtered my sister, and he did it for fun. What matters is how he speaks about that crime today. He doesn't say he is sorry for what *he did* to my sister. He says he is sorry for 'what happened', as if it was an event that he witnessed and not one he caused. True remorse requires bold and unflinching ownership, and an understanding of the magnitude of the crime committed. If Orwell Glass had that understanding, he would not be here asking for a second chance. He would know that he is exactly where he deserves to be and should remain, and that his second chance is that he gets to live and not be tortured to death at the whim of someone else."

Keep going. It's almost over. Keep going. It's almost over. Keep going.

"Please, members of the board, I do not ask you to consider my words today. I beg you to. Do not free this man. He is not only a danger to society but an embarrassment to have among our ranks, and he should rot behind a lethal-force fence until the last breath leaves his body. It is my sincere belief that only when he is a cold, rotted corpse in a dirty pine box, will he have paid for his crimes against my sister and my family."

Jennifer braced herself. This was it. Anticipation returned in full force despite having already met his eyes once before. A needlelike prickling scored her arms and legs, and her jaw began to ache. *Fuck. Just turn around.* She breathed deep and steeled her nerves, told herself she wasn't going to cry or scream or fall apart. She was going to say her piece, and she was going to have her peace, and he was going to die in prison.

She turned around, and their gazes locked. Immediate. His empty eyes weren't so empty anymore, and Jennifer felt a shock of familiar fear, so old and ingrained that it felt like a memory. Or something close. Jennifer thought of the way he had looked at her that day and refused the urge to shudder. He would not have power over her, not ever again.

"You were never good enough for my sister," Jennifer told him, enunciating every word so he was sure to feel the bite of the truth. "You aren't good enough for anyone. Such a pretty, privileged childhood, and look at you now. I pity your parents for the vile, embarrassing monster they brought into this world and the life they must now lead having to be associated with someone so truly and deeply disgusting, disturbed, and cowardly. You are not worth the tax dollars we waste to keep you alive, but I will still gladly spend them to ensure that you *never* have the opportunity to do to someone else's sister what you did to mine. I would gladly spend every last cent I have to ensure that your imprisonment and misery lasts as long as is humanly possible before you wheeze your last foul breath and move on. And when that happens, I want you to know this: no matter how hard you convince yourself otherwise, there will be no redemption for you on the other side. You will die, and you will disappear, and no one, *no one*, will care."

His lips parted, eyes wide, but Jennifer had nothing more for him. No words. No time. He deserved nothing more than what he'd gotten, and what he'd gotten was all she had. Her hands shook so intensely that she barely managed to pocket her papers as she strode back through the gate, trying to keep her head up. Her eyes were on fire as she passed her row of seats and kept walking, burning gaze fixed on the door.

She was done. It was done. She did it.

And she was going to vomit.

With the help of a CO, Dosie found Jennifer in a small women's restroom down the hall from the hearing. There were three stalls, and only the middle one was occupied. Dosie could see Jennifer's loafers under the door, toes pointed toward the toilet.

"Jen?"

The toilet flushed, and the stall door opened. Jennifer emerged with smudged eyeliner and bloodshot eyes and a small wad of toilet paper held against her mouth. She didn't look at Dosie as she crossed to the sink and turned the water on.

"They called a recess to deliberate," Dosie said as Jennifer stared into the steaming water and washed her hands three separate times before drying. "Your aunt went out for some air. She wanted to check on you, but I asked her to let me instead."

Jennifer gripped the edges of the sink and let her shoulders slump inward. "Dosie." Her voice was weak and gravelly from the strain of throwing up. "I need this to be over."

"Oh, honey, I know." Dosie went to her, wrapped her arms around her from behind, and lay her cheek against her back. "It almost is. I promise."

"I can't feel half my body," Jennifer whispered as she leaned back against her.

"You're just overwhelmed," Dosie told her. "It will pass. Come here." She led her to a plain wooden bench under the obscure glass of the only bathroom window and sat with her. Jennifer lay against her shoulder and took slow, measured breaths as Dosie stroked her arm. "You were amazing in there, Jennifer."

"I was scared. And angry."

"And brave," Dosie said firmly. "And I am so proud of you. I am *so* proud of you."

Jennifer sobbed, one harsh blip of heartbreaking sound before she sucked it back down with an audible squelch that made Dosie's throat hurt just hearing it. "I thought I was going to hurl mid-speech."

Dosie kissed the top of her head. "But you didn't. Because you're amazing and also a little terrifying," she said and felt Jennifer's small tremor of a laugh. It transformed into another sob that, once again, she swallowed.

"I fucking hate crying."

"I know, but tears or no tears, you were a total bad ass in there."

"I feel like just the ass part," Jennifer said and tucked her face into Dosie's neck. "I can't stand hearing his fucking voice. And for him to say, for him to *dare*—" She sat back again as if she couldn't hold still and blew a harsh breeze up over her eyes. "And now I need a fucking toothbrush."

"I have mints in my purse, but my purse is in the locker."

"And that *woman*," Jennifer growled, shaking her head in disbelief. "That absolute fucking cunt of a woman."

Dosie rolled her lips together to keep from gasping or laughing or both. Jennifer could barely focus long enough to finish a thought, so she certainly wasn't going to filter herself. Dosie could see in her body that she was fried, that she needed to get out of the prison and out of the past and *rest*. Whatever came next, she'd earned that much.

"How could she do that?" Jennifer said, staring across the room at the empty air as if waiting for it to answer. "How could *anyone* do that?"

"You really don't think it could be a coincidence? Maybe she was assigned his case."

Jennifer's eyes cut sharply toward her. "It *wasn't* a coincidence."

"But how do you know?" She pulled Jennifer's hands between hers to massage her palms. Anything that might comfort was worth a try. "Tell me what happened with her."

"It was years ago," Jennifer said, "when I was still based here in Boston."

"She hired you?"

"We had three sessions, and she became increasingly affectionate and personal with each one. During the second, she started asking me a lot of questions about my personal life, and I could tell that she had a bit of a crush on me, but she was really understanding when I shut down the questions, so I thought that was it. But then she schedules a third session, and ten minutes into it, asks me to roleplay like we're a married couple, and that's when I ended it. I told her I wasn't comfortable with that type of play and obviously was not a good fit for her needs, and then I said I wouldn't book with her anymore."

"Ah, yeah, that was a fun conversation for us, too," Dosie said, and Jennifer dropped her head into her hands and snorted.

"She did *not* take it as well as you did."

"I took you upstairs, if I remember," Dosie teased and knew it was worth it when Jennifer turned her face in her hands and smiled at her.

"Yes, you did," she said and leaned in for Dosie's kiss before remembering her breath. She offered her cheek instead, which Dosie happily kissed. A small red print of it remained behind, and she swiped it away with her thumb.

"So, what happened?"

"She said I was running from our connection, and that I would regret it."

The words caused a chill to trickle down Dosie's spine. "Do you think she meant *this*?"

"I don't know. All those years ago? I doubt it. But maybe something like it. She's clearly held on for a long time."

"Did you feel like you had a connection with her?"

"Not at all," Jennifer said, "and I tried to tell her that, that she was projecting what she felt onto me, that I didn't feel that way, but she wouldn't hear it. It didn't matter what I said. She just kept saying that she knew what she felt and wouldn't let me deny myself happiness."

"That's unnerving."

"That was just the start."

Dosie's heart kicked into a rapid rhythm. "What do you mean?"

"I got a delivery," Jennifer said. "It was maybe three weeks, maybe a month, after I struck her from the client list. Eighteen long-stem red roses and a card with no name, just a hand-drawn heart. Delivered directly to my apartment by courier."

Directly to Jennifer's apartment? But that would mean.... Her stomach dropped. "She stalked you?"

Jennifer's sigh was heavy and long. "Name. Phone number. Address. Email. She probably had a list of every parking or speeding ticket I'd ever gotten, too. She had it all. And the deliveries kept coming. Flowers, cards, chocolates, teddy bears. Fucking strawberry-flavored lube. She never identified herself as the sender, but I knew it was her. The timing was just too coincidental. But without any proof, I couldn't do anything about it, so I just waited. And then the emails started. All from bogus addresses and all harmless stuff like 'I miss you,' and 'Thinking of you.' 'Give me another chance.'"

Dosie's chest felt as if it was made of glass. If her heart beat any harder, it might shatter. She had no idea Jennifer had been stalked by a client before, and the thought not only horrified her but broke her heart. For Jennifer to experience that after everything she had already been through was devastating, and Dosie couldn't even begin to imagine how scared she must have been. It was no wonder she'd always kept people at such a distance. "You must have been terrified."

"Yeah," Jennifer huffed and massaged the back of her neck. Her French twist was slightly disheveled but not enough to be noticeable from any distance. "That's an understatement. It went on for weeks with me blocking every new email address and refusing her deliveries, and then she actually called me. I didn't answer, but she left a voicemail and said that even though I ignored her call, I still looked beautiful, and then she described exactly what I was wearing that day."

Dosie's stomach jerked and then sank as if anchored. "She was actually watching you? Oh my God."

"I completely fucking panicked," she said, voice dropping to a near whisper.

"I would have, too," Dosie told her. "Anyone would. You're supposed to be afraid in situations like that."

"I didn't go to the police. I thought about it. If I'd had more solid evidence, maybe, but as it was, I knew there was no way I could have her arrested. I didn't think I'd even be able to get a protection order based off what I had."

"So, what did you do?"

"I did the same thing she did to me," Jennifer said and shook her head as if she hated to admit as much, as if she was ashamed of herself. "I got her information from the file she set up when she booked. It wasn't a lot, but it was enough to find her on the internet. That's how I learned she was in law school, at Harvard, no less. A fucking law student at one of the most prestigious schools in the country actively stalking someone."

Jennifer stood and returned to the sink, wet a few paper towels with cold water and wiped them down the back of her neck. "She posted about one of her classes, so I went."

"To her class?!" Dosie's eyes bugged before she could stop them. "Really?"

"No, not her class," Jennifer said. "I just went to the campus and found where the class was and waited outside the building."

Dosie rubbed her chest. "Oh my god, baby, my heart is racing."

"Welcome to my fucking life for the last however many terrible days it's been now," Jennifer said and leaned over the sink again, arching her neck down so she could cover more skin with the cold towels. "Anyway, I confronted her, and I... I wasn't very nice about it."

"You didn't need to be."

"I didn't have to be callous either."

Dosie hated when Jennifer tortured herself this way, especially over past decisions. She knew how hard it was to let things lie, but she had also learned that dwelling on the past was the fastest, easiest, and most effective way to remain trapped in it. "Were you cruel?"

"No." Jennifer wadded the wet towels and tossed them in the nearest bin. "I mean, I don't think I was. But I know I didn't have to do it the way I did." She let free a gust of frustrated breath and ran the water again to slurp a bit into her mouth and rinse. "Maybe she wouldn't being doing this."

"Tell me what you did that you think was so terrible."

"I didn't even approach her," Jennifer said. "I spoke *at* her from at least thirty, forty feet away. And she wasn't alone. There were other people around, other students. I still don't know if any of them were with her, but I know a lot of them heard what I said." She returned to the bench and dropped heavily into her seat again. "I told her that she was acting like a psychopath who didn't understand the meaning of the word no, and that a law student should know that stalking was a crime." She turned her head as if she didn't want to look in Dosie's eyes. "I told her I was never going to be her girlfriend or her partner or her wife, and that no one in their right mind ever would be if that was how she conducted herself, and then I threatened her with a restraining order if she ever contacted me again in any way. And I left."

"Hey," Dosie said softly and squeezed her arm. "Look at me,

please." Her blue eyes were so conflicted. "Why are you afraid I'm going to judge you for that? Honey, I don't even understand why you're judging yourself for it."

"I humiliated her," Jennifer whispered. "That's why this is happening."

"No, this could have happened with or without her," Dosie countered. "You know that. You protected yourself, and it probably did embarrass her, but she *stalked* you. She forfeited her right to respectability when she ignored your no and violated your privacy and sense of safety. Please, put this guilt away, baby. You aren't responsible for her choices."

A deep comfort eased through her body as Jennifer took her hand and brought it to her chest. She lay it over the thump of her heart and pressed as if she intended to make a print. Her pulse was familiar to Dosie now and felt like the early notes of a favorite song, and in seconds, she was soft and lazy, heavy like a weighted blanket. She wanted to be in bed, or anywhere else, anywhere cozy, stretched alongside Jennifer in the dark and quiet, looking at each other as if into the stars.

"You are so beautiful," Jennifer said, and it floated through Dosie like morning birdsong.

She pulled her in and kissed her jaw, her cheek, the dip of her temple. "I love you, too," she said and felt as if she could live off Jennifer's easy, grainy laugh forever. She stood and held her hands out. "Let's go check on Carine." She helped Jennifer up and smoothed her shirt and jacket. "You're sweaty."

"I know. I'm dying for a shower."

"Soon," Dosie promised and opened the door for her. "We've been in here so long; the guards probably think we've got food poisoning."

"Or that we're smuggling drugs."

"Oh my God. Don't even joke about that. They probably have cameras in here."

The extraordinary relief of making it through her speech did not last, nor did the relief of spilling her guts, hiding in Dosie's arms, or reminding herself that it would all be over soon. Jennifer sat in the same seat as before, knee bouncing under Dosie's hand, and whatever calm her courage had earned her ceased to exist. She watched the board members return to the bench, one by one, and felt the lump in her throat grow with each. Seven times the size of her airway, she was sure she wouldn't survive. *What if he gets out?*

"Breathe," Dosie whispered.

What if he gets out? No, she couldn't breathe, not until she knew.

"Mr. Glass, would you stand, please?"

Jennifer gripped the wooden edge of the pew as Glass stood and bundled his hands neatly behind his back. She dropped her gaze and focused on Dosie's hand instead. *What if he gets out?*

"Thank you," said the board member at the center of the bench. "Mr. Glass, after careful consideration of all records, materials, and pleas presented here today, this board finds that despite your promising record while incarcerated, which we applaud, you have not demonstrated sufficient remorse for your crime and have displayed a troubling and inadequate understanding of the heinous nature, magnitude, and consequences of your criminal behavior."

Jennifer's body turned to jelly. All the tension raced free, and she sank into the pew as her breath grunted out of her and the tears she had been fighting all day shot down her cheeks as if in competition to reach her chin. Two hands clutched her, Dosie from one side and her aunt from the other.

She didn't look for Glass's reaction, or Kim's. Neither mattered. Jennifer hoped to never see either of them again.

"This," the representative continued, "coupled with the sheer brutality of your offense, indicates a high risk of re-offending upon release. As it stands, this board is not convinced that you are currently capable of safely re-entering society, and it is for this reason that your petition for parole is denied."

Carine collapsed against Jennifer's side as if she, too, had been holding her breath, flexing every muscle, for nearly half her life. She said something, but Jennifer couldn't hear. All the sounds in her ears were warped. All the colors around her blurred. For a moment, the room was a spinning top, and she was merely along for the ride. And then it stopped. It toppled. It righted itself.

And finally, she was able to get up. She was able to feel the ground beneath her feet again. It was over.

***

"It was worth it, you know."

They stopped two steps from the warm waiting car that had just pulled around to get them. Jennifer's hand hung in the air, already reaching for the door handle. It dropped to her side, and Dosie quickly grabbed it as they turned to face the loathsome source of the voice.

Kim Pritchard stood only a few feet away, close enough to kick given the length of Dosie's legs. She wasn't a violent person, had never been a violent person, but this woman made her want to kick. Like a mule. A really stubborn, angry mule.

An unearned smugness turned Kim's features sour and made Dosie feel gross from head to toe. She stared at Jennifer like a hungry predator would, as if trying to decide if she wanted to eat her first or kill her; as if she expected both to happen either way. "Just to see the look on your face."

Oh. Dosie's nerves ignited like a box of matches all stricken at once. *I do* not *like this woman.* She reached for her necklace, relieved to have it in place again, and ran her fingers along the pearls. *Don't start your first-ever fist fight outside a prison, Dosie.*

Jennifer's eyes were flames, bright blue heat lapping at the air as she stared Kim down and seethed. She stepped toward her, hand tethered behind and squeezing Dosie's bloodless, and bared her teeth as if preparing to growl her next words. Or bite.

Dosie's eyes widened. *Don't let your girlfriend start a fist fight outside a prison, Dosie.* But then Jennifer straightened her spine and stepped back again. She made a slow show of smoothing her coat and clearing her throat and said, "I actually felt sorry for how I handled things with you, Kim, but now I just feel sorry for you. You're not well. And if this is how you conduct yourself, you shouldn't be practicing law. You should be behind bars yourself."

"Oh, please," Kim said with a sneer. "A law-and-order lecture from you? You're a pimp, Jennifer. A madam."

Jennifer bristled, but Dosie *raged.* "Just stop it," she snapped, and all eyes set on her. "You're being unfair."

"Oh wow," Kim laughed, unbothered. "The new Audrey Hepburn fetish doll even speaks. How much did you shell out for that feature?"

"Come on, love," Jennifer said and tugged Dosie by the hand toward the car. "We're done here."

"Are we?" Dosie heard the unnaturally high pitch of her own voice but couldn't level it. Her blood was suddenly rushing in her ears like a river.

"No, seriously," Kim said and met Dosie's eyes, "where did she find you?" Hers were russet and angry. "1952?"

The muscles in Dosie's upper arms and thighs tightened as if bracing for imminent use. Jennifer let go of her hand to open the car door, and it turned itself into a fist. Her insides were lava.

"Dosie," Jennifer said and sat herself inside the car. She shifted over to give space for Dosie to follow. "She lost. Now she's throwing a fit." She held out a hand. "We don't have to listen."

She was right. Dosie knew she was right. There was no reason to endure the woman's insults or her foul attitude. Letting her bait them into a fight, even one strictly of words, wasn't necessary or smart.

"You know she's a whore, right?"

The cold air rose to a boil in the span of a heartbeat. Dosie shut the door before Jennifer could get another word out and turned to face Kim again. She clenched her teeth so hard that she was afraid she might chip one, but she couldn't stop.

"Piece of advice?" Kim said, still smug as Dosie's heels tapped over concrete, and she stepped into her space. "Don't fall in love with a whore. You'll never get anything more than her body, and she'll give that to everyone else, too."

Dosie's chest heaved with each breath. *Words.* Her knuckles hurt from holding her fists so tight. *Words, Dosie.* Her brain had some sense left, at least, a good thing since her body seemed to have become a living lit fuse. *Use words.*

"Unlike Jennifer, I don't feel sorry for you," Dosie said, and she didn't care that her voice was strained. She was proud she was using it at all. "What if that man had been granted parole, and he went out, and he killed another girl? How would you live with yourself?"

"I would live with myself fine," Kim said and crossed her arms over her chest as if bored of the whole affair now that the object of her disdain was no longer present. "He's entitled to representation. You don't like it, take it up with the Sixth Amendment. I was doing my job."

"So was she," Dosie snapped and had to stop herself from jabbing a hand into Kim's chest as she made her point. "*You* turned it into something it wasn't, not her. She didn't humiliate you. You humiliated yourself. And you're going to keep humiliating yourself until you learn how to deal with your *obvious* issues. So why don't you freaking get it together and *deal with them already?*"

She stepped back with a huff and fanned the heat from her face. Kim stared at her, seemingly struck silent with her bottom lip hanging open and her mad eyes conflicted. Dosie felt like a skyscraper in a pretty dress, a million feet tall and made of steel. She smoothed down her skirt and the back of her hair and cleared her throat as her heart's angry rhythm calmed. "And *don't* call my girlfriend a whore."

No response was needed. Dosie returned to the car and opened the door, found Jennifer sitting right at the edge of her seat. Her gaze was sharp sky blue and hungry. Or adoring? Either made her feel invincible. *Did she hear every word?*

Dosie glanced back to see the lawyer hadn't moved. Her sneer returned as Dosie met her eyes again and said, "Piece of advice?" She stepped one foot inside the car. "And this one is genuine: Let go." Jennifer moved aside again, and Dosie sat herself down, reached for the door. In the cold gap before she closed it, she gave one of the truest lessons she had ever learned and hoped the woman took it to heart. "Or be dragged."

14

The white sun floated high to the west in the cloudy, colorless sky. It was still early in the afternoon, but Dosie crawled into their hotel bed as if it was ten past midnight and she had had too much to drink. Her clothes lay strewn atop Jennifer's on the armchair in the corner, shed in exchange for a baggy T-shirt, cotton briefs, and fuzzy socks. Jennifer, who hadn't yet emerged from the bathroom, had replaced her outfit with nothing and taken a quick shower.

The cold of the untouched sheets felt like an ice pack pressed to Dosie's arm and thigh as she wiggled into the center of the bed like a worm trying to escape a slab of concrete. "Why did we turn the heat off before we left?" she whined and squeezed the covers around her like a snug cocoon.

"Because it would have gotten too warm," Jennifer called through the open crack of the bathroom door.

Dosie kicked her legs, rubbing her feet back and forth against one another like she was an enormous grasshopper trying to make sound. "But now it's too cold."

"It will warm up quickly."

"It would warm up faster if my girlfriend was in here with me,"

Dosie said, and as if she had guessed the correct sequence of words to unlock a prize, the bathroom door pulled wide, and a naked Jennifer appeared.

A faint reddish hue tinted her skin from the heat of her shower, and her damp, towel-wrung hair lay over her shoulders in a rumpled waterfall of inky black. She had smudged charcoal lines around her eyes, making the blue of her irises brighter, and her lips had a reflective sheen, as if she'd just applied a balm. A drop of water lingered in her shallow bellybutton and a few in the dark tuft between her legs. She was stunning, and Dosie stared at her as if entranced, as if frozen on the deck of a sinking boat as a siren swam closer and closer.

"You have the best ideas," Jennifer said as she lifted the blankets and slid inside the chilly bubble.

Her body was a piping hot tidal wave, moving closer and closer, warming everything it touched. When it washed over Dosie's shivering form and sapped the cold away, Dosie moaned so loudly and intensely that anyone walking by their room would have called it indecent. But she couldn't help herself. Nothing had ever felt better than the hot, soft, soap-scented embrace of the woman she loved.

"Wow," Jennifer said, chuckling. "Maybe we should try temperature play sometime."

Dosie tried and failed to get closer. There was simply no 'closer' left for her to get. They lay laced together like a half-naked braid— Jennifer being the naked half—with their legs tangled and their arms crossed over each other. Their foreheads touched, noses bumping. Dosie could feel Jennifer's pubic hair tickling her thigh. She was as close as possible, and she wanted closer.

"What's temperature play? A sex thing? Wait. Have we talked about it before?"

"Yes, but remind me to tell you again another time," Jennifer said. "I'm too tired to talk about sex."

"Are you too tired to *have* sex?"

Jennifer's laugh was low and raspy and sent electric tingles down the backs of Dosie's thighs. "Yes, but I find it delicious that you're asking."

"I was joking," Dosie said, "but I find it delicious that you wish I wasn't."

"What if I had said I wasn't too tired?"

Dosie grinned. "Then I was going to say, 'Well, too bad, so sad, because I am.'"

"You are unbearable."

"Unbearably adorable?"

Jennifer yawned as she said, "Something like that."

"Do you want to sleep?"

"I don't know." Jennifer closed her eyes and began a slow series of strokes up and down Dosie's back, her short nails dragging and scratching and making Dosie want to moan again. "I'm not opposed if it happens."

"Do you want me to put the TV on?" Dosie twirled Jennifer's damp hair around her fingers. "We could probably find something to watch until we fall asleep."

"No. Just lay here with me."

"Okay."

"Warmer now?"

"So much. Thank you."

"Welcome."

A comfortable quiet curtained over them as they lay looking at one another, rocking themselves in a mild sway that barely constituted motion. The ambient noises in the room seemed to magnify for a moment. The heat's hum became a loud drone. The car traffic from the streets below, a discordant symphony. But then they melted back into the background again, and Dosie forgot all about them.

"I thought I would feel better," Jennifer said after a while, her voice stirring Dosie from the daze she had drifted into.

"What do you mean?"

She heaved a sigh, and her fresh, minty breath floated over

Dosie's face. "I'm so relieved," she said, "but I thought I would feel something. A sense of closure or...."

"Different somehow?"

"Maybe. Yes."

Dosie kissed her and said, "Give it some time." Healing could be a lot like getting a pretty, but rigid, brand-new pair of shoes. The mind and body needed a period of adjustment before the change could start to feel good. "You've barely processed any of it."

No reply came, only quiet acceptance, and their warm, sleepy bubble took hold. Dosie let herself daze again, and then she dozed, whether she let herself or not. The room and Jennifer smudged like wet paint as her eyes blinked slower and slower, sleep dragging her toward darkness.

"Dosie?"

Like before, Jennifer's voice caught her right at the edge and pulled her back into the light. "Hm?" Her eyelids fluttered until her eyes were clear, and she was able to focus properly again. When she did, she found Jennifer watching her, eyes tired but alert. "What is it, baby?"

"Are you too tired to talk?"

The slight worry in her voice woke Dosie in a snap. "No," she said and propped herself up on an elbow so she could get a bit of space from Jennifer's intoxicating body heat. "About the hearing?"

"No, it's something else I've been thinking about for a while."

"Oh." Her stomach rolled. *Don't assume the worst. It could be anything.* "Okay."

"I want to cut back on my sessions," Jennifer said, but before she could take another breath, corrected herself. "A lot. I...want to stop, I think."

For a second, Dosie failed to understand a single word, let alone what they all meant when strung together. "Your work sessions," she said as comprehension hit. Her eyes widened before she could stop them. "Really?" She lay her hand over Jennifer's chest, right at its center. "Why?"

"A lot of reasons," she said, "but the main one is that I've been finding it harder and harder to enjoy them. I don't look forward to them anymore. There's no anticipation except for it to be over, because all I can think about is...."

"Is?"

Jennifer looked up at her, unadulterated affection in her eyes. "You," she said. "I don't feel like I'm present anymore, because all I really want is to be home with you, putting all of that time and energy from my sessions into *us* and our relationship and our sex life."

Dosie felt like a hot-air balloon, floaty and on fire. Any time Jennifer talked about her feelings, it excited her, but when she talked about her feelings specifically for *her*, Dosie may as well have been made of helium. She would drift into space if Jennifer wasn't always holding her hand. "You're saying you want to retire?"

"I'm saying...." Jennifer blew a loud raspberry of a breath and nodded. "Yeah, I think that's what I'm saying."

They looked at one another, frozen and quiet for two staggered beats of their hearts, then Jennifer smiled, slow and slight. It echoed onto Dosie's face as if they were a mirror of one another, and in seconds, they became two cheesy grins and one beautiful blue set of rolling eyes.

"Must you always look at me like that?"

"Like what?"

"Like you're...just...."

"Super in love with you?"

Jennifer groaned and rolled onto her side, put her back to Dosie. "You're turning me into mush. I was not mushy before I met you."

Dosie laughed and enveloped her from behind. "I think you were already mushy," she said. "You just had a hard candy shell. It was delicious." She bit the back of Jennifer's neck, gnawing playfully like a dog with a bone. "So crunchy."

"You're ridiculous."

"I know." Dosie ran a line across the curve of Jennifer's shoulder with her fingertips, followed it with chaste kisses. "Will you be okay with just me?"

Jennifer flattened onto her back again and looked at her. "What do you mean?"

"If you stop, will you still be getting all your, um, needs, I guess, met? With just me?"

"Why would you think I wouldn't?"

"I don't," Dosie said. "I'm just asking. I know you're used to doing stuff with other people that you don't do with me, and you have to take things slower with me sometimes. You don't get to be as rough or bossy."

"I am plenty bossy with you."

"Okay, that's true," Dosie laughed. "But you let me boss you back sometimes."

"A rare privilege," Jennifer said. "Wield it wisely."

"I just want you to be happy," Dosie told her. "And satisfied."

"I am," Jennifer said, grabbing Dosie's hand. She pulled it to her mouth and kissed her knuckles, her palm, the tender interior of her wrist. "Yes, I have everything I need with you, love. You have to remember that most of what I do is client preference. Just because I'm comfortable and consenting or even enjoying myself doesn't mean what's happening is what *I* actually desire or prefer. What you and I have is what I want. The sex we have is just as new and different and sometimes even intimidating for me as it is for you. The emotional intimacy of it is unlike anything I've ever had before."

"That's my favorite part," Dosie said and crawled on top of her, struck silly again with the urge to be closer than physically possible. She lay herself atop Jennifer, cheek to the middle of her chest, and hummed with pleasure when Jennifer's arms came around her.

"Mine too, much to my surprise."

Dosie propped her chin on Jennifer's sternum, looked up at her, unable to stop from smiling. Jennifer glanced down at her. "What?"

"You're in love with me."

Jennifer pursed her lips as if suddenly fighting her own smile and looked away. "Meh, I like you fine."

"You're completely smitten," Dosie teased as Jennifer groaned and pushed away her tickling hands. "Jennifer Dupont: Smitten as a kitten." Then she gasped.

Jennifer jerked as if bitten and shouted, "What?!"

The chaos catapulted Dosie into the most obnoxious laugh. She capped her hands over her mouth to try to tame it, but it would not be controlled. "I'm so sorry," she wheezed between gasps for air and harsh snorts that made her nose burn.

"What is wrong with you?" Jennifer shoved her over and onto the mattress. In her glorious birthday suit, she propped up on her hips, grabbed her pillow, and whopped Dosie right in the face with it. "Do you want me to piss myself in this bed?"

Cackling, Dosie batted away the pillow and shouted, "I'm sorry! I'm sorry!"

Jennifer threw her weapon aside and launched herself onto Dosie instead. "You're forgiven," she said from above, one hand planted on each side of Dosie's head, then dropped down to kiss her laugh away. She pulled Dosie into her arms again, half on top of her and half beside. "Care to explain?"

"I just suddenly remembered something," Dosie said as she pulled up her T-shirt to wipe her cheeks, each lined with tears from laughing, "and I don't know. I—"

"Gasped like you saw the fucking boogeyman standing in the bathroom," Jennifer supplied, and Dosie had to pinch her nose to keep from laughing again. "Do I even want to know what you remembered? Should I go pee before you tell me? I don't want to risk the sheets. They just put these on this morning."

Dosie's cheeks flamed under her hands. Jennifer loved to act as if she wasn't a jokey person, but she frequently made Dosie laugh until she cried. "Stop before you get me going again."

"Fine." She pulled Dosie's hands away from her face to kiss her. "Tell me."

"Okay, but try to have an open mind. Okay?"

"I'm fully open," Jennifer said then winked at her. "Put something inside me."

"Oh my God." Dosie groaned and covered her face again. When she peeked between her fingers, Jennifer pumped her eyebrows at her and smiled as if she'd won something. A breezy laugh swept through her, like a sweet little dessert from her earlier outburst, and she kissed away Jennifer's toothy, self-satisfied grin. "Okay, so, remember how I said I didn't want to be a mom?"

"Oh, no," Jennifer said quickly. "*Not* a baby. You can put something inside me, but definitely not that."

They looked at one another and burst into raucous laughter again. Dosie was sure that at least some of it had to be the fact that neither had slept well in days. They were travel weary and emotionally spent, flooded with relief and a little deliriously in love, and it made for a potent combination. Every time Dosie laughed, she felt a little loopier, and everything that was funny got funnier.

"How do you feel about cats?" she asked, and Jennifer narrowed her eyes.

"That would depend on the cat. Why?"

Well, she didn't say she was deathly allergic to them. She didn't even say she hated them. I'll take it! "So, there's a possibility that you *could* like a cat?"

"What is happening? Why do I need to have an open mind about cats? Do you want us to get a cat?"

Dosie latched onto Jennifer's word choice like a raft at sea. *Us.* As if it was a foregone conclusion that if Dosie got a cat, then Jennifer would, too, because they were a pair. They were sharing their lives together. *Stop,* she told herself before she could get carried away with her dreamy conjecture. How her heart had managed to remain so tender and fanciful after all she had endured, she would never know. She did her best to rein it in every now and then and sometimes wanted to roll her eyes at herself, but she was also exceedingly grateful. What a terrible fate it would have been, she imagined, to have turned to stone over clay.

"Yeah, so, the thing is, we kind of already *have* the cat," she admitted. "He's at the house with Natalie."

Jennifer's brow scrunched. "Is he a stray? Did he show up on your property or something?"

"Um. Not exactly. He *was* a stray, but he didn't show up at the house. I found him at the shelter that first day after you left, when I did Natalie's shift with her."

"You couldn't go inside a pound without getting a pet?"

Dosie smacked her hands to her cheeks and dragged them down, felt her lower eyelids stretch like a hound dog's. "I was upset. And worried. And you had just left. And he was so sweet to me."

Jennifer leveled her with a look that made Dosie's stomach stir and the back of her throat tickle. "Please, tell me more about how I pushed you into the furry arms of a kind, understanding cat."

"I'm just saying," Dosie said through her laugh, "I was vulnerable."

"Susceptible to pussy?"

"Oh!" Dosie jabbed Jennifer's stomach as it began to vibrate with her amusement. "My!" Then her naked thigh. "God!" She climbed on top of her again. "Jennifer!"

"I haven't slept!"

"You're the one who wanted to talk. I was almost asleep before."

"Details," Jennifer said and ran her hands up and down Dosie's thighs. "What does our cat look like?"

"Really?" Dosie bounced on Jennifer's hips, causing her to grunt. "*Our* cat? You want to be a cat mom with me?"

Jennifer curled her lip. "Well, not if you're going to call me that."

"You're going to love him. I promise. He's super sweet and shiny and all black except for a teeny tiny bit of gray around his face. And he's a senior, so he mostly just sleeps a lot. Also, he has no claws, which I think is probably sad for him but good for your fancy furniture."

"A senior? You got us an old man cat?"

"Natalie said the seniors and the black cats hardly ever get adopted, and he's both. It broke my heart. He's been living at the shelter for two whole years. I couldn't take it."

Jennifer gave a resigned sigh. "Well, I do love a good taboo," she said and pulled Dosie down until their chests mashed together and the tips of their noses bumped. "And I love your soft heart."

"Even if it turns us into old cat ladies?"

"Even if it turns us into zookeepers," Jennifer told her and prodded Dosie's dimple. She tweaked it like a key as if unlocking a bigger smile, and Dosie gave it gladly. "But let's avoid that if possible."

"You know you don't really have to be responsible for the cat if you don't want to be, right?"

"I know," Jennifer said and smoothed her hands down Dosie's arms. "Are you going to tell me our feline friend's name?"

Ugh. Dosie's joy plummeted. Her face squashed with her displeasure. "No."

"What? Why?"

"It's bad."

"It can't be that bad."

"I can't say it. It's child abuse. We have to come up with a new name for him."

"Just tell me."

"Fine," Dosie whined, "but then we're never speaking it again. Deal?"

"Deal."

With a tragic huff, Dosie stuck her lips right to Jennifer's ear and whispered the terrible name their cat's previous owners had given him. She cringed as she said it, and Jennifer did too. "See?"

Jennifer's face twisted with disgust as she said, "Let's hope it's someone's terrible idea of sweet instead of something he's known for."

Their volatile week of pinball emotions and surprise confrontations caught up to them. Jennifer pulled the blackout shades on the windows, and for seventeen hours, she and Dosie slept like two hibernating bears in the dead of winter. When they finally awoke, it was morning bright outside, and Dosie dragged Jennifer out of bed for a yawn-riddled yoga session in the sitting-room floor. They drank room-service coffee while Dosie packed up their things, and Jennifer booked them a flight to Sacramento for later that day.

They showered and dressed, and Jennifer curled Dosie's hair for her, and when Dosie asked if she wanted to see her aunt again before they left, Jennifer was surprised to realize that she truly did. She had already seen the woman more in the last several days than in the last several years combined. But things were different. Jennifer felt changed; again, in this place, she was changed. One minute, she was as she was, and the next, she was someone new, more, hopefully better. And she *wanted* family. She wanted closeness and connection. She even wanted affection; well, in moderation.

She could never have what she once had. She couldn't repair or remake it, and she couldn't hang onto it. But if she could let go of her fear and allow it, she could have something new, something all its own and just as special, and she finally could. She finally wanted it and believed she deserved it. She believed Carine deserved it, too.

They met for lunch at an older Irish pub in town with a mellow vibe and an even mellower crowd and passed a few hours together. Carine brought a box of her assorted pastries and broke Dosie's heart by telling her she had to wait until the flight to have one. Jennifer snuck her one anyway when Carine went to the bathroom and kissed away the crumby evidence so she wouldn't get caught.

For two peaceful hours, they shared tidbits and wine over the wooden Scrabble board Carine brought with her. They talked on and off, but for the most part, it was quiet as they focused on the game, and Jennifer was amazed at how easy it was for the three of them to simply be together, whether or not someone was speaking. It was as if they had been meeting for years for a game of Scrabble at the pub.

The final word was SQUEEZE, and it netted Carine enough points to take the game by six. Dosie rewarded her by covering their bill.

The pub's warmth had chased away the memory of winter, and it came as a shock when they pushed the door open and reentered the world. Jennifer gritted her teeth and pulled her coat tighter. She was ready to be home again. She wanted the Bay Area's version of cold, not eastern Massachusetts's. She wanted to be drinking coffee from her favorite coffee shop in her favorite seat by the window in her condo. She wanted her space and her things, her scents and her soaps and her lotions and her teas. She wanted her own shower and her own bed and Dosie naked in the middle of it, wearing her sheets like lingerie. She was more than ready to be home, but when it came time to say goodbye, she realized she also wasn't quite ready to go.

Carine took her hands and kissed each cheek. She followed the latter with a swipe of her thumb and looked into Jennifer's eyes. With a sigh, she said, "Après la pluie, le beau temps. Oui?"

In a flash, Jennifer was right back with her father, his voice uttering those same words as he soothed away a nightmare or bandaged a bloody knee or picked Jennifer up after she fell off her bicycle. *After the rain, good weather. "On this, Jennifer, you can always count."*

"Oui," Jennifer agreed and promised to speak with her again soon, promised herself she would be better at keeping in touch. She would be more diligent with her care and more willing with her heart, even if it was hard. She could do hard things. She had always been capable.

Carine held one of Dosie's hands as she said, "Keep making her smile, darling. Please. It has been so long."

Dosie's own smile was the only sun in Boston's dreary sky, bright despite the gray around her. "It's my favorite thing to do," she said, and Carine looked back at Jennifer as if to say, "*Mon Dieu, this face!*"

Exactly, Jennifer thought and laughed a cloud of fog into the air.

"Maybe you can come to California sometime and visit us," Dosie said. "We'd really love to have you any time. For the holidays, maybe.

Or is that too soon?" She looked to Jennifer, who felt a sudden urge to kiss her or cry, or both. Dosie offered time and affection to her aunt with such genuine ease. She barely knew Carine but spoke to her as if she'd been part of their family for years. Jennifer didn't know that was something that would matter to her, but it did, because it felt so much like a future wrapped in words, and Jennifer wanted a future. Good and bad and between, she wanted it all, and she wanted it with Dosie.

Carine promised to consider a visit, and the three said their last goodbyes. Jennifer linked her hand with Dosie's, and they walked quietly back to Ned's waiting car. When they got inside and were buckled in, Jennifer directed Ned to head for the airport while Dosie opened the applications store on her phone.

Jennifer watched her type into the search bar: *learn a language.* Her brow tilted upward, pulling the corner of her mouth with it as joy glowed like embers in her chest and turned her hot with affection. "Learning a new language, are you?" she asked, and Dosie looked up at her with eager eyes.

"I want to start learning French, so you have a reason to speak it again," she said, then she frowned as if torn by a sudden thought. "Is that okay? Would you like that, I mean?"

Jennifer's smile widened as she bumped their shoulders together and said, "Now who's smitten as a kitten?"

Dosie laughed and knocked her knee against Jennifer's. "Can you say that in French?"

"Probably not," she admitted with a snort. Then she leaned in and kissed the back of Dosie's jaw, the outer curl of her ear. "But I can say this: Je t'aime, Dosie." She kissed her slower now, longer. Once at her temple. Then the swell of her cheek. The corner of her eye. "Je t'aime."

Dosie buckled herself into her seat as Jennifer stored their carry-on luggage. She watched her rattle off a whisky order to the flight attendant then change it to a ginger ale, and for some ridiculous reason, was struck dumb with attraction. Jennifer was chic head to food in a loose-fit obsidian suit and white silk blouse, black leather boots and silver bangles and micro chains. Her hair hung low in a loose ponytail that she tossed out of the way as she finally took the seat beside Dosie, fastened her seatbelt, and casually crossed one long leg over her knee. Her makeup was minimal, a touch of charcoal to brighten her blue, and her hard, angled jaw made a regal silhouette against the afternoon light coming in through the window. Dosie had been looking at her all day. Not a stitch on her had changed, but Dosie felt a tremor run through her and a catch in her chest. The sight stalled her lungs for a split second, and she must have made some sound, because Jennifer looked up at her as if she'd said her name.

She smiled, and Dosie's tremors turned to quakes. "What?"

"You take my breath away," Dosie said, because the words were there. They were there, and they were true, so why shouldn't she say them?

When Jennifer's slim cheeks tinted the barest pink, Dosie felt as if she had won the lottery. Something so rare, and it was just for her. Jennifer looked at her and despite the season, her blue eyes sparkled like a summer sea. It spurred Dosie's romantic soul, and she didn't try to tame it.

"I really am smitten," she said and brought Jennifer's knuckles to her lips, "and I'm okay with it, because I am so proud to be with you."

Jennifer looked away for a moment and cleared her throat. She adjusted her position and pulled their clasped hands to her lap. When she found Dosie's eyes again, she lowered her voice to a near-whisper and said, "You know I'm a whore, right?"

Oh. A runaway pain streaked a ring around Dosie's heart. Had Kim Pritchard's words been lingering in Jennifer's mind since they were said? Did they make her feel some kind of shame where she previously, and rightly, had none? Dosie couldn't let that lie.

"I thought you were retiring," she teased and brought a hand up to frame her love's cheek, her slow-growing smile. "Jennifer, you are a queen."

Jennifer stared at her for a long, still moment, and all the world but her gaze disappeared. The movements behind and around her blurred. Voices became thumps of sound with no definition. She could have stayed there a while, much longer than she ever imagined she would find reason or care to stare into someone's eyes. Sometimes, when Jennifer woke her from her nightmares, Dosie would be too tired to talk but too upset to sleep, so they would simply stare at each other from inches away. Every time, as she came back to herself in Jennifer's eyes, as she found her center and floated back to calm, she felt the most profound sense of rightness. As if she was exactly where she was meant to be at exactly the right time with exactly the right person, and it was the safest she ever felt.

"Your ginger ale, ma'am."

Jennifer looked away long enough to take her drink and set it aside then turned her attention back to Dosie. "I'm proud to be with you, too," she said and sweetly kissed Dosie's cheek. "A nice, normal girl with a nice, normal past."

A small laugh tickled Dosie's throat. "Oh, the normal-est," she said as the plane began to taxi out of the gate.

The flight attendants made final preparations and gave a safety demonstration that always made Dosie nervous, because no one else ever seemed to be watching. But Jennifer held her hand and shared her ginger ale and queued up the same movie on their screens, and she was able to relax again. When the plane took off, and they tilted into the air, Dosie peered out the window a final time. Boston became its own bright but cloudy sky, a gray-white expanse as surreal as the last week had been. She didn't say goodbye to the city. She was sure she would be back again. Perhaps sooner than later.

Corrie MacKay

15

The house smelled like lemon zest and bleach, and Dosie knew right away that Natalie had gotten bored. She wouldn't have been surprised to step into her kitchen and find all her dishes, measuring cups, and spices rearranged. If her upstairs closet was better organized, she wouldn't complain. Her chaotic collection of shoes had been driving her up the wall for a while, but she'd been too lazy to do anything about it.

Natalie welcomed Dosie with an animated hug, dancing her from side to side like one of those wacky inflatable tube guys always wiggling around outside of car dealerships. When she was done with Dosie, she turned to Jennifer and stuck out a fist. Jennifer's awkward reciprocation made her appear like an alien attempting to blend in.

"Yeah, so," Natalie said and clapped her hands together, "welcome back and all that. Everything here's been fine. Except the power went out last night and didn't kick back on until early this morning, and it was way too quiet without the fan, so I couldn't sleep. And then my phone died, and I couldn't charge it, so I just—"

"Got up and cleaned the whole house?"

Natalie shrugged. "Pretty much," she said through a yawn. "But I'm good. I slept the whole day to make up for it."

"Yes, your hair gave that away," Jennifer told her, and Dosie capped a hand over her mouth that did nothing to mitigate her loud laugh.

"Aw," she said as she wrapped her arms around Natalie's sleepy frame to console her. "I personally wasn't going to say anything about the weird bird nest on the side of your head. Or your sleep breath, which I've just become aware of."

"Mmhm." Natalie knocked Dosie off her with her hip, and Dosie bumped her right back. They made an impromptu competition of it, knocking one another back and forth, first with their hips, then their shoulders. "I think Jennifer's mean-girl energy is rubbing off on you, Dose."

"Excuse you," Jennifer said. "I do not have mean-girl energy."

Dosie bopped Natalie into the wall with one particularly rough shoulder ram then ran and hid under Jennifer's arm. "I don't think you have mean-girl energy, honey. I think you're just a little intimidating."

"Scary girl energy," Natalie corrected as she pointed at her eyes with two fingers then turned those fingers toward Dosie to say she was watching her.

"Even better," Jennifer said with a droll voice and kissed the side of Dosie's head. "I'm going to go shower." She looked between the two of them. "Unless that will offend or terrify anyone?"

"I'm a little offended that I'm not invited," Dosie teased and was happy to see Jennifer's mouth twitch into a tiny smile.

"And I'm a little terrified that she will be," Natalie added, and Jennifer rolled her eyes until the red beyond the white was visible. Natalie snickered as if pleased with herself. "Oh, come on. I know you like me."

Jennifer crossed her arms over her chest. "In small doses, sure."

"Hey, I'm with you. Like, a teaspoon of me goes a long way, for sure."

The words turned Jennifer's grin into a grainy, small laugh that made Dosie's heart sing. Seeing her love with her best friend, teasing back and forth, made her feel a sense of nostalgia despite never having had anything like it. Strangely, it made her feel homesick for what was right in front of her: one growing branch of the tiny family tree that she had planted herself and tended from seed. Or perhaps for the old stump in the ground beside it, for the tree it used to be and the branch that housed her swing and the notches in the bark where Mother measured her and her siblings.

"Dosie?"

"Hm?" Dosie pulled herself out of her head, found Jennifer's curious, concerned eyes. "Sorry. I got lost in my thoughts for a second." She nudged Jennifer toward the stairs. "Go on. Go shower."

Jennifer didn't seem to want to move for a moment, but then she nodded and made for the stairs with one of her bags still slung over her shoulder. Three steps up, she stopped again. Her hand froze on the banister as her gaze fixated on the upper landing.

"Jen?" Dosie peeked around to see a shadow with eyes standing at the top of the stairs. For a split second, she almost screamed. Then she remembered that shadows didn't have eyes, but shadow-colored cats did. "Oh! There he is!"

"What? Who?" Natalie said, bewildered, and shuffled over to look as well. "Oh, yeah, Doody—" Dosie gave her a sharp look that served as a reprimand, and she corrected herself with a laugh. "I mean, DB. Yeah, he likes to creep around like a little vampire. I keep finding him in your room, so I guess he's decided it's his favorite. He's almost never downstairs, except when there's a fire going, then he likes to take a toasty nap."

"Aw." Dosie melted at his sweet, big eyes, like two yellow-green moons in a night sky, and the thought of him snoozing by the hearth. "Now I want to build a fire."

"Yes to a fire," Jennifer said and continued her journey up the stairs.

Dosie clapped her hands. "Okay, I'll start it. Think about names in the shower!"

At the top of the stairs, Jennifer stopped and flicked on the light. She took a moment to adjust her eyes then looked down at the cat. His silky little neck craned back as he met her gaze, and the two seemed to have some sort of silent exchange.

"Um, is this, like, witchcraft?" Natalie whispered beside Dosie. "What is happening?"

In a calm, crisp voice, Jennifer said, "Sit."

"*Pffft!*" Natalie's disbelief was riddled with laughter. "He's a cat, Jennifer. He's not going to—"

The cat sat.

"What the *actual* shit, bro?" Natalie stared, open-mouthed, at the pair. "No. Total coincidence."

Jennifer looked down at them and arched her brow in challenge. It was so sexy that Dosie was torn between laughing at what had happened and flushing at Jennifer's relentless appeal. The result was both.

"Yes," Jennifer said as her gaze met Dosie's. "I could like this cat."

Dosie bounced on her heels. "Cat moms!"

"Still no." Jennifer looked at the animal again. "Come on then," she said and carried on down the hall out of sight.

"No way he's going to...." Natalie's jaw dropped open as the cat stood again and followed Jennifer down the hall. She looked at Dosie in awe. "Do you think I could talk her into volunteering at the shelter?"

"Based on the smell I remember, no," Dosie said, "but you're welcome to try anyway. Has he been adjusting to the house okay?"

"DB? Oh, yeah, he's been super easy. Unlike us, he isn't prone to anxiety. He's a cool guy."

"Yeah, I've never been cool."

"Never, not once," Natalie agreed, and Dosie's chest hurt preemptively as if her body knew she was about to laugh until she ached.

Natalie took her hand and pulled her toward the living room, made a beeline for the hearth. "Everything go good over there? You okay?"

"I'm okay," Dosie said as Natalie handed her a few logs from a nearby basket, and she stacked them on the grate. "It's been heavy, really heavy, but yes, good. And I've been having some flashes and a few bad dreams, but I'm okay." She stuffed a bit of paper between the logs for kindling.

"And her?" Natalie nodded her head toward the foyer to indicate the woman not in the room. "She okay?"

The long-stemmed matches rattled inside the box as Dosie shook one free. "She is," she said and dragged the match across the rough striking board. It crackled and sizzled as a flame burst to life at the head and created a subtle burning scent Dosie loved. She stared into the flickering orange as it began to eat its way down the matchstick. "She will be." The kindling caught, and the first small wave of warmth emanated from the fire. Dosie tended it carefully so it could grow. *She will be.*

It was late. The fire burned low and no longer crackled. Dosie didn't think she had bones anymore. She lay on Jennifer like a puddle on the ground, not an ounce of tension under her skin as they lazed in front of the embers and filled the silence with sporadic conversation.

Natalie was sprawled on her air mattress, flicking through social media on her phone. She opened a new post from Kaylia's page and turned it toward Dosie. "If she posts half a guy's face, does it count as a declaration of love?"

"That does seem serious," Dosie said. "She only posted the hand of the last guy she thought she had feelings for."

"New York guy? Yeah, not even his whole hand. It was like two fingers around a coffee mug. That was it."

"Sometimes all you need is two fingers," Jennifer said, eyes serenely closed, head lolling against the back of the couch as she dozed on and off.

"What are you? A naughty little mosquito?" Natalie asked. "Just buzzing in and out of the conversation at random?"

"Careful," Jennifer warned, still not bothering to open her eyes. "I bite, too."

Natalie turned her attention back to her phone. "Dosie, I think your girlfriend is flirting with me."

"It can be hard to tell," Dosie said. "Her threatening voice and her flirting voice sound the same."

Jennifer tickled her until she nearly squirmed them both off the couch and onto the floor. Then she wrapped her arms and legs around Dosie like she was one long pillow instead of a person and said, "Your girlfriend's ready-for-bed voice sounds like this, because I'm ready to go to bed. Please."

"Aw," Natalie cooed. "She said please. Take her to bed, Dose."

Dosie sat up. "We have to walk up all those stairs now."

"The sooner we start, the sooner it's done," Jennifer said and nudged her on.

"Fine." She tousled Natalie's hair as they passed. "Love you, best friend."

"Love *you*, best pal," Natalie said through a long yawn and cocooned herself tighter in her blanket. "And best pal's girl."

"I have a name," Jennifer said.

Natalie squinted her eyes as if confused. "Oh wait. I remember. Jeanette, right? Or was it Jessica?"

"Fuck off," Jennifer laughed and used her foot to kick Natalie's blanket-cushioned behind.

Natalie launched one of Dosie's small decorative pillows and cackled when it whacked Jennifer in the head before tumbling to the floor. "Goodnight!"

The old stairs complained under their weight as they lazily hiked to the second floor. Jennifer's hand against Dosie's lower back was like a warm pulse of energy, stirring her on with the thought of that warmth being everywhere. She wanted Jennifer's naked body blanketing her in bed, lulling her into the heaviest, most comfortable sleep.

As if sensing the desire, Jennifer traded her simple touch for enveloping Dosie from behind the moment they hit the second-floor landing. Their synchronized steps became a jumble that nearly toppled them as she glued herself to Dosie's back. Her hands settled over Dosie's bellybutton and her mouth over the side of Dosie's neck, turning her nerves on like a light.

"Jen," she quietly huffed, pushing back against her as if they weren't already as close as they could be. "We're not going to make it if we can't walk without falling down."

Jennifer tightened her hold, dropped into a squat, and scooped Dosie right off the floor. She waddled them down the hall and into the bedroom to the tune of Dosie's delighted giggle, then dropped her, unceremoniously, onto the bed. A second later, she dropped herself right on top of her.

With their noses pressed together, Jennifer's two eyes merged into one. "I'm so tired," she groaned, kissing Dosie's lips between each word. "I don't want to move anymore."

"I would say that's fine, but I think we would both regret sleeping in this position come morning."

Jennifer's one big eye rolled. "When I was in my twenties, I could sleep in any position without issue. Now, I sleep with my head slightly turned and am paralyzed in the morning."

"Poor baby," Dosie said. "So old and achy."

Jennifer grumbled. "Old, my ass." She launched herself up with renewed vigor and arched an eyebrow at her girlfriend. Slowly, she pulled off her shirt, then her bra, never breaking eye contact. Her sweatpants went next, pooling around her feet, and she stepped out in nothing but her smirk and underwear. Then she dropped those, too, kicking them off her toe so that they smacked right into Dosie's face.

The scent of her hit Dosie next, and her mouth watered. Desire stirred hot and low in her belly. She tamed it, knowing they were too tired, but still grinned like a kid in a candy store about to have a delicious treat.

"Now," Jennifer said with a slow turn that put her smooth, toned back and shapely rear on display, "I'm going to go brush my teeth. You can watch this ass walk away, then try to tell me it's old."

Dosie's cheeks were hot. One glance in the mirror showed they were a joyful pink, and her smile couldn't be tamed. "How old is perfection?" she called, and Jennifer peeked around the bathroom door to wink at her.

"You just earned yourself a prize," she said, and Dosie knew exactly what the prize would be. "In the morning though, because I am very old and tired."

Dosie laughed until her eyes watered and said, "Deal." Then she shimmied backward on the bed to rest against the headboard and wait for Jennifer to finish her bathroom routine. She would start her own after. They had tried it side by side before, but it felt a bit like trying to play musical chairs with the sink. Both liked their space when getting ready, for bed or otherwise. "Did you think of any cat names, by the way? Natalie suggested Felix."

She glanced at the door as Jennifer peeked around again and asked, "What do you think of Laurent?"

Dosie's chest warmed at the sight of Jennifer's sweet, sincere gaze and the sound of her voice wrapped around a name chosen in tribute. She couldn't put into words how it made her feel to know Jennifer wanted to name their cat after her sister, a topic she often avoided. Such a choice suggested an incredible, healing shift in her, and Dosie was so happy, she could burst. "I think it's perfect," she said, smiling as Jennifer disappeared around the door again. "As long as you don't mind me sounding super *not* French trying to pronounce it."

"You will get the hang of it," Jennifer replied, a bodiless voice floating through the room like an echo.

Dosie wanted to get the hang of it right away and figured it was as good a time as any to start her French lessons. Her phone lay on her bedside table where she'd left it hours before, plugged into the charger. She tapped the screen and saw she had a missed call. At the sight of the unknown number, her body went rigid. Her heart began to thump, harder and harder as her gaze dropped from the call notification to the one beneath it. One new voicemail.

As usual, Dosie's first instinct told her it was press. Some journalist or documentarian had hunted down her number again, seeking interviews or authorizations or her participation in a project. But then she remembered. *Ira.*

"Love, where is the lotion?" Jennifer appeared around the bathroom door again. "The pomegranate one. Did we use it all?"

Dosie looked up, heart slinking into her throat. She could feel how wide her eyes were but couldn't make them relax. "I.... Lotion?"

"What's wrong?" Jennifer crossed the room in three quick strides and sank to Dosie's side. "What is it?"

Dosie tilted her phone toward her, the notifications still lingering unclicked, and Jennifer guessed her worry right away.

"Your brother?"

"I don't know," Dosie whispered. She couldn't explain it, but she suddenly felt like she was being watched, listened to. Violated, somehow. It made no sense, but some part of her was certain that if she went to her window and peered out, she would see the outline of a man hovering by the old gate. A living ghost straddling past and present, there to draw her back to the latter and keep her there. *No, no, no.* She felt sick.

"It's just a call," Jennifer said, resituating herself onto the bed to wrap an arm around Dosie's shoulders and draw her into her soft, nude embrace. "And you don't have to return it."

"There's a message," she squeaked out, and Jennifer nodded.

"I see that. Do you want to check it?"

"I don't know." She hated the way her voice cracked. "Should I?"

"Oh, darling, there is no 'should' in this situation," Jennifer told her and combed Dosie's hair back to kiss her temple, then her cheek. "It's strictly about what you want and feel comfortable with. You do not have to be available to someone just because you're related to them."

Dosie knew she was right, but her body didn't seem to care. Panic sat at the edge of her composure like a wrestler waiting to be tagged into the ring, and all because she'd gotten one little voicemail. The idea of hearing her brother's voice again so soon, or at all, made her feel outside of her body and outside of her life. Time dropped away, and Dosie became convinced that, at any minute, she would wake up and discover she had never escaped any of it. She was still there, not only in that house but in that life. And everything that came after was just an impossible dream.

"There is nothing to be afraid of," Jennifer whispered at her ear. She rubbed Dosie's chest over the mad beat of her heart, the warmth of her hand seeping in through Dosie's shirt. "I am here, and you are safe."

Dosie took a deep breath. *There's nothing to be afraid of,* she repeated in her head. *I'm safe.* Then she swiped the notification and hit the play button.

For a second, there was only silence, but then a robotic voice spilled through the speaker. "Hello. This is a collect call from Pelican Bay State Prison in Crescent City, California. An inmate—" The automated voice cut out, and another voice took its place, one that sent an icy chill down Dosie's back. "—your father, Samuel Fisher—" The automated voice returned. "—is attempting to contact you. If you would like to accept—"

The voice went mute as Jennifer snatched Dosie's phone away and smashed the button to end the message. Dosie couldn't move. Her blood was ice. Her stomach had dropped out of her or shriveled and died. Something in her was rotting, she was sure.

"Breathe," Jennifer said, because she wasn't. Dosie wasn't sure she would ever breathe again. Her lungs were so tight, they felt like they might explode. "Breathe, baby."

Dosie's body went liquid as she suddenly dragged in one colossal breath, held it another second, then exhaled with a cry. She turned sharply in Jennifer's embrace and pressed into her neck and chest. "Hold me," she begged despite Jennifer's arms already snug around her. "Please."

Jennifer held her tighter, locking her so firmly in place that it nearly took her breath again. But Dosie needed it. She needed the compression to calm her nervous system. She needed Jennifer's scent in her nose and Jennifer's hands on her back and Jennifer's lips at her ears, whispering, "I've got you," and "you're safe," until she could make herself believe it. Because there was another voice in her head now, rising to the surface from the depths where she'd buried it. *Dosie-girl.*

Hearing her father's voice for the first time in years and in her own voicemail, no less, was like being plunged into a frozen lake without warning. Shock. Pain. *Fear.* All of it amplified by the realization that her brother had done this to her. Ira had indeed gone to see their father, which broke Dosie's heart, but he had also clearly told him about Dosie and given him her number, which didn't just break her heart. It annihilated it.

She knew what it was like to be in Samuel Fisher's presence, to have his eyes on you as he implored you to do something, how he could make everything seem so simple or so innocent. How easily he could bend his children to his will. She knew, but it made her no less devastated. More than that, she was *furious.* Despite everything in her body telling her not to, and despite her last experience with him being a gun in her face, she had still tried to reach out to her little brother and offer him something. Companionship. Family. Or a chance at it, at least. And what did he do? He gave that opening to their father instead, and Dosie could not forgive him.

She slowly calmed in Jennifer's arms. Her lungs found their rhythm again, and her heart eased to a softer beat. She cried, unable to stop, but that was okay. She had cried countless tears over her family before and would likely cry countless more. What she couldn't abide anymore was the fear. The anger. She hated the way both felt in her body and realized, as she lay there, that she would never be free of either if she allowed her past back into her life. It didn't matter if she felt obligated or guilty or concerned. It wasn't her place. Her siblings weren't her children, and she needed to let them go, wholly, both those who were gone and those who still remained. She needed to live the life she had *now*, in the present, and the only way to do that was for her to say a lasting goodbye to the one that came before.

"Are you okay?" Jennifer asked as she finally relaxed her muscles and let Dosie ease out of her arms.

Dosie stood on unsteady legs and wiped her cheeks with the heels of her hands. "Yeah," she said, her voice as dry as her throat. "I just want to wash my face and go to sleep."

"Okay." Jennifer stood as well, and Dosie looked at her, confused. "What are you doing?"

"This," she said and walked to the large window on the far side of the room and pulled it open. A cool breeze filtered in as Dosie's phone flew out, tossed from Jennifer's hand like a boomerang she had no intention of recatching. Then she shut the window again, and crawled back into bed.

Dosie was stunned, gaze darting between the window and her girlfriend. But then a gurgle of a laugh crawled up her throat and out, breaking her gloom like a sunbeam through a dark cloud. "Did you just throw my freaking phone out the window?!"

Jennifer laughed, too, her expression torn between satisfaction and surprise, as if she hadn't known she was going to do it until the doing was in process. But she wasn't mad about the result. "I'll buy you a new one," she promised. "That one was malfunctioning."

"It was?" Dosie snorted and shoved her over on the bed. "You don't think I could've just gotten a new number?"

"Mmmm, no, I don't think so." Jennifer pulled her down on top of her. "But I'll get you one of those, too."

A laugh or sob caught in Dosie's throat. She wasn't sure. It didn't matter. Sometimes, they were the same. "I love you so much," she whispered as she sank into Jennifer's warm, naked embrace again and felt she was exactly where she was meant to be.

"Run, Dosie. Just run and don't stop."

The ground didn't feel solid anymore. She bounded off it like it was made of rubber, running faster than she ever had in her life. Then she heard it: a scream. Screams. There were screams all around, flying as fast as bullets now, but this scream.... This scream sank into her back like claws and tore her open.

"Mother?" she weakly cried as she stumbled to a stop, already turning. She whirled in every direction, searching for the source in the cacophony. Another wail emanated from the haze of smoke encircling her, and Dosie barreled blindly toward it. "Momma?!"

Sweat soaked her face and neck as the flames devouring the bunks grew higher and higher, painting the sky in angry reds and oranges and grays. Her eyes felt like hot coals, and she could hardly see a thing. Her hands hit the chapel barn before she even knew it was there.

She pushed at the doors. Something heavy was holding them in place. It yielded with a few more shoves, and Dosie careened inside. It still smelled like incense from the last chapel blessing. The scent hit her nose only a moment before another did, one she quickly identified. Blood. It was coppery and sharp, and in the span of only a breath or two, Dosie felt she had it everywhere. She could smell it in her nose and taste it in her mouth, feel it coating the back of her throat.

On the floor, she saw what she had struggled to push aside, and all her insides turned to ice. The weight against the door was a body. The limp legs trailed to those of another, then another. Like paint spatter, women and children speckled the floor left and right. Kids Dosie read to and made treats with. Mothers who treated her like their own. All dead. And in the center of the chapel, at the heart of the massacre, stood her father, the Prophet, a still-smoking rifle in his hands. At his feet sat Dosie's mother, now silent and unmoving and slumped against his calf as if, even in death, she needed him to prop her up. She needed him to be there. She needed him.

Dosie stood gaping, fixated on her mother's empty eyes. Her knees shook, hands too. Only when the stench of urine hit the already foul air did she realize she had wet herself. Her heart thrashed like something wild tossed in a cage. She didn't know what to do. *Run*, she thought, commanded herself, but she couldn't. Her feet wouldn't budge.

"Dosie-girl," her father said, winded from his work with the rifle, and smiled at her. It wasn't genuine but unhinged, as if he had turned something off in his brain and was left with some sort of disturbed, senseless joy.

Run. Her muscles jerked. Something in her face must have given her away. *Or he really can read my mind.* Her father's voice seemed to jump the air between them and land sharply at her ear, as if he was right behind her instead of ahead. "Don't," he said, and Dosie's heart sank into her burning belly and sizzled.

She didn't. She was rooted against her will now, by fear or her father's command, she wasn't sure. The thought bloomed before she could nip it. *I'm going to die today.*

"Why?" Dosie managed to stutter. Then she shouted it over the din. "Why are you doing this to us?!"

The Prophet's voice turned to a dance, the sweet ballad he'd been soothing her with all her life, before and after he tore her apart. "Oh, my angel," he said and lowered the rifle. He stepped toward her, and her mother's body flopped to the ground without his support. His heavy work boots tread over the flesh and bone of his own family, and he hardly seemed to notice. He barely wobbled, and he never looked down.

"This is the only way to save us," he told her and sounded so incredibly certain that Dosie, for a few terrible beats of her heart, believed him. He petted her hair the way he had always done, from the top down to the very tips, then gave the end a tug. "We have to keep the family together, don't we?"

Corrie MacKay

She had no answers and a billion questions, and she still felt no inclination to demand he resolve any of it. She felt only the duty to hand herself over to her father and let him tell her that what was when and why was how and that there was nothing to fear at the end of a gun. Everyone was dying. Everyone was going. Everyone was already gone.

"I won't leave you behind," her father said as if once again reading her mind, and Dosie was sure the moment had come. She could feel the mouth of the rifle near her arm, the metal still warm as it bumped against her skin. *I'm going to die today.*

Run. She wasn't going to run. She didn't even know why she kept thinking it. Her legs were done. Her body was done. She had seen too much, lost too much. *Run. No, it's okay. It's okay. Father says it's the only way.*

When the gun went off, cracking in the air like lightning, Dosie grunted and grabbed her gut. It was instinct, and it was wrong. She took a deep breath, unharmed, and watched her father stumble backward. His hand jumped to his side, blood spilling over his fingers faster than he could catch it. His rifle dropped to the ground, and he followed.

"Down! He's down!" A voice shouted from outside the open door a second before the place was swarmed, and Dosie was swept into someone's arms before she could process a bit of it.

"We've got you." Someone carried her away, because she couldn't move. "It's over now." It wasn't. It would never be. Her mother's empty eyes followed her until the barn was out of sight. "It's over."

"Dosie."

She hadn't wanted to wake her, but nothing else seemed to work. She tried petting her hair and arms to no avail. Soft humming at her ear didn't soothe. Even holding her close only helped for the span of a breath or two. Then the whimpers came back, pained little cries like those of a wounded animal emanating from Dosie's throat as her brow creased and her lips frowned, and her hands curled into the sheets like she was terrified. Jennifer couldn't bear it.

"Dosie," she said again as she gently shook her shoulder.

Relief blew through her like a warm breeze when the whimpering stopped, and Dosie's puffy eyes fluttered open. For a brief moment, she appeared utterly confused, then her gaze found Jennifer's, and she reached for her. Her hand molded around Jennifer's cheek, and Jennifer topped it with one of her own.

"What is it, baby?" she whispered. "Are you okay?"

God, Jennifer thought, struck silent. Even after crying her eyes out and exhausting herself to sleep, Dosie's first concern was *her.* Jennifer felt that familiar tingle course through her, the same one that had been turning her life upside down since the moment she first met Dosie Fisher.

She had always known how layered and complex intimacy could be, but she had never known or experienced the reality of it the way she had with Dosie. The littlest things felt like love letters. There was romance in a glance caught in a mirror. A casual touch while passing in the kitchen felt like a promise. Zipping up a dress. Smoothing down a collar. Clasping a necklace. Turning a light on so the other could see better while reading. Waking up covered after falling asleep bare. A spur-of-the-moment foot rub or a kiss on the cheek. A lingering hand on the small of a back. "You look nice," whispered breathlessly on the way out the door.

There was heat in every bit of it and a steady heart thrumming along in constant rhythm. Jennifer had been learning what love was, truly, and *that* was what she discovered. It was everything, every little turn of the wheel once committed. Love was the absolute magic of a connection that turned all things, even the smallest things, the most ordinary of things, into gifts both galvanizing and soothing. Into moments that stole breath and promised pleasure and commanded the heart to beat faster. Moments that eased pressure and calmed nerves and swayed like a slow dance under the skin.

Corrie MacKay

Love was Dosie Fisher looking at her as if nothing and no one else in the world existed, touching her as if she needed it to thrive, telling her she was with her no matter what or where or when. Love was that little feeling in her chest, that tingle, that rush, that sent Jennifer's heart soaring up her throat, so that when she opened her mouth to say she was okay, to say that Dosie had just had a bad dream and needed waking, what came out instead was, "I want us to live together."

She hadn't meant to say the words, but the moment they left her lips, she knew they were true. In a matter of seconds, they became all she could think about, and somehow, that didn't scare her at all. Instead, Jennifer felt alive, wide awake in the dark, in Dosie's bed, waiting for the girl who had her heart to give her an answer. Or at least process the question.

Dosie stared as if she wasn't entirely sure she was awake yet. She rubbed her eyes and blinked, then looked at her again. "Is this real?" she asked, and Jennifer couldn't help herself.

She chuckled and bopped Dosie's chin with her finger. "It is very real," she promised, and a wide grin broke over Dosie's face.

"Really?" Her eyes watered as her hand found Jennifer's cheek again. "Really, Jen?"

"Really."

"Oh, wow," she whispered, voice small and tight. A tiny laugh blipped across her lips, and she shook her head against the pillow. "What a thing to wake up to." She thumbed Jennifer's bottom lip. "What brought this on?"

"I don't know," Jennifer admitted. "You were having a nightmare, so I woke you." She pulled Dosie's hand down to her chest and held it there, just over her heart. "I want to be here to wake you when you have bad dreams. I want to be here when you need me and when you don't."

Dosie's lip quivered. "Say more," she whispered, inspiring another laugh.

"Fine," Jennifer said. "For you." She squeezed Dosie's hand and let everything she felt bubble to the surface and out. "I want you so much, Dosie. I want you there when I fall asleep, and I want you there when I wake again, and I want that every day. I don't want to drive three hours to kiss you. I don't want to tell you I love you over the phone, because I can't have you right in front of me whenever I want."

Dosie blew a long, heavy breath and wiped her cheeks. "Keep going," she said, and Jennifer knew she needed it. Every word. Every emotion. It had been a hell of week and a hell of a life, a whirlwind where a slow breeze was needed, and they were both fragile. This wasn't just a confession or a request; it was comfort. It was connection. It was liberty at the tip of a tongue.

"When I come home at the end of a day, I want it to be to you," Jennifer told her, "not an empty apartment. And if I can't share my day with you, then I want to end it in your arms. I want us cooking dinner together and telling each other stories and taking showers together where we never get clean, because we can't keep our hands off each other long enough to wash. Dosie, I want to kiss you goodnight every single night, and I want to fall asleep to the sound of your breathing. I want—"

"Okay," Dosie cried, sniffling as she pressed her tear-streaked cheeks and lips to Jennifer's and kissed her. "You have to stop now. My heart feels like it's going to burst."

"So does mine," Jennifer said, "and I'm sure it will if you don't tell me what you're thinking soon."

"Oh, God," Dosie laughed. "I didn't even realize. I'm so sorry. Yes! Yes." She rolled Jennifer onto her back and climbed on top of her, settling on her naked hips. She ran her hands up Jennifer's bare torso, over her soft nipples, causing them to strain. Her fingers curled around the back of Jennifer's neck, and then Dosie was drawing her up, up into a kiss so deep and so hard that it almost hurt. Yet nothing in Jennifer's life had ever felt better. "I really, really want that, too."

An incredible relief flooded her, washing away her doubt and all her insecurities and clearing the way for unmitigated bliss. "Yeah?"

"So much," Dosie whispered into her next kiss. She looped

Jennifer's neck with her arms, legs wrapped around her waist. "Where will we live?"

"I don't know," Jennifer said. "I haven't thought that far. Have you?"

Dosie's smile was small, almost shy. "I've thought about a lot of things. A *lot*."

Jennifer slipped her hands under Dosie's T-shirt to rest on her warm back. "Oh? And?"

"And I think your place, maybe," Dosie said and glanced around her dark room. "I don't need this house anymore. I want to finish it. I might even keep it, but I don't think I need to be here anymore."

"We could get a new place," Jennifer offered and smoothed her hand over Dosie's bed-mussed hair. "Something wholly ours."

"Really?" Dosie asked, voice riddled with surprise. "But you love your condo."

She did. The place was her first big purchase and still the largest she'd ever made; one she had worked her ass off for and barely afforded. Years later, it was her longest-lasting refuge, but it was no longer her only. She didn't need it the way she needed it before. Now, her favorite sanctuary, her safest place, resided in a different home: the living, breathing home currently occupying her lap.

Even as they tested and sometimes terrified her, each new path her love for Dosie took her down turned her world a little brighter, stretched it a little wider, and colored it a little richer. Life had been so much before her—both brilliant and beastly—but since Dosie, *with* her, life was *tremendous*. It was limitless. There had rarely, if ever, been a thing in Jennifer's world since her first terrible taste of loss that she couldn't see the eventual end of, but with Dosie, she saw no end. Like an easy current rolling along the sea, they went on and on, no edge to tip over, no finish line to cross. Just the two of them, going on as they were forever.

"I love you," Jennifer said on a sigh, as if it was the simplest answer to everything. And maybe it was.

She had grown so much since they first met. Dosie had too. In many ways, she felt like she was meeting herself for the first time. Herself in love and in intimacy, freely and enthusiastically committed. Herself unfettered and open, and Dosie too, neither of them bound or suppressed by any ideals or beliefs, by any gods or men or the monstrous minutia of their pasts. Growing up, neither had imagined much for themselves, but now, Jennifer's imagination was as boundless as a child's. The child she never truly got to be. The child Dosie never got to be. She could picture so much for them. Transposed over every dream, every scenario, every little whim, there they were. Enduring together. Loving each other. And it was as simple and incredible as that.

Jennifer had no idea what the future actually held, what pains and joys awaited, but she didn't care. She wasn't worried. She had everything she needed. "And I'm starting to think I could go anywhere as long as you're there, too."

"Oh, God," Dosie whispered and lay their foreheads together. "I wish I knew how to tell you. I don't think there are words."

"For what, darling?"

"For how incredible it feels," she said, "to love you and to be loved by you."

The words kissed at Jennifer's heart, encouraged it to beat a bit faster. "I know exactly what you mean."

They sat in silence for a while, simply breathing one another in. Touching whatever flesh their fingers found. Kissing away tears and painting little smiles into each other's skin.

"Jen?"

"Hm?"

"Everything really is going to be okay," Dosie said. "Isn't it?"

Jennifer looked in her eyes and felt certain. "It's going to be incredible." She thumbed the shallow dip of Dosie's dimple. "Do you believe me?"

A sweet, knowing grin spread Dosie's lips. "Yes."

"You know," Jennifer said and slid her hands down to the bottom of Dosie's shirt again and under, "I might spend an indecent amount of money on décor."

Dosie closed her eyes as Jennifer's palms slinked up and over her breasts. "You already do that," she said, breath hitching mid-sentence as Jennifer pinched one stiffening nipple between her fingers. "I might barge in on you in the bathroom without thinking."

"You already do *that*."

They shared a soft kiss. Dosie giggled giddily against her lips, and Jennifer felt drunk. On her, on them, on the future they were choosing to share. *This is happening. We're doing this. We love each other.*

"You realize you've just made this one of the best days of my life, right?" Dosie said, and Jennifer finally pulled her shirt up over her head and tossed it aside.

"Hold that thought." In one swift move, she flipped Dosie onto her back and pressed her into the bed. "Let's see if we can't make it even better," she whispered and slinked down the length of her, making promises without words that they both intended to keep.

About the Author

Corrie MacKay is an American writer with an extensive background in genre writing and editing and an inability to sit still for long. New adventures are always calling! She is a proud lesbian and feminist using her fiction to explore the themes that have dominated her life and to share the lessons that she has learned along her journey. Her stories are maps of wonder, hardship, and healing. And heat. Don't forget that!

More than anything, MacKay seeks to leave her readers with a rich and enduring sense of hope and a desire to live and love.

Other Works by Corrie MacKay

The Lay of You

Jennifer Dupont lives a successful solitary life as crème de la crème of San Francisco's most elite escort service. To clients, she is the Director, an imposing beauty with a fondness for expensive whisky, tailored suits, and uncompromising control. It's a fitting persona even outside work, as old wounds have left her unwilling to risk her heart. That is, until she meets her newest client.

Jennifer Dupont lives a successful solitary life as crème de la crème of San Francisco's most elite escort service. To clients, she is the Director, an imposing beauty with a fondness for expensive whisky, tailored suits, and uncompromising control. It's a fitting persona even outside work, as old wounds have left her unwilling to risk her heart. That is, until she meets her newest client.

Over a decade has passed since Theodosia "Dosie" Fisher was rescued from an isolated, abusive cult founded by her father, and while years of therapy have earned her an emotional maturity most never acquire, her body remains neglected, riddled with questions she has long been afraid to confront. So, when her two best friends suggest she hire an escort as a pressure-free way to explore, she decides to go for it.

The attraction is immediate, the curiosity and connection even more so. Every exchange is electric. Every touch sparks. Every kiss siphons secrets and edges them nearer a level of intimacy that Dosie has sought all her life. Jennifer, on the other hand, has only ever wanted the opposite.